Savage DESIRE

Watch for the newest historical romance from
ROSEMARY ROGERS
and MIRA Books

Available December 2001

ROSEMARY ROGERS

Savage DESIRE

MIRA®

ISBN 0-7394-1490-9

Printed in U.S.A.

To the Righteous and the Truthful and the Honest.
May they always win out!
WALK IN THE LIGHT.

THE BEGINNING
May, 1876

1

Despite a cheery fire burning behind brass firedogs it was cold in the parlor, a chill that had nothing to do with the fusillade of rain blowing against leaded-glass windowpanes. Outside Steve Morgan's London town house, gusts of wind swept around pink sandstone corners with a hollow moan that only added to the sense of gloom inside. Heavy velvet drapes of dark green shrouded windows flanked by Chinese pots of delicate ferns. Two wingback chairs of rich gold brocade sat on each side of the hearth, the sweeping lines of their ball-and-claw legs cushioned atop thick Turkish carpets patterned in green, gold and umber.

Virginia Brandon Morgan perched stiffly on the brocade ottoman, with its dangling fringe, her hands clasped in her lap in an effort to appear calm under the unnerving, steady gaze directed at her from the man in the chair angled against the warmth of the fire.

Tension hovered as if alive, as tangible and dangerous as a lion prepared to pounce. But then, Steve had always had the power to make her feel uncertain, ever since their first meeting nine long years before.

The fragrance of roses was almost overpowering; a huge bouquet dripped loose petals atop a gleaming parquet table next to the ottoman. Velvety crimson petals lay like drops of blood against the wood. Ginny suppressed a shudder and glanced up, her eyes briefly meeting his hard blue gaze.

Even while she struggled for words to break the sudden awkward tension between them, she resented the necessity for it. Why must he regard her so closely, his eyes shuttered, his face unreadable as if— As if *she* had chosen to stay away from the children? After all, she had been on her way to them when she'd left New Orleans and then had been injured before she could reach them. It wasn't as if she had wanted to be taken so far away from them. And Steve knew that.

But he had still taken them from France to England and hidden them in the countryside with his old flame, so Ginny could not see them without his permission. If not for this attempt at reconciliation, she would no doubt never get to see her children again.

In truth, that was not the only reason she wanted to be with Steve, to try again. She *needed* to renew the love they had once felt so strongly for one another, and that fact was both frightening and promising.

Could they renew the love they had once shared after everything that had come between them? There was hope....

Yet now he regarded her so intently, his dark face set into harsh lines, black brows a straight slash over eyes that held volumes of unspoken censure.

He had often told her how much he admired her ability to always survive. Yet there were times it seemed as though he resented that ability. Her throat tightened. The tension was so palpable it throbbed like a live beast.

Across the room Steve sprawled in a wingback chair, his long legs stuck out in front of him and crossed negligently at the ankles. He looked far too comfortable when she was so ill at ease. Oh God, she was so nervous! Why? Why could she not be as unaffected as he obviously was? But she couldn't be, of course, for this was too important.

This first meeting, with children she had not seen since they were infants, terrified her. Laura and Franco—her own children—twins born when she and Steve had been separated by distance and conflicts. The children had been left in Mexico, then sent to stay with Tante Celine in France for far too long.

It was unintentional, of course, for Ginny had never dreamed of all the events that would take her so far away from them....

Hazy images danced in front of her eyes: the lush green beauty of the harbor town of Gibara in Cuba, the earthquake that had temporarily blinded her, Richard Avery's rescue of her, his kindness and love on the journey that ended in the sultan's palace in Dolmabahce, the dark days of blindness mixed with fear and relief and despair. All that was behind her now, part of her past. Her present was here with Steve and their children. Their future together stretched before her with bright promise if she could just grasp it and hold on.

Childish laughter shattered her reverie, and for a brief panicked moment she caught and held Steve's opaque gaze before the sound of the parlor door opening drew her eyes and riveted her attention.

Ohh... They had changed so, these exuberant children with faces still round and cherubic. Gone was the light fuzz atop infant heads, replaced with thick dark hair that held only faint hints of copper like her own tresses. Chattering and laughing, they ran to their father, arms outstretched with joy despite the murmured reprimand of their nursemaid.

And Steve— The cold mask he'd worn only a moment before had vanished, replaced by a softly tender light in his eyes and a genuine curve of his mouth into a smile that was at the same time loving and indulgent as he greeted his children.

All this Ginny saw in the space of an instant as the children heeded their nurse's instructions and curbed their first wild joy into a more sedate greeting.

"Good morning, Papa," Laura piped, her childish treble quavering with suppressed delight as she strove for self-discipline. "It is very good to see you."

"And you, poppet." An affectionate drag of his hand through her curls tousled them. Adoring eyes gazed up at her father, that love mirrored in the blue eyes so like hers.

Laura Luisa Encarnación Morgan—the name was larger than the child, Ginny thought irrelevantly. Her gaze shifted to Franco, who stood beside his sister with a grave solemnity that reminded her suddenly of Steve's grandfather, Don Francisco, the old martinet who was the regal and demanding head of the Alvarado family. But, of course, he was named after him—Francisco Alvarado Morgan—so perhaps it was only fitting that he should remind her of the old gentleman.

Already Franco was a bit taller than his sister, his dark head a shade above hers, his bearing that of a young soldier.

Ginny's heart lurched. She didn't know them—her own flesh and blood. These children she had carried beneath her heart for nine months, had fought so fiercely to protect...and she did not *know* them.

Steve was talking to them, asking questions and listening to their answers with an interest that could not be feigned, and they chattered without reservation. Ginny watched with her heart in her throat, aching to reach out but unwilling to intrude. She felt suddenly like an interloper in a clique that excluded her. Could this be the man she had always considered coldly dangerous? This man who had gone to one knee on the floor to help a child button her hightop shoes? Impossible to believe, if she had not witnessed it for herself. The ruthless gunman of her experience was a gentle, loving father to his two children.

Tears stung her eyes, and she did not know if they were for her loss or the fact that Steve had finally become the man she had never thought he wanted to be....

A soft voice murmured in her ear, "Be patient, Ginette, and they will learn to know you soon. After all, it has been so long since they last saw you, and they were so small."

Tante Celine. A gentle hand was on her shoulder, the soft squeeze familiar and comforting. Her aunt's reminder eased some of the pain Ginny felt at the realization she was a stranger to her children, and she managed a nod. It was true, yet to wait, quietly watching while her children seemed oblivious to her existence, was the hardest thing she had ever done.

Another rose petal fell soundlessly to the gleaming tabletop, a bloodred tear that felt as if it came from her heart. Would they accept her? Or had she been gone from them so long they would resent her absence? Oh, how could she tell them of all she had endured, the nights she had longed for them, planned their futures together?

The enormity of her past soared like a specter to haunt her as she watched them quietly, regret deeply scouring her with razor-sharp talons. It was not regret for what she had done, but what she had not done—the nights she had not been there to tuck them into their beds, to sing them to sleep and to comfort childish tears. *Oh, please God, do not let it be too late!*

Then finally Steve glanced up at her, his mouth slanted in the half-mocking smile that had the power to make her heart drop to her toes.

"Laura, Franco," he said, "we have a guest with us this morning."

A guest! Ginny's eyes flashed, but she held her tongue and her breath as two pairs of childish eyes turned toward her with frank curiosity.

"She is very pretty," Laura blurted, then caught her lower lip between tiny white teeth. "I mean, good morning, madame."

Amazingly, Laura sketched a graceful curtsy, her hands even holding out the folds of her short dress as she dipped slightly. Franco matched his sister's gracious gesture with a brief bow from the waist, and his gaze was just as frank.

"*Bonjour, madame,*" he said, the French words smooth and fluid on his tongue, an obvious challenge to his sister. Green eyes flecked with gold regarded her gravely from beneath his lashes.

"*Bonjour,*" Ginny replied just as solemnly. "It is very nice to see you both again."

She restrained the urge to go to her knees and gather them into her arms, uncertain how they would respond. Did they not remember her at all? Had they completely forgotten their mother?

Then Laura took a step forward, placing her hands on Ginny's knees, dark-blue eyes so much like her father's staring up earnestly.

"Madame, I do know you, is it not so?"

"Yes, Laura, you do." Ginny took a deep breath and put her hand over the child's. "Though it has been some time since I was able to see you, or hold you…you and Franco have always been in my heart."

But will they understand why I was not with them, why it was better for them to stay in Mexico with Don Francisco than to be with me, when I am not certain I understand it myself?

"But I have seen you— I know! You look just like the portrait that Papa has hung in his study."

Stricken, Ginny glanced up to meet Steve's amused gaze, her first thought of the painting so recently done by Alma-Tadema that hung in the Royal Academy. Surely Laura had not seen *that* painting, the one of her as *The Sultan's Captive* where she wore practically nothing save a few wisps of strategic gauze! Why had she not thought that one day her own children might see the painting?

"Don't worry," Steve drawled, his amusement evident in the grooves that bracketed his mouth, "the miniature in my study is not too—revealing. It's quite suitable for young children, and a good enough likeness. I had no idea Renaldo was an artist of sorts. It must be Missie's influence."

Of course! His cousin Renaldo was a gentle, kind man who had been very generous to Ginny, and worried so that his wild cousin Esteban would actually kill her one day. It must have been his idea to send the painting to remind the twins they had a mother. How like him to be so thoughtful.

"Did you like the painting?" Ginny asked, and Laura studied her with a slightly furrowed brow.

"Yes, very much. But the painting is of our mother, Papa said. Did you know her?"

"As well as anyone could, I think, though there are times I do not think I know her well at all…." She stopped and bit her lip, emotion making her voice quaver and her lower lip tremble slightly, uncertain what she could say to this child staring up at her with such innocent trust.

It was Franco who stated the obvious, his tone flat. "You are the lady in the painting, so you are our mother."

She glanced at him, reminded suddenly of Steve by the wary, reserved gaze the boy directed at her, so different than his twin's openness.

"Yes," she said, taking a deep breath, "I am your mother."

"Where have you been?"

Taken aback, she flashed Steve a rueful glance, saw from his face that he had no intention of helping her and said quietly, "I was on my way to you when I became very ill. As soon as I recovered and could travel again, I came to be with you."

Franco's steady gaze did not waver. "It took you a long time, *ma mère,* to join us."

"Yes." Her throat tightened so that she could barely force the words past her lips. "Far too long."

Silence settled briefly, broken by Laura's impulsive forward motion into her lap, her small body squirming close as she said, "We are glad you have finally come! I have a new puppy. Would you like to see her?"

"Yes...yes, I would like that very much," Ginny got out past the lump in her throat. Laura's sweet face was a blur beyond the hot tears that stung her eyes.

Blindly she allowed the child to pull her up from the ottoman, watched as Laura remembered her manners and turned briefly to her father to ask permission to leave and heard his gruff consent. Her eyes swept over Steve, saw the faint smile on his hard mouth.

"It's always been easy for you, green-eyes," he said softly. "Welcome home."

She caught her breath. *Home.* Strangely, she always thought of Mexico when she thought of home, instead of France, where she had been brought up. Perhaps soon they could return, to bring up their children in the warmth and beauty of Mexico. After all, she still had the Hacienda de la Nostalgia, a marriage gift from Don Francisco, and of course Steve owned a house and extensive land as well. They could take Laura and Franco to Monterey, where the beautiful house overlooked the ocean and the slick black rocks along the California coast, where sea spume laced the air with salty tang and it felt so clean.... Yes, there was much they could do as a family now.

Laura's impatient tug on her hand reminded her of the new puppy, and with a laugh she followed the exuberant child from the parlor and down the hall toward the kitchen where she could already hear excited yaps. Franco was slower in following, his wary reluctance reminding Ginny so much of his father. There was so much of both of them in these children, and her heart leaped with the prospect of their future together. All would be well now. *It had to be....*

"*Maman!*" Laura broke free and raced to kneel beside the small spaniel puppy that bounced enthusiastically against her. "*Maman,* come and see how soft Silky's ears are...."

It was the first time one of her children had called her Mother, and Ginny could not stop the happy tears that rolled down her cheeks as she knelt beside the child to stroke the spaniel.

"Yes, my love," she whispered, "they are very soft."

Laura slanted her a frowning glance from eyes that were slightly uptilted at the corners, unusual eyes like her mother's, with the same gypsyish slant that made Ginny's green eyes so remarkable and exotic.

"But you are crying, *Maman*...."

"Because I am so happy, my sweet. Only because I am so happy...."

And I hope nothing happens to take that happiness away again....

2

Music swirled above the glittering jewels and gas lamps that brightened the vast ballroom filled with the elite of London. Aristocratic heads turned to watch the striking couple that seemed oblivious to the stares, though they were certainly used to them by now.

Of course, Steve Morgan—also known as Esteban Alvarado—the American millionaire who had somehow been appointed as Mexican ambassador, always stood out in a crowd, with his tall, lean good looks and the air of danger that attended him.

"Yes," a dowager whispered behind her jeweled fan, "he does *look* Mexican, I suppose, with his dark skin. And it is said that his grandfather is a rich Mexican landowner descended from Spanish aristocracy, though I think all of them claim a heritage they do not possess."

"Perhaps," her companion remarked, eyeing Steve Morgan with an appreciative smile, "he is aristocratic, though if you look at his eyes—" She shuddered deliciously. "So very wicked, those blue eyes, and the way he looks at a woman. Why, it makes one feel disrobed!"

The dowager countess laughed. "I am not so old that I do not recall how it feels to have a man look at me that way, my dear Amelia, and neither are you. Is it true, do you think, that he *still* has his famous Italian opera singer as mistress even though his wife has just returned? I cannot imagine why he would not be more discreet, though his *wife* has hardly been very discreet herself. My dear, the most delicious *on-dits* claim that she actually lived in a Turkish harem, and then there is that painting that hung in the Royal Academy, the one by Alma-Tadema that is scandalously revealing. It is her, I have heard it said.''

A light tap of folded fan against her companion's arm accompanied the significant glance and whisper. ''It is *said* that the Prince of Wales purchased it from the Academy for his own private collection.... What do you think of that?''

''I think,'' the dowager replied with a sniff, ''that it is far too obvious there is much mystery and rumor about the ambassador's wife, and not all of it can be just the latest gossip. Mrs. Morgan has had her own share of admirers, I am told.''

''Oh my, yes! When she first returned to London, she was seen in the company of Herr Metz, the Swiss banker. Much has been rumored about his preference for *boys,* though it is claimed that he is only a friend of her cousin, Monsieur Pierre Dumont. Very interesting, I think....''

The jeweled fan fluttered more gossip, their boa feathers studded with emeralds and sapphires, intricate patterns of gilt wafting speculation between the women with relish.

''And now Morgan has been appointed as the Mexican ambassador, though I hardly see why it is necessary. There is always revolution in that country, and England should not be involved. Ah, but these politicians must have their intrigues, I suppose. Do you think it true that his wife's former husband, the Russian prince, was actually *killed* by him? He does look as if he could do murder, looks very dangerous despite the fact he's dressed so impeccably.''

As conjecture swirled around them, Steve and Ginny danced a waltz, his arm around her slender waist as he held her against him. His hand spread on green satin the exact shade as Ginny's emerald eyes, lean brown fingers pressed firmly into the small of her back.

Exotic eyes tilted up at him, and a sparkle lit their depths as she smiled provocatively. ''They are all making guesses about us, I am certain.''

"And do you care?" His hand tightened briefly. "Let them talk."

"Shall we give them something else to talk about?" Her soft murmur was accompanied by a subtle shift of her body, so that he felt the press of her breasts as a seductive reminder against his chest.

He gazed down at her through narrowed eyes, amused by her defiance of public convention. Ginny, his green-eyed temptress, his nemesis, the woman who bedeviled and tempted him, the one woman he had never been able to get out of his mind for long. It was just this sort of thing that made him want her, her unexpected flouting of all the rules society expected to be followed, her fiery nature and passionate little body that he knew so well—yet hardly knew at all.

No matter how many times he'd made love to her in the past, there was always something new and surprising when he was with her.

"Have I told you how lovely you are tonight?" he said in a soft drawl, deftly turning her toward the open French doors at the far end of the ballroom. "And how much I would like to kiss you all over?"

"No, you have not." Her murmur and the tempting pout of her mouth reminded him once again how sweet her lips were and how long it had been since they'd made love. He had spent their first night together with Ginny in his arms, but not made love to her since then. He knew she wondered why, as he did himself.

There were so many memories between them, so many times they had fought one another, the verbal spats no less vicious than the physical ones. He still bore the scar from where she had stabbed him so long ago, that time in the desert when he had forced her into submission, taking her on the burning hot sands with only a thin blanket beneath them, not caring if she wanted him—until she had shocked him into taking her seriously. Then she had yielded to him, his passionate little gypsy. With the fresh knife wound bleeding in his side, he had taken her again….

Ginny. When the news had been given to him of her death

in an earthquake in Cuba, he had thought—*known*—it couldn't be true. How could such life, such beauty and passion die without his knowing the exact moment of its death? First a kind of grief, then anger overwhelmed him, until he had moved by rote, living each day because he had no other choice, because he had two children who looked to him for their survival. It had been the children who had kept him from the road to his own destruction, the anguished thought that they were all he had left of Ginny.

So many times in the months he had thought Ginny dead he'd remembered his cruelty to her, her frustration, her fury and, yes, her own brand of vengeance. She knew how to hurt him in return, with a careless shrug of her shoulder and a new admirer on her arm. Now it was time they ended the games, time they came to *know* each other instead of indulging in the constant warfare that always seemed to lead to bed.

Yet he felt so awkward with her now, so damnably like a callow youth instead of her husband. Her lover. The man who had introduced her to the passionate side of her nature—and who had watched her blossom into an alluring woman he had not been able to forget even when he had tried.

Guiding her in a sweep of satin skirts across the ballroom floor, his hand shifted lower, palm testing the contours of the stiff corset binding her beneath the silk. He preferred the softness of her bare flesh beneath his hand, her smooth, flawless skin a welcoming cushion instead of layers of cloth and bone. Why must fashion dictate women hide their bodies behind rigid whalebone and yards of satin?

"What are you thinking about, Steve?" Her elegant head was tilted, her eyes curious as she gazed up at him, and he gave a careless shrug, his tone light.

"I noticed that the Prince of Wales could not take his eyes off you earlier. Is he another of your conquests?"

"Could he be? Oh, don't look so black at me, Steve. I'm only teasing you. The prince is a terrible flirt, but he talked mostly about his tour to America and Canada. It is so difficult to understand his thick German accent at times."

Not replying, he swung her about and through the open

French doors onto a narrow veranda. Strains of the waltz were softer here, and his hand shifted on her back to slide down to the shelf of bunched skirts caught up with bows and lace in the ridiculous fashion called a bustle.

"Steve...?" There was a question in her eyes and tone, the pressure of her hand light on his arm as she looked up at him through her lashes.

"It's more quiet out here." A poor excuse. He just couldn't stand the crowds anymore, the smell of too much perfume, the ennui and desperation that was so evident in the high voices and nervous laughter. It always made him impatient, made him want to ride out where the air was fresh and there were no staring, avid gazes. The impulse to leave the ball was nearly overpowering.

Moonlight filtered through lacy tree branches, pouring molten silver onto the veranda just off the ballroom, and the soft air was spiced with the fragrance of night-blooming flowers. A huge urn at one side dripped soft white blossoms that reminded him of moonflowers, a tropical vine in Mexico that exuded sweet scent and exotic blooms, round and lucent—pale as the moon, as beautifully intense as Mexico.

"You're ready to leave here now, aren't you, Steve?"

He looked down at Ginny, saw the frown gather in her eyes and on her brow. She was far too perceptive at times. He put out a hand, his finger brushing over the gleaming jewels around her neck, vivid against the creamy expanse of her skin. Once her pale skin had been a lovely peachy color, a vibrant tan acquired from days of riding in the hot Mexican sun. His hand fell away and his tone was abrupt.

"You should know something, Ginny."

She tensed beneath his hand, eyes suddenly dark and wide.

"Oh God! You're not going to tell me bad news tonight, Steve, when the music is so gay and the champagne chilled. I am having too good a time and I refuse to allow it."

Despite her flippant words, there was a note of genuine distress in her tone. For all her bravado, Ginny was far too fragile lately. The resilient woman he'd known—had battled across half of Mexico at times—had changed since she'd come back to England for her children. Since they had agreed to reconcile. But hadn't he changed, too?

He forced a smile, dragged his fingertip across the lushly glowing necklace around her throat, up to the heavy earrings dangling from her lobes.

"Ah, hell, sweetheart, you know I just want to tell you how the moonlight makes your eyes glow like stars...."

"Liar." A soft laugh vibrated in the air between them, and she wore a resigned expression on her lovely face. "I know you better than that. You once told me not to expect pretty words in the moonlight from you."

"And I haven't disappointed you."

"No, there have been few pretty words from you, that's true." She moved to lean against the stone wall, a graceful drape of her body that reminded him of the Alma-Tadema painting. In the pale light, her eyes looked huge, darkly mysterious, bewitching. "You hate it here, don't you, Steve? Don't bother denying it. I can see how restless you are, can feel it in the way you hold me. Is it *here* or is it us?"

"London can be stifling at times."

It was the truth—and a lie. The city bound him, tied him down, but the restlessness came from being forced into a role he didn't relish playing.

"I see." Ginny faced him quietly. "I think there's more to it than that. Is there something you don't want to tell me, something to do with us?"

"Not tonight." He bent, took her chin in his palm and kissed her swiftly, more to silence the questions than to serve a need, but that swiftly altered when she caught his lower lip in her teeth, a gentle, warning nip.

"Don't lie to me, Steve Morgan," she whispered when she relinquished his bottom lip, "Honesty, remember?"

He touched his lip with one finger, faintly amused by her vehemence. "Vicious little hellcat."

"I would think you'd remember that."

"And I was beginning to think you'd grown timid lately. I see how mistaken I've been in thinking you have tempered with time."

She smiled. "Let's just say I've grown wiser and less patient. Shall we go back inside? After all, we came to be seen, I believe. We're quite the talk of the town now, I understand, the scandalous Mr. and Mrs. Morgan, with rumors about us as thick as a swarm of bees. I've had no less than three gentlemen ask me tonight if it's true that I am a Russian princess."

"And what did you reply?"

"That of course I am, and I expect to be treated as royalty."

He palmed a fat, loose curl of coppery hair that lay upon her bare shoulder, shining against her alabaster skin like bright silk. Feathery strands curled around his finger in a soft caress. Regretfully, he released her hair, his hand remaining on her shoulder.

"I have to leave you for a little while, Ginny. Try to miss me."

"Leave the ball?"

"No, I have some business matters to attend upstairs. I won't be long, so don't think you're rid of me that easily."

"I wish I believed that."

"You should," he said lightly, "because it's true."

On the surface, it was true. A few of the cabinet members were in attendance tonight, and in his new role as ambassador from Mexico, he was expected to join in the discussion about a possible international crisis. Since Juarez's death in 1872, his successor, Sebastián Lerdo de Tejada, a chief justice of the supreme court, had been unpopular. Lerdo was a liberal anticlerical, hated because he did not flinch from using the power of the state to enforce his policies. Porfirio Díaz had risen again to grasp power from him, and now revolution seethed.

"Disraeli will be here," Lord Sedgwick had murmured to him earlier, "instead of dancing attendance on the queen."

Disraeli, prime minister of England and newly made earl of Beaconsfield, was a powerful man in the confidence of Queen Victoria. His predecessor, Gladstone, had been hated by the widowed monarch. It was likely that England would lean toward the policies favored by Disraeli in regard to the civil unrest in Mexico. Peace was always tenuous.

Since the *Alabama* affair three years before, when U.S. claims negotiations resulting from the British arming of Confederate warships during the Civil War had finally been peacefully resolved, relations between the two countries had been excellent. The warship *Alabama,* most famous of the Confederate raiders, had captured or destroyed over sixty Northern vessels during the conflict. After the war ended, the United States insisted upon compensation for damages from England for reneging on their neutral status. The arbitration tribunal in Geneva awarded damages, England had promptly paid the fine and cordial relations had been restored again. New turmoil on the U.S. border could affect both nations, if England chose to ally with Mexico.

Damn politics! He was more comfortable with action than the interminable speeches and intrigues that suited men like Jim Bishop.

Bishop. The U.S. government agent was as much of an enigma now as he had been when he first came to Steve and offered him a chance at life, instead of the hanging that faced him as the result of a duel. Of course, he'd nearly been killed more times than he could count since then, and all in the name of the United States government.

But he was damned if he knew why Bishop had seen to it that he be appointed an ambassador based in England, other than the fact that it brought him to London at a convenient time for the United States.

"I can count on you, I am certain," Bishop had said in his usual dry way, "to regard the interests of the United States as highly as Mexico's in your duties."

"Don't I always?" he'd answered, and they both knew the answer to that.

Now here he was, balanced on a tightrope between two countries again, and at the same time trying to reconcile with his wife.

Ginny, of the fiery hair and temperament. The young girl he had first met had evolved into this composed, beautiful woman who seemed so confident and poised. He'd married her twice, both times to assuage scandal, yet still did not know her. She eluded him, the essence of her like a wisp of fog, always just beyond his grasp.

Yet her ethereal nature was what had captured his heart so long ago, intrigued him more than any woman ever had. Even after he'd abducted her and taken her with him into the mountains of Mexico, she'd not lost her allure for him. Not until his grandfather had forced him to marry Ginny, had he taken the time to explore his reasons for keeping her with him. And then it had almost been too late....

His activities as a *Juarista* nearly cost them both their lives. That separation, when he had been sent to a hellish prison, was only the first of so many since then. Yet somehow they always managed to survive, to end up in each others arms again. Even after this last separation, when Ginny had stormed out of New Orleans with Andre Delery and he'd thought he would never see her again, part of him had known he would. Maybe that was the reason he had taken their children from Ginny's aunt in France, bringing them to England. He knew she would search for them once she left Stamboul.

It rankled that, until so recently, she had been living in a sultan's harem with Richard Avery, Lord Tynedale—his grandfather's son. It had been Avery who was responsible for informing the Russian ambassador to Turkey of Ginny's need to leave Stamboul when revolution loomed. As the Russian tsar's illegitimate—but favored—daughter, she incurred ongoing interest from both the tsar and Russian authorities.

Steve had gone to Stamboul to find her when news of the impending Turkish revolution was given to him, and he had missed her. Instead, he had met General Ignatiev, a Russian officer sent by the tsar, who had helped Richard Avery arrange for Ginny's flight from Stamboul when it became apparent she was in grave danger.

She always seemed to emerge from disaster unscathed, a phoenix rising from the ashes.

It was difficult to recall that she had been blind for a time, that Avery had been the man to take care of her. Now she gazed up at him with a familiar sparkle in her clear green eyes, a half smile curving her sensuous mouth.

"As long as you are meeting with *gentlemen,* and not one of the ladies who look at you so greedily, I will share you. But do not forget that you are going home with me, Steve Morgan."

Though she said it playfully, tapping him with her folded fan, there was steely determination in her tone. He grinned.

"I have a feeling I would regret it very much if I were to find companionship elsewhere tonight. Would you use the little knife you no doubt still carry?"

"Perhaps...or perhaps I would come after you."

"It would not be the first time."

"Ah, and has Concepción—I mean, Lady Marwood—ever forgiven me for that? I did not hurt your old *friend,* after all, though I was greatly tempted."

Steve laughed softly, and spread his hand atop Ginny's shoulder, fingers digging gently into her skin. "No, I don't think Concepción will ever forgive you for besting her. She did not expect a *gringa* to outfight a gypsy."

Green eyes narrowed slightly. "It seems that she wasn't the only one to underestimate me."

So Ginny still had not forgiven him for taking their children to Lord Marwood's house in Devon, but he had no intention of explaining himself again. After all that had gone between them, he'd known he could trust Concepción to keep his children safe, whether she hated Ginny or not. Or perhaps *because* she hated Ginny, it would have given her great satisfaction to withhold her children from her.

He cupped his hand under Ginny's chin to forestall the question he saw simmering in her eyes. In no mood to field jealous demands, he bent to kiss her. Immediately, she melted into him, her body firm and lithe, her lips half-open beneath his mouth, passionate and demanding.

Christ, he had forgotten for a moment how easily she could arouse him with a kiss, the pressure of her small, firm breasts against him a reminder of what lay beneath her elaborate gown and female underpinnings. Heat surged, the old fires as hot as ever, and as high. If he didn't back off now, he'd end up causing a true scandal. He broke off the kiss, saw from her swift glance of satisfaction that she was well aware of his reaction and shook his head grimly.

"Go and dance with your cousin, little hellcat. I see him looking for you. I'll be at your side when we go in to supper."

Mutiny flashed in her eyes, but she gave an acquiescent shrug. "If you insist. Pierre is too infatuated with the lovely Miss Prendergast, whom *you* escorted to England, to take much notice of me at the moment, but I'm certain I can find a dance partner without too much trouble. Perhaps even an escort into supper if you do not return."

"I'm certain you can." His hand clamped down on her arm in a vise, but he only lifted her hand to his lips, his gaze lazy and mocking. "As long as he's agreeable about being replaced when I return, there will be no trouble."

He left her just inside the French doors, where the music was loud and the vast ballroom, with its glittering crystal chandeliers, stuffy and crowded, giving her hand to Pierre Dumont with a meaningful lift of his brow.

Pierre was no fool. He would keep an eye on Ginny to be certain there were no more scandals. There was already too much conjecture, too many whispers floating around London about them, and he hoped his volatile wife remembered that.

3

But Steve needn't have worried about Ginny.

She was the model of decorum, taking great pains to play the part of doting wife and mother, even while she worried that Steve had resorted to his old ways. If he had— If he had, she would be desolate. The past years had taught her how much she wanted peace in her life, a real family, with husband and children around her, not the tempestuous tumult that she had lived in far too long.

And oddly, even though she was nearly thirty years old now, she felt as if she had just grown up. It was a shocking realization, the knowledge that she had been so selfish and self-absorbed these past years, so caught up in the private struggle with Steve, that she had failed to notice how her own actions were to blame for many of her tragedies.

Not all of them, of course, for she hadn't chosen to be taken hostage by Steve so long ago, and certainly had not chosen to be taken prisoner by that fat Colonel Devereaux right after marrying Steve. Those events had been thrust upon her. And so had Tom Beal. *God!* She still shuddered in horror at the memories of his cruelty, and was fiercely glad that she had killed the mercenary. He'd deserved it.

But the girl she had been then had become the woman she was now, more mature, aware of what she wanted finally—Steve, of course.

Steve was the only man she had ever really loved, though

she had thought she could forget him with others, thought for a time—with Richard Avery—that she could pretend he never existed. But it was all a lie, for she had not been able to forget Steve even when she'd hated him, even when she had thought him executed in the revolution and her life no longer worth living. Nothing seemed to matter after that: not the men, the gaiety of life in Mexico City, nor when she danced for Emperor Maximilian in Chapultepec.

And Steve had survived after all, had been one of the *Juaristas* who fought against the French invaders in Mexico, finally driving them out of the country. Steve, a fierce *Juarista,* alive and hating her then for what he had thought was her betrayal. But she hadn't allowed him to hate her, had followed him to the small hacienda where Concepción waited for him, had fought the Mexican gypsy for him and won the right to wait for his return. After that, Steve had looked at her with new respect, and a wariness that was more revealing than any confessions.

There was the same look in his eyes at times now, as if he were reassessing her. As if they were still in Mexico.

Mexico!

She inhaled sharply, so that Pierre, who had been scanning the crowd for the lovely Lorna Prendergast—the American girl whose father was a friend of Steve's and his partner, Sam Murdock, and who had accompanied Steve to London with her mother—turned to glance at her with surprise.

"What is the matter, Virginie?"

Quickly, she hid her sudden apprehension, for Pierre would only dismiss her misgivings if she voiced them.

"Nothing. Oh, except that I read this morning in the *Times* that there is trouble in Mexico between Lerdo and Díaz again. I had thought—hoped—that perhaps we could return soon, so the children can grow up with their heritage."

"Leave England with the children? What does your husband have to say about that? Now that he is ambassador—a farce in my opinion—isn't his presence required in London?"

"Oh, Pierre, I am certain that he will not stay here long. When has he ever remained in one place for long? Only Mexico has ever held him for any length of time, and then only because of his grandfather.'' She tapped her folded fan lightly against her cousin's arm, a playful smile on her lips masking the sudden narrowing of her eyes. ''But *you* would know what Steve plans to do, would you not?''

''How would I know? Your husband does not confide in me, Virginie.''

''Does he not? I thought perhaps he spoke to you of his plans—of a possible return to Mexico.''

A flush darkened Pierre's fair face, and he shook his head. ''Do not involve me in your marital discussions, for you know how I feel. My God, you have only been back a month and already you are talking of leaving here!''

''But London is not my home. Pierre, I want to go home again, back to Mexico with my children, where they can grow up in the warm sunshine and life is less complicated.''

''Your life will never be uncomplicated,'' he replied bluntly. ''You will not allow it. I suppose you intend to take the children and leave if your husband does not agree? Or will you leave them behind again, as you have done far too often in the past?''

For a moment she was silent, stung by his accusation and aware of the truth behind it. Then she said quietly, ''I have no intention of trying to take them away from their father, nor do I wish to leave them again. Oh, you may look at me skeptically and I don't blame you, but it's the truth. I'm tired of it all, tired of the uncertainty, of not knowing if he loves me or if I will ever see him again. I want a *home,* Pierre, can you understand that? A home of my own, where I can watch my children grow up and know that my husband will be there at my side. I think that it's all I have ever wanted, but I never knew it until recently.''

''Then you should tell that to your husband, not to me.''

''Yes. You are right, of course. I fully intend to do just that.''

Pierre's expression softened and he managed a smile that looked faintly rueful. ''Virginie, *petite cousine,* of course you will do what you must. Forgive me.''

"There is nothing to forgive. Pierre—"

Lorna Prendergast, a spoiled, willful girl much too certain of her youthful beauty, and *far* too enamored of Steve, chose that moment to appear at Pierre's elbow, her lovely face set into a mask of polite inquiry. Auburn hair gleamed under the glow of crystalline light, and her tawny eyes were frankly curious and malicious as she greeted Ginny with a smile.

"How generous of Mr. Morgan to allow you to stay with the children for a time," she said sweetly as she tucked her hand into the crook of Pierre's arm with a proprietary air, "for I am certain you must have missed them a great deal."

"Yes, I did. But then, Steve doesn't want any of us to be parted again." Ginny lifted a brow, her smile coolly polite as she added, "I would have preferred staying at home with them tonight, but he insisted I accompany him. I'm sure you realize how *forceful* Steve can be when he's determined to have his own way."

Her implication had the desired effect; crimson stains marred the ivory purity of Lorna's face and her lips twisted as if she had just bitten into a sour lemon. Poor Pierre wore the look of a man struck with a pole. He wavered, his eyes beseeching as he looked from Ginny to Miss Prendergast, but she took no pity on her cousin.

"I am certain Pierre can tell you how difficult a time it has been for our family lately, Miss Prendergast, and how relieved we all are to be together again after so much time apart."

Lorna's eyes narrowed thoughtfully, but her smile recovered. She had the air of a woman accustomed to having her every whim granted, for whom a refusal would not be tolerated, and being ignored would be unbearable.

"Yes, there must be *much* the two of you have to settle between you, especially after the scandalous painting of you that was recently hung in the Royal Academy—or does your husband know about that yet?"

"Your curiosity is misplaced, Miss Prendergast. And quite impertinent. If I thought my cousin susceptible to your self-indulgent charms, I would be greatly concerned."

Lorna glanced up at Pierre, who looked nearly desperate

with discomfort. She tapped him lightly with her folded fan. "Why, Monsieur Dumont, I am grieved that you think of me so little."

"In truth, Miss Prendergast, you have been all I have thought of since meeting you," Pierre replied gallantly, and he flicked a warning glance at Ginny as if to demand she not create a scene.

He might well save himself distress, Ginny thought with growing boredom, for she had no intention of being drawn any further into a discussion of Steve Morgan, nor did she desire to remain a witness to Lorna Prendergast's flirtation with Pierre. There were much more important things to think about than this rather spoiled young woman.

"Excuse me," she murmured, "I see my aunt is looking for me."

Before Pierre could protest, Ginny had moved away from them and crossed the ballroom, weaving her way through full skirts of satin and silk, the glitter of jewels and the drone of conversation a familiar background. Snatches of gossip fluttered in the air on wings of suppressed excitement.

"...but my dear, you *must* know that he was seen in an intimate *tête-à-tête* with an opera singer..."

"Such a handsome man, but dangerously wicked, don't you agree, my dear Lady Epson?"

A delicate shudder accompanied the dowager's gossip, and she leaned forward to say in a loud whisper, "An Italian opera singer—Francesca di Paoli, I believe. She was so enraged by his defection to his wife that she threw an absolute tantrum and promptly began seeing that German duke. I heard that she was to attend this ball tonight, and if she does, what a delicious scene *that* would be!"

Laughter followed their conjecture, and they both turned to watch as Ginny moved past them on her way to the far end of the ballroom where Tante Celine stood with some of her friends.

Damn Steve, he *would* abandon her to the gossip of old cats, she fumed as she made polite replies to her aunt's queries and sipped champagne punch more freely than she should. Why did he always do this?

And the gossip about Francesca di Paoli, his former mistress and a thorn in her side.... Surely she would not be here this evening! Oh, that would be just *too* much to bear if the haughty Italian diva made an appearance!

"Ginette," Tante Celine leaned forward to say with a slight frown, "are you unwell?"

Ginny flashed a bright smile to hide her turmoil. "No, no, of course not. Just a bit weary. The twins were quite insistent that I join them on their picnic today, and it began to rain and we had to run back to the pony trap. I hope Laura does not take a chill."

"I'm certain she will be just fine. She is stronger than she appears, and Franco is such a sturdy child."

Diverted by the thoughts of her children, Ginny nodded in agreement, her smile growing pensive.

This past month getting to know the twins had been the best days of her life, but though Laura readily accepted her, Franco was more guarded. He was so like Steve, and she thought ruefully that she now knew what Don Francisco had meant when he had said his grandson was a hellion as a child. He must have been, for she saw the same reckless streak in Franco.

Just yesterday he had climbed to the top of one of the huge old trees in the back garden, defying his nurse's pleas to come down until she came to Ginny in hysterics. It had been terrifying to see the small boy so high, clinging to a thick limb and pretending he was not afraid, stubbornly refusing to come down until Ginny had shrugged carelessly and said that he must be very brave to be so high, but his father would be home soon and he must come down so he could tell him how far he had climbed.

Then she had held her breath as Franco made his way down the tree, limb by limb, until he was on the ground again and the footmen were allowed to put away the ladders that Madame Dupree had summoned. Yes, he was very like Steve, she thought with a mixture of resignation and dismay, just as daring, just as reckless.

As if her thoughts had summoned him, she saw Steve enter the ballroom and pause just inside an arched doorway. His lean build and dark features were achingly familiar, and still had the power to quicken her heartbeat. It was all only a thin veneer, the urbanity he donned as casually as a silk jacket to hide his true nature. And it was that trait women seemed to recognize in him, the air of repressed danger that made Steve Morgan an exciting challenge.

Too often, the eager women who tried to tame him found to their sorrow that he could not be domesticated like some feral cat. But perhaps that was what drew them.

Ginny waited, frowning slightly as she heard the buzz of excited voices escalate and her aunt's sudden, muffled exclamation.

"What is it, *Tante?*"

Celine seemed flustered, her eyes anxious, her smile too quick. "Do not react hastily, Ginette!"

"But why should I, *Tante?*"

Then she saw the reason, and her fingers tightened into a vise around the fragile stem of her wineglass. As the crowd shifted, she saw Francesca di Paoli enter to stand at Steve's side, a hand on his arm as she leaned close to whisper into his ear.

Diamonds glittered in the Italian singer's hair and on her earlobes and around her neck, reflecting lamplight in sparkling-hued rainbows. She was slim and very beautiful, with the pale skin of a madonna and classically oval features set off by large, flashing dark eyes and thick masses of glossy, dark-brown hair coiled at the back of her small head. She radiated arrogance and confidence in her appeal to men—especially the man on her arm.

Fury clogged Ginny's throat and burned her eyes, but she forced herself to remain outwardly calm as she lifted her wineglass and sipped the smoky, brisk wine that did nothing to cool her rising temper.

Garbed in a snowy brocade fitted to her voluptuous curves,

di Paoli ignored everyone but Steve, her attention trained on his handsome face. Paco Davis, Steve's old friend and long-time partner, had told Ginny about her, admitting without words the intimacy of the Italian singer's relationship with Steve, as if she had not already known it. Hadn't she seen newspapers touting them as a couple? Yes, and though it had been when she was entangled with Prince Ivan Sahrkanov, she had still been furious with Steve for flaunting the Italian diva so openly.

Apparently, he had not severed their relationship.

How difficult it was to break old habits. Would Steve resist the obvious allure of di Paoli? After all, he had once told her that Francesca was more of a friend to him than anyone had ever been. That taunt had rankled for a long time. It still did.

Foregoing the temptation to react rashly, Ginny ignored her aunt's worried glances and instead turned to the dowager at her side, chatting casually as if nothing were amiss.

Behind the flutter of a jewelled fan, the dowager's eyes sparkled with open curiosity, but her conversation was as mundane as afternoon tea.

"I understand that your husband is from Mexico, is he not, Mrs. Morgan?"

"Yes, he is."

"Odd, he certainly doesn't look very Mexican, though he *is* rather dark complected. All that bright sunshine in Mexico, I would think. It is hot there, I understand."

"Yes, it is very sunny in Mexico, and warm. And my husband is only half-Mexican. His father was American."

"Ah, I see," the dowager commented, and her shrewd eyes shifted to the little group dominated by Steve and Francesca that stood by the portico. "Do you attend the opera often, Mrs. Morgan?"

"Only with my husband, Lady Wooddale." The old cat! She knew very well the rumors that were running amok about Steve and the opera singer! It was time to defuse them. Her smile was mechanical and polite. "Please excuse me."

Gliding through the crowd that seemed to magically part for her, Ginny approached the little group by the open door of the portico. Steve saw her first, his blue eyes crinkled the smallest bit in amusement as she held his gaze, her chin up in customary defiance.

This was familiar footing, this cat-and-mouse game they had always played with one another, much more comfortable than the awkward courtesy of careful reacquaintance.

"Mrs. Morgan," Lord Grayson said when she reached their group, "it is an honor to have you join us."

Though she murmured a polite reply to the baronet, her gaze held Steve's eyes with relentless tenacity. She would not allow anyone to intimidate or ignore her ever again, she vowed silently, and finally shifted her attention to the woman on Steve's arm.

Francesca di Paoli watched her with dark eyes that burned like banked coals, not attempting to hide her disdain for the wife of her former lover.

"Stefano, is this your little wife?" she asked with a haughty lift of her brow. "She is not at all as I expected her to be, *caro.*"

It was not, Ginny knew, meant as a compliment. Green eyes clashed with black, fiercely competitive.

"No? Yet you are everything I thought you would be. Steve, darling, it is getting late and I'm worried about our children. Don't you think we should be going home?"

"Leaving?" the man at her elbow protested. "Surely not so soon, I hope! I have not yet had the honor of a dance with so lovely a lady. If your husband does not mind, of course."

As the viscount turned toward him, Steve shrugged, the suggestion of a smile touching his lips. "My wife has a mind of her own, Lord Hartsfield."

Hartsfield turned back to Ginny. A tall man, with large brown eyes that reminded her of Laura's puppy, he had an eager, boyish expression and manner, and she found herself in the awkward position of being rude or forced into a dance she did not want.

Courtesy demanded she acquiesce to Hartsfield with a gracious smile, and as he swept her onto the dance floor to the lovely tune of a Strauss waltz, she caught a glimpse of malicious triumph in Francesca's eyes.

"I understand that your husband supports the opera most generously," Lord Hartsfield remarked. "It was his efforts that brought Signorina di Paoli to London to appear in a production of *Caglisotro,* the Strauss operetta, was it not?"

"My husband has a great appreciation of the arts," Ginny replied with a smile that felt frozen on her lips. Damn Steve, had he brought that...that *creature* to London? Oh, it would be just like him to do such a thing, careless of the consequences, or how it affected her. She felt like scratching that smug smile from the Italian whore's mouth!

As if reading her mind, Steve suddenly appeared at their side on the dance floor as the waltz ended. "I believe this next dance is mine, my love. I'm certain you don't mind, Lord Hartsfield."

If Hartsfield was disappointed, he didn't show it, but relinquished Ginny's hand with a murmur of gratitude for her company.

Steve pulled her against him, his eyes dark blue and glittering with amusement as he looked down at her. "You look as if you could rip me in two, Ginny-love."

"Why is she here, and with *you?* Is that the important business you had? I swear, Steve, I just don't think I can—"

"Not here." His hand tightened briefly around her waist, a warning squeeze that reminded her where they were. His tone was soft, a lazy, amused drawl. "The arrangements were made months ago, before I knew that you would ever return from Stamboul."

"And now that I'm back?"

"Everything has changed, green-eyes."

She caught her breath at the sudden intimacy of his tone, the intense glance he gave her. "What do you mean *everything?*"

"Ginny, we've danced around this subject for the past month. This is hardly the time or place to discuss it now."

He was right, of course. But it was the first sign he had given her that he truly wanted her to stay, to be with him.

Ginny's hand trembled on his shoulder, her fingers pale on the dark cloth of his coat, the emerald ring she wore a great, winking green eye.

Carelessly, as if he did not care if she accepted it, he'd given her the ring the week before, saying, "I bought it a long time ago for you, and almost forgot it until my valet found it with some pieces of my mother's jewelry."

Any comments had stuck in her throat, the desire to blurt out questions overriding her appreciation of the beautiful, square-cut emerald that looked so large on her small hand. She had been too cowardly then to ask the questions that were always on her mind, but now?

"Steve, it's getting very late. We aren't expected to stay here all night, are we?"

"Tired of the wealthy elite already?" His mouth crooked in a teasing smile. "You've always looked quite at home with the aristocrats, my love."

"Yes, I'm sure I have, but tonight I find them boring. I *do* get tired of being stared at and gossiped about, and I see little difference between these people and others who feel free to pry where they're not wanted."

Over his shoulder, she saw Francesca di Paoli dancing with Lord Grayson, her dark head bent close as if hanging upon his every word. Languid eyes lifted, clashed with Ginny's, her smile infuriatingly confident before she was swept away in the steps of the dance.

"Or be where they're not wanted. What did you tell her, Steve?"

He didn't pretend to misunderstand, and shrugged.

"'Cesca? I told her that I was going to dance with my wife." He moved effortlessly, taking her with him across the floor, his steps moving them closer to the door. His hand on her back was warm, firm. "After supper, we'll make our farewells to our hosts and I'll have the carriage brought around. The problem with these affairs is that they last too damned long."

"And are too crowded, perhaps."

His eyes crinkled slightly at the corners. "Yes, perhaps it is getting a bit crowded here. Too many gossips."

"And old lovers."

His hand tightened, fingers pressing into her skin, a hard reminder. "Let's keep this civilized, shall we?"

Ginny bit her lip, angry at herself for bringing up his former relationship with Francesca. It was hardly the way to reconcile, if she couldn't even control her unruly tongue!

So much had changed between them, so many old hurts and suspicions still had the power to destroy them if they allowed them. Could they get through all this?

The past month had been so...strained, as if they were strangers living under the same roof, sharing a love for two children but still feeling their way cautiously in their own relationship. There had been no discussion between them, no disagreements. And no resolutions.

Later, she decided, a mechanical smile on her face as she felt the curious gazes on them, I will confront Steve. I'll risk it all—my pride and my heart. Will he see that I really want nothing more than to be with him and our children, to make a new life together?

Yes. It had been a month, far too long to continue as they were. Tonight when they were alone, she would be very direct and ask Steve what he planned. It was a new thing, to contemplate honest conversation between them, a discussion that did not involve screaming accusations or snarled insults.

Yes. She would talk to him, would bare her soul and tell him that she loved him, ask him if they could soon return to Mexico with their children and start a life together all over again.

4

It was late when they arrived at the house that Steve had leased in a fashionable section of London, one of the comfortable houses on Bruton Street that were not ostentatious but spacious and welcoming. Pink sandstone gleamed in the pale glow of the moon that peeked from behind swirling wisps of cloud, dimly illuminating the street as their carriage rolled to a halt. A gas lamp sputtered fitfully against the shadows.

Midsummer was usually warm in London, but tonight it was cool, and Ginny pulled her silk shawl up around her shoulders as she descended from the carriage and went into the house. Small pools of lamplight gleamed on black-and-white tile floors of the entrance hall, and out of the shadows stepped the maid to welcome them.

"You are up late, Berthilde," Ginny said with a slight frown. "Are the children all right?"

The tiny woman built like a sparrow nodded as she took Ginny's silk shawl. "*Oui, madame.* It is just that Laura woke and the lamps were out, and Madame Dupree asked me to fetch her some warm milk to calm her."

"Another nightmare?" Steve started toward the stairs.

Ginny followed, lifting her skirts in a whispery rustle of satin as she tried to keep up with his long strides. Feet clad in emerald satin the same shade as her gown skimmed up the stairs, but Steve took the stairs two at a time, and she was breathless by the time they reached the nursery on the second floor. A soft breeze belled lace curtains over open windows. The lights were on and bright, revealing a tousle-haired Laura sitting up in bed and Madame Dupree trying to coax her to lie down. The nurse turned to Steve, exasperation in her eyes.

"She is quite all right, Monsieur Morgan," she said briskly, "except that she is stubborn to a fault. She refuses to go back to sleep unless you are here. It is not a trait to encourage in the child, and I suggest that you—"

"Madame Dupree, I suggest that you close that window and then go back to your room. I will take care of my daughter now. If you have any more suggestions, you may make them to your next employer."

Madame Dupree grasped his meaning immediately, and her mouth closed with an audible snap. Wisely, she made no other comment, but went to close the window and then left the room.

Laura had quieted immediately upon seeing her father, and dimpled as she smiled up at him. "You are very late, Papa. Was the party nice?"

"You little imp, what are you doing awake at this hour? Was it the dream again?"

"Yes, only this time, I got away." A shadow flickered on the child's face, and her eyes darkened. "It was a bad man who would not let us go, even when I told him I wanted to go home."

Ginny bit her lip at the swift, accusing glance Steve flung at her. Herr Frederick Metz, the Swiss banker she had been involved with when she first reached London, had sent men to snatch the children from the country house while Steve was away. The hired thugs had not counted on Steve's early return, nor anticipated that Laura would recognize her father and wave to him as their carriage passed him on the road. The result was inevitable, but for them to watch their father battle— Oh, she remembered too well how Steve fought, viciously and with no restraint. It would have been even more frightening to two small children, and it was all her fault.

Her gaze shifted from Laura to Franco's bed across the room. He was sitting up, sleepy-eyed but observant. What must he think, as well? In the past weeks she had tried so hard to penetrate the shell he kept around him, but the boy resisted her every effort.

"I told you Papa would come," he said now to Laura, "and he did. He always keeps us safe. Go back to sleep."

Was there an unvoiced rebuke in that comment for his mother, perhaps? Ginny couldn't blame him. She had not been there for them when they needed her, had not kept them safe as Steve had done.

When Laura was finally settled, Steve accompanied Ginny to her bedroom, reaching around her to open the door. A low fire eased the chill, the coals a flickering glow in the grate. Ginny draped her silk shawl over the graceful lines of a Sheraton chair and turned to watch as Steve shrugged out of his evening jacket to toss it carelessly onto the coatrack in one corner.

Lately, he left her at her door, going down the hall to his own chamber, courteous and remote, as if they were complete strangers again. No—even when they *were* strangers, he had never viewed her with the same dispassionate gaze of the past month.

Her resolve to draw him into an honest discussion intensified, and she was slightly surprised to find that she was nervous and on edge. Clumsily, she began to fumble with the buttons of her gown, more to gain time than anything else.

"Dismiss your maid," he said, eyeing her, "and I'll help you with the rest of your dress."

"No, thank you, this dress is far too expensive to allow you to rip it," she retorted with a faint smile, "and I recall very well your methods of removing my garments for me."

A flash of humor glinted in his eyes, his mocking smile reminding her of the many times he had stripped away her clothes without regard for their expense, or her protests.

"Do you think I cannot buy you another gown, Ginny my love?" He tugged loose his tie, his fingers efficient and swift. "I've purchased more gowns from Worth than he has no doubt sold to the entire country of France."

"Yes, but not all of them were for me." It was an automatic

response to his teasing, but she regretted it the moment the words were out. Why remind him of all the women in his life?

His dark brow lifted and his eyes narrowed slightly as he met her gaze. "They should have been," he said quietly, leaving her momentarily speechless.

There was something so *different* about him. Oh, yes, he had changed. He looked the same, with his wicked eyes and smile, his air of danger and darkly lean good looks that were still a magnet for women of all ages. But there was a difference now. Beneath the outer hardness of his face and manner there was a taciturn regard that baffled her.

They had slept apart since the night when he had pulled her into the house she shared with Pierre and Tante Celine, but there had been no explanation. That night he had brought her to his house and his bed, and she had spent it in his arms, feverish kisses, caresses, hungry words of love and reunion all that was between them until the early hours of morning.

But after that, a careful distance, a polite detachment between them, as if they were still protagonists instead of husband and wife trying to find common ground again. It was awkward, a courteous fiction as transparent as morning mist.

At first, she had been so weary in body and soul, still tentative in their new relationship, that she had not wanted more from him. But now she could not help but wonder if he wanted her at all. Did he? Or had he tired of her? After all, she was nearly thirty now and had been through so much. But her mirror told her she was still firm and youthful, her skin barely showing signs of motherhood. The marks she'd gotten while carrying the twins had faded to faint silvery tracks like pale spiderwebs, barely perceptible on her belly and thighs.

A little clumsily, feeling damnably awkward, she said, "I suppose you managed to finish your business this evening? You must have, for I hardly saw you the rest of the night, not until our late supper."

"Complaints, Ginny?"

"Questions." She unhooked the emerald necklace circling her neck and placed it in a velvet box, then removed the matching earrings that dangled from her lobes. They clinked softly as she dropped them into the box, splashes of green against soft black velvet.

Turning to face him, she saw his eyes narrow warily at her. A mask seemed to drop over his face, as if he expected the worst, and she remembered suddenly all the times she had raged at him, screamed at him like a virago, half-wild with rage and anguish.

Inhaling deeply, she calmed herself with the reminder that he was here with her because he chose to be, and that she was with him for the same reason. They had their lives ahead of them, once they got past the lingering resentments and old ghosts.

"It's too easy to suspect the worst, I suppose," she began, but a discreet knock at the door interrupted her. It was Berthilde with her dressing gown, eyes sleepy in the dim light of the hallway lamp as she held out the yellow silk.

"It was being cleaned, madame. Shall I assist you?"

"No, Berthilde, go to bed. I won't need you tonight."

The door closed softly behind the girl and silence fell as she turned to look at Steve, saw his fleeting frown disappear to be replaced by a carefully blank expression.

Altering her earlier decision to be direct, she said instead, "You promised to help me with my gown, I believe."

As he came to her she turned, and his fingers brushed against the vulnerable nape of her neck as he tugged at the top button. Cool air whisked over her skin, made her shiver. She caught a glimpse of their reflection in the mirror across the room, his dark head bent, a vivid contrast to her bright hair as he worked the buttons of her lovely gown.

Oh, the memories, of the many times he had undressed her, of the times they had fought one another and loved one another. And now here they were, pretending a courtesy neither felt, while unanswered questions formed a barrier between them.

It was time for answers.

"Signorina di Paoli did not look very happy when we left tonight," she observed, and saw his reflected shrug. "I think she was most unhappy when you did not escort her in to supper.''

''She seemed happy enough with Lindhaven. They're old friends.''

It was on the tip of her tongue to point out that once *he* had been close friends with her, as well, but she said instead, ''How long do you intend to stay in London, Steve? I mean, this ambassador position, it's not really what you like to do, is it?''

His soft laugh stirred the hair over her ear as he leaned forward, flicking open the last button. ''Are you worried about my happiness, Ginny-love?''

She pulled away, tugged at the bodice of her gown to peel it away and stepped out of the glittering material that slid to a puddle around her ankles. Clad in only white silk undergarments, she draped the gown on a padded hanger, kept her hands busy to avoid looking at him.

''Your happiness affects mine,'' she said evenly. ''Of course I would worry that you're happy.''

She hooked the gown on the dressing room door, then allowed Steve to untie the laces of her corset. The stiff garment was so constrictive, forcing her to remain upright, binding her ribs almost painfully now. Ginny heaved a sigh of relief as the laces were freed and she could breathe more easily. Slipping on the silk dressing gown, she moved to the small mahogany table cluttered with bottles of expensive perfume and powders. Deftly unfastening the combs that held her hair atop the crown of her head, she eyed him in the mirror when he didn't respond. Nothing showed in his face, only that careful attention that was like a mask.

Oh, I feel so awkward, so uncertain!

''We have the children to think of,'' she pointed out as her hair fell free, a copper cloud that framed her face and made her look far too pale, so that her eyes resembled glittering bits of green glass. ''I admit that I haven't done what I should for them, but I want to start over. I want *us* to start over, Steve. I want to go home, home to Mexico. I think that's where the children need to be, and—''

Disbelief flashed in his eyes, and his brow shot up. "Mexico? Christ, Ginny, you can't be serious. Or haven't you heard it's a battleground now that Díaz is fighting for power?"

"Yes, of course I have." She tugged the silver-backed hairbrush through her hair, her eyes focused on Steve's reflection in the mirror. "But Lerdo is president now, isn't he? If the fighting is nearly over, it should soon be safe. I do not see why we can't make plans to return—"

"Maybe your memory is shorter than mine," he said harshly, "because I can damn well remember how it was when Maximilian was in Mexico. Have you forgotten the *Juaristas,* the revolution, the *soldaderos?*"

An involuntary shudder tracked chills down her spine, and Steve's voice softened a little at her visible reaction.

"Ginny, the fighting is not yet over. I won't risk the children in Mexico right now, and for that matter, I won't risk *you* there until I make sure it's safe."

Her fingers shook slightly as she placed the hairbrush carefully on the dressing table; silver gleamed in the soft lamplight. "Does this mean that you intend to go to Mexico?"

A faint, rueful smile tucked one corner of his mouth inward, but his eyes were watchful. "You've always had a way of getting straight to the point when you choose. Yes, Ginny love, that's exactly what I mean. As ambassador—"

"Pierre said your appointment was a farce," she broke in as she turned back to face him. "Is it? Is that why you're in London? Is this appointment due to Jim Bishop's machinations again? His dark intrigues?"

"Dammit, Ginny—"

"I *knew* it! It is Bishop. He's here, isn't he? In London? Like he was in New Orleans, and in San Francisco, and every other time things have gone so wrong.... Will it ever end? Will you ever just want to be with *me* and not go running off trying to save the world?"

"Save the world? How melodramatic you can be, Ginny my love. If men like Jim Bishop didn't try to *save the world,* as you put it, there would be total anarchy. Bands of mercenaries running wild—"

"As you did?"

Blue eyes narrowed fractionally at her, a cold glitter in their depths that reminded her how ruthless he could be.

"I assume you're referring to my time spent as a *Juarista. Juaristas* weren't mercenaries."

"Weren't they?"

"No, not like your beloved French soldiers, who raped, murdered and looted with impunity from Maximilian. At least the Juaristas were fighting to protect their own country."

"Yes," she said quietly, "and it will happen all over again if you're right. Steve, please, if Mexico is in danger of having another long revolution, we'll stay here. Or we can go to France, or even Russia. We could visit my father—he sent for me, and if not for the trouble in Bulgaria, I might be there now. Oh, Steve, it was chance that took me back to France, and then of course, finding out you had brought the children to England—"

When he remained silent, she said almost desperately, "We can go anywhere we'll be together and not torn apart again. I don't think I could bear it if we're separated, or I must be away from the children again. They are just beginning to remember me. *You* are just beginning to remember me...."

The wariness in his eyes altered subtly. He reached out, touched a blunt fingertip to her cheek, scrubbed his thumb over the moisture he found there and lifted his dark brow.

"Tears, *mi amante?*"

"Steve, I want a *home,* a real home, where we can watch our children grow up and know that we'll always be there together. It's all I've ever wanted, but I never knew how much until recently. Until I saw you again, and saw how the children love you and how you love them. It—it showed me a side of you I hadn't suspected was there."

His hand dropped to his side and he didn't respond. Ginny felt the beginning of despair well inside at the futility of wanting that elusive security and love she'd searched for since she was only a child. First, her mother had died, and her father was always absent. Though she had known herself well-loved by Tante Celine and her cousins, it had not been the same thing at all. Not even when she'd left France to join her father in America, had she felt as if she truly belonged. Always an outsider, always feeling as if she had somehow lost something precious. And she had spent far too long in search of it.

The mistakes she'd made, the men in her life—the futile search for acceptance, for unconditional love to fill the void. Now she was a woman grown, with children of her own, and she still felt as if she was that lost, lonely child inside.

Steve put his palm against her cheek, his skin rough and warm as he stroked her face gently.

"Ginny, I wasn't going to tell you now, but I guess it's best to get it over with. I'm leaving next week for Mexico."

"Next week? When *were* you going to tell me? As you walked out the door? Oh God, Steve, I thought this time it would be different, that—"

"Listen to me, dammit. With Porfirio Díaz fighting for control and Lerdo resisting, Mexico is in danger of another full-blown revolution. You remember the last one. It wasn't pretty. This time, there's no leader like Juarez to guide the country in the right direction."

"Then take me with you." She leaned into him, intense desperation engulfing her as he began to shake his head with a frown. "If you leave me behind, our lives together will never recover. I just know it. And I could help. I knew Lerdo, and Díaz, too, so it's not as if I would be a liability. Oh, Steve, don't leave me behind again!"

After a silence that seemed far too long, he shook his head, a faint smile crooking his mouth. "I suppose if I don't take you, you'll just follow me anyway."

"Yes," she said, "I will. And I'll make certain that I'm an inconvenience."

He laughed and hooked his hand behind her neck to pull her hard against him, his breath wafting across her cheek as he bent to kiss her.

"Little hellcat. You may be of some use to me, after all, though I'm willing to bet Jim Bishop won't agree."

"To hell with Jim Bishop," she said faintly as his mouth brushed across her lips.

And then Bishop was forgotten, and Mexico, and even Italian opera singers, as Steve scooped her into his arms, carried her the few steps to the wide canopied bed against the wall and tossed her onto the mattress, his lean body following her down as he slid his hands beneath her silk dressing gown. She arched upward, hungrily, reaching for him and twining her arms around his neck.

''*Bruja,*'' he muttered against her throat, ''my green-eyed witch. You'll probably be the death of me one day....''

Her hands raked up his back, shoving impatiently at his shirt until she felt bare skin, her fingers spreading out to hold him close as she shuddered with reaction. Lamplight cast a rosy glow across the room. Lips and hands made new and remembered discoveries as their bodies moved apart, then joined again, the passion that was always between them reignited.

There was no more talk as they came together with a savage intensity, not even undressing. The restraint of the past month was gone, replaced by the familiar need that always consumed them, that had driven them to desperate acts at times, this overpowering passion between them. It was a relief and an answer, and as Steve thrust inside her, his body a hard, driving force that took her past the realm of coherent thought to mindless sensation, Ginny knew that she would do whatever she had to do to stay with him.

He was her past, her present, her future....

5

Steve Morgan was ushered into a large anteroom with gleaming marble floors beneath thick Turkish carpets. Dark mahogany panelling boasted gilt-framed paintings of austere faces beneath white powdered periwigs. A stifling room, with only one tall casement window flanked by heavy draperies allowing in thin light, it seemed to close in around him. Shadows hovered in far corners like guilty secrets untouched by the glow of lamps or truth.

Restless, Steve resisted the urge to pace. Damn Grayson for committing him to a meeting with another anxious investor. Mexico's current situation made rich men who invested in land or silver mines nervous, gave them a high stake in the future of the country's leadership. To make it worse, this investor, he'd been told, owned extensive property in Oaxaca, and needed discreet advice on the advisability of supporting Díaz.

Christ, he had too much to do to waste time pretending interest in a bored aristocrat's political machinations. With his return to Mexico only a few days away, he realized just how impatient he was to leave London.

It wasn't just the fact that the city had begun to swallow him; that was bad enough. He wanted to be in the thick of things, in Mexico, where he could protect his grandfather if need be, conserve what was left of the old man's strength.

The last time he'd seen Don Francisco, his grandfather had looked frail, though an indomitable will still shone from his eyes, as piercing and clear as ever. His new wife, Teresa—former wife to Lord Tynedale and Richard Avery's mother—watched over Don Francisco with a protectiveness that Steve found irritating. He still hadn't quite forgiven the old man for marrying, nor for keeping the weighty secret of an unmentioned son.

What would it have been like if he'd known? Nothing would have changed, but he wouldn't feel as if he'd somehow been betrayed.

Footsteps echoed on the marble floors; he turned as the door swung open. Richard Avery, tall, lean, with pale skin and burning deep-blue eyes, entered the room and regarded Steve Morgan with a lifted brow.

"It is good of you to come."

"Lord Tynedale, I admit that I was not told it would be you I was to meet."

"Would you have come if you'd known?"

"Maybe." This was the man who had taken Ginny from Cuba to Mexico to France and finally to the Ottoman Empire. Avery had loved Ginny, and she had loved him in return. He'd saved her from death twice—but Steve was damned if he could summon up a deep sense of gratitude. A lingering resentment usurped more appreciative emotions.

Richard Avery motioned to chairs in front of a small table. "Shall we be seated? What I have to say won't take long."

"If this is about Ginny—"

"It is and it isn't. Please. Grant me the courtesy of a few moments of your time. There are things I'd like to ask you, things I do not feel I can ask anyone else."

Despite himself, Steve found Avery's manner inoffensive and disarming. He accepted the offer of a glass of dry sherry, a civilized invitation to a camaraderie neither felt.

Stretching his long legs out under the table, he sat back and regarded Avery over the rim of the small glass, observing his careful movements, the slight frown etched in his brow as he twirled the wineglass between his fingers.

Finally Avery looked up. "Do you love her?"

Steve's eyes narrowed slightly. "I don't see that it's any of your business. Ginny and I have known each other a long time. How we feel about one another is no one else's affair."

"Yes. I am aware of that. I am also aware that you have not always chosen to remain with her, for various reasons."

"If you asked me here to condemn me for—"

"No, no." Avery put up a hand when Steve started to rise from his chair. "That is not my intention. I simply seek to reassure myself that she is happy, not just content. I have my own reasons for it."

"Guilt?" He hadn't meant to sound so mocking, but saw from Avery's startled glance and quick, angry flush that he had come near the truth.

"In a way. You mock me, but I loved her. It was not her fault that I had to divorce her. And yes, we were married in the eyes of the law of Islam."

There was an innate dignity to him that halted Steve's terse reminder that he was not married to her now, and Avery must have sensed it, because his tone altered slightly, became impassive.

"It was necessary for me to force Ginny to leave me, but I did not want to part from her. I was caught in an untenable situation. You are aware, I am certain, of the political implications. Sultan Abdul Aziz was deposed in May, after Ginny was safely away. He killed himself by slitting his wrists with a pair of scissors, it is said. His successor, Murad, has been declared insane by his brother, Abdul Hamid, who seeks to take the throne. Since the massacre of the Bulgarians by Turkish troops, Russia will no doubt soon declare war on Turkey. I barely escaped with my own life, even though my mother is Persian and distantly connected to the sultan. That alone can be a death sentence when there is a struggle for power."

In the soft hush that fell as he paused, Steve regarded the man who was his mother's half brother; his uncle, though younger by a few years. There was a definite familial resemblance between them, evident by the dark blue of their eyes and lean build, but Richard Avery was as alien to him as an English aristocrat.

"And so," Avery continued softly, his tone reflective, "after I sent Ginny to safety with Colonel Shevchenko, I did what had to be done to survive.'' His eyes flicked up, caught Steve's gaze and held it. ''You, I understand, are an adventurer. A man who takes risks. I am not. I prefer books to danger, the exploration of civilized cities to the threat of the wilderness. But I'm not unappreciative of its beauty. Nor am I immune to the beauty of a woman.''

Steve set down his glass, his tone hard. ''If you wanted me here to tell me about your relationship with Ginny, she's already told me.''

''I am fully aware of that. Do not mistake me— I found her very beautiful, very vulnerable, but I knew it was not me she wept for at night, nor dreamed of, nor wanted with her. It was always you, Esteban. May I call you that? I have heard Don Francisco mention you so many times, it is how I think of you.''

''Have you? Until recently, I had never heard of you. I find it intriguing that you were aware of me all this time, yet I had no idea of your existence.''

''Until my father died, I did not know that the Esteban of whom I had heard so much was related to me. You see, I did not know Don Francisco was my true father until Tynedale died. *Tynedale.* It seems so cold to refer to him that way, when I always thought of him as my father. You do know, do you not, why it was that Don Francisco was my father? It was not an impetuous affair, as you seem to believe. My father asked him to produce an heir. He had been badly injured in a riding accident after my sister Helena was born, and without an heir, his title would pass to another. He could not bear the thought of it. Don Francisco was always such a wonderful friend, and it was to him that he turned for this most special of requests.''

The taste of the dry sherry on his tongue was heavy, and Steve did not refuse the offer of another glass to wash it away, to drown the distaste he felt. If it had been any other man, he would have left by now. But for some reason, he could not bring himself to reject Avery's explanation. Had he been waiting for this, wondering, without admitting it even to himself?

''My mother,'' Avery continued in the same soft monotone,

"was a beautiful woman. She still is. Don Francisco, being the gallant gentleman that he is, agreed to my father's request. Once successful, he left Cuba. It would have been too awkward to remain, to visit often, you see. So, I'm Lord Tynedale now, heir to title and lands as my father wished, but grateful to Don Francisco for the gift of life, and for nothing more."

"Do you think I'm concerned with my inheritance? My grandfather has disowned me so many times that it's never been something that worried me. It doesn't now, either."

"No, it would not. You are a millionaire several times over, I've heard, from careful investments. It is partially because of that ability that I wanted to meet you, to bring this out into the open between us. I know you will care for your wife as she should be cared for, and I want you to know that it was always you she wanted—"

Steve set his empty glass on the table between them and rose to his feet. "How long do you intend to be in London?"

Tynedale understood. He stood up, smiling slightly. "The prince desires to travel to Russia, and has asked me to accompany him. He made the acquaintance of the tsar on his last tour of France, and has accepted his invitation to the summer palace. It is beautiful, I understand, named for Catherine the Great, and very opulent. I expect to be most intrigued. It should take my mind off the recent death of my wife."

The reference was to his Turkish wife, the woman who had supplanted Ginny, and no doubt been responsible for the attempt upon her life as well. Living in a harem had its drawbacks, it seemed.

"Why are you telling me all this, Tynedale? You didn't arrange for me to come here just to find out how I feel about my wife."

"Perhaps not." A faint smile pressed at the corners of his mouth as Tynedale watched him. "I felt we should meet privately before we meet publicly. Tomorrow evening you are to attend a soiree given by the Prince of Wales. So will I. It is inevitable that we meet, so I leave it up to you to prepare Ginny for my presence there."

* * *

Ginny was surprised and a little shaken when Steve told her that Richard Avery would be attending the same soiree.

"He's *here?* Oh, I knew he was supposed to be in London, but I wasn't sure...didn't know if he would even think of me or would prefer not to see me again."

"I think he'd like it too much."

Sprawled in a chair, one leg thrown carelessly over the arm, Steve watched her through lazily narrowed eyes, a faint smile on his mouth. Ginny knew that look. He was waiting for her to react.

She arched a brow as she reached for the cup of hot, sweet tea she favored. Delicate china rattled with a light, tinkling sound, tiny roses vivid against the creamy white background. It was a habit lately to drink tea in the afternoon, a practice that was growing in popularity in London. She sipped the hot brew slowly, taking her time before she responded to Steve's news of Richard.

"It will be delightful to see him again. He was very good to me, and I cared a great deal for him."

It was true. She *had* cared for Richard. But he'd never supplanted Steve in her heart, and he'd been intelligent enough to know that.

She looked up in time to catch the skepticism in Steve's gaze, and was startled. It was gone so quickly, she wondered if she had imagined it, for he gave another careless shrug, his smile revealing nothing.

"You can renew your acquaintance tomorrow night at this damn soiree we're committed to attending. I'll be glad to leave London. It's become nothing but a round of social events."

"Yes, my only regret is having to leave the children here for a while. Oh, Steve, what if they feel abandoned?"

"Your aunt has been with them so long, they won't feel abandoned. And it's only for a few months, until I'm sure the danger in Mexico is over. We can live at Hacienda de la Nostalgia, if you like, or investigate my new holdings in Chihuahua, then decide where to live with Laura and Franco."

"So you think the rebellion will end that quickly?"

"I won't know that until we arrive, but from what I know

of Díaz, the man is an excellent military leader. I rode under his command for too long to think he will lose a military conflict to Lerdo. But politics is another arena, one not as natural to him as to Lerdo. The outcome is uncertain at this point.''

Ginny bit her lower lip, remembering too well the last revolution in which she'd been involved, and the horrors of it. Could she go back and take the risk of becoming caught up in it again?

As if guessing the direction of her thoughts, Steve leaned forward, and his tone was soft. ''If you're having doubts, green-eyes—''

''Maman!'' The childish interruption dragged her attention from Steve to the impetuous Laura, who burst into the room with Franco at her heels, an indignant expression on her small face, while Franco's eyes burned with frustration.

''*Maman,* Franco said you're leaving us again, and I told him that was not true. Tell him, *Maman,* tell him that we are staying together!''

Dismay made Ginny's hand shake as she set down her teacup and folded the little girl into a warm embrace. ''Franco is right, my darling, but only for a little while. Oh, don't cry, Laura, my sweet girl. Papa and I are just going to get our new home ready for you and Franco to join us.''

Her wailing cry brought tears to Ginny's eyes, and she pulled Laura onto her lap, cuddling her close as her throat closed with emotion. Steve sat like a stone, his face closed and impassive. Franco was a smaller version of him, the round features of a child blurred with the effort to mimic his father's stoicism.

Laura's sobs slowed to an occasional sniffle as Ginny described some of her favorite places in Mexico, told the children how warm it was there, and how their great-grandfather would be so glad to see them again.

''He has missed you so, and writes long letters asking when we will bring you back to see him. You don't remember Mexico, I know, but it's your home. *Our* home. There is lots of sunshine, and wide-open spaces where you can ride your ponies and play with your dogs. Yes, my sweet, you can take Silky with you, of course! She will be happy there, too."

"But why can't we go with you now?" Franco asked suddenly, and in his green-flecked eyes, Ginny recognized the return of anxiety.

"We have to make arrangements, son," Steve said when Ginny floundered. "There is a lot to do, and it's best that you come later with Tante Celine."

"Besides," Ginny said then, smiling, "you love to go to the seashore, and I heard *Tante* say that she is taking you to Brighton next week. You will like that, won't you?"

Both children brightened; the tension in Franco's face eased and he turned to his father as if for confirmation of the promised treat.

It was a small reaction, but that her son filtered any of her promises with his father's corroboration still pierced her to the heart. Would Franco always be so wary of her? Had she ruined any hope of his ever trusting her again?

Ruffling Franco's dark hair, Steve assured him that it was true. "Tante Celine and Pierre are taking you on the train to Brighton."

"Will Miss Prendergast go, too, Papa?" Franco's gaze was hopeful, a reminder that he had formed an admiration for the lovely Lorna since she had been so much in Pierre's company of late.

It rankled that her own son would prefer Lorna to her, but Ginny betrayed nothing of her feelings as she said, "If Pierre should invite her, I am certain she will go, too."

"Then I shall talk to Uncle Pierre and tell him to invite her," Franco said, "for she likes to play with us."

"Perhaps because she is still so near your age," Ginny couldn't resist saying, and saw the amusement spring into Steve's eyes at her spiteful comment.

It wasn't true, of course, for Lorna Prendergast was nearly twenty, but still too young for Pierre in Ginny's opinion. She was beautiful, well-mannered, and certainly came from an excellent background if her mother's demeanor was any indication, but Ginny found Lorna to be far too immature and overindulged to care much for her company.

It was obvious that Lorna resented her as well, though that had more to do with Steve than anything else. After all, the girl had made it quite plain that she had been interested in Steve as more than just an escort from New Mexico to London. There were times Ginny felt very much like boxing her ears, but as her father was good friends with Sam Murdock, Steve's partner, that would never do. Too bad. It might help knock some sense into her head if Lorna realized that the world did not revolve around her own desires.

Yet even feeling as she did, Ginny was glad that Franco enjoyed Lorna's company; it was important for a child to feel wanted and appreciated.

"Come," she said impulsively, rising to her feet with Laura in her arms, "let's go for a ride in the park. Your papa has a fine new phaeton and pair of matched bays that need to be exercised. Shall we?"

"May we take Silky with us, *Maman?* Oh, and a basket, as we did last time? I love to feed the swans on the lake."

Meeting Steve's gaze, she saw him nod, and laughed. "Yes, you may, my little duckling. We shall have Cook prepare a basket of food for us, and bread for the swans."

It was a beautiful day, with soft sunlight and a fresh wind that smelled sweet and clean once they were free of the congested streets. Steve handled the horses with careless competence. Hyde Park, with its majestic trees, serpentine roads and winding streams, was unexpectedly peaceful in the midst of the chaotic city. Flowers cascaded in tended beds, and a fountain spewed torrents of water that glistened in the light like diamond drops. London was decked in summer finery, with masses of lavender, forget-me-nots and roses spicing the air with fragrance and brilliant color.

Ginny, garbed in a light gown of green-striped cotton, trimmed in grosgrain green ribbons to match her gown and Laura's, thought that she had never been as happy as she was at that moment. With her children and her husband at her side, she could conquer anything the world might toss her way....

And indeed, they made a lovely spectacle as Steve, so darkly handsome in his casual jacket and trim trousers, handled the reins with relaxed expertise. Ginny was the very image of a doting mother, an exquisite creature laughing with her children as they sped past pedestrians.

"Do you see them?" inquired an observer of his comrade.

The second man, taller than his companion, did not take his eyes from the phaeton as it passed them where they stood in the encompassing shade of a towering oak. "Yes. I know him. It is the woman who interests me, however. She is the one we need."

"They are all tools, my friend. Weapons in our battle against injustice."

As the phaeton sped past, none of the occupants noticed the men watching them with such intense scrutiny. One day, they would notice them—but by then it would be too late.

6

It was to be their last official social event before leaving London, and Ginny took great care with her toilette. Berthilde, looking distracted and harried, scurried from the dressing room to the bedchamber with another gown, finding at last the one that they both liked, while Steve waited impatiently.

"If we are to get there before the late supper tonight, you'd best choose a gown, Ginny."

From amidst the bouquet of crimson-and-yellow silks scattered on the wide tapestried bed like wilted flowers, Ginny's voice sang out, "I chose the one I'm wearing. I'll be ready in just a moment!"

By the time she emerged, Steve considered the results well worth the wait. Standing in the entrance hall, he heard her coming down the sweep of stairs and turned to comment on her tardiness.

A shimmering copper skirt floated around her legs, reflecting lamplight, and the snug bodice clung to her breasts and small waist with cunning efficiency. A filmy wrap seemed to drift around her bare shoulders.

She wore a necklace of gleaming topaz, stones of a rich amber set in gold filigree, with matching earrings so long they brushed against her shoulders.

Berthilde was still fussing around her, following and straightening folds of the skirt, rearranging one of the ribbons that streamed down the back, tucking another flower into the mass of curls atop Ginny's head, clucking under her breath when she was finally told to stop.

"Enough," Ginny said, tugging at an elbow-length glove, "the ribbons will only be crushed in the carriage. You may have the rest of the night off, Berthilde. We'll no doubt be quite late returning."

"*Oui, madame.*" Berthilde looked pleased, and pursed her mouth primly.

Ginny seemed to sparkle. When they reached the sprawling mansion that was brilliantly lit, even in the gardens where Chinese lanterns dangled like fireflies above neatly clipped yew hedges and overflowing urns of fragrant flowers, she stood out vividly in the sea of more sedate gowns. As usual, Ginny received admiring glances from the men as they entered the house and were announced in dulcet tones. They made their way down the receiving line, where the Prince of Wales greeted them with gruff good humor.

"Ah, Ambassador Morgan, it is pleasant to see you again, as always. Will you be visiting the racecourse tomorrow? I hear Lord Hartsfield has a prime bit of horseflesh entered."

Bowing slightly from the waist, Steve reminded the prince that he was leaving for Mexico in two days.

"But I am certain you will be back, Ambassador Morgan! You cannot deprive us of your beautiful wife's company for too long. Or is she remaining here, perhaps?"

The profligate prince regarded Ginny with an avid admiration; it was no secret that he conducted many affairs, not bothering to be discreet despite his wife's chagrin. It did not matter to Prince Edward if the object of his desires was married, as long as the husband had the good sense to look in the other direction.

Steve Morgan gave no indication of being that kind of husband, and Ginny had no intention of being another Alice Kepple. She tactfully rejected the prince's suggestion that she accept English hospitality while her husband was away on business, and moved gracefully along as those behind her moved forward.

Then Steve felt her falter, heard the strained note in her

voice as she greeted the man standing next to the prince in the line.

"General Ignatiev, I see you did not return to Russia after all."

"Not yet." Tall and spare, with vigorous mustaches that swept out to the sides, the Russian general who had helped arrange Ginny's flight from Stamboul regarded her with icy eyes that held no hint of welcome. "And I see that you did not go to Saint Petersburg though you professed such eagerness to see the tsar again."

"Plans change, or are changed by fate."

"And did you find Colonel Shevchenko...efficient?"

"I am here, so I would say that he was most efficient, General."

Ignatiev's gaze moved to Steve. He nodded in recognition and then shifted away as they moved along.

"I got the distinct impression that the general wasn't very happy to see you, my love," he said when they reached the crowded ballroom. Strains of a waltz were playing, barely discernible over the noise of the crowd. Ginny's face was pale, her mouth stretched into a taut line as he moved her toward the windows that opened onto a wide verandah.

Her shoulders lifted in a light shrug. "He wasn't very pleasant when I last saw him, so I don't think his opinion of me has changed greatly."

Steve studied her for a moment. Incongruous color that had nothing to do with cosmetics brightened her cheeks. It wasn't like Ginny to get upset because of rudeness. Damn, he had seen her face an entire room full of hostile men with a composure he wouldn't have been able to manage under similar circumstances.

"Ignatiev often travels with Tsar Alexander, but he's here as an envoy to assist in making travel arrangements for the prince to visit Saint Petersburg." He paused, then added, "Lord Tynedale will be in the entourage traveling with Prince Edward."

"Will he?" She turned luminous eyes to him, a faint smile

lifting the corners of her lush mouth. ''Russia is lovely in the summer months.''

It was a noncommittal reply, but what had he expected? Ginny had always been adept at hiding herself from him, as he had always been just as proficient in concealing his own thoughts from her. It was a vicious cycle at times, neither of them quite ready to relinquish old habits, to fully trust the other's intentions. It would take time to ease the habit of licking old wounds, he thought wryly, and he was as guilty as she of harboring mistrust.

He snagged Ginny a glass of champagne punch from a passing footman's silver tray, pushed it into her hands and said casually, ''Lord Tynedale approaches.''

Ginny's eyes widened slightly, dark pupils expanding as she lifted her champagne glass. If not for the slight quiver of her hand, he would have thought her completely unaffected by Tynedale's presence.

It was hard-earned composure that kept the smile on her face as Ginny turned to greet Richard Avery.

''Richard, you're looking quite well,'' she said lightly when he took her free hand and bowed over it in a courtly, old-fashioned manner that was so indicative of his nature.

He straightened, dark-blue eyes so similar to Steve's holding her gaze.

''You are more lovely than ever, though I once thought that impossible. I see that life with Esteban agrees with you most heartily.''

''Yes. It does.''

''I am so glad, Ginny.''

The sincerity in his tone was unmistakable, and she drew in a soft breath of relief. There would be no constraint or silent reproaches between them now, for after all, each had chosen the path more suitable for their lives.

''Will you dance this waltz with me, Ginny, with Esteban's permission, of course?''

Steve took Ginny's empty champagne glass from her hand as Richard escorted her onto the crowded floor. The music was loud, but not deafening, so that they did not have to speak loudly to be heard.

"Ginny, are you as content as you seem?"

"I am very happy, Richard. I have my children with me at last, and Steve and I are trying to work out all the problems of our past. It's not easy, of course, but I knew it wouldn't be. So much has happened between us, and to us, that it will take time to sort out our feelings, to come to terms with everything."

"Ah." His hand on the small of her back flexed as he guided her in a sweep across the floor. "You may not recall, but when I used to ask you if you were happy, you always said you were content. Now I ask if you are content, and you tell me you are happy. Oh, do not look distressed, Ginny, for I always knew I didn't have your heart, not the way I wanted it. And I suppose it's just as well, after all that happened."

She thought of Gulbehar, the wife Richard had taken at the sultan's wishes, and the vindictiveness of her attempt to kill Ginny and her unborn child so that she would be the first wife, and her child, his heir.

"I do not see your wife with you tonight. I presume she is still in Persia?"

"Steve didn't tell you— Gulbehar and our son died of a fever."

"Oh, I'm sorry." It was a reflexive sympathy, murmured automatically, but she *was* sorry, for Richard's loss if not for the woman who had tried to kill her.

She should have known Richard would perceive her true thoughts, for he squeezed her hand, smiling sadly.

"You are not sorry she cannot hurt you anymore, I'm sure, Ginny, for what she did to you was truly terrible. There are no pardons for it, no penances to atone for her actions. You lost our child, and nearly died as well. Now she has died, and so did our child."

She looked up at him, saw in his eyes the sorrow he felt, the loss, and said, "Yes, but I have forgiven her. If she had not poisoned me, perhaps I would not have regained my sight, and perhaps I would not now be here, but still in Stamboul instead of—''

When she halted, he smiled. ''Instead of with the man you love. Yes, I know. I always knew.''

He sounded so sad. Ginny searched his face, the fine features that were so like Steve's yet so different; his skin was paler, slightly pockmarked with old scars from a bout of the pox as a child, and his eyes, so dark a blue like Steve's, but that held none of the ruthlessness, only compassion.

''It's true, Richard. I do love Steve. I've always loved him even when I didn't want to. I'm not sure why, except that he and I have been through so much together now.''

''There are ancient beliefs that say a man and a woman must find the one true love, that when they do, that love will last for all time, through strife and even death. I think that is the sum of your relationship with Esteban. No matter how many others you might think you love, he is your only true love. You were fortunate that you found one another while you were so young. Now you have the rest of your lives to be together.''

''Oh, Richard, I knew you would understand. How I wish you would find your true love.''

''Perhaps I will. One day. Perhaps I will even find her in Russia, a woman with green eyes and copper hair.''

His smile was teasing, his hand on her comforting, and Ginny felt at ease in his arms as the waltz took them around the floor. Another barrier had been hurdled, another avenue chosen, another chance offered on the path to happiness. It was as if pieces of a puzzle were falling into place.

Steve, standing beside a pilastered column and talking with a man she recognized as Lord Beaconsfield, the prime minister of England, was her fate. She had always known it, even in the darkest of times.

I just pray that whatever happens in the future, we can face it together....

NEW ORLEANS

7

It was all so familiar; a lingering sense of *déjà vu* hovered over her as Ginny leaned against the frame of the French doors that opened onto Royal Street below. New Orleans. A teeming city of diverse culture, gracious and bawdy, like an elegant lady clad in tattered silks.

Sunlight graced the day with soft, moist heat. It was still early; servants washed off narrow *banquettes* before the traffic of the day, chattering in soft tones that sounded like lilting music while soapy water washed over the previous day's accumulation of dirt and horse droppings.

Ginny only half listened, thinking of her children and how she missed them so much already. Leaving them with Tante Celine until the unrest in Mexico was ended had been wrenching, but best for them. Still, she had wept halfway across the Atlantic until Steve had sworn softly and muttered that the ship had as much saltwater belowdecks as surrounding them.

Tante Celine had taken them on the outing to Brighton, promising them long days spent on the beach to assuage their disappointment at being once more separated from their parents. It had been a tearful farewell, though the sadness was tinged with excitement at their promised treat. They were so young that the time would not be real to them, the realization that two months was a long separation. If all went well, it would pass quickly and she would soon be with them again, though Tante Celine was not at all certain she wanted to go to Mexico.

"It is a barbaric country," she had said with a light shudder and sigh of resignation. "I cannot bear to think of my precious Laura and Franco living there."

"It is their home, *Tante,*" Ginny had reminded her gently, and then hugged her. "This is so hard, but I must go with him. I cannot be apart from him again, especially not now, when it has been so long. Do you understand?"

"Yes, Ginette, you know I do. Perhaps this is best, that you and your husband have this time of reconciliation alone, with nothing to distract you from each other. And it will not be so very long until you are reunited with the twins, after all, only a few months. I will care well for them."

Some of the anguish at leaving them behind was diluted by the knowledge that her time with Steve would give them the opportunity to reacquaint themselves with one another. The three-week long voyage from England to New Orleans had been a revelation of sorts, for both of them.

It could not be her imagination that Steve's wary reserve had altered to a more open acceptance, and the guarded expression in his eyes had faded almost entirely away now.

Yes, she had made the right decision to come with him, and for the first time, had confidence in their futures together. When he held her in his arms, the ghosts between them evaporated as if they had never existed.

Instead of lodging in her father's house in the quiet section of the American district, Steve had leased a house in the Old Quarter, near the corner of Royal and Hospital Streets. Painted pink with green wooden shutters over windows and doors, the house was small but gracious.

"It's more private," he'd said, but Ginny thought that was only part of the reason for his wanting to be away from the scrutiny of his in-laws. Upon their arrival in New Orleans just two days ago, he had left immediately to meet someone, but would not tell her who or even where. Probably some dark place like Maspero's Exchange, where men could meet without drawing too much attention from unwanted sources.

The situation in Mexico was even more serious than she had thought it would be. The conflict had not ended, but grew more dangerous every day. Sebastián Lerdo de Tejada was chief justice of the supreme court, a liberal and anticlerical, heartily disliked for using the power of the state to enforce his goals in Mexico. Mexicans resented his, to them, excessive concessions to the United States railway interests.

But to the United States, the potential for huge profits lay in keeping Lerdo in power, and American senators like William Brandon, Ginny's father, had keen interests in making certain that Porfirio Díaz did not gain power.

Brandon made his position clear that night, when he and his wife Sonya met with Steve and Ginny for an evening meal at Antoine's Restaurant in the Vieux Carré.

Leaning forward, he fixed Steve with a gimlet gaze that belied his smooth tone. "Since Juarez died, Porfirio Díaz has come out of hiding to lead the country. His revolts against Juarez failed, so now he seeks to gain control of Mexico by ousting Lerdo. It's a goal that I sincerely hope is quickly extinguished. It would do Mexico no good to continue another revolution."

"It's a relief to hear you say so, Senator, especially as the United States government helped fund the French in the last revolt in Mexico," Steve replied coolly, earning a fierce glare from his father-in-law.

Aware of Sonya's soft exclamation of dismay, Ginny shot her a warning glance. It would be futile to become embroiled in their discussion; it always was. The man she had always thought of as her father was confident, even brash, she had heard people say, as befitted a United States senator more comfortable in the elegant drawing rooms of Washington than he had ever been in the raw, open lands of Mexico, or even Texas. He was known to be shrewd when it came to politics and money—not always a popular choice.

Yet it had been because of Brandon's determination to send a shipment of gold to Emperor Maximilian during his brief rule in Mexico that she had met Steve Morgan in San Antonio. It was so long ago, yet she could recall that moment as if it were only an hour before, how the gunslinger calling himself Whitaker had stood in the arid dust of the street below her hotel room, facing a man bent on killing him. The duel had been brief and shocking, seared into her memory as if with a hot iron. Whitaker—Steve Morgan—had been as cool then as he was now in an elegant restaurant with snowy linen tablecloths and crab bisque.

Could William Brandon have forgotten that? Could he have forgotten how dangerous and lethal Steve could be when he chose?

It would not have made Ginny feel a bit better to know that Brandon was fully aware of Morgan's penchant for danger and survival. It was that very nature that had prompted him to hire the man to guard wagonloads of gold—only to have them stolen, along with Ginny.

Ah, it may all be behind them, and he may wear this polite mask now, but he had not forgotten for an instant how Morgan worked, and he knew instinctively why he was here in New Orleans, though the pretense of returning to ready their home for their children was the prevailing story of the moment. Nor had he forgotten that when New Orleans was occupied by Union soldiers, then Union Captain Steve Morgan had seduced Sonya into his bed. It was not a thing a man was likely to forget, especially when Sonya became a shivering wreck in Morgan's presence.

But politicians were adept at hiding their true feelings, and even now he could smile blandly as he said, "Mexico still enjoys peace with Spain, though relatively precarious. Díaz would threaten that peace, and send the entire country spiraling into chaos and revolution."

"Spain is not the greatest enemy to Mexico, sir." Steve lifted a dark brow, his smile just as prosaic. "At the moment, American politicians are the greatest threat."

Damn the smiling bastard, did he really believe what he was saying? But what could one expect from a man so ruthless as to abandon his own wife to the riffraff life of the *Juaristas,* after all?

Schooling his tone, he said, "The United States has only

Mexico's best interest at heart, while her own citizens would destroy the country with greed."

"And that has nothing at all to do with the fact that you, personally, stand to gain a fortune with your railroad interests, I presume."

Brandon's mouth tightened. "If I recall correctly, you own quite a few shares of Union Pacific and Central Pacific railroad stock yourself, Morgan."

"True. But I have no intention of exploiting Mexico to increase the value. More wine, Senator?"

A waiter clad in spotless linen hovered at the table, solicitous and yet not overly so as befitted a well-trained sommelier. Wine, a crisp white Reisling, sparkled in crystal glasses. Taking his cue, Brandon turned the conversation to more mundane topics though he made a mental note to do some more investigation into Steve Morgan's presence in New Orleans.

"Sonya, dear," he said lightly to his wife, noting her pallor and quick, startled glance, "have you told Virginia about our new house yet?"

Looking almost guilty, Sonya shook her head. "No, I have not had—we have been so busy catching up on all that has happened since last we were together, that I have not mentioned it. You tell her about it, William, since it is all your work."

Watching Ginny over the rim of his glass, Brandon caught the slight frown that puckered her brow; candlelight gleamed in her green eyes, exotic eyes that had been inherited from another man. It had been painful to realize that he was not her real father, had not been the love of her mother's life, as Genevieve had been of his. But he could not change that, could not change the fact that most of the world knew Ginny as his daughter. He had been too long in the habit of considering her as his child to stop it now.

Twisting the stem of the wineglass between his thumb and fingers, he smiled faintly. "I purchased the old Delery plantation, out on the River Road. It has been neglected for far too long, but was in surprisingly good condition. I've been restoring it as best I can, though it is difficult for me to personally supervise the workmen as much as I would like.''

It was an oblique reference to the limp that still dogged his every step, and though he should thank God that he could walk at all, for the rest of his life he would struggle with pain because of the bullet still lodged in his back. An assassin's bullet, meant for another man, perhaps, though for a long time he'd had his doubts.

But that, too, was behind him, and he had resumed his seat in Congress, reelected by voters grateful and relieved that he blunted as much of the effects of Reconstruction for them as possible, while still promoting the New South of the post-Civil War. As a native Virginian, he walked a tightrope between North and South, both factions believing him to be in their corner. It was a delicate balance, held on to with grim tenacity at times, and at any moment capable of being wrested away from him by a careless decision.

''Andre Delery?'' Ginny's face was pale, gemmed eyes like brilliant emeralds wide and shocked as she stared at him.

''Yes, the old Delery mansion. Since Andre's death, it has been vacant, and went for taxes this past year. I bought it for a paltry amount. The craftsmanship is exquisite, and there are few like it left now. You must come out to see it, Ginny, for I know you appreciate rare beauty.''

''Yes, yes, of course,'' she murmured as she looked down, fanned lashes veiling her eyes.

So it is true.... He had wondered if the rumors about her leaving New Orleans with Delery over a year ago when he'd been shot were valid; now he knew they were. Ah, tempestuous Ginny, as passionate and untamed as her mother had been cool and contained. He envied Morgan almost as much as he pitied him at times.

''Sonya,'' Ginny said after a few minutes of desultory conversation, ''I must visit the convenience. Would you care to go with me?''

Senator Brandon managed to rise courteously from his chair, and watched them leave with an indulgent smile, idly wondering why it was that females always felt the need to travel in pairs on such occasions.

But as he took his seat again, Morgan remained erect. He bowed slightly from the waist, and said tersely, "I see an old acquaintance I must greet, Senator. If you will excuse me for a moment?"

Frowning as his son-in-law walked away without waiting for a reply, Brandon shifted uncomfortably in the chair and sipped French brandy brought by an attentive waiter. Amber liqueur left legs on the concave glass, slipping lazily down the sides as he slowly twisted the snifter.

For all his surface refinement, Morgan was still just an uncouth gunslinger beneath that veneer, a killer and an outlaw. It amazed him that Virginia—reared to be a lady despite all that had happened to her once she'd come to America—still loved him. But then, Morgan never seemed to have trouble attracting women.

In the years since he'd first met him, Brandon had become well aware of the effect Steve Morgan had on women. He had noticed how female eyes tracked Morgan, observant, even hungry at times, widening as they watched him cross a room. It was the unknown, the savage in him; women sensed it.

For a long time, the senator had found it vaguely amusing to watch women throw themselves at his son-in-law. It usually had the same ending—Steve bored easily, had no patience with light flirtations or even secret assignations with restless wives. Nor did he allow women to divert him from his purpose, though there had been a few who had managed to interrupt his life—and his marriage.

But lately, there was an undercurrent to Morgan that made Brandon uneasy, made him regard the man with even more wariness than ever before. The first wild recklessness that had characterized Steve's actions a few years back had tempered now, melded into a sense of purpose that made him far more dangerous than he had been then.

Eyes narrowed when he saw Steve Morgan pause by a table in the far corner; two men sat in the shadows provided by a folded screen and potted plant, hidden from his view. It sharpened his misgivings. Morgan was an unknown quantity, a man he could neither predict nor avert from his purpose. There was far too much riding on the future in Mexico, and he was damned if he'd allow Steve Morgan to interfere.

His hand tightened on his glass, and he lifted it to his mouth in a swift, angry motion. Brandy coated his tongue and throat, liquid heat, redolent and welcome.

Not this time, by God!

Sonya had changed. Her china doll prettiness was still as delicate as always, but sadness lurked in her blue eyes and in the discontented droop of her mouth. She was garbed with exquisite care. Her elegant gown of dark cream-colored faille and overdress of cream-and-white-striped India silk was trimmed with bows of cardinal red and cream-colored lace. Her creamy chip hat bore a cluster of red roses on the turned-up brim, with lush feathers drooping elegantly forward to brush against blond ringlets on her forehead.

"You look lovely tonight," Ginny remarked as they made their way back to the dining room. The silence between them was oddly tense. Why had she invited Sonya to come with her? Perhaps she'd just been flustered by the reminder of Andre Delery, another ghost from her past, and wanted only to escape. Yet this was nearly as bad, for her stepmother looked as if she were about to burst into tears or hysteria at any moment. The tension marking her pretty features was eased only slightly when Ginny added, "That gown suits you."

"I wish I could wear that color," Sonya said suddenly, and gestured at Ginny's gown, "but it makes me look washed out."

"You would look quite pert with more color, I think." Ginny paused to allow a waiter to pass, biting back the words that trembled on the tip of her tongue. The last time she had seen her stepmother, Sonya had been wailing in her bed with remorse. Guilt, long repressed, had boiled over when her husband was shot and lay in serious condition, and Sonya had blamed herself for it, certain her dalliance with Steve Morgan so long before had invited such a tragedy. It had been a shocking discovery, and had sent Ginny bolting from the house and New Orleans. She had fled with Andre Delery, intent upon going to her children but ending up in Gibara instead, where an earthquake had left her temporarily blind and defenseless—if not for Richard Avery.

The muted clink of silverware and crystal provided a soft hum as they lingered in the bricked passageway between dining rooms. Fluted iron columns braced the low ceiling. So much had happened, so many old wounds that nothing could ever truly heal. She saw in Sonya's eyes that she suffered still.

Smoothing a hand over the myrtle-green silk skirt of her gown, Ginny managed a smile that was almost genuine. "I remember you wearing a lovely shade of rose that was so deep it was almost red. It was very flattering on you."

"Yes. Yes, well...it seems rather *brash* now, and draws too much attention."

So that is it...she's trying to hide.

"It is a centennial year," she said lightly, "and there have been dozens of festive celebrations for you to attend. I'm certain you draw attention no matter what you wear."

Sonya shuddered lightly. A faint stain colored her high cheekbones, making her blue eyes bright. "Since...since William's *accident,* I've found it more agreeable to remain in the background."

"Are you afraid?" Ginny stared at her in surprise. "It was all a mistake, you know. The assassins shot the wrong man. They meant to shoot Don Ignacio. All that unrest in Cuba should have warned him, for he is a man to earn many enemies."

"Perhaps." Her lips were tight, a look of strain marking her face. "It just seems that...that *no one* is safe anymore, doesn't it? I mean...during the war here, it was expected, but still, because I was married to William, a Virginian and a United States senator, no one *dared* accost me. And then it just seemed that there were not as many criminals running loose, or men who don't mind risking all for so little, as they do now. I—I don't know anymore, where, *if,* there's a place that's safe."

She looked up, a beseeching gleam in her eyes, as if she were a child needing comfort and assurance.

At a loss, Ginny didn't answer for a moment, unsure how to soothe her stepmother, or even if she wanted to. Idly pleating a fold of her cream-colored polonaise between her fingers, she inhaled deeply to stem the old resentment.

Years of wariness were too deeply ingrained to confide in Sonya now, or to allow herself to be drawn into a more intimate discussion despite the first impulse to comfort Sonya's fears. Her reply was mundane, her assurance uncertain.

"My father would never allow anything to happen to you. You'll feel much better in the morning, I'm sure."

Sonya reached for her, fingers curled into claws that gripped Ginny's arm with surprising strength, digging into green silk as she whispered fiercely, "Ginny, you must not go to Mexico! It's...it's too dangerous for you."

"What...what are you talking about? I know there is civil unrest now, but not like before, when the French were there and Juarez was struggling for power."

Sonya's gaze darted around the room, past the low brick archway that shielded them from prying eyes before returning to Ginny, her tone rife with urgency. "There are always men who are greedy and ruthless. Think of your past, of everything that happened to you then. It might all happen again."

"Sonya, I do believe you're being far too pessimistic about this. Steve has assured me that the situation is not as grim as it was then. Yes, of course there will be some tense moments, but nothing like the *Juarista* revolution."

Recoiling slightly, fine white lines formed around her lips as Sonya frowned. "You won't listen to me."

"Really, I don't think it's as bad as all that, but I will be careful, I promise."

"They'll be wondering where we are." Sonya's hands twisted nervously in front of her, knuckles white as sun-bleached bones. "Please, don't say anything to William about this. He'll think I'm just being a hysterical female again."

"No. No, I won't say anything to him." Ginny managed a reassuring smile to hide her own private doubts. She had already voiced her concerns to Steve, and he had shrugged them aside. Now the doubts surfaced again. Sonya looked a wreck, her pale face and trembling hands conspicuous.

As they neared their table, Ginny said calmly, "I have a lovely morning dress in the Pompadour style and colors, a pale-blue silk and white flowered brocade with pink bows. It does not suit me, and with a few alterations, I am positive it would be lovely on you."

Sonya looked startled, then nodded her understanding as they reached the table where Senator Brandon sat alone and alert. "That would be very nice, Ginny. Thank you."

Her father looked pleased to see them so amicable, and as he struggled to stand, she put a hand on his shoulder to push him gently back down.

"Where's Steve?" she asked as she tucked the elegant back of her polonaise to one side so she could seat herself. It was bulky, with a rich green passementerie, fringe and double loops of green silk, not really made for sitting, but more for strolling.

"Your husband went to renew an old acquaintance, I believe," Brandon said dryly, and Ginny followed the direction of his glance.

At first, she did not see him, then caught a glimpse of Steve's lean form half-hidden by a potted palm. He was so elegant in his evening wear, the black broadcloth coat and stark white linen shirt suiting his dark good looks to perfection.

When he glanced around, her heart leaped, then dropped like a lead ball as she recognized the men sitting at the table behind him—Jim Bishop and Paco Davis.

Sonya's fears of earlier didn't seem quite so childish to Ginny now, for full-blown panic rose sharply to almost choke her as she stared at the two men who had always meant danger to her. Oh God, she had thought perhaps this time it would be different.

As Steve headed back to their table, his face was set in a carefully blank expression that gave away nothing. Jim Bishop returned her stare with his usual grave passivity, but Paco had the grace to give a sheepish shrug and halfhearted grin that she was too irritated to acknowledge.

"What a coincidence to see them here," she said when Steve took his seat. He gave her a bland smile.

"I had the same thought. You're nearly out of wine, my love. Shall I order more?"

Defiantly, Ginny stared at him as she drained the last of her wine, then set the glass on the table with a distinct thud. "Yes, but do make it champagne, Steve darling. You know how I adore it."

"Among other things," he said easily, and beckoned for the sommelier to attend them.

Champagne was brought, an excellent vintage that was dry and bubbly, and she sipped it steadily as her mood grew dark and anxious. It seemed that every time either Bishop or Paco were anywhere near, the worst happened. It wasn't that she particularly disliked either man, but only the turmoil they always brought with them.

It's starting all over again…the uncertainty, the danger…I can feel it. Oh God, what if Sonya's right?

Steve looked up and his eyes met hers, a clash of blue beneath his ridiculously long black lashes. A faint smile tucked one corner of his mouth inward, a wry gesture as he lifted his champagne glass.

"To the future, green-eyes. Wherever it takes us."

It was, she thought with a mixture of despair and resignation, the précis of their relationship.

8

When the evening finally ended, Ginny found herself trapped into riding in a carriage with her father and Sonya. Dismay outweighed anger as Steve handed her into the open door of the waiting brougham and stepped back. Light from a coach lamp flickered over his face; she saw the grooves in his lean face deepen as he smiled.

"Aren't you coming, Steve?" She leaned out and put her hand on the still open door when he made no move to get inside. His eyes were unreadable in the thick purple shadows as he shook his head.

"I'll be home later. There are a few things I have to do first."

Aware of her father and Sonya on the plush velvet squabs beside her, Ginny stifled the sharp comment on the tip of her tongue. Damn him, he was leaving her to field the inevitable questions from her father, and she didn't think she could bear the strain of keeping up the appearance of nonchalance that would be required of her in their company.

"It's late. Perhaps you should come home now," she said pleasantly, and saw from the slight tuck of his mouth that he was all too aware of her irritation.

"You know I always hurry home to you, my love," he said with the wicked, careless grin that reminded her of far too many times before. "I know you want to spend as much time with your father as you can before we leave again, and I won't bore you with my tedious duties. Good night, Senator. Mrs. Brandon.'' He inclined his head politely and stepped back from the brougham.

Ginny was neatly trapped, and he knew it. She sat back with a flounce, glaring at him as the door was shut and the brougham jerked forward.

It was an uncomfortable ride to the little house near the corner of Royal and Hospital Street, but thankfully brief. A single gas lamp illuminated the narrow street, and a light rain had begun to fall, glistening on cobblestones and misting the air when the brougham rolled to a smooth halt before the house. Ginny was reminded once again of a layered cake, the house's pink brick walls and delicate iron balconies like ornate frosting decorating the second story.

As the coachman leaped down and came to open the door, the vehicle dipped slightly. Ginny paused with her hand still clinging to the leather strap that dangled from the frame. Her father said, ''I hope that my unpleasant conversation with your husband did not cause you any trouble, Virginia.''

Awkwardly, she half turned. ''I was unaware there was any unpleasantness until now.''

''Ah, well, I would not quite call it unpleasantness, perhaps, though he and I certainly do not agree on the tense situation in Mexico. There will be another revolution unless it's prevented. This time it could affect all the landowners there. As you are one of them, I would think you would be a bit more concerned about your holdings.''

There was a note of censure in his voice.

''William…'' Sonya put a hand on his arm. ''I do not think this is the right time or place—''

''My dear, there is always a right time or place for a discussion that may well affect Virginia's future and even her well-being.'' Beneath his mild tone lurked an icy rebuke, and Sonya's hand dropped from his arm as if burned.

''It is not necessary to worry about me,'' Ginny said to him firmly. ''Steve is more than capable of seeing to my safety and the security of our holdings. After all, Don Francisco is still an influential man in Mexico, and is well-acquainted with both Sebastián Lerdo de Tejada and Porfirio Díaz. For that matter, so am I.''

''While I admire Señor Alvarado's political connections, I do not think Steve's grandfather has as much influence as you presume. He is an old man now, and has kept out of the political fray as much as possible. If I remember correctly, he was unable to keep you safe from that French Colonel Devereaux. Or am I mistaken?''

Sonya swallowed a gasp, and Ginny shuddered at the memory of the events that had changed her life so radically. Nightmares still haunted her sleep on occasion, snatches of painful memories that came only when she was powerless to hold them at bay.

Her chin came up and her gaze was direct. ''No, you are quite correct. But that was not Don Francisco's fault. It was mine alone. I made the choice. At the time I thought it was the right one.''

Ginny stepped from the brougham and turned back to meet the senator's eyes. ''Now, if you don't mind, it's late and I'm quite weary.''

Once inside the house, shivering at the dampness that lingered in rooms unheated by a welcoming fire, she knew that she had not heard the last of this from either her father or Sonya.

God, would the past always come back to haunt her? It didn't matter where she went, there were all these reminders of painful losses, events that had molded and shaped her life and her love—*Steve.*

Of everything, he was the only constant, and at the same time, the most unpredictable aspect of her life. She wanted to be certain of him, always certain of their love and their future together.

And just where *is* he tonight? Damn him, he knows how I hate being uninformed about his actions—especially when it is my future that's involved. Does Steve ever think of that, or of me, or only of what he wants…?

* * *

It would have gratified Ginny to know that Steve was thinking of her at that very moment.

Green-eyed temptress! His copper-haired wife had led him halfway around the world, and he still did not really know her. Not even after all these years and the wild, savage nights she had spent in his bed, a tigress that was all passion and abandon. Their attempts to become reacquainted were still awkward, the old habits dying hard and slow.

He vacillated between anger at her stubbornness and the familiar passion that was always there, always compelling. At times he thought that he would not be able to get enough of Ginny, of holding her and stroking her passionate, squirming little body, tasting her mouth, and the soft spot beneath her ear that made her shiver and cling to him, moaning like a cat in heat. It was a constant emotional tug-of-war, an internal struggle to rid himself of the old barriers between them.

Rain pelted cobblestones beyond the *banquettes* and gutters, a steady driving downpour that sent refuse rushing in a fetid river toward Royal Street. No gaslights lit this area; it was dark, save for wavering glows from windows and open doorways. Muted laughter, ribald songs, snatches of raucous music mingled with the sound of rain against stone, drifting on the brisk wind to where he stood.

As a younger man, curiosity had taken him to the Swamp, an area known to be infested with every low character that came to New Orleans. But now he barely paused at the corner, and turned in the other direction toward the row of neat houses a world away from the degradation and danger that lay on Gallatin Street.

Barrelhouses and concert saloons lined Gallatin, all through the Vieux Carré and the area above Canal Street. Along Saint Charles Street, the half-dozen blocks between Canal Street and the city hall at Lafayette Square boasted nearly forty-five places where liquor was sold, and nearly every one was dangerously disreputable. Gallatin in the French Quarter, and Girod Street in the American quarter, retained an evil reputation that had been acquired in the tough days of the rowdy flatboat crews.

Barrelhouses and concert saloons had been introduced to New Orleans by the Northern riffraff that swarmed into the city in the wake of Farragut's victory, adding dubious talents to a criminal population already numerous and dangerous. No lower dive existed. Strictly a drinking place, the barrelhouse occupied a long, narrow room, with rows of racked barrels on one side, and on the other, a table stacked with heavy glass tumblers or a bin of earthenware mugs. For five cents, customers filled a mug or tumbler at the spigot of any of the barrels; failure to immediately drink and refill earned prompt ejection from the guzzle-house environs. For those who drank to capacity, the reward would be a quick trip to the back where he was robbed, or if unlucky, a tour of the alley to be stripped of clothing as well as coin. Only the suicidal resisted.

A gust of wet wind scoured the street. Steve should have hired a hansom cab, but he'd wanted time to think before he met with Bishop again.

Bishop. The man had an uncanny instinct for finding him, for ferreting him out like a bloodhound. It was no coincidence that Bishop and Paco had been at Antoine's this evening, of course. With Bishop, nothing was ever a coincidence—including an invitation to play cards.

An inevitable poker game, seemed innocent on the surface, but was merely a ruse to gain information and cooperation. It never failed.

"There will be some familiar faces, and one or two you won't know. It's been a long time, but I'm certain you'll find the evening most—beneficial."

Oblique as always, Jim Bishop's carefully uninflected voice carried a message.

The apartment where Bishop waited for him was in a block of rather shabby buildings, nearly indistinguishable from the others. Inside, cigar smoke drifted in hazy layers through the room, and several men were already at a table covered with an oilcloth. Thin walls did not keep out the sounds of other tenants, nor the squawk of a badly played fiddle seeping through peeling wallpaper and boards.

"All this and music, too," Steve murmured with a wry

smile as he joined the men at the table. Bottles of wine and bourbon filled a small table at one side.

"I expected you earlier," Bishop responded, never taking his eyes off a hand of cards. It was no surprise when he won the pot, raking coins toward him as others sat back in glum silence.

"I decided to walk. Where's Paco?"

"He'll join us soon. He had some errands to attend. Are you in?"

Steve pulled out a wooden chair, the legs scraping loudly across a bare plank floor, and sat down at the table, his back to the wall instead of the door. It was an old habit, learned years ago when he wore his .45s low on his hips and sat in far too many dangerous saloons playing cards with men who thought nothing of killing a man for five dollars.

For a short time they played cards in silence, Bishop, as usual, taking most of the pots. Steve knew one of the men at the table, a Westerner he'd met years before in Texas, but the others were strangers to him, introduced only by first names: Charley, Johnny and Tige. It was Tige's place they were using for the meeting.

When Steve lost three aces to Bishop's full house, he tossed down his cards in disgust and leaned back in his chair, balancing it on the two rear legs. "I'm beginning to think this night is going to be a total waste."

Cool gray eyes flicked up to study him for a moment. Casually, Bishop said around the cigar clenched between his teeth, "Your dinner seemed pleasant enough."

When Steve didn't reply, Bishop continued. "Senator Brandon seems recovered from his injury now. I understand that he has acquired another home outside the city. Such a shame that he was incapacitated for so long while he recovered from that assassination attempt. But then, it was not meant for him at all, it seems, but Don Ignacio. A pity. So many bullets go astray these days."

"Get to the point," Steve said shortly, and met the cold gray gaze that came to rest on him. "I assume you have one. You always do."

"Yes, I do. Your wife is acquainted with Porfirio Díaz, I believe."

"As you well know, she worked with him as a French interpreter after Juarez took control of Mexico."

"And she has also become acquainted with Lerdo. During her time spent in Mexico, she managed to make the... ah...acquaintance of quite a few influential men. But then, a woman as lovely as your wife would be a magnet to powerful men. It's always that way."

Steve's eyes narrowed slightly, cold and blue, as he studied Bishop's bland countenance. Coins clicked, sounding suddenly loud in the smoke-shrouded silence. Bishop dealt out cards with swift efficiency, speaking around the cigar stuck in one corner of his mouth.

"Do you still own land in Chihuahua? A ranch convenient for the Union Pacific to run their rails through?"

"As you no doubt know, I still own interests in both. I'll take two cards."

Bishop slid two across the table toward him. "Now that the United States has railroad tracks being laid in Mexico—due in large part to Lerdo's generous concessions—the current state of affairs in Mexico is uncertain, to say the least. In the north, Luis Terrazas, as governor of the state of Chihuahua, has the support of the locals. The fact that he has gained their support by his rather generous use of federal taxes to establish a strong militia to fight the Apache, and has acquired a personal fortune, has not been missed by certain officials in Mexico City."

"Nor by Díaz." Steve leaned over and scraped a match across the floor, lit a cigar and squinted at Bishop through the curl of smoke rising in the air. He shook the match and tossed it into an ashtray. "Terrazas supports Lerdo as president. It will cost him if Díaz succeeds in his coup."

"Yes, so it seems. See you ten and raise ten." A crisp banknote slid atop the growing pile in the middle of the table. "It might be beneficial to any interested parties to have a foot in each camp, so to speak."

"Mexico is already in chaos. I suppose it would be too much for our government to keep out of it."

Bishop's wintry gaze studied him dispassionately for a moment. "If I thought you were serious in your sudden distaste for our policies, I would be vastly concerned."

"Hell, I am serious. Has it ever occurred to any of you that maybe we're part of the problem, not a cure? It would make more sense to educate the citizens rather than kill those who disagree with the current regime."

"'Know in order to foresee, foresee in order to work,' I suppose? Positivism at its best. A 'Triumph and Study over Ignorance and Sloth' motto that works well in theory, but is not always practical. You see, I am familiar with Gabino Barreda as well. A brilliant man with most intriguing hypotheses, but shortsighted in applying them to modern life, I fear."

"Juarez didn't think so."

"Juarez is dead. And so, for the most part, is his effort to educate an entire country in Positivist philosophy. Despite Barreda's noble efforts, it is far more practical to the rural youth to have enough food than it is to follow elitist dogma, however virtuous in concept it may be. I'm surprised you'd think it practical."

"Not practical, just idealistic." Steve grimaced. "I find that the thought of my own children growing up in a world where the first solution to disagreement is all-out war is somewhat daunting."

"Ah. Yes, of course. You've become well-acquainted with your children now, haven't you? How old are they?"

"That's not the point." Steve folded his cards, shoved them toward the middle of the table.

Bishop's cigar made an arc, gray ash drifting to the table to lie in a fine powder over cards and oilcloth. "Then what is the point?"

Impatiently, Steve reached for the bottle of bourbon, poured a half glass in a dingy tumbler and sipped it. "It should be fairly obvious. I'm ready for peace, not war."

In the thick silence that descended on the room, Bishop

regarded the men with an opaque gaze, his eyes moving from one to the other before coming to rest on Steve's wary face.

"The situation in Mexico is dangerous. A few years ago, when the French were involved, the outcome was never really in doubt. We knew the French would not stay in a country that was not their own once the tide turned against them. But this is different. Díaz is Mexican, an Indian from Oaxaca just like Juarez. It's *his* country—he'll fight to keep it.

"There is an ancient principle of politics that a revolution devours its children. It happened in France during the Terror, and it happened to Maximilian in Mexico. During the Reform War and the French intervention as well, Díaz distinguished himself as the strong right arm of the Liberal cause. By the time the French were ousted, he was a general and well-known throughout Mexico. It was a matter of great pride to him that he was so influential, a staunch ally of Juarez until their estrangement."

When Bishop paused, eyes squinting against the curl of cigar smoke, Tige tossed his cards to the table. "What happened to estrange them, if Díaz was so close to Juarez?"

A ring of smoke drifted into the air above the table as Bishop pursed his lips. "It was the kind of misunderstanding that causes wars and revolutions. When Juarez was making a triumphal entry into Mexico City after beating the French, General Díaz rode out to meet his old friend and mentor, wearing a brilliant uniform and riding a splendid white horse. It was a statement of pride, a triumphant moment when he expected, and rightly so, to be greeted with courtesy and gratitude. After all, he had been wounded twice, escaped capture three times, and for three years led forces that inflicted nine defeats on the imperialists. Not only that, he had gained a reputation for honesty by returning to the government an eighty-seven-thousand-peso surplus that had not been spent during the long Juarez campaign against Maximilian.

"But when he rode out to meet Juarez, the new president extended no greeting, no gratitude, but merely nodded curtly and signaled for his coachman to drive on. It was a crushing blow to Díaz's pride, an undeserved humiliation."

Tige whistled softly. "Did Juarez suspect him of treachery?"

"No, I think it was more a case of principle. Juarez was antimilitary. After the defeat of Maximilian he dismissed two-thirds of his army, as Morgan can attest. But after that, Díaz was no longer in Juarez's camp. He resigned his commission and retired to La Noria, a hacienda in Oaxaca that the grateful state awarded him in 1867. And from there, he began plotting to overthrow Juarez. His attempts to be elected president failed, as Juarez narrowly won against Díaz and Lerdo in '71. Then Díaz claimed that the election was fraudulent, and demanded the overthrow of Juarez.

"That revolt failed, and when Juarez died in 1872, Lerdo, as chief justice of the supreme court, succeeded him as president. Since Lerdo has been so unpopular, it was easier for Díaz to revolt this past January. It seems that he will succeed this time."

Frowning, Tige, a beefy man with close-set eyes and a good-natured face, shook his head. "What is the United States' position on this? Do we want Lerdo or Díaz?"

"Either one can be manipulated, or bought, into acceding to our interests, but Lerdo has been particularly generous with his concessions. What we must do, gentlemen, is ascertain that Díaz is just as amenable should he succeed in his coup—and we must be ready."

Steve leaned forward, crushed his cigar into the glass ashtray. "And that is where I come in as ambassador, I presume. I'm to humor the victor."

"Not necessarily." Bishop's smile was thin. "There are, shall we say, certain *factions* that have invested heavily in Lerdo. Díaz is an unknown quantity to some of these men. He could destroy them if he chooses. Some of these investors are powerful. Lust for wealth and domination is a dangerous motivation. Unscrupulous men are capable of endangering the peace efforts and negotiations underway, and at this time, we do not want to risk another war between Mexico and the United States. I'm certain we all agree on that, gentlemen. It is even more risky when the diverse actions of some are sanctioned by the law of a foreign power that lies so close to our borders. The threat of losing land and wealth can make men act—precipitately.''

''You mean, they'll fight to save their holdings before Díaz takes them away.'' Butch Casey, the Texan that Steve had met years before in California, leaned forward, elbows on the table and his fingers forming a steeple under his bearded chin. ''If Lerdo is ousted, the lands he sold could be reclaimed. If Americans fight back, we've got a war on our hands with Mexico.''

''Yes.'' Bishop shoved aside the cards to clear a space on the oilcloth, and began to draw a map of Chihuahua. ''I happen to know that a certain senator from Virginia has purchased a large hacienda right here, along the border. It's being mined for silver and copper, and stands to be exceedingly profitable. I am certain he would stop at very little to save his interests. Right now, the senator has a private railroad, but the Central Pacific has recently purchased rights to run tracks through the property, giving the American government the perfect opportunity to supervise the situation as ore from the mines is transported north. It has also incurred the avid interest of the Mexican faction, and needs to be monitored.''

It didn't take a map to see the direction in which Bishop was heading the conversation.

Steve sat back in his chair, mouth curled into a wry smile as he met Bishop's opaque gaze. ''Since Ginny's father is involved, it stands to reason that her presence in Mexico City is expected and perfectly natural.''

''Exactly. And since she insisted upon coming with you, how better to learn what each side is doing than to have a foot in both camps?'' Bishop coughed discreetly. ''Of course, our government cannot acknowledge any part in this, as everyone here is aware. But there is backup available. Casey is known in a few towns along the Mexican border, and Charley has taken a job at the mines. All that remains now is for a man accepted as a Mexican landowner and ambassador of goodwill to be included in the Mexicans' confidence. It could avert a full-scale war between the two countries, which would only end badly for Mexico, especially since the country is already in the throes of a struggle between Lerdo and Díaz.''

''Damn you,'' Steve said without rancor. By now, he should be accustomed to Bishop's machinations. And the man was right. Another war between the United States and Mexico would be disastrous for both sides, too newly recovering from catastrophic civil wars.

''When do you plan to leave?''

Steve poured another half glass of bourbon, downed it in one shot and shrugged.

''I'll let you know. Don't bother with the usual reminder about being on my own—I never forget it.'' He stood up, chair legs scraping loudly on the floor. ''But this time, I want you to stay out of it. Let me work alone. That means that I'm not involving Ginny. It's too dangerous.''

''Of course.''

But despite Bishop's too swift agreement, an uneasy suspicion lingered. It wouldn't be that easy to keep her out of it. Not once they arrived in Mexico. He had learned the hard way that no plan was perfect, no scheme safe.

What the hell would Ginny say?

9

"William, I do wish you would find a way to talk Ginny out of going to Mexico."

William Brandon frowned slightly. "I agree it is unwise of her to go, especially now, with Díaz threatening to take over the presidency. Damn him, it could ruin everything I've worked for this past year if he does manage to overthrow Lerdo. Another revolution endangers my new investments."

Sonya paused in brushing her hair, her arm still lifted and lamplight gleaming on the silver-backed hairbrush in one hand. "You have investments in Mexico as well?"

"Of course. It's legal, and quite profitable. Since Congress passed laws allowing railroad access into Mexico, it's smoothed the way to transport raw and smelted ore back into the United States. I stand to make more money than ever now that President Grant's Specie Resumption Act has made greenbacks redeemable in gold or silver coin. Dr. Durant's lobbying has paid off for all of us, it seems."

In the sudden silence, he laughed wryly. "Don't tell me you disapprove? But my dear, that would be so hypocritical of you. It's the money I've made from Mexican mines that purchased the Delery plantation, and even that hairbrush you're using."

Sonya dropped the hairbrush as if burned, and whirled to face him, her pale face rigid with distaste. "Do you have any scruples at all, William?"

His tone hard, he said, ''More than you at times, my dear. After all, it was you who slept with your son-in-law, wasn't it?''

''Damn you! You know very well that was a long time ago, during the war when you were so far away and he...he was so persistent. And that was before he'd even met Ginny, so don't pretend otherwise.'' Hugging her arms around her body, clad in a silk peignoir that floated around her like soft ivory mist, Sonya turned away again and moved to the long windows that looked out on a small balcony. ''Oh God, it seems that my penance for it is to be forever haunted by him. I wish he *would* go to Mexico and stay there! It would be better if I never had to see him again, hear him call me *Belle-Mère* in that drawling contemptible voice, and know that he remembers everything—''

Halting abruptly, she whirled back around to face her husband, still seated in a straight-backed chair near the fire. ''You have no excuse, William. Whether you want to admit it or not, the world knows Ginny as your daughter. You still love her, I think, though at times I wonder what you really do love. Did you ever love *me,* I wonder....''

''You're talking rubbish.'' He stamped a foot irritably on the thick carpet spread near the hearth. ''Plain rubbish.''

''Am I? I don't think so.''

''Do you think it's easy for me, constantly walking a fine line between factions that are out for blood? And I do not mean just a figurative manner of speech, but a literal one as well. Steve Morgan is one of the most ruthless men I've ever met in my life, and God only knows what drives him to do the things he does, or why Virginia keeps coming back to him. Christ, after that debacle two years ago, then the rumors that nearly ruined me before, in San Francisco with her Russian prince... I do what I have to do to survive, my dear, as you should appreciate instead of condemn.''

Sonya shuddered lightly and turned back to the window. Rain slid down glass panes, tiny rivulets like crystal, forming spidery tracks. She thought of the Beaudine plantation that she had inherited from her first husband, wild and impetuous

Raoul, whom she had loved so much. She could hardly bear to go there anymore. There were too many memories, first of Raoul, then of Steve Morgan, the young Union captain who had taken what she'd so freely given, hating herself at the time but unable to resist the urges of her own body.

Yes, she had told William she hated Steve Morgan and she thought she must. He had humiliated her, preferring a quadroon girl to her, even fighting a duel over the girl! And then, even worse, he had married her stepdaughter so that she could never be completely free of him.

So why did it suddenly matter to her that Ginny not go to Mexico? Why should she care if the girl endangered herself?

Perhaps because, despite their differences and the frequent times she didn't even *like* Ginny, she recognized in her a resilience and courage that was to be admired. It was a grudging admiration, for after all that had happened to her over the years, Ginny had survived. Some of the stories of her past were too horrible to contemplate, the indignities she'd endured far more humiliating than anything imaginable. Yet Ginny didn't surrender. She kept her head up and her eyes on the future.

It was, in a strange way, inspiring.

Some of the despair of the past weeks began to lift, and Sonya turned away from the window. Even after William had fallen asleep beside her, she could not sleep for the restless thoughts spinning in her head. Memories of the last time Ginny had been in New Orleans summoned all too familiar premonitions.

Something terrible was going to happen. It always did when Steve Morgan was involved. If only Ginny had stayed safely in London with her children. Disaster loomed, and there was nothing Sonya could do to prevent it....

"Really, Sonya," Ginny said with a lift of her brow, "I am capable of making my own decisions. While I appreciate your concern, I assure you that the situation isn't nearly as bad as you may think."

It was quiet in the drawing room, the servants having already brought a tray of hot Louisiana coffee and the small pastries that Sonya loved. Dustings of sugar frosted steamy pastries, the sweet smell almost cloying. A low fire burned, and the sharp light of late summer streamed in through floor-to-ceiling windows that opened onto a wide gallery.

Frustration creased Sonya's brow, a slight furrow in a face that was rarely allowed to reflect her emotions. Her gown was a flattering deep-rose silk, her pale skin flawless still, save for a tiny network of lines at the corners of her blue eyes as she looked at Ginny.

"I told William you wouldn't listen."

"Listen to what? Vague warnings of doom should I go to Mexico? Steve's grandfather is still influential there and has many friends in high places."

"Yes, and he was influential the last time, and it did you no good. Ginny, listen to me! I don't know why I feel this way, but I do. No, don't turn away, please! It's all so wrong, don't you see? The rebellion going on, the threat of another revolution, and then the unrest along the borders. You know far better than I how dangerous it can be. Why will you risk your life?"

Ginny took a sip of the hot chicory coffee; it scalded a path down her throat, strong and bitter. "Because I do not want to be separated from my husband again."

The truth of her reply stunned them both. For several moments the only sounds were those of the logs in the fire and the distant hum of servants beyond the closed doors. It was an illuminating self-discovery.

The delicate Limoges cup Sonya held rattled slightly in its saucer, breaking the spell the truth had cast. "I see. Even if it greatly endangers you?"

"Yes. Even if it takes me from my children for a time, even if I risk grave peril. Oh, don't you see? I've changed. I don't know how or why, but after all this time—the years I've resisted what I felt, hated him, distrusted him, wished I'd never met him—I've realized that he's the *reason* behind all I've done, even if indirectly. I can't help what has happened to me beyond my will, but I *can* help what I do now. I intend to go with him.''

Sonya gave a helpless sound, a mixture of a sigh and a sob. Carefully, she set down the delicate cup and saucer, slender fingers arranging it on the tray as if it were vitally important that it sit exactly right. Then she said, ''At least be careful. The situation in Mexico is volatile. There's more at stake than just the resignation of one president in favor of another. There are men who will stop at little to hold their interests, and who may be involved in the efforts to keep their choice in power.''

''I didn't realize you cared about politics in Mexico, or even in the United States,'' Ginny said.

''Normally, I don't.'' A tiny frown creased her brow, and she lifted her shoulders in a dainty shrug. Blond hair caught the light from the window, a soft gleam that framed her face; she looked worried, somehow, something not usually associated with Sonya. ''You'll do what you want, of course.''

''Yes.'' Ginny leaned forward, set her cup on the tray next to Sonya's and rose, her hands smoothing the soft bronze folds of her cotton riding habit over her slender hips. ''It's getting late. I have so much to do before we leave, and I promised I would not be too long. Do you like it here? It's lovely, and much closer to the city than I thought it would be. It took hardly any time at all to ride out—''

Sonya had risen, too, and said quickly, as if to forestall any questions, ''You will go up and bid farewell to your father before you leave, won't you?''

''Yes, of course. He seems to tire easily these days. I suppose it's taken him much longer to recover from his injuries than even he thought it would. After all, he almost died from that bullet. I'm sorry I wasn't here for him.''

''Yes. He used to wonder where you were when he was still so feverish. It took some time for him to realize that you were missing. And, of course, we thought you dead for a long time, until—until we learned you had survived.''

''I imagine it was quite a shock for all of you.''

''You sound so mocking. Must you ridicule me when I'm trying to understand, trying to—build a bridge?''

"Build a bridge? Between you and me? That's not at all necessary, Sonya. There's nothing to bridge."

In a brittle tone, Sonya said, "We both know better than that."

Ginny caught the undercurrent in her voice. The memory of the last time in New Orleans swept back, sharply.

Sonya, delirious after the senator had been shot, hysterical in her bedroom, defying all efforts to calm her. Adeline Pruett, an avid witness, Steve holding Sonya by the wrists; Sonya in her white nightgown clinging to him, babbling, "No—I don't want to hear any more. It doesn't matter.... Why do you keep standing there? You weren't so slow that day of the storm when you took me by force! What's stopping you now? Aren't I more beautiful than she is? My skin's whiter, look—"

So much was a blur after that, even her own cold voice dredged up from the icy pit of her stomach as she had stood in the open doorway and said, *"He's really no damn good—and not at all worth yearning for, you know."*

But she was wrong. She'd known it even as she said it, even when she thought she hated him....

"Maybe I'm wrong," she said stiffly and saw Sonya's brows lift in surprise. "There *has* been a certain amount of constraint between us. We both know the reason for it. Not enough time has passed since...since I learned about you and Steve. Oh, I know it was before I met him, before I even met you. But you must understand how I felt, how it shattered me when I learned of it."

Sonya flushed; an ugly shade of bright pink stained her cheeks and made her eyes a hot blue. "Yes, of course I can understand that. I have no explanation for my actions."

An awkward silence descended.

Finally Ginny said, "It's time to put it all behind us. This is a new beginning for me, and a new beginning for my marriage. I see no reason why it can't be a new beginning for us, as well."

"If you really mean that..." Sonya paused; tears made her eyes glisten. She lifted a fine lace handkerchief to dab at her eyes, a graceful gesture that was oddly touching.

"It's time to bury the past. Let's not resurrect it again. It's too defeating."

Maybe it really *was* time to bury the past, Ginny thought as she mounted the stairs to the senator's study. *My father,* she reminded herself. *It's so hard to think of him as anything but my father.*

Brandon was sitting in a huge wingback chair, with wire-rim spectacles perched on the end of his nose as he perused a sheaf of papers in one hand. Ginny paused in the open doorway to study him a moment before he took notice of her, and the familiar mask dropped over his features.

He'd aged in the last three years, more so than she had first thought. Now, seeing him in the bright morning light that streamed through the window, she noted the sagging jowls, the deeper creases in his face and around his eyes. His hair was thinning on the top, yet still thick, and sprinkled with gray at the temples. A handsome man still, now showing his age for the first time.

A lump formed in her throat. Regret? Sorrow for what had never been, would never be, perhaps?

"Good morning," she said briskly, and entered the room with a smile pasted on her face.

The senator looked up, obviously startled. Immediately, he crumpled the papers in his hand, folding them over in a clumsy bundle. "Virginia! My dear, I did not expect you this early. Weren't you to come later this afternoon?"

"Yes, but it was such a lovely morning I decided to ride out on my own."

"On your own?" A brow rose. "A rather foolhardy act these days."

"Not exactly all on my own. I'm well aware of the inadvisability of a woman riding alone, even in the city. No, I had an escort."

Brandon tucked the papers he'd been reading into a book and put it on the floor beside his chair. "Your husband, I presume."

Ignoring his sour tone, she managed a light shrug and reply. "Steve is not the only escort available."

"I do hope you're not up to your old tricks again, Virginia. It can be damned embarrassing."

"Well, I can see that you're in no mood for my company, so I shall take my leave now. We'll be departing tomorrow for Mexico, so I shan't see you again before I go."

As she turned to leave, the senator said, "Please, I didn't mean to sound so offensive. I just worry about you. And I fear my mind was elsewhere when you surprised me."

Ginny turned, green eyes clashing with her father's as she faced him fully. "I'm not the foolish young girl I once was. I've learned some bitter lessons in the past years, and now that I'm a mother, I've realized there are many things more important than being worried about what someone else thinks of me."

"That includes me, I suppose."

"Perhaps especially you. I've never lived up to your ideal of what I should be, have I? You've made that clear enough. I suppose in some ways I deserve your low opinion, but at least you cannot say I've been a hypocrite. What I've done in my life, I've done. Not all of it was my choice, but I survived because I had to. Tell me, did you ever love me?"

"Virginia…my God." The senator sounded aghast, and he squirmed in his chair, scowling. "I've always loved you. Why do you think I would not? Christ, it must be something in the water around here. No, don't look at me that way. Sonya asked me the same thing. Don't either one of you understand what I've had to do to survive as well? Do you think I've done all I have just for myself?"

"Yes, in a way, I do think that," Ginny said frankly. "I don't believe that you would never have run for your seat in the Senate or acquired a fortune if I didn't exist. Nor does Sonya. But you're a man accustomed to power, a man who *enjoys* power and wealth. Sometimes I think that's all you really do care about. Is that why you didn't stay with my mother?"

Scraping a hand over his jaw, her father sat quietly for a long moment. The sunlight picked out silvery strands of hair, gleamed brightly on polished mahogany furniture and the gold rims of his spectacles.

"The truth of the matter," he finally said calmly, "is that your mother did not love me. Before we met, she loved another man, as you now know. I thought I could make her love me, my sweet, sad Genevieve, but nothing I did made her happy. I felt so helpless. Do you know what it is to love someone and not have that love returned, to have your insides twisted into knots all the time, and know that nothing you ever do will be enough? You—you were the only happy thing that came out of our marriage, and while I may not have been the best of fathers, I tried my best to give you all I could. Apparently, it wasn't enough."

Ginny stared at him. Hadn't she said just a few minutes ago that she intended to start over? That it was a new beginning for all of them? Yes, and if she was to be honest with herself, she had to admit that she hadn't always been a daughter who was easy to know. After all, she hadn't seen him while she was growing up, not until coming to America when she was twenty-one. They'd both missed out on so much.

"You were—are—a good father," she said, and saw his face change from guarded to cheered, a subtle shift of facial muscles that suddenly made him look younger. "I don't want to quarrel with you, especially since we're leaving early tomorrow and I don't know when I'll see you again."

"You're determined to go?"

"Yes. I don't want to be separated from Steve again. There has been too much of that in our lives, and I won't risk our futures any longer. We have children. We have to forge a life together now, before it's too late."

"I see. Well, I cannot say I'm happy to hear that you're going into a country seething with revolution, but I know the futility of trying to stop you from doing what you've set out to do." His mouth twisted into a wry smile. "It's never worked before, and I'm certain would be a waste of my time now to try to convince you otherwise."

"Steve has diplomatic immunity. I do not anticipate any problems that can't be safely resolved."

"Perhaps. I assume Don Francisco is aware of your intentions?"

She bit her lip, uncertainty obvious, for her father gave a shake of his head. "Ah, Virginia. At least inform him of your plans before you arrive. He should be made aware."

"Oh, I'm sure Steve has taken care of all the details. He usually does."

"Yes, he does have a nasty habit of tying up loose ends—even those that should remain untied."

Another silence fell, brief and pregnant with meanings that Ginny sensed were not meant for her to know.

She started to ask, but then her father said, "I would never do anything to hurt you. I'm sure you know that. Just be careful while in Mexico. Promise me that."

"I promise. And I know you never mean to hurt me, just as I've never meant to hurt you."

"Yes." He struggled to his feet and grabbed his silver-headed cane in one hand, using it to propel himself to her side. A faint smile curved his mouth as he reached out to touch a stray copper tendril that dangled against her cheek. "You look so very much like your mother, yet you're much stronger than Genevieve. You have all her goodness inside you, but I think you have learned my strength of purpose. Remember that. As long as you depend upon yourself, nothing can destroy you."

"You sound as if I'll be traveling to the mouth of hell instead of to a familiar home. Have you forgotten my time in Mexico City? In Orizaba?"

"No, of course not." His hand shifted to lay on her shoulder, a warm, heavy weight. "But places change. People change. Goals change. I just want you to be prepared for whatever may happen."

"Don't you think I know better than most how things change? God, when I think of all that's happened to me in the last ten years— But that's not what we're discussing, is it? No, I feel as if I'm being warned. What *is* it? What are you saying to me? Be frank. I'm not a politician, and I don't like having to read between the lines. If you have something to say to me, for the love of God, say it!"

"Ah, Virginia, Virginia—you make it so difficult. No, my child, I'm not trying to warn you of anything, save your own impetuous nature."

"Are you not? It seems as if you are."

"Perhaps you aren't aware of the political situation, not just in Mexico, but in the United States. The scandal of the Whiskey Ring is still a sharp memory in most minds, and even though Babcock was acquitted of conspiracy to defraud the Federal government of liquor taxes, the taint on him, as well as those connected with him, remains. President Grant may have intervened on behalf of his secretary, but too many people believe that the Whiskey Ring is part of a plot to finance the Republican party by fraud. It's not easy getting bills through Congress or to earn public approval. My influence is not what it once was, I fear, should you find yourself in need of it."

Ginny frowned as the senator turned away to stump back to his chair and sink down into it again with a muffled sigh of pain. Despite his seeming fragility of health, an aura of strength emanated from him, an indomitable will. She moved to stand close to his chair, studying him in the revealing light through the window. "Is that why you're so worried lately? Were you involved?"

"Really, Virginia, what kind of question is that!"

"One that needs an answer. You're right when you say I haven't kept up with American politics. I've been gone so long that it hasn't mattered to me. But now I find myself wondering if your concern for my safety has anything to do with more of your plots. I haven't forgotten how you used me and Sonya to disguise the shipment of gold you were sending to Maximilian. I was such a fool. It all seemed so exciting and romantic. Poor Max. It wouldn't have helped him in the end anyway. But you never thought of *my* safety then."

"You're wrong," the senator said testily, and thumped the end of his silver-headed cane against the floor. "If not for Steve Morgan, you would have been perfectly safe. He did more damage by abducting you than he did by taking my gold."

She couldn't refute that. Ginny gazed down at her father for a long moment, then asked softly, "Were you more worried about me, or about the gold he took?"

"Don't be ridiculous, Virginia. You've always been worth more to me than any amount of gold."

It was a facile reassurance, made with the aplomb of a politician, but lacking in sincerity. Brandon didn't meet her eyes, but kept his face stubbornly averted.

Ginny didn't stay much longer. When she left, she bade him farewell and gave him a perfunctory kiss, then called for her escort to bring her mount.

"Must you leave so soon, Ginny?" Sonya looked worried. "I would feel better if you would allow me to send Franklin with you as an additional escort."

"Girard is quite capable, thank you. Steve hired him, and I have faith in his judgment."

Sonya slid an uncertain glance toward the lean young man bringing Ginny's horse, but only nodded. Their farewell was only slightly less awkward than the one with her father, and Ginny was unsettled and agitated as they left.

It was not a very comfortable departure, Ginny thought as she rode back along the curving river road that swept from the old Delery plantation along the banks of the Mississippi and down to New Orleans. Both Sonya and her father had acted so strange, as if—as if trying to tell her something. Perhaps she should have talked more to Sonya, or listened to her. But really, in light of all that had happened between them, it was difficult to trust her completely.

"Madame Morgan," Girard said respectfully as their horses slowed to a trot at the city limits, "it is best if we ride along Magazine Street until we reach Canal. I do not think it safe here."

A brisk wind had sprung up, blowing Ginny's copper hair loose from the confines of the straw bonnet tied upon her head. The smells of late summer were in the air, vying with the more pungent scent of river debris and the mélange of cargo being unloaded on nearby docks. It was noisy, the serenity of the road behind them dissipating in a beehive of activity and swaying masts and the belching smoke of riverboats and steamers. Rough boatmen swarmed the clutter of cargo stacked along the wharves, some of them pausing to turn and look as they drew near.

As she pushed her blowing hair from her eyes, Ginny saw a familiar face among the men, and drew her mount to a halt. "Wait a moment, Girard. I see someone I know."

He saw her at almost the same time, and a cheeky grin split his face as Paco Davis climbed the bluff to approach her where she waited on the rise overlooking the docks.

"You're as beautiful as always, Ginny. Have you forgiven me yet?"

"No." She tapped him lightly with the riding crop she held in one hand. "Tell me, I know there's something strange going on. What is it? You owe me an explanation of some sort, so don't look at me like that. After all that we've been through in the past, you should know you can trust me."

Warily, Paco fixed her with an intense stare, his black eyes half-lidded. "I can't tell you any more than Steve has told you, I'm sure. I'm just an errand boy."

Ginny's mount shied a bit when Paco put a hand on its bridle, dancing away from him. She lifted a brow as she calmed the horse. "I doubt that very much, but I can see you have no intention of telling me anything. Very well, I'll just ask Steve. Is that the ship we're taking?"

Paco nodded. "Yeah, it should get us there pretty fast, unless there's another hurricane. It's the time of year for them."

The *Liberty* rode at anchor at the end of the dock, a small, two-masted schooner that looked neat and trim. Burly stevedores were loading cargo, huge boxes and crates that were lifted by a crane and swung on ropes to be lowered into the hold. The vessel dipped with each new burden, straining at thick chains and coils of rope holding it to the dock while men shouted orders and curses.

"Will you be sailing with us, or can you answer even that question?" Ginny asked. Paco flashed a white grin.

"I'll be going along, at least at first. I've friends of my own to visit once we reach Mexico. But then, you'll be visiting Don Francisco so shouldn't miss us."

"Us? I hope you don't mean that Steve is going with you instead of staying with me. You *do!* I can tell by your face that's what he plans, damn him. After promising me we would not be separated again. Where is he?"

"Ginny, *por Dios,* I didn't mean… Look, you can't blame him for something he didn't say. Damn, my big mouth is going to get us all in trouble one day. Just wait and see what he says, all right? I don't know if he's going with me or staying with you. Steve hasn't made any such decisions, or told me about it anyway."

"Then I suppose Jim Bishop has told you that he has plans for Steve to go elsewhere?" Anger boiled inside her, coupled with dismay, hurt and uncertainty. How could he? *Would* he? After all the promises, the assurances that they'd stay together this time? Wasn't that why she'd come with him, leaving behind their children once again?

Steve Morgan, I can't live in uncertainty…. You will tell me the truth this time, by God!

Humid air lay in a cloud on Gallatin Street, oppressive and muggy, so that breathing left a bad taste in the back of Steve's throat.

"Here, *amigo,*" Paco said, holding out a tumbler full of whiskey, "this should kill the taste of the air."

"Or me." Steve eyed the tumbler with distaste. "I don't know how you drink this rotgut."

"Quickly."

Feeble light flickered from open doors of dance-hall saloons and barrelhouses, the only illumination provided in this dingy, dangerous section of the Vieux Carré. It was the haunt of pickpockets, cutthroats and thieves, riverboatmen and prostitutes. A short thoroughfare of only two blocks from Ursuline Avenue, through Hospital and up to Barracks Street, it contained some of the roughest dives in all of America, as well as New Orleans. The district was the natural habitat of the men they had come to meet.

The overflow of this vicious underworld spilled into adjacent Levee Street and Bill Swan's Fireproof Coffeehouse. The coffeehouse was the only establishment in New Orleans where the Live Oak Boys were welcome, Swan having been a member of this formidable gang of ruffians himself before he managed to amass enough money to purchase his own, different brand of thievery. The Live Oaks took his resort under their protection, partly for old times' sake, and partly because he was wise enough to give them free liquor. It was an arrangement that worked well, for the Live Oaks were known to take great pleasure in intimidating and raiding other resorts, either on commission from a rival establishment or because they just took pleasure in it.

"Bishop must have lost his mind," Paco muttered when they entered the coffeehouse; he was fortified with whiskey and determination, but still had reservations. "A man can get himself killed in this place."

"It's the only place we won't arouse too much suspicion by meeting our contacts."

"*Sí,* but we look more like easy marks than patrons," Paco grumbled.

Steve grinned. "You always look like an easy mark. It's your innocent face that gives you away."

"*¡Mierda!*" Paco swore, then laughed. "Only you would think I have an innocent face, *amigo.* Your wife sees right through me. I saw her today, down at the docks as she was riding back with Girard. She has a way with her, you know, and somehow I let it slip that you would not be staying with us the entire way to Mexico. *Por Dios,* but she can make me say things I had no intention of saying, and then I stand there like a fool trying to explain it away."

"I know the feeling. Don't worry, I'll handle Ginny."

It was said more confidently than he felt at the moment. Christ, Paco was right. Ginny had a way of making him say things he regretted later.

"Is that O'Brien?" Paco indicated a beefy man with a scarred face; he was carrying a huge oak cudgel and with him was a man who looked equally rough, both of them cut from the same coarse cloth.

"Yeah, looks like both of them."

Matt and Hugh O'Brien had grown up in the Live Oaks gang. Their father had died five years before while drunkenly trying to rob a fisherman from a rowboat on the Mississippi River. In their midtwenties now, the men were notorious troublemakers around Gallatin Street, always ready to make money at any task except an honest living. They had the kind of connections that could be useful in this hellish underworld of crime.

After buying a round of drinks—the Irish whiskey little more than neutral spirits with a half pint of creosote dumped into it—Steve got right down to business.

"I'm told you gentlemen have the merchandise we need."

The older O'Brien, Hugh Jr., looked at him with narrow eyes that were as flat and black as a lizard's. "Maybe we do. Maybe we don't. I ain't seed no money yet."

"You were paid a conscription on order. You get the rest when the merchandise is delivered to the docks."

Steve met his gaze with the same cold expression. It was a familiar game, a poker bluff to see who blinked first.

"Yeah, well, we had more trouble than we thought we was," O'Brien growled. "That warehouse was locked tighter'n a whore's purse, and we had to git rid of a guard that we didn't expect."

"That's not my problem." Steve eyed him, aware that the younger man was shifting from foot to foot, his hands still wrapped tightly around the neck of the heavy cudgel capable of taking off a man's head in one blow. "We had a deal. It's up to you if you want the rest of the money."

After a short silence, O'Brien jerked his head in a nod. "I'll git the rifles to the dock. You just git me my money."

"How many?"

"Two thousand, maybe more. Hell, there's enough crates to reach from here to Canal Street, end to end. Somebody at the Custom House is going to be pissed as hell that they ain't there no more. Took us damn near all night to load them sonsabitches on wagons and git 'em took off and hid. We should git a bonus fer that."

A heavy layer of smoke drifted in the close, dark saloon, smelling of tobacco, whiskey and stale sweat. It was rife with danger as well, and belligerence that could prove deadly.

"Your efforts won't go unrewarded, gentlemen," Steve said easily. "Just have the rifles at the dock by midnight tonight. We sail in the morning."

It was ironic, Steve thought, that the United States government was providing ammunition to a Mexican dictator—or to his successor. Whichever man promised to come out the victor in this latest rebellion would receive the sanction of the powerful nation to the north. He could remember how discreetly Juarez had been given assistance in his struggle to keep the French from taking Mexico, to ensure that Mexico was kept in the hands of the people instead of a foreign power that might be a threat to the security of the United States.

As usual, it had to be silent aid, with no overt tones of interference. "A most delicate situation," Bishop called it in his typical dry understatement. "Of course, if you are discovered..."

It went without saying that they were on their own. Steve, with his connections to Mexico, would be assumed to be acting in his own interests, as would Paco Davis. They were the natural men to assign this task, and as appointed ambassador, Steve was less likely to be searched or suspect upon his arrival in Mexico. Yes, it was perfect.

Except for the complication Ginny could provide if she balked or created a scene when she learned that he would be more involved in the rebellion than he had told her.

"I begin to think it most inconvenient that you brought your wife with you," Bishop had said, his gimlet gaze holding no hint of the disapproval he voiced. "She has been known to be a *distraction* in the past."

"If I'd left her behind, she was liable to come after me and be even more of a distraction," Steve replied shortly. "And you know what she can do when she's angry."

Paco had smothered a laugh quickly at Bishop's sharp

glance, but it was obvious they shared the same opinion: Ginny was always an unknown quantity.

"Keep her happy, Mr. Morgan," Bishop had said then, but his meaning was plain. "She will be useful to us with Lerdo and Díaz, but only if she is content. I trust you will do all in your power to affect that end."

"Keeping Ginny content is my main mission in life," he had replied dryly, and saw a faint, rewarding flicker darken Bishop's eyes. "She creates too much havoc when she's not happy with me."

But there was more to it than that. Dammit, didn't he and Ginny deserve some kind of peace? Once all this was over and Mexico was not in turmoil, he meant to see to it.

10

On their last night in New Orleans, her trunks were packed and stood against one wall in the sitting room on the ground floor, but Ginny paced the thick gold carpets of the second-floor bedroom, waiting for Steve to return. A lamp burned with low light; the windows were open to allow in fresh air and the sound of his arrival. He'd been gone all day. No doubt by now Paco had told him about their meeting, warned him that she'd be waiting for him with questions.

How like Steve, to avoid her when he didn't want to deal with inconvenient questions!

She intended to be calm when he finally arrived, but this time she would not let him distract her from finding out his intentions, no matter what he did. This time, there would be *no* secrets between them.

In spite of her resolutions, however, Ginny found her temper and her patience strained when Steve arrived. He did nothing to avoid it, of course, sauntering in well after midnight when she had long given up and gone to bed, waking her as he shut the bedroom door. A single lamp illuminated the room, leaving it in pale light and deep shadows.

Ginny considered feigning sleep, but she somehow gave herself away and saw through slitted eyes that he knew she was awake. Indignant, she sat up, glaring at him.

"Did you know, my love," he said softly, "that your eyes glow like a panther's in this light? All green fire and hot flames. Is that passion I see, or should I prepare to defend myself?''

''You should prepare to answer my questions,'' she began tartly, but he shrugged and yawned, obviously intent upon ignoring her as he sank onto a chair and tugged off his boots, then let them drop to the floor.

''I'm surprised you're still awake, Ginny, when it's so late and we have to get up early. I hope you're packed, and that you aren't trying to take half of New Orleans's dress shops with you.''

''Tessie finished packing for me.'' She pulled the coverlet up to her neck, eyeing him narrowly as he stood up and shrugged out of his shirt, then began to unbuckle his belt. The muted clink of his buckle sounded loud in the soft gloom. ''Where have you been? With Bishop? Have you decided yet if you're going to stay with me, or if you're going to go running all over Mexico or wherever it is he wants you to go now?''

Pale light gleamed on his bare chest and shoulders, softening the patchwork of scars from knives, bullets, a whip—that memory was far too cruel, and she shuddered as he said, ''I hear you've been talking to Paco.''

''Yes, I have. Well? Do you deny it? *Do* you intend to leave me behind? You promised that we'd be together, Steve. This time there were to be no secrets between us, nothing to keep us apart. Have you forgotten, or did you ever mean those promises?''

''It's late, Ginny. I'm in no mood to get into this discussion. We'll have plenty of time on the ship to talk about promises.'' He eyed her darkly for a moment, a frown hardening his mouth. ''You aren't turning into a shrew again, I hope.''

Rising to her knees in the middle of the bed, she glared at him with renewed ire. ''You're avoiding the issue. This is important, Steve. What are you *not* telling me?''

He dropped to the bed next to her and rolled to his side without replying. Goaded, she put a hand on his shoulder and pushed him back to face her.

Immediately, his hand clamped onto her wrist, held her in

a steely vise, fingers digging into her skin firmly but not painfully. "Let it rest, Ginny."

"I can't— I have to know if you're going to run off on me again, or leave me to the mercy of whatever forces come along. Oh, let go of my arm, Steve."

To her surprise, he did, eyes narrowed and glinting darkly up at her. He stretched lazily like a big cat, folded his arms behind his head and lay there with a maddening half smile on his mouth.

"You're quite fetching in that gown, my love. It shows off your breasts and that creamy skin. You know, I think I prefer you looking all white and soft—virginal. How do you manage to look so innocent after having two children?"

It was an attempt to cloud the issue, and she sat back, legs folded, crossed arms holding her knees against her chest as she stared back at him.

"I refuse to be drawn into a discussion of anything but an answer to my question. *What are your plans?*"

Before she could avoid it, his hand flashed out, snared her wrist again and yanked her forward so that she fell across his chest in an inelegant sprawl. He held her, one hand splayed on the back of her head, his fingers tangled in her hair to hold her still. His skin was warm; he smelled of bourbon and tobacco.

"I plan," he muttered against her mouth, "to make love to my wife."

"Steve, damn you—stop that!" But Ginny found herself swiftly pushed onto her back with him over her, his weight holding her down despite her angry struggles.

Oh, why did she bother to fight? He held her down so easily, with a competent strength that summoned memories of all the other times he had done this, of the times he had taken her against her will, and the times they had come together like two animals....

She closed her eyes, blotting out the sight of his shadowed face, the merciless blue eyes narrowed at her and the mocking twist of his mouth. His hand slipped over her breasts, caressing them beneath the cotton nightgown.

"I don't want to stop, love. And if you were being honest with yourself, you'd admit that you don't really want me to stop. This is the one thing we've always had between us, this obsession with each other. Christ, I fought it long enough, tried to pretend it didn't exist, but I was only fooling myself. I want you, Ginny. I always have."

Half despairing, knowing that she was fighting a losing battle, that her body would override her anger with him, she made no protest when he kissed her, a long consuming kiss that roused her to unwilling passion.

"Damn you," she said again, but it sounded like an endearment even to her own ears. Steve laughed softly.

"Yes, I'm damned, but so are you. We're both damned. It's our natures. Open your eyes, Ginny. Look at me. Yes, like that. I want to watch you while I make love to you...."

Her gown was gone suddenly, pulled away to land in a white drift on the floor. Steve sat back, legs bent under him, his eyes half-narrowed with desire as he stared down at her. His voice was hoarse. "God, you're so beautiful—so goddamn beautiful."

"Steve..." Feeling choked by emotion, she lay still as he touched her, his hands dark against her palely gleaming body, caressing her small breasts, the flat of her belly and then the red-gold curls at the juncture of her thighs. For a moment he was a stranger again, the man who had taken her virginity so long ago, the same man who had abducted her, tormented her, loved her with such violent intensity for nine long years. The breath caught in her throat painfully and her chest rose as she dragged in air.

She wanted to protest, to demand answers to the questions plaguing her, but suddenly his tongue was in her mouth, seeking, ravaging her senses and driving out every thought but the rising need to be one with him. Relentless hands on her body, cleverly finding her secrets, touched her intimately, sliding inside her to thrust with lingering strokes that summoned gasps. Then he pressed her thighs apart and pulled her legs over his shoulders while she lay in helpless surrender and need....

Looming over her, his face shadowed, fickle light from the

lamp casting a subdued gleam on his shoulders and highlighting him against the gloom beyond, he held her with his hands on her breasts, palms shaping them, his lean fingers teasing her rigid nipples into hard knots. When she was gasping, writhing under his touch, he bent, his tongue searing into her like a hot iron.

Ginny cried out, her hips arching, and she found her hands tangled in his dark hair, holding his head as she moaned and shook helplessly. Release burst in trailing, fiery streamers, and he slid his body upward to cover her with his own as she collapsed in a shuddering heap.

"Hold me, Ginny."

Obeying, feeling heavy, as if her body were weighted with lead, she lifted her arms to wind them around his neck. He entered her then, with a swift, savage thrust, his body pounding into her with relentless urgency until she began to respond, the fire reigniting, banishing lethargy and shadows, banishing everything but Steve.

It's always like this... I'm lost when he touches me....

11

Sleepy drifts of fog slipped over the wet cobblestones leading down to the docks, muffling the sounds of hooves and wheels. Ginny stood in the shelter of their carriage in the dark hours before sunrise. Her face was pale in the murky light, eyes green and sleepy, lashes casting a faint shadow on her cheeks as the fitful glow of a lantern swept over her. Misty fog dampened the folds of her hooded cloak and skirts so that they clung to her legs, outlining the curve of hip and thigh. Tendrils of copper hair had escaped from her hood and clung wetly to her cheek.

Even in the dim light, her mouth looked bruised, still passion-swollen. Steve looked away from her, from the swift, questioning glance she flung him. Damn Bishop anyway. It always ended like this; Ginny was right.

"*Amigo,*" Paco said, coming up behind him, "we can board as soon as you're ready."

Familiar shipboard sounds closed in around them in the soupy light of glass lanterns. Ginny hadn't said a word to Steve since they'd left the leased house on Royal Street. He'd done his best to exhaust her, and seemed to have succeeded.

A crewman escorted Ginny to their cabin, and she didn't even glance back at Steve as she followed, disappearing down the narrow hatchway with a silence that left him both relieved and suspicious. It wasn't like her to be so quietly accepting.

Anger was expected, temper flashing in her eyes as she railed at him, not this unnatural silence.

"She has changed, *amigo.*" Paco said aloud what Steve was thinking. He gave him a swift glance.

"Maybe. Or maybe she's just changed tactics. I'm still not sure what her motives are, or if she'll end up being more trouble than help."

"Bishop may think she'll be useful, but I never have liked involving women. They're too unpredictable, and your wife is one of the *most* unpredictable females I've ever met. I've never forgotten that day in Mexico when she drew her knife on Concepción, or how well she could handle the weapon."

Steve grinned. "I've always wondered—what were *you* doing when Ginny and Concepción were fighting? Why didn't you take the knife away?"

Shuddering, Paco shook his head. "I have a strong sense of self-preservation that does not permit me to be fool enough to try to take a knife away from an angry woman who knows how to use it."

It was a sentiment that Steve understood. His untamed tigress, his siren-nemesis wife, was the kind of woman who kept a man curious as well as cautious. He was living proof of that.

Yes, he understood Bishop's desire to use Ginny as a means of gaining information from Lerdo and Díaz, much as he hated the thought of it. She was the kind of woman who would always be noticed by men, and by jealous women as well. Even 'Cesca, who was one of the most confident women he had ever met in his life, had admitted to a twinge of jealousy. "*Caro,* your wife is a bitch, but a beautiful bitch. I can see how she would attract a man such as yourself, though I think you a fool for going back to her."

Ginny would not have appreciated the Italian woman's dismissive assessment of her, but she had voiced her own opinion of Francesca that was even less flattering. Being in the same room with them in London had not been an experience he cared to repeat; he'd been on tenterhooks waiting for one of them to start an angry, spitting catfight, and had been amazed by Ginny's restraint.

Maybe she had changed, as Paco said, but he was damned if he knew how permanent it would be. He didn't trust her not to revert to her old ways.

Hell, he couldn't trust himself not to lapse into his more familiar role as an indifferent husband. It would be far too easy to forget their recent vows to revive their marriage for the sake of the children as well as their own mutual need. With Ginny, he always felt as if he were walking a tightrope, balanced precariously between heaven and hell.

The dragging creak of chains was suddenly loud, and diverted his attention to the fact that the ship was about to depart. Steve left the rail and Paco, and headed down the passageway belowdecks. The pungent scent of damp wood and cargo was thick in the air, redolent with vestiges of spice and tobacco, even whiskey.

The *Liberty* made frequent voyages to the Texas-Mexico border to deliver cargo, some of it not as legal as the ship's manifests recorded. It was sleek and silent, a vast advantage over the noisier, more visible steamships of the line, and able to slip into port without much notice.

Ginny was seated on the narrow bunk that served as their bed. She looked up when he entered, her eyes a cool green in the bright light of a lamp on the opposite wall.

Their eyes clashed briefly before he crossed the small cabin to open the round porthole. "Even damp air is better than none," he said casually, but she didn't respond to his comment.

Shouts and curses filtered into the cabin on the rush of brackish air; chains rattled and ropes shrieked as sails were hauled. Ginny stood up, put a hand against the wall to steady herself as the ship lurched and met his gaze.

"I have been thinking about the political situation in Mexico. It occurred to me that I could be of use in meeting with Don Porfirio and Señor—President Lerdo. If your intent is to be a mediator between them, remember that I know both men, even worked for Don Porfirio at one time. There's no reason for us to be separated from one another—unless you just don't want me with you."

Beneath the mask of indifference she wore like a banner he sensed her uncertainty, her apprehension.

"You're quite clever, love. Why would you think it wise for you to meet with Díaz or Lerdo?"

"Because Don Porfirio was quite pleased with me when we were in Puebla, and he enjoyed my educating him in French and even English. And Señor Lerdo was nice to me in San Francisco. I think he even tried to protect me from—the prince. That was at first. He tried to warn me about Ivan, I think, and it was Lerdo who told me that you had agreed to the annulment of our marriage."

"That was your father's decision, not mine." Steve leaned back against the wall and crossed his arms over his chest, deliberately cool and remote. Ginny had removed her voluminous cloak, and the silk gown clung to her curves. It was a soft yellow that brought out the copper tones in hair loose and waving around her serious face. She looked like a gypsy, with her slanted eyes and high cheekbones, familiar, yet as mysterious to him now as she had been the first time he saw her.

How beautiful she was.... It still mystified him that she had crept under his guard as she had, and made herself indispensable to him. Even now, knowing that she would be angry when he finally told her what he had to do, he could admit the depth of his feelings for her. Hell, he loved her. He had for longer than he could remember.

If he did what Bishop wanted they'd be separated again, and that was when trouble always seemed to keep them apart. Was it worth the risk? Maybe he owed her honesty, owed her the chance to make her own choices....

"When we get to Mexico," he said abruptly, "I'm to leave you at my grandfather's and go on to Mexico City."

Ginny's brow shot up. "For how long?"

"Not long, just long enough to see which side is going to come out the winner in this coup. From what I've learned, Lerdo is losing, but we can't be certain until it's over. My job is to find out all I can, then make sure the victor keeps the best interests of the United States in mind."

"Was leaving me behind your idea or Bishop's?"

Her chin came up in that familiar, stubborn tilt that always meant trouble, a defensive gesture that he recognized from long experience. She made him think of a wild forest creature, ready at a moment's notice to flee or fight.

"Christ, Ginny, why would you ask me that?"

"It's a reasonable question. You can't pretend that all of your disappearances have been Bishop's fault, after all. There were the times you wanted to disappear. Which is this? Am I to languish at your grandfather's *hacienda,* waiting for you to come back—if you come back?"

A lift of her shoulder was casual and indifferent, but her green eyes burned with banked fires.

Steve knew what was worrying her. It had crossed his mind, too, the danger that was always inherent in a revolution, but there was little he could do about it. And even if he could, he wasn't sure he would. Another revolution would drain Mexico of her resources, leave the country vulnerable again to her enemies. If Spain decided to take advantage, it would put them on America's doorstep. Then both countries would be at risk.

He told himself these things, justifying his decisions, but there were times, like now, when he wondered if he was only fooling himself. In the past it had been the excitement and element of danger that attracted him. Was that still the reason? Was that the reason he'd been so restless lately, and frustrated by delays? He had thought he was ready to settle down now that he had a wife and two children he was only just getting to know?

Once, Ginny had accused him of deliberately flirting with danger, and he'd teased, "I guess I've just got a restless devil soul, sweetheart."

Maybe that was still more true than he wanted to admit, even to himself.

"Ginny, I'd rather keep you out of this," he said now and saw her eyes narrow speculatively at him. "I can't tell you what you want to hear. I have my own details to take care of first, then we'll be together again in Mexico City. Paco will escort you there from my grandfather's. It will give you a chance to visit with Renaldo and Missie. Didn't you say not so long ago that you wanted to see them again?"

"Yes, but I thought it would be with you and the twins at my side." She took an irritable step across the small cabin to shove at the open porthole hatch. It swung wider, admitting the effluvium of a river port on the breeze that washed inside. "This is not what I expected."

"As you know better than anyone, plans change. Hell, my plans weren't to get mixed up in another bloody revolution. Do you think I want to get involved, to be away from you?"

"Yes," she said frankly, and when he swore at her, said in a rush, "Maybe not be away from me, but you do want to be involved. You might as well admit it."

"All right, maybe I do want to stop another long, useless war that only profits politicians and not the citizens. Is that so damn wrong? It affects you and our children as well as the rest of Mexico, and even America, if outside interests get involved."

"Oh, Steve…I know that. I suppose what I'm asking is if you're already tired of me, already wanting to be gone. If you think about it, we haven't been together this much in a long time—maybe since we've known each other. Not, at least, without some sort of crisis separating us, putting miles and anger between us."

An impatient reply formed, but then he saw her eyes, the naked honesty gleaming from her face, and held his tongue. He wouldn't do as he had the last time—hell, *every* time they parted. It had made it easier to part if he drove her away with cruelty and indifference, but it had torn them apart, too. He shrugged, said lightly, "Hey, green-eyes, you know I never get tired of you. Not even when you're nagging me like you are now. But there are some things I can't tell you. You know that. Just be content with knowing that I have no intention of letting anything or anyone ever come between us again."

In the soft silence that fell, he heard what sounded like a sigh of relief, but her eyes remained fastened on his face with intensity.

"I hope you mean that," she said finally, and there was a

slight husky note in her voice before she turned away to gaze out the open porthole. "It's long past the time for us to make our marriage work. I'm so weary of running, of being lonely and uncertain. Perhaps I am behaving as you've said I am before—a nag, but only because I don't want us to fall into that trap again."

"We won't. Have some faith in us. Just don't try to talk it to death, Ginny."

She turned back to face him; growing light spread over her face, illuminating the spare cushion of high cheekbones and the straight, slim nose above her deliciously tempting lips, the mouth of a demimonde curving into a faint smile. A dimple flirted at one side and the cleft in her chin deepened as she laughed softly.

"I'd forgotten how blunt you can be when I least expect it. I suppose I should be grateful you're not your usual sarcastic self."

Her smile eased the tart words and she shook her head the smallest bit when he shrugged.

"Yeah, I've been told that I'm not always so charming."

"I have no doubt of that, and by more women than I'd care to know about, I'm certain. Oh, don't look at me that way. I have no intention of asking for names and places. It would take far too long. You have had far too many women in your life."

"But none of them ever haunted me like you have," he said, an attempt at levity that fell flat. It was faintly surprising to realize he meant it. No woman had ever stuck in his mind like Ginny...not even the other woman he had once asked to marry him.

Elizabeth Cady Burneson stepped out onto the porch of the rambling ranch house and stared at the black hills outlined against a red sky. Sunset was beautiful, a time of peace for her, as the day's chores were nearly finished and the children ready for bed. She sagged against a weathered post, weary but content. Lingering scents of a fresh apple pie drifted on the soft air, late summer blending mellow light and fragrances most pleasantly.

A muffled giggle drifted out the open door and then a childish shriek; she smiled as she heard Martin's laughter.

He was so good with the children, as he had promised he would be. Even with the child who was not his own, but another man's son, the child that his real father had never seen, or even knew about. The only legacy of his parentage was in his middle name. He had been christened Matthew Morgan Burneson, at Martin's insistence, for he said that the boy should inherit something of his real father, even if only a name.

"One day we'll have to tell him the truth, Elizabeth. When he's old enough, he'll deserve to know about him."

Steve Morgan. His face remained a vivid memory still, the blue eyes so intense in a hard face, his lean competence and drawling, husky voice.... She shivered. He came to her in dreams on occasion, and it was as frustrating as it was perplexing. Why? Why should she think of him at all? Martin made her happy. He was a good husband, a good provider, a good father to their three children. Emily was nearly two, and the baby less than a year old. Matthew was almost three now, a lively boy who possessed his father's reckless streak.

Perhaps that was why she thought of Steve Morgan. Each time she looked into her child's dark-blue eyes fringed with long black lashes, she saw Steve looking back at her—the man she had called Smith, the man she had fallen in love with and yet never really knew. Had never forgotten. Yet it was a bittersweet memory when she thought of him, for she knew that he could never have given her what she needed in life—stability.

No, Steve Morgan was too restless and reckless, too much of an adventurer. Had he ever remarried? Somehow, she thought not. His eyes, when he had told her of his wife's death, had been too haunted.

And perhaps it was that, more than anything, that had convinced her she should not accept his request to go away with him, the knowledge that his heart did not truly belong to her and never would. Perhaps she could have borne the life he led as long as she could be with him, but never could she have endured knowing she did not have his entire heart.

It was far easier to lose him than to share him....

"Beth!" Martin was laughing, calling out to her. She turned away from her view of the hills and the past, smiling as she went back into the house, to her husband and her children, to the security she craved.

12

The *Liberty* sliced through the gulf waters easily, its prow cutting cleanly through choppy waves. A squall had blown up and threatened to blow them off course, rocking the vessel violently and keeping most passengers belowdecks.

Ginny lay on her bunk while the ship pitched and rolled from side to side. Despite the thud of feet above, she heard and recognized Steve's step in the passageway outside their cabin. She sat up and swung her legs over the edge of the bunk as the cabin door opened.

He stepped inside, bringing with him the fresh scent of rain and saltwater. He'd forsaken the garb of an English gentleman again, and was clad in dark corduroy pants, a blue shirt open at the neck and an oilskin that crackled as he shrugged out of it and hung it on a peg fastened to the back of the cabin door. Even with the oilskin, his shirt was damp, outlining smooth muscles in his arms and back. All he needed now was his hat and familiar gun belts to complete the familiar image of a gunslinger.

His mouth quirked in a smile. "Got your sea legs, I see. Does nothing ever faze you, green-eyes?"

"A few things." She slid off the bunk and stood up, but the ship rose sharply, hung for an instant on the crest of a wave, then plunged into the trough like a bucking horse, knocking her off balance. Steve caught her easily, his arms hard around her waist, holding her against his chest. He laughed softly.

"If you want me, just say so, *querida.* You don't have to throw yourself at me."

With her hands against his chest, she looked up at him. His damp shirt smelled like wind and rain.

"If I wanted you, I know how to get you," she replied with a teasing lift of her brow. "You're easy enough."

"Now you've hurt my masculine pride." He released her and she curled one hand around the frame of the bunk to stay on her feet, watching as he crossed the small floor with an enviously easy grace.

"Steve—" She paused, suddenly feeling foolish as he turned to look at her. How did she say what was on her mind? How did she say to him that when they'd boarded this ship he had still been as much a stranger to her as he'd been the first time she met him?

Though she was as familiar with his body as she was her own, she knew nothing about Steve, who he was, what he wanted to be or perhaps had once intended to be. Nor had she ever told him about her own dreams....

Soon they would be in Mexico, and the time for talking, for the sharing of souls, would be lost in the inevitable duties and chaos of traveling. She may never have a better time to talk to him, to bare her own soul.

"Steve," she said swiftly before she could change her mind. As he turned to look at her, she blurted, "I have some things I want to tell you, that I *must* tell you."

Slowly, she began to tell him about what she'd done while they were apart, making no apologies and expecting nothing from him. If ever they were to survive together, he had to know everything. No more secrets, no more surprises or men from her past. If he left because of it, he would have left anyway one day if—when—he knew the truth.

"Because the truth has a way of destroying the lie when you least expect it," she said, meeting his eyes with a show of confidence she didn't feel. Inside, her heart was madly thumping, her nerves stretched so tautly that she thought he must be able to feel the tension inside her. "You already know most of this anyway. You deserve to hear the little you don't already know from me."

Amazingly, he accepted it all without comment, no harsh words or sarcastic criticism when she told him about Andre Delery, with whom she had left New Orleans after finding out Steve had slept with her stepmother, and she told him that she had loved Richard Avery, but not with the wild, sweet passion she felt for him. She even confessed about Boris Shevchenko, the burly bear of a Russian who had escorted her from Stamboul when Richard sent her away. She spared herself nothing, unflinching from harsh facts.

"I don't expect you to reciprocate," she ended flatly, "or to tell me about all your past *amours.* I just wanted us to start our new life together with no more lies between us, no secrets, no swords hanging over my head."

Darkness had fallen while she talked, so that the tiny cabin was lit only by the soft glow of a single lantern on the wall opposite the bunk where they lay. The storm had blown itself out and the ship glided swiftly toward their destination—and their future.

Steve's eyes were dark, a midnight blue in his lean, tanned face, narrowed at her with an expression of fierce attention. She couldn't tell if he was angry, disgusted or hurt, and dismay clogged her throat so that she found it difficult to swallow rising panic.

Finally he moved, his long, lean fingers brown against the pale skin of her hand as he reached for her, curling them around her wrist to force her clenched fist open. He held her hand, silent, only a muscle leaping in his jaw to betray his tension as he studied her face in the gloom.

"Christ, Ginny," he said at last, softly, "did you think I would stop loving you if you told me all this? You look like a scared rabbit. You know I've been no saint myself. I know you don't expect details, like names and places, but I can give them to you. What I remember, anyway."

"No," she said, surprised to find she meant it. "That's behind us now. The important thing is that we never really loved anyone else, that our hearts have always belonged to each other. Oh, Steve, it's *all* that's important!''

''Ginny—''

''You don't need to remind me of all that's happened between us, because, believe me, I remember it far too well to ever forget. But I do know that despite everything—or, maybe in some strange way because of it—we've always loved each other that much stronger. I'll admit that I've been jealous of you, of your women like Concepción and Francesca di Paoli, even the arrogant Miss Lorna Prendergast and her obvious designs on you. Does that surprise you?''

''Only that you admit to it.'' A wry smile twisted his mouth as he stared at her, his eyes half-lidded and slightly wary.

''Well, why shouldn't I? This is a night for confession, for the truth. No more ghosts, Steve.''

''Yeah, maybe you're right.'' After a pause he said, as if to himself, ''I haven't always made the right decisions. For a long time I thought I knew what I wanted from life, from myself. It was enough to do what was right at the moment. If I hadn't met you, maybe I would never have felt any differently. But you, green-eyes, changed everything.

''When I was in Cuba, I was told you were dead. Maria Felipa, Cuban leader Julien Zuleta's daughter, took great pleasure in informing me of your death. I felt responsible. It didn't matter that you weren't with me when you had your accident. You were my wife, and I should have protected you, should have been with you instead of letting you go off with Andre Delery. I blamed myself for a long time. It ate at me...turned me into a man I didn't know anymore. Hell, for the first time since I was a kid, I felt utterly lost and bereft.''

His eyes met hers. ''I wanted you and knew I'd never have you again. It was the worst time of my life. I tried to forget you even though I knew that I couldn't, that nothing and no one could replace you. But I still tried.''

When he drew in a deep breath, she put her fingers over his lips and shook her head. ''I know. You told me about her. The woman you asked to go away with you. But now I'm here, and we're together. Nothing can hurt us if we refuse to let it. Don't, Steve, don't tell me anymore. I can't bear to hear it...."

Silence fell between them, the creaking of the schooner a familiar counterpoint. Water sluiced against the sides in a steady whoosh and the muted snap of canvas sails was like the beat of giant wings against the wind.

When he reached for her, it was the most natural thing to fall into his arms. This time their lovemaking was tender and sweet, an absolution and a benediction after confession. It was the first time in her memory that he had ever been so gentle with her, bringing her to release several times before he sought his own...whispering soft words that were erotic and loving at the same time as he touched and caressed her, kissing her eyes, lips and breasts until he slid inside her at last.

As the ship plunged into the waves in a wild rocking motion, his mouth moved against damp strands of hair that straggled over her cheek. "I love you, green-eyes. Don't you know that?"

"Yes...oh Steve, yes!" Arching upward, she shuddered at the rough friction of his body inside her, the exquisite torment of his powerful thrusts. Inside the cabin, it was warm and stuffy, the humid air that filtered through the small round porthole over the bunk smelling of the sea and wind. It was a voyage into sensual discovery, an exploration of the senses and, ultimately, of their souls.

By the time the ship docked at Point Isabel below Brownsville, Texas, Ginny felt for the first time that she held a piece of Steve Morgan's heart.

MEXICO

13

The *Liberty* docked at Point Isabel around midnight. The lights on the shore were dimmed by heavy fog, faint blurred pinpricks against black velvet shadows. They spent the night aboard ship, disembarking at first light the next morning, while their baggage was being unloaded.

Ginny waited in the warm morning air that pressed down like a heavy hand on her, the humid dampness clinging to her hair and face, filling her lungs. Seabirds swooped and cried over the harbor, a familiar melody punctuated by the groan of chains hauling baggage from the hold of the ship, and the bellowed orders of the stevedores unloading it.

Wagons rattled on wooden docks, lumbering vehicles that would carry Ginny's trunks and personal belongings to Don Francisco's *hacienda.* The things she had purchased in London shops to furnish their home, even some of the children's new furniture and toys, would be stored until they had decided where to live. The Hacienda de la Nostalgia was her favorite home in Mexico, but Steve had suggested they inspect his new estates before they made a final decision.

''Hearst tells me that the *rancho* is situated in a prime location, and we may find it more accessible to the United States, Ginny.''

So she had agreed, reluctantly, for she truly loved the home she had been given as a wedding present, but they could always travel between the two homes if they chose to do so. So much depended upon the political situation in Mexico, upon the revolution that was still raging between Díaz and President Lerdo.

Frowning, she couldn't help but notice that Steve had hired a villainous-looking group of men to escort their baggage train to Don Francisco's *hacienda.*

"They look like bandits," she said frankly, but Steve only laughed.

"I'll be sure to pass on your compliment, Ginny."

But then, she thought, watching him as he went to meet with the ship's captain, he looked rather like a bandit himself, wearing his guns again, slung low on his hips and tied to his thighs with leather thongs. It reminded her of all the times she had seen him use those guns, his ruthless proficiency and dangerous reputation as a gunman. He seemed to have reverted once he wore them again, becoming as hard as he looked.

At his insistence, she had packed only a single leather trunk, a small one that held just her necessities, a few gowns and toiletries, for their journey. "I still don't see why we cannot travel with the baggage," she'd protested, but Steve was impatient.

"We don't need anything hindering us, Ginny. Besides, I remember when you used to wear *calzónes* and a *sombrero* and be glad to have them."

"Yes, I remember that, too, but I'm not as foolish as I used to be," she'd replied tartly. "And I have no desire to arrive at your grandfather's *hacienda* dressed as a peasant."

"Pack carefully then, because most of your trunks will go with the rest of the baggage. Paco hired dependable men to get it there safely."

"I don't understand why we can't take it with us. It's not as if it would be that much trouble. And why hire so many men to guard trunks full of clothing and household goods? What *else* have you got in there, for heaven's sake?"

"I'd like to be there for my grandfather's birthday fiesta, and if we have to drag your trunks halfway across the country we're liable to miss it by a month," he said in a mocking drawl, ignoring her question about the trunks.

Now curiosity prompted Ginny to inspect the baggage for herself, and she made her way down the docks to the stacks of wooden crates that were being loaded aboard heavy wagons. Long narrow crates that she'd never seen were being loaded, and she moved closer to inspect them.

To her indignant surprise, she was swiftly stopped by one of the guards.

"That's close enough, ma'am. This is private property."

"Excuse me, sir, but I am Virginia Morgan, and this is *my* private property that is being loaded."

"Yes, ma'am, I know who you are. But I have my orders. No one is allowed near this cargo."

Irate, she snapped, "What is your name, sir? I want to know just who is keeping me from my own belongings."

"Butch Casey," he said with a shrug that conveyed his indifference to her anger and her questions. "My job is to get your baggage to Mexico in one piece, ma'am." The glance from his cold blue eyes was neither hostile nor cordial, but strangely wary.

"Just what else are you supposed to get to Mexico *in one piece,* Mr. Casey? Do you think I'm blind or deaf? I know how many trunks I have and how many wagons it takes to carry them. I may allow my husband to think I haven't noticed there are a lot more crates than necessary, but I have."

Casey's attention was riveted on her; his head jerked in a nod. "That's between you and Mr. Morgan, ma'am. Good day."

Their brief confrontation only served to strengthen her convictions that there was much more going on than Steve would admit, but she did not ask him about it again. Recent experience proved he would only avoid answering.

She should be used to it by now, the mysterious events and secrecy. But why did Steve still feel he must be so…so furtive!

Ginny barely had time to catch her breath before they were on a steamboat up the Rio Grande to Roma, a town clustered on steep sandstone cliffs above the river. They disembarked, then continued by horseback up the rutted road that ran parallel to the Rio Grande; the twisting river formed the border between Mexico and Texas, shallow enough to walk across in places.

Though the journey was calm and uneventful, there was an element of tension behind Steve's easy, casual manner that made her wonder why he and Paco had been in such a hurry to disappear once they reached Nuevo Laredo, leaving her alone with no explanation.

I suppose I should be glad that I'm staying in a nice hotel instead of someplace like—like Lilas's again, she thought with a trace of irritation. Steve seemed to have a penchant for choosing houses of ill repute—where he was far too well-known for her preferences.

The American town of Laredo was just across the thin, sluggish red ribbon of the Rio Grande. Fort McIntosh faced Mexico, perched on the high bluff overlooking the river, a warning and reminder of former conflicts and the current friction. It seemed quiet, with no sign of civil unrest along the border despite the rumors.

Yet uncertainty dogged Ginny as she tried to rouse from the torpor brought on by the lull in their tiring journey. With some of the journey made by boat, it was not as arduous a trek as it once was, but it was still exhausting.

Sunlight seeped through half-shuttered windows in the whitewashed adobe walls to fill the room with heat. Ginny blinked against it, lethargic after her noon meal. She lay on the narrow bed alone. Steve was still gone. He was almost mysterious, evading questions with a careless ease that was infuriating. If she wasn't so tired, she might have demanded an explanation. But every muscle in her body seemed to ache and she wanted to just lie on the soft feather bed until she could summon the energy to take a hot bath and wash away the trail grime that was no doubt imbedded in her skin forever.

God, how did I ever survive riding for days—weeks—in the dust and heat? It was so long ago now, as if it had been someone else who had ridden—had been forced to ride—at a grueling pace over brush-studded, arid land relieved only by an occasional seep hole. Hot in the deserts, cold in the jagged-toothed mountains that ringed the flat plains, her introduction to Mexico had been less than pleasant.

But now Mexico was so familiar. She remembered the first time she had seen this country, with Michel Remy. They had ridden along the contours of the Rio Grande then, too, but it had been south from El Paso. It had seemed such an adventure at the time, a high drama with gold hidden in the beds of her father's wagons, gold meant for Maximilian to further his efforts to secure Mexico against the *Juaristas*—and to further William Brandon's dream of creating an empire that would straddle the border of the United States and Mexico. She'd believed in her father then, in the dream that he could keep a foot in both camps and emerge unscathed and victorious. Ah, she had been so young, so foolish. And it had all seemed so romantic!

Riding beside the handsome French officer she had first met as a girl in France, it had seemed as if nothing could harm them, for they were accompanied by skilled French soldiers, and, after all, the *Juaristas* were only a ragtag bunch of guerrillas instead of highly trained soldiers like these picked by Marshal Bazaine himself.

But, in Mexico there were many deceptions, and she had quickly learned—as had Michel—that it was wise not to believe in appearances. The high rocks of a quiet mountain pass had suddenly sprouted menacing armed bandits, led by a blue-eyed *bandido* draped in crossed gun belts.

And her life had changed forever.

Ginny sat up, swung her legs over the side of the bed and rose to cross to the window. She wore only a thin shift of white lawn, loose and cool as it swished around her bare legs. Sunlight pricked her eyes sharply, turning the air to molten gold as she pushed open a shutter to peer out at the street below.

It was quiet during the afternoon *siesta,* except for a few stragglers on the streets. Thick dust hung in a soft haze on the still air, heat shimmering up in iridescent waves. There were things about Mexico that would never change, even when politics and politicians changed fortunes and lives in the blink of an eye.

It was all so complicated, the tortured convolution of Mexican politics so frustrating and frightening at the same time, that Ginny tried to focus instead on the future—her future with Steve.

There were moments it seemed as if nothing had changed, yet everything had changed. She was so different…and Steve had changed in so many ways. Outwardly, he seemed to be an entirely different man, yet beneath the calm facade she sensed the same violent nature.

But there had been no confrontations between them, no heated arguments, not even when Steve suggested she go to Don Francisco's *hacienda* instead of the *rancho* in the province of Chihuahua that he had purchased from Hearst.

"You can go on to my grandfather's with the wagons and baggage," he'd said, but she quickly refused.

"And be separated from you again? No. We'll stay together and arrive together. Things have a way of happening when we separate."

Shrugging, he'd only stared at her, amusement glinting in his dark-blue eyes. "Suit yourself, Ginny."

"Don't I always?"

Laughing softly, he had pulled her to him and kissed her, a swift, hard kiss that removed any objections she might have thought of.

"You won't believe me when I say this, but you are so predictable when you're unpredictable, Ginny."

So now here they were, in Nuevo Laredo on the border of Texas and Mexico, instead of across the Meseta Central in the province of Zacatecas. So close to home, and yet still so far away.

Don Francisco planned a fiesta, of course, to welcome home his prodigal grandson. And Teresa would be there, the woman he had loved for so long—and who had given him a son to be claimed by another man. *Richard.* How ironic that the only other man to even slightly touch Ginny's heart was Steve's uncle. Did Don Francisco understand about Richard? But how could he, when she wasn't certain she understood it herself?

Don Francisco had come to visit her at Richard's soon after she had first been blinded. She recalled him gently asking questions of her, and she had detected the concern and sympathy in his tone even though she hadn't been able to see him. He must have recognized that she still loved Steve, and been patient with her. What would he say when he saw her again?

Steve was his grandson, but Richard was his son. She had rejected one for the other. How strange that they were all so connected, even when unaware of the reasons, the true relationship. It must be a measure of the old man's strength of character that they were so different, yet so similar, Steve and Richard both strong men in their own dissimilar ways. As was Don Francisco, an important man in Mexico even through all the political turmoil.

No doubt the fiesta would be a grand affair; guests would arrive from faroff provinces as well as neighboring *haciendas.* There would be music and dancing, wine—probably *aguardiente* as well—long tables of food, and all the aunts to fuss over Steve and scold them both for not bringing the children.

Thoughts of her children brought a familiar ache. It was terrible to miss them so much, even though she knew they were happy with Tante Celine. Sometimes at night she woke up, thinking she had heard Laura call out, or that Franco needed her. Then she would realize that it had only been a dream, that they were far away in the English countryside. It was comforting to know they were with *Tante,* and that Pierre would never allow them to come to harm.

And perhaps, by the time they join us here, I will at last be certain of Steve, of myself and our love.... Weren't all the secrets behind them now? All the ones that really mattered? Yes. And while it was *very* annoying that he didn't have enough confidence in her to confide the details of Jim Bishop's plans, it wasn't as important as personal honesty between them.

A clatter in the street below snagged her attention for a moment as a cart drawn by a small burro lost a wheel. The cart was piled high with produce for the market, and initiated an immediate flurry of activity as children suddenly appeared to snatch ripe melons from the cascading pile dumped into the street. Two men in wide, dusty *sombreros* stopped to help the driver right the cart and chase away the laughing thieves. Ginny watched idly, then it was quiet again, the excitement subsiding as the children vanished and the cart was propped drunkenly on a wheelless hub.

Restless, she closed the wooden shutters again to blot out the bright light and dust, then turned away from the window, stirring the sticky air with a small lacy fan she had bought at the French market in New Orleans. The heat was growing oppressive; a bath would cool her off, and she would have her gown pressed while she was bathing. Steve had said they were to have supper later at the fort across the river in Laredo.

She frowned. He'd been gone for hours. Just where *was* he? So many things could happen. She hated worrying, and there was no point in thinking about it any longer. It would do no good and only make her irritable.

A bath was brought up for her, hot steaming water with a sprinkle of scented salts, and she relaxed in the tub for over an hour, until the water cooled and she felt refreshed.

There would be few opportunities for baths for a time. The easiest portion of the journey was behind them. From here, the trip would be long, hot and hard, for they would have to cross the Sierra Madre Mountains on horseback, sleeping in small, rustic *posadas* along the trail and even on the ground beneath the moonlight and stars.

It was a trip she'd made many times, but it never got easier, she remarked that evening at the fort after supper was over and they sat out on the long porch of the dining hall where it was cooler.

"But Mrs. Morgan, soon the railroad will make travel so much easier," Uriah Lott, a guest of the colonel's, said as he leaned forward to stare at her earnestly. "I have already laid tracks from San Diego down to the Gulf Coast at Corpus

Christi in order to transport sheep to market, and will be extending the line even farther.''

''San Diego?'' Ginny's brow shot up in surprise, and Mr. Lott laughed ruefully.

''Oh, no, I see I've misled you. San Diego is twenty-five miles north of Corpus Christi. But it's a start. Why, I have investors behind me now, and plans to lay even more tracks across the plains and the border. That's one of the reasons I'm here in Laredo, you see. It's the perfect gateway into Mexico. When a permanent bridge is built to link with Nuevo Laredo across the Rio Grande, we will soon be able to travel all the way to Mexico City by rail! I envision tracks laid all the way up into Canada eventually, and it's not just a dream. It's the future.''

''So your railroad is going to compete with the big boys of Union Pacific and Central Pacific?'' Steve regarded Lott over the rim of his brandy snifter. ''I assume you have all the funding in place for this.''

''Well…part of it. I do have a major investor who is interested in my plans. I think the Rio Grande Railway could successfully compete in the market. There's room enough for all. Which is one reason that I'm so pleased you agreed to meet with me, Morgan.''

''I'm no longer involved with the operations of the Central Pacific or the Union Pacific, Mr. Lott.''

''But you *are* a major stockholder.'' When Steve said nothing, Uriah Lott sat back in his chair, brows raised. ''I was told that you are the man I should talk to about this, for you have influence with men like Jay Gould. Look, I'm a businessman. Railroads cannot continue operating at a loss and taking government subsidies. We both know why this has happened—track was laid too fast, shoddy rails that have had to be pulled up and relaid before the first train could even run it. Builders ignored quality and economy just to get more track laid ahead of the others so they could rake in the most government subsidy money. It's a fact. I don't intend to operate the same way. My tracks are going to be made of the new Bessemer steel, not iron. The rails are more durable, will support greater loads, and save money by cutting down on the number of accidents due to broken rails.''

Cigar smoke wreathed the air; the commanding officer at Fort McIntosh, Colonel Nathan Prime, summoned an enlisted man to bring more wine for Ginny, who had stubbornly refused to be relegated to a parlor with the officers' wives and boring discussions of children and recipes.

''I'm afraid I'm not accustomed to the heat yet,'' she had said politely but firmly, ''and I simply *must* sit outside where it's cool.''

Besides, she thought wryly, it was the only way to stay close to Steve. She was beginning to wish, however, that she had pleaded a headache and returned to their hotel, for she found Colonel Prime annoying. *Must* he stare at her like that, pretending that he wasn't when she happened to glance his way?

The colonel turned back to Steve, cheeks puffed out as he sucked on his cigar, deliberately blowing smoke in her direction, Ginny was certain, to show his disapproval of a woman who did not know her proper place.

''Ah, so you know Jay Gould, Morgan? He's quite a robber baron, I'm told. Is that why you're in Laredo? Planning on laying railroad tracks of your own?''

''Not exactly.'' Steve glanced at Ginny. ''Just passing through.''

Like a dog with a bone, Lott was not to be diverted from his topic. He emphasized his points with the tip of his cigar making a glowing arc in the soft night air. ''I met James J. Hill last year, and he has some most intriguing ideas. He has big plans to build a transcontinental railroad across the northern region of America. Oh, I know, they call it Hill's Folly. But Hill has built several local railroads and he knows what he's doing. He's a good businessman. It's all in the talking stage right now, but I think one day he'll succeed in doing it.''

''He's got stiff competition for very little business, taking it through unsettled territory,'' Colonel Prime said with a laugh. ''Hell, there's nothing up there but Indians and goddamn bears! 'Scuse me, Mrs. Morgan.''

More interested in the intriguing prospect of railroads criss-crossing America and into Mexico than the colonel's deliberately rough language, Ginny nodded politely.

"But I think the idea has merit, Colonel. It wasn't so very long ago that Texas was largely unsettled. Look at it now. In ten or twenty years, there will be towns full of people all over America. And a privately owned railroad would not have to rely on government subsidies to fund the company, but on private investors who are more interested in business dynamics than politics."

The colonel looked slightly surprised at a woman having any interest in a business conversation. Steve smiled.

"My wife owns a considerable amount of railroad stock herself, so you'll pardon her for having such a keen interest in how her money's being spent."

Lott smiled slightly. "Then, with a woman's inherent wisdom, I imagine she sees the advantages to a privately owned railroad."

Ginny shrugged. "Perhaps. But I have a few questions. How will you compete with the Northern Pacific, the Union Pacific and the Santa Fe? All three of those railroads were financed by the federal government, and as such, have their expenses paid for by the government. Have you considered how long it will take to recoup building and operating costs before you begin to make a profit? Is there a comfortable margin of error in your estimations of construction costs in building a line far enough to pay for itself?"

Chuckling, Lott shook his head. "I see you have made a study of it, Mrs. Morgan. I read Hill's proposals in which he concludes that building one extension at a time would keep costs down and pay for expenses. If farmers are moved in from back East to settle the land along the railroad, they would use my trains to ship produce to markets back East. It would take time. Without giving in to government subsidy, each extension would have to build up red-to-black business before another extension could be built. Plus, by utilizing short, direct routes, it minimizes operating costs."

"Do you intend to go into a partnership with Hill?" Steve's

eyes were narrowed against the curling smoke of his cigar. "I understood him to prefer the north country to the south."

"No, we have different areas of interest. I plan on providing reliable, low-cost farm-to-market rail service in Texas and Mexico, and eventually join with Hill's planned routes to go up into Canada. Goods will be able to move all over the North American continent by rail. Americans will be more prosperous than ever."

Steve asked, "And your investors? Are they aware of the risks? Or do they prefer government subsidy?"

A slight frown marred his forehead, and he pursed his lips. His dark beard was sprinkled with gray, bushy brows a shelf over deep-set, penetrating eyes. He puffed silently on his cigar a moment, blew out smoke and shook his head.

"Only one man has suggested it, but he has a vested interest, I believe. Still, he is powerful, and has enough wealth to help finance feeder lines to his mines if we make a deal."

"A word of advice, Mr. Lott. If your investor is connected with Congress in any way, look elsewhere for your financing. When politicians run things, a simple business decision can get hung up for months or years before it receives the approval of Congress. And make no mistake, it would be Congress granting approval to build a feeder line even twenty feet from the main line to the stockyard."

"You sound as if you speak with experience, Mr. Morgan."

Steve shrugged. "I have experience with politicians."

"And Mr. Gould? Is your experience with him profitable?"

"Let's just say that I found it to be my best interest to get out of the railroad business, Mr. Lott. A man needs a strong stomach to deal with politicians and the labyrinthine workings of railroads."

Lott leaned back in his chair, studying Steve. The colonel cleared his throat and turned to Ginny.

"Your husband tells me that you've spent some time in Mexico, Mrs. Morgan."

"Yes. My home is there."

"But—pardon me if I am too bold—you are not Mexican?"

"No, I was born in France but choose to live in Mexico. It's a beautiful country."

"Yes, it has its beauty, that is true. Do you not fear losing everything in the current rebellion?"

"A person cannot lose what was not theirs to begin with, Colonel. Mexico is not mine alone."

"Nor does it belong to Lerdo or Díaz, yet they fight for it and people lose their lives and property."

"Rather like the war between Texas and Mexico, I would think. Or even the more recent war between the Union and Confederate armies."

"Or the French and the *Juaristas?*" Prime smiled. "And some on both sides lost everything. Lerdo is slowly losing his struggle with Díaz. Mexico is in danger of another bloody revolution, and I'm here to see that it doesn't spill over into Texas."

"Yet if Díaz emerges as the victor, Colonel," Uriah Lott said, "I predict that commerce with Mexico will open up new doors, and the need for railroads will be more vital and profitable than ever before."

Lott turned to Steve again, eyes glistening in the light afforded by the glow of lanterns. "Mr. Morgan, while I appreciate your reluctance to commit to anything without more information, a friend of yours suggested I talk with you."

It didn't surprise Ginny to hear him add, "Mr. Bishop was quite certain you would be able to advise me, as you are on good terms with American senators and Mexican officials."

"Was he? There are times even the invincible Mr. Bishop can err."

Steve sounded so cool, as if he were unaware that Jim Bishop had sent Lott to him. Was there a hidden message in there for her? After all, her father was a Congressman, and had interests in silver mines—though she thought they were all in New Mexico.

Growing bored, and still weary, Ginny tried to catch Steve's eye, to signal to him that she was ready to leave the army post. He ignored her, but the colonel did not.

"I understand you are familiar with Mexican politics, Mrs. Morgan."

"Not exactly, Colonel. I am acquainted with Lerdo and Díaz, but not involved in political intrigues."

Lerdo had introduced her to Prince Ivan Sahrkanov, "as a translator," he'd said, since she spoke French and Spanish so fluently and the Russian prince was not at all conversant in Spanish. It had been a mistake from the first, but she hadn't known that then, had only discovered after it was too late what kind of man he was.

Steve had come to her rescue then, too, though his methods had been harsh at times. But she could also remember those times he'd taken her on a carriage ride, or out on a ship in the San Francisco harbor, fed her delicacies and expensive champagne, as if he were courting her. It had been the first time he'd ever treated her as a woman worthy of respect—*his* respect.

Each day brings us closer together, she thought, and more pieces of our lives fall into place. Soon, we'll put all this behind us and make new lives together....

"Of course Mr. Bishop was extremely helpful," Lott was saying, "and suggested I talk to Richard King from Santa Gertrudis near Corpus Christi. He has a huge spread there, a former Spanish land grant."

Steve sat back in his chair. "I'm acquainted with King. He's a solid businessman, and may better serve your needs than most. Talk to him about investing."

Colonel Prime snorted. "Richard King is a former steamboat captain who had a lucky streak."

"It wasn't luck that made him recognize possibilities in a desert, Colonel, it was intelligence and aptitude. A man can do a lot when he works at it." He stood up. "Now, if you gentlemen will excuse me, it's been a long day for my wife and she needs her rest."

Relief flooded through her, and Ginny murmured a polite farewell as Lott and Prime rose to their feet.

"Colonel Prime is a bit opinionated," she said when they were back at the hotel. Steve pushed open the wooden shutters to allow in a soft breeze. It was cooler at night now, the heat of the day evaporating quickly.

"Typical military officer." Steve shrugged out of his coat and tossed it on the back of a chair. "They'll name a fort or street after him when he dies, and talk about what a good leader he had been. In a few years, no one will remember who he was."

"You're in a strange mood." She began to remove the pins from her hair, letting it fall around her shoulders and face. Her head ached; too much cigar smoke and stuffy conversation, she thought. She felt so irritable and on edge.

As she brushed her hair, perched on the edge of the small tufted chair that seemed oddly elegant in a hotel that provided only the minimum of luxuries, she watched Steve at the window. He braced himself on one arm, staring into the street below as if watching for something—or someone.

"Where's Paco?" she asked.

"Probably in a *cantina* telling some pretty girl how brave and strong he is. He has better sense than to agree to attend supper at a military post."

"Yes, why *did* you accept the colonel's invitation, Steve? It must be because of Jim Bishop. Oh, I'm right, aren't I? Did you know when you went there that this Mr. Lott would be waiting to talk to you, to ask your advice about his railroad?"

"Ginny love, you ask far too many questions. It's late. Get some sleep."

"Are you coming to bed—? Where are you going, Steve! You *can't* be going out again! Ever since we arrived in Texas, you've been secretive and—and sneaky." Frustration made her careless, and her vow to hold her tongue was forgotten as he began to buckle on his gun belts. "Just *tell* me what is going on. I'd like to know why you sent our baggage on with those armed guards who look like bandits. There's more to it than you're admitting to me, and I know that, too. Why did you feel you had to meet with Colonel Prime and that Mr. Lott? This is all Bishop's doing, I know, but do you think I'm so foolish as to tell anyone things that aren't supposed to be told?"

"Christ, Ginny, it's not that and you know it. You know how mysterious Bishop likes to be. If it makes you feel any better, I didn't know who was going to be there tonight. I just had a message that I was to accept the colonel's invitation to join him for supper."

He raked a hand through his hair. He looked very tired. She rose from the chair and went to him.

"Come to bed. Don't go out again."

"I have to meet Paco." He met her eyes, a faint smile twisting his mouth. "I won't be out too late."

"Will Bishop be there?"

"He damn well better be. I want some answers myself. Now go to bed, Ginny. I'll be back in a little while."

He grabbed her close, his hands on her shoulders hard and compelling as he held her against him, his mouth pressed close to her ear. "Trust me, Ginny. Just take a chance and trust me."

Swallowing the questions that begged for answers, she managed a nod. "All right, Steve. I will. Just—just be careful. I don't want to lose you."

"Believe me, sweetheart, I'm like a cactus burr you can't lose." He kissed her, swift and hard, his mouth a burn on her lips, the pressure lingering even after the door had closed behind him.

She sighed. It was the best she could hope for after losing her resolve not to ask questions or make demands on him. She had to trust him.

But it was so hard at times, when past experiences had made her wary. Yet what choice did she have?

14

Thick smoke drifted in hazy layers from the floor to the naked, blackened beams of the ceiling. It was little more than a mud-and-cane hut on the steep, crumbling slopes of the Rio Grande, hidden behind a stand of scraggly mesquite trees that clung precariously to the top bank.

From this vantage point, Fort McIntosh was within easy sight, just across the sluggish river. Bare wooden bones of an old steamboat thrust above the waterline where it was too shallow to allow passage above Laredo, glistening in the moonlight. The hills were rocky and full of rapids too dangerous to allow river traffic to flourish this far north.

''A rather primitive place,'' Bishop observed in his usual colorless voice, and sipped from his own flask of aged bourbon, preferring it to the risky fare offered by the *cantina.*

''No one asks questions or cares who comes here, as long as they pay for their drinks and don't bust up the chairs and tables,'' Paco commented. He was not as fastidious as Bishop, and drank from a rough wooden cup, though sparingly. ''You were right about Lott, it seems.''

''And Prime. The colonel has a fine disdain for men who have new ideas.'' Steve sat with his back to the wall, across from the door. It felt comfortable and familiar to be wearing his guns again; old habits died hard.

''Yes, well, Colonel Prime is not involved in this. He just

happened to be useful in arranging a meeting with Uriah Lott. So what did you think of him?''

This last was directed at Steve and he shrugged. ''He has some innovative ideas that will work if he doesn't get caught up in politicians' greed. If Brandon is the senator who has offered to fund his railroad, he'll end up getting burned.''

''Yes, well, as you have assumed, that is exactly who has made an offer. A very generous offer, I might add. Poker, gentlemen?''

Without waiting for agreement, Bishop shuffled a pack of cards and began to deal, his expression bland in the glow of soot-grimed lanterns.

Steve picked up his cards and studied them idly. ''I suggested he go to Richard King. He's connected with Mifflin Kenedy, and both men are shrewd businessmen. Tough, maybe, but more honest than the senator. Brandon just wants feeder lines to his coal mines, he doesn't care how he gets them.''

''Silver.'' Bishop glanced up, eyes hooded. ''Not just coal mines, *silver* mines. He's sitting on a fortune in ore and pretending he's dealing in coal.''

Paco whistled softly. ''No wonder he's anxious!''

''Yes, getting the ore out by train would be the most efficient—and private—method, as well as the safest.''

''Does the Mexican government know he's mining silver instead of coal?''

''I have no doubt that there are a few officials who are well aware of it, and probably on his payroll. But Senator Brandon has been clever enough to pay them well for their silence and cooperation. His biggest problem has been getting the ore out of Mexico and across the border without being apprehended by either country. Of course, we are aware of his activities on a *confidential* level. At this time, we cannot interfere without possibly alienating Lerdo or Díaz, both of whom have their hands full just dealing with the struggle for power.

''But we are trying to keep informed about Brandon's operations as best we can, while being discreet. A full house, gentlemen.''

As Bishop raked in the small pile of coins in the middle of the table, Paco tilted his chair back on the two rear legs, frowning. "So what is it we're supposed to do? Sign on with the mine? Find out what's going on?"

"No, that is too risky. You two are known to Brandon, and possibly to men in his employ. Besides, we have some men there already. It would be best if we had someone familiar with Brandon and his methods, someone in his confidence, perhaps, who might be able to discover his future plans. I know that the senator has renewed his acquaintance with Sam Murdock."

Silence fell. Steve glared at Bishop across the table. It was just like him to throw in that name while raking in the pot! Damn the man, he had ice water in his veins and the damndest luck. He leaned forward to take more cards, words more casual than he felt.

"Just where is Murdock these days? Last I saw of him he was staying at Jack Prendergast's place in New Mexico Territory."

Prayers End. And Beth.... God, he hadn't thought about her for so long, until she had popped into his mind the night that Ginny decided to tell him everything about herself. Then, out of the blue, Elizabeth Cady's name had loomed, once a bright flame in the darkness that had followed the news of Ginny's death. Bleak days when he hadn't cared if he lived or not, hadn't quite known why he was still alive. It had taken nearly dying to bring him back to living.

That, and Beth.

He wondered if she was happy with Burneson, and hoped she was. She was just the kind of woman for a man like Martin Burneson—steady and reliable, surprisingly passionate beneath her shell of reserve. And she'd known better than he did that she wasn't the woman for him. There had only been one woman in his life who never failed to intrigue him, all too often infuriating him, but never boring him.

And it was that woman who would be furious if he did what it was obvious Bishop wanted him to do.

"There are telegraph wires strung all the way out to San

Francisco, you know.'' He tossed his cards down to the scarred tabletop. ''If you want Murdock, all you have to do is wire him.''

''He's a busy man. Besides, as you have no doubt guessed by now, he is visiting Prendergast's ranch. It would be an excellent opportunity to draft a plan without a lot of attention being drawn to your meeting.''

''If you think my arrival there would go unnoticed, you are dead wrong. Remember, I had a little trouble there once before.''

''Yes, well, I'm certain that you're imaginative enough to find a way to speak with Murdock without a lot of notice being taken. More cards?''

''Hell, no! I'm not playing cards with you, and I'm not going to see Murdock. Get yourself another man. I'm supposed to be going to my grandfather's, then making sure the rifles get safely to Mexico City and into the right hands, remember? That was the plan.''

''Plans so frequently change. Circumstances arise that make it necessary to be flexible, Steve. Of all the men who report to me, you are the one that Murdock trusts most. And Brandon trusts Murdock.''

''And Ginny is back at the hotel expecting me to go with her to my grandfather's. What in hell am I supposed to tell her?''

''That is a matter between husband and wife, but I'm certain she would not begrudge you the opportunity to see an old friend. Or two.''

Behind the bland surface of Bishop's expression lurked a hidden meaning, and Steve's eyes narrowed.

''I think,'' Bishop added unctuously, ''you might find it quite *instructive* to renew old acquaintances.''

It was just like Bishop, Steve thought impatiently, to change tactics and leave him to deal with the results. Hell, it would take at least two weeks to get there, meet with Murdock and then get back. Ginny would never believe that he hadn't known it from the first.

* * *

Instead of the explosion he expected, Ginny stared at him with wide green eyes when he told her he had to leave for a while.

"It won't be long. Christ, don't look at me like that. I told you that it wasn't my decision."

"Yes, but you haven't told me where you're going."

"You know I can't."

There was a long pause, then she said softly, "I suppose I should be grateful that you told me you're leaving this time instead of just going without a word. But don't you ever get tired of Jim Bishop running your life?"

"Not nearly as tired as I get of being nagged about it. Dammit, Ginny, you've always known how it's been. This is what I do, what I've done since before I ever met you."

"I thought that by taking a position as ambassador, you would be able to have a *normal* life instead of disappearing for days, weeks, months at a time like you do, going God only knows where and doing God only knows what. One of these days I expect to see Jim Bishop at my door instead of you, telling me that this time your luck didn't hold out, that this time the bullet was fatal."

She drew in a deep breath, eyes wide and glistening with anger and distress. "How do you think I feel, always waiting, always knowing that you might not come back to me at all? Do you think it's any easier not knowing where you go and what you do? It's not! I imagine things that are probably ten times worse than the truth. It's not fair, Steve. It's just not fair to do this to me again! What about your promise?"

"Hell, do you really think I want to go? I don't, but it's necessary. You'll have to go on to the *hacienda,* make the excuses to my *abuelo* for me, tell him that I was delayed and I'll be there as soon as I can. Paco will go with you."

"Oh, I'm certain Don Francisco didn't really expect you to be there on time. You never are. And it's always left up to me to make your excuses for you. *I* have to be the one to face him!"

"Self-pity, green-eyes?"

"Don't you dare mock me, Steve Morgan! For all I know,

you're going off to some woman, and just using Bishop as an excuse. It would be so easy for you, and I'd never really know, would I?''

''Is this the trust you mentioned?'' He said it quietly, and saw her startled glance at him before she turned away, cheeks still flushed with anger and eyes bright with tears. He felt only the slightest twinge of guilt for not telling her about Elizabeth Cady, but hell, Beth was married and it was unlikely he'd ever see her again anyway.

Relenting, he said, ''The *man* I'm supposed to meet is someone you know very well, Ginny. Sam Murdock. Shall I give him a message for you?''

Some of the frustration faded from her eyes. ''Yes,'' she said. ''Tell Sam next time he wants to meet with you, he can come to you instead of making you come to him!''

Steve laughed. When he went to her and put his arms around her to pull her close, she didn't resist but leaned into him with a shaky sigh. Her hair was fragrant, a teasing scent like exotic flowers, light and sensual, filling his senses. He was supposed to leave in an hour, but he didn't want to leave her like this, not without making sure she understood.

It was only natural to sweep her into his arms and carry her the few steps to the wide bed, the mattress dipping in a squeaky protest as he laid her on it and leaned over her.

''This doesn't rectify anything, Steve Morgan,'' she said as she lifted her arms to wind them around his neck, ''so don't think you can just make love to me and all will be forgotten!''

''If any man ever knew that, it's me, love. I still have the scars from where you convinced me of it.... Look, wait here for me if you want. I'll get back as soon as I can.''

''No. Laredo has bad memories for me.'' She sounded so dejected. He blew softly on her ear until she sighed and stirred beneath him.

''Then Paco will take you to the new *rancho* in Chihuahua and I'll meet you there.''

''You haven't even seen it yet! It could be a mud hut with no roof.''

''I doubt it. Hearst said he stayed there for a time.''

"And if I prefer going to Zacatecas, or maybe on to Mexico City?"

"Ginny love, you can't go with me."

"I didn't ask to go with you, Steve Morgan!"

"No, but you're trying to make me crazy thinking about what you'll do if I leave you on your own. It won't work this time...." He stopped her protests with his mouth, a harsh kiss that smothered them effectively.

He was late riding out of Nuevo Laredo, taking the road that led to El Paso and then on to New Mexico territory, but it was worth it. He'd left her sleeping, after she drowsily kissed him goodbye and told him she had no intentions of waiting on him or making excuses for him to his grandfather.

Paco had business in Ojinaga on the border, then he'd take her on to the *rancho.* Paco would keep Ginny safe enough until he could get back, Steve thought. Then he grinned, thinking of Ginny's stubborn surrender that was more of a challenge. She never gave in graciously, but always fought to the end. It was just as well he'd never told her about Elizabeth Cady. It would only make her fret about what was past and over.

There had been enough of that.

He intended to conduct his business with Murdock, then get back to Ginny as quickly as possible. Dammit, he felt like a lovesick calf, missing her when he was away from her, irritated as hell most of the time when he was with her. It was a lethal combination.

15

Sam Murdock greeted Senator Brandon inside the study of his opulent Pullman coach that had pulled onto a side track just outside El Paso.

"It's good to see you again, Senator. It seems you're doing much better now."

"Yes. Taking a bullet is not something I would recommend, but it certainly has the effect of making a man analyze his priorities in life." Brandon took a seat in the wide cushioned chair beside Murdock's desk, leaning heavily on his cane as he lowered his weight.

"I must say, I was a bit surprised to learn you were in Texas," Murdock was saying, his tone noncommittal. "The last time I saw you was in San Francisco, I believe."

"Yes, when my daughter and her husband created such a scandal." Brandon grimaced. "In fact, one of the reasons I wanted to meet with you while I'm here is your partner, my son-in-law. I was recently informed by a man named Uriah Lott that any further negotiations with him concerning the railroad I wish to build are ended, thanks to Steve Morgan. It seems that he was advised to seek financing with Richard King or Mifflin Kenedy instead, but I need that damn track laid in order to increase production efficiency. You're connected with the railroad. What are the chances of Central Pacific laying track in Mexico?"

"Right now? Almost nonexistent." Murdock steepled his

hands and gazed at the senator over his fingertips, frowning slightly. "Private financing versus government funding—it would certainly eliminate unnecessary costs and regulations. I've thought of it myself."

"Good God, man, I didn't come to you for confirmation of the occasional idiocy of congressional acts. We all agree that some laws are designed to profit the government more than citizens. It's a fact of life."

"And some are designed to profit government officials more than citizens," Murdock said quietly, smiling slightly when Brandon frowned. "It's true, William, and you know it. Even you profited by the whiskey scandal."

This was not going at all as he had hoped. Disconcerted by Murdock's unfortunate reminder of past transgressions, he struggled for an effective argument that would persuade the millionaire investor to stop Steve Morgan. He was well aware that Steve was capable of retaliation, but Murdock was not a man who had to answer to voters. *And* he was Steve's partner. Could he convince him to interfere, or at the least propose a way to block Morgan's influence?

Brandon eyed Murdock for a long moment, then said, "Morgan has gone so far as to try to ruin me! It's almost a personal vendetta. We've disagreed over politics or policies before, but I never thought he would act upon his threats. It seems he's quite capable of impoverishing me if he's not stopped. Sam, I appeal to you, as his partner and my friend as well, to do something to stop Steve Morgan from ruining me."

Sam Murdock quietly drummed his fingertips atop the gleaming surface of his ornate mahogany desk, eyeing Brandon thoughtfully. "It would be a conflict of interests were I to involve myself in either of your interests, William, as I am sure you must realize. Steve has his own pursuits, and would not listen to me in any case."

"But you must certainly see the advantages to the current situation in Mexico. You're a shrewd businessman. In a few years, the railroad will be the main way to ship goods all over the continent. The man who builds the first commercial railroad in Mexico will practically rule the country!"

"That doesn't seem to be a job with longevity," Murdock observed wryly. "Mexico has a history of bloody revolution against its rulers."

"A puppet-head ruler would be valuable, with the real leader behind the scenes pulling his strings." He leaned forward, hands clasped atop the silver head of his cane. "We could be the power behind the throne, make decent laws. But we won't succeed if Díaz is not as amenable to American involvement as was Lerdo. The country is rampant with outlaws like Juan Cortina running loose, crossing the border at will to steal from American citizens."

"Yes, but Juan Cortina is in jail now, caught by the Texas Rangers and imprisoned for his crimes," Murdock reminded.

"You know as well as I do that the Mexican government won't keep him there long. He's as involved now in political schemes as he was when 'free' as an outlaw." Brandon scowled and shook his head.

"Díaz came to power as a champion of liberal principles such as municipal democracy and no reelection. But now that he has assumed the presidency it's become clear his main concerns are internal stability and foreign investments. While I agree that a law-and-order program is desperately needed to counteract the depredations of the bandits, he has at least taken measures to put an end to the outlawry."

"The *Rurales* are nothing more than legalized bandits! Most of them were notorious outlaws themselves until Díaz drafted them into his paramilitary force."

"Perhaps, but you must admit that they are far better trained and paid than the reluctant men conscripted into the army by force. And if they were bandits, they know how to find the bandits."

"Yes." Brandon looked up, suddenly alert. "They would certainly know how to find another notorious bandit. You've given me an idea, Sam."

Murdock's eyes narrowed slightly.

"I hope it's not what I think it is. If you send men after

Steve Morgan, he will come after *you.* Personally, I wouldn't want to risk it. Besides, what of Virginia? Your daughter does not deserve to have her father hunt down her husband as if he were a criminal.''

''Steve's activities have not always been legal, and my daughter is far too well aware of that. She was warned. I begged her not to come to Mexico, to go back to England or at least stay in the United States. If she chose not to listen to me, then she will have to face the consequences, as the rest of us are forced to do on occasion.''

''William, I cannot compel you to listen to me, but I will offer this advice. Don't provoke Steve Morgan. He can be as dangerous as a tiger.''

''Even tigers can be caged, Sam.''

''That's true, but I'm not at all certain I'd want to be around if this particular tiger got loose.''

''I'll keep that in mind, Sam,'' he said, a genial smile replacing his brief frown. ''And you're right, of course. It would be too awkward. Will you be in El Paso much longer?''

''No, I'm just here checking on some of my cattle investments. The last Indian raid decimated a great deal of my herd. I'm thinking of moving the herd farther north for a while, to a friend's ranch in New Mexico.''

Conversation moved to cattle and the price of beef on the hoof at the markets. By the time Brandon left for his own hotel, he was fairly satisfied that Steve Morgan would not be a problem much longer.

Prayers End—a cross between heaven and hell in Steve's mind. He stood for a moment on the weathered boards of the depot platform. The hinged sign swung creakily in a constant wind that blew across flat, brush-studded plains. He didn't know why he'd gotten off here, instead of riding on, going straight to Prendergast's ranch.

It was the same thing he'd done last time, gotten off too early because there was something about the place that had drawn him. In the morose frame of mind he'd been in then, it was probably the name of the town that had grabbed his attention.

At that time the news of Ginny's "death" was still fresh in his mind, and he'd been searching for relief from the haunting images of her that crowded his thoughts. It had been almost a relief to be confronted in the saloon where he'd gone for a drink, but it had turned out to be deadly for Jared Cady.

He had made Elizabeth a widow that day, and his lover a month later.

Striding across the platform, Steve's boots made a loud hollow sound on the boards, a vibrating echo. The train huffed smoke into the air, belching steam and cinders like tiny red stars. Metallic groans and the heavy scrape of the baggage car door opening were followed by the snorting disapproval of his horse; stiff stalks of straw littered the tracks and ground as he persuaded the skittish horse from the car.

"Hey, mister, don't I know you?"

Steve barely glanced at the old man. "Maybe. Maybe not... Look out...!"

The horse finally decided to leap free of the car, and would have bolted if Steve hadn't had a tight grip on the reins. He flipped up the stirrup and tightened the cinch, then led the animal to the side of the station house. Wind whistled around the corners, a keening sound, high-pitched like a woman's sob. The old man followed him.

"Yeah, I *do* know you! You're that gunslinger feller, the one that shot up Jared Cady a few years back, ain't ya? Yeah, you're him all right. I niver fergit a face. It's the eyes. A man's eyes are what I niver fergit...and I damn sure would niver fergit your eyes, mister. Nope. Like two cold pieces of dark sky."

He swung the old man a glance again, and the garrulous voice quavered to a halt. For an instant, he saw fear leap like flames into red-rimmed eyes.

"Last time I was here, you recommended a hotel."

"Uh, yeah, sure...Denver House. All Jack Prendergast's friends stay there when they come this way."

"Thanks." Steve mounted and turned the restless horse in

the direction of the town that lay west of the depot. It was all too familiar, playing out just like the last time, with the same old man to greet him. Hell, didn't the old-timer have anything better to do than hang around the railroad station and talk to strangers?

It was eerie, the way it all came rushing back to him, as if it had happened only yesterday: the saloon with the belligerent men crowded around the bar, Jared Cady's taunts, even the way he'd felt a weary sense of fatalism, knowing he was going to have to fight his way out or draw his gun. Then the brief, vicious confrontation with Cady before he made it out the door…only to be ambushed from all sides, bullets smacking into him and the thought that he was dying before it all plunged into dark oblivion.

If not for Elizabeth Cady, Jared's widow, he might have died. But she'd wanted to see him hang for murder, not take the easy way out by dying.

And he'd been obliging enough to live.

Even once it was proven that he'd acted in self-defense against Cady, there were plenty of folks in Prayers End who distrusted him. Beth had ignored them, ignored propriety and her own instincts and allowed him to stay with her. But in the end it hadn't been what she wanted. *He* hadn't been what she wanted. And he'd known it, too.

Now he was back, and the town didn't look to have changed all that much; still the same huddle of ugly wooden buildings strung haphazardly like a broken necklace. Fading light knit a sullen glow behind the outlines of the town.

It baffled him why people wanted to live here, out in the middle of nowhere in an inhospitable land. Ranchers grazed lean cattle on scrub and rock, fought over land and water rights, formed granges and went to church, made more children and died worn-out and hollow inside. Most of them never left the territory, except maybe to go to El Paso or a neighboring town.

Dust rose, drifted on the wind in stinging gusts that peppered his bare skin in a stinging assault. He reined in and dismounted in front of the livery stable, caught his saddlebags and hefted them over one shoulder.

When he turned, the livery owner was staring at him, his red face gone chalky white in the swiftly darkening dusk that promised a threat of rain.

"Steve Morgan..."

"Yeah. Si Barker, right?"

A terse nod made Barker's heavy jowls quiver. He rubbed one hand over his face, managed a forced smile that showed tobacco-rusted teeth.

"What brings you back here, Morgan? Gonna help out with the Association again?"

"I didn't know it needed help. Last time I was here, it was doing fine." He slid his palm over the black's dusty neck, gave him a pat. "Give him an extra ration of oats tonight. He deserves it after that train ride."

Flipping a coin at Barker without bothering to look at him, Steve pivoted on his boot heels and strode toward town. Barker would spread the news like wildfire that the hired gunslinger was back in town, the man who'd killed three men and cleared leather faster than any man here could remember seeing before.

Still shouldering his saddlebags, he checked in at the Casa Loma Hotel; it was smaller, clean and had good food. There was no point in stirring up folks by staying at the town's best hotel. They'd have a lot to say anyway, and he was damned if he knew why he'd come back here. He should have ridden on, got off the train in El Paso and been at Prendergast's ranch by this time tomorrow. It was a damn fool idea to come back. A man could never go back. Hell, he didn't want to go back anyway.

After all that had happened, in a strange way he felt almost disloyal to Ginny to even wonder what had become of Beth. Before, even when he hadn't thought Ginny dead, he'd taken other women, enjoyed them without a thought for anything but the moment. But hell, he wasn't a callow youth any longer, reckless and selfish. Maybe his grandfather's lectures had finally sunk in, penetrated his conscience. How Concepción would laugh if she ever heard him say that! The fiery gypsy had been his careless mistress whenever they met, enjoying each other's body without a thought for anything but their own pleasure. She had once told him that Ginny had changed him.

"She is a bitch, that one," she'd added frankly, "but I understand her because I am a bitch, too. You need a strong woman, but *ay di mi,* she will end up killing you one day!"

A cold wind was blowing up with the promise of an early winter. It had a bite to it, sweeping down the slopes to blow tumbleweeds down the middle of the street.

He found himself at the Red Sky Saloon again; it was close to the livery stable and not that far from the hotel. Only a few men were inside, two playing a card game at a rickety table in one corner, and another nursing a drink at the bar. Tinny music plinked on the old piano, and the same ancient black man sat hunched over the keyboard, gnarled fingers picking out tunes with surprising deftness.

A couple of Mexicans sat at a table near the door, intent on a hand of poker. The barkeep looked up, his face reflecting astonishment when he recognized the newcomer.

No one said anything, not even the barkeep as Steve walked to the bar. He dug into his vest pocket and pulled out a coin, flipping it to the bar.

"Whisky."

But the barkeep was already pouring it, a generous splash into the glass he'd just cleaned and wiped dry. It had gotten quiet. He glanced toward the piano. The old man was getting up, one hand against the top of the piano for balance. He moved away, toward the back of the saloon, steps wobbly but certain.

"He's just taking a nap."

Steve glanced back at the barkeep; blue eyes were wary and hard when he met the curious gaze.

Shrugging, the barkeep said, "He's getting old, I guess. Can't play as long as he used to."

"That happens." He tossed down his drink, felt it sear a path to his belly. It wasn't the rotgut that he'd had here before, but the better stuff, smoother and not as harsh. *Bert.* That was the man's name. Bert.

"Yeah," Bert said with another shrug. He looked nervous and a bit chagrined. "If he wasn't so damned good, I'd find me a new piano player, but ole 'Lijah's the best around. He can play any tune you name."

The same curtains that had swallowed Elijah fluttered, and a woman sauntered into the saloon, an overly bright smile pasted on her face. Pausing at the end of the rough wooden counter stretched between huge barrels that passed for a bar, her smile couldn't disguise the bored, petulant look in her eyes. She was new since the last time he'd been here, younger and prettier than Lottie.

Light hair, a kind of dark blond, was crimped into curls that swept back from her forehead, and the dress she wore was gaudy purple satin trimmed in black ruching that had come loose over her breasts, as if torn by eager hands. The matching satin slippers had seen better days, with stains and rundown heels. If not for the sulky expression on her face, she could have been appealing.

One of the men at the table said something to her in a low voice, and she lifted one shoulder in a shrug that sent a thin strap of her dress sliding down.

"You still owe me for the last drink, Stan. Go on home with you before I tell your wife."

Pulling free of the hand he'd put on her arm, she turned, and her gaze raked over the tall, lean man at the bar. Her eyes widened when she saw him, the smile growing brighter, and her expression changed.

"Well hello, stranger," she said, coming toward him, satin skirts making a whispery sound as she walked. "I don't think I've seen you here before."

A faint smile tugged at the corners of his mouth, but he didn't reply, only sipped at his drink.

Bert leaned forward, a warning note in his voice. "Janey, better leave this one alone. You try any of your tricks with him, you're liable to regret it."

Close up, Steve saw that she wasn't as young as he'd first

thought. Maybe it was her hard life. A tiny web of fine lines radiated out from the corners of her eyes, and one eyelid drooped slightly, giving a lopsided appearance to her face.

"If he's as smart as you think, Bert, I won't need to use any tricks, now will I?" Her arch reply was directed at Steve rather than the barkeep, and he turned finally to face her.

Something in his eyes made her pause, and the smile wavered slightly. "Buy a lady a drink, handsome?"

Steve tossed a coin to the bar and pushed away.

"For the lady," he said, and touched the brim of his hat with one finger as he turned toward the double batwing doors.

His progress was unremarked, and it wasn't until he was outside on the wooden sidewalk that he realized he'd been half expecting trouble. A confrontation of some kind, maybe even another ambush. It was almost an anticlimax, a sense of relief mixed with disappointment that no one had shot at him or challenged him.

Taut muscles relaxed slightly, and by the time he reached the Casa Loma, he wanted nothing more than to eat a hot meal, go to bed and sleep. It was unsettling. What had he expected when he came here? An apology? A parade? He felt slightly foolish and more than a little let down.

Hell, he'd be gone tomorrow. It didn't matter about the first time he'd been here. Not anymore. For a long time he'd dreamed about it, violent nightmares with bullets and orange spurts of flame, ropes that cut into his throat and slowly choked the life from him...cold, deliberate voices spouting hate and vengeance while he lay helpless.

The dining room was nearly empty when he went into the hotel, and he took a table in the corner opposite the door, casually checking out all the exits. A hot meal of steak, potatoes and baked apples was ample and tasty, followed by a mug of steaming, bitter coffee and a cigar.

"You'll have to smoke outside, mister," he was told, and he paid his bill and took his unlit cigar out to the porch, leaning against a support post.

The wind was colder now that the sun was down, and rattled a few loose shingles on the roof in a clattering sound that made him a little jumpy. Yellow lights gleamed in the windows, casting wavering squares of light on the wide street.

Cupping his hand over the flame, he struck a match and lit his cigar. The tip glowed red. In the distance, a coyote howled, a wavering, lonely sound in a night surprisingly quiet. The smell of dust and decay was in the air. It was a dying town. Not even the avoidance of a range war had kept it alive, it seemed. He wondered if Milt Kehoe and the others still met in the Smallholders Association. Had any of them been stupid enough to take on Prendergast, or had they stuck to their agreement to lease land in exchange for water rights?

Big Jack Prendergast wasn't the kind of man to fool around once he decided he wanted something, but he was honest enough to keep a bargain he'd made. And he'd been made to see the advantages to dealing with the smallholders instead of fighting them.

Dropping his cigar to the wooden sidewalk, he crushed it beneath his boot heel, then went inside the hotel. Down the street was the Denver House, the hotel where Prayers End had celebrated the successful negotiation of the deal with Jack Prendergast. It boasted crystal chandeliers and a fine kitchen, with thick carpets in the lobby floor and hallways, and a real East Coast chef preparing the meals. He'd spent part of his last night in Prayers End there, and didn't intend to set foot in it again.

After a restless night, he went downstairs and ate a light breakfast, then paid his bill before heading for the livery stable. Weak light spread a thin glow over the hills, chasing shadows from deep crevices and valleys as the sun rose higher.

The black was fresh and eager, pawing the ground and tearing up chunks of hard dirt with his hooves as Steve mounted.

"Still ride a barefoot horse, I see," Barker remarked, and Steve met his eyes for the first time. "The 'Paches, they ride 'em that way, too."

There was a note of derision in his tone that set Steve's teeth on edge. He leaned forward, tossed a silver coin in the air so that it caught the light in a glittering spiral. Barker missed catching it and had to bend down to retrieve the coin.

He straightened, and looked resentfully at the man watching him, eyes narrowed when Steve smiled.

"I learned a lot from the Apache, and Comanche, too. I used to live with them, ride with them, raid with them. If I'd met you then, I'd probably have a red-haired scalp hanging from my belt."

Barker blanched, and Steve nudged his horse into a trot that took him out of Prayers End without a backward glance.

When he was about a mile out of town, he saw the dust from an approaching wagon ahead. It came closer at a high rate of speed, a double team drawing it.

As it got near enough for him to make out the driver, he realized that this is what he'd really been waiting for since he'd gotten to New Mexico Territory. He reined in his mount and waited, hooking one long leg over his saddle horn and rolling a smoke.

The wagon rumbled to a halt beside him, horses blowing noisily. "Were you going to leave town without even bothering to come and say hello to me?" Elizabeth Burneson demanded.

The wind had flushed her cheeks pink, and it was obvious she had dressed in a hurry; she wore a plain gown of dark-rose wool, pretty but simple. Her hair was half-loose and straggling over one shoulder, dark curls tangled.

"It seemed best." Steve licked the edge of the thin paper to seal it, and stuck the smoke in one corner of his mouth.

"You still have bad habits, I see." Her eyes were wide and dark with emotion, and he noted the slight trembling of her hands on the reins.

"Is that what you rode so hard to tell me?" Amused, he saw the flush rise higher in her face, her high sculpted cheekbones wearing color like flags.

"No. I—I do have something to tell you. It's—it's not easy, but Martin— We got married not long after you left town."

"I figured you would. He's the kind of man you needed, the kind of man who would make you happy."

"Yes, you're right about that." Her gaze was steady, and her hands didn't tremble quite so much now. The wind tugged at her hair and the hem of her gown. "He makes me very happy. He's a good man, a decent, hardworking man who would do anything for me." She paused, then added, "And anything for our children."

"I'm glad to know that, Beth, really I am." He meant it. Maybe he should feel remorse, but he hadn't thought of her much after leaving, and not at all once he'd discovered that Ginny was still alive. Only recently had he thought of her, reminded by Ginny's confessions.

One of her horses shied slightly, spooked by Steve's horse, and the wagon rolled forward. Instinctively, he reached out to grab the reins. Elizabeth had lunged to grab them up, and swayed precariously over the seat of the buckboard.

"Sit down before you fall out and a wheel rolls over you," Steve said roughly, and reached over to set the brake.

She glared at him. He could smell her now that he was so close, the woman-smell of fresh-washed clothes, soap and a faint powdery fragrance.

"Steve..." Her voice faltered and she took a deep breath to steady it. "When Sheriff Blaine came out to tell us that you had come back, I didn't want to see you again. I just didn't see the point in it, in raking up old memories."

"So what changed your mind?" He watched her closely. He had always been able to tell when something was bothering her. She got fidgety, like she was now, plucking at her skirts, restless fingers moving from her gown to her hair, hands fluttering like sturdy birds in the air.

"Martin changed it. He said...he said you should know, that it wasn't right to keep such a thing from a man. Even when I told him that you wouldn't care, that you didn't even want the two you already had, he— Well, he's a good man, and he says I must do the right thing. He left it up to me." Her mouth twisted slightly. "He knows that I always want to live up to his high expectations of me."

Steve was quiet now, and wary, his blue eyes narrowed and watchful as he waited, sensing before she said it what she would tell him.

"You—I—*we* have a son, Steve. And I knew about it before you left. I kept it from you because you had told me that you weren't cut out for parenthood. There. I've said it. You're free to hate me now for not telling you."

Carefully, he took the unlit cigarette from his mouth and tossed it to the ground. "How does Martin feel about him?"

Apparently, it wasn't the question she'd expected him to ask. She folded her hands in her lap, knuckles white with strain.

"He adores him. And Matthew adores his father. Martin *is* his father, Steve, in every way but one."

"I'd like to see him."

All color drained from her face, leaving it ashen. She began to shake her head, her voice a kind of moan.

"Nooo...he's too little to understand!"

"Then it won't hurt if I meet him. He doesn't need to be told anything but that I'm a visitor. Christ, Beth, it's the least you can do after not bothering to tell me about him!"

Her eyes flashed. "Not bothering? You told me you have twins, a boy and a girl, that *you* had never bothered to even see! Why should I think you'd feel any differently about this child?"

"You shouldn't." He eyed her a moment, then said, "You married Burneson because you knew you were pregnant."

"I would have married him anyway, I think. I always knew, deep down, that you weren't the kind of man to stay around, to make a family and a life. You only confirmed it."

"This may not make any difference to you, but I thought about my children after I left you. I found out my wife was alive after all, and that she'd taken them with her to Europe. I went after them. Hell, I think I might have known I was going after her, too, but at the time all I could think about was that I hadn't even met my children and I'd lost them."

"Your wife is alive? You must have been very happy to hear that."

Steve laughed ruefully. "I didn't know if I wanted to kill her myself or was relieved she wasn't dead. I did know I wanted my children. Laura and Franco. They're beautiful, smart and just mischievous enough to escape sainthood."

A faint smile curved her mouth. "I have three now. Two boys and a girl." She put a hand on her belly and he saw that it was rounded, swelling out the front of her dress. "And another one on the way. Odd to think now that I once thought I was barren."

"Will you let me see him, Beth?"

It was said quietly, and the smile faded from her mouth to leave her expression strained. After a moment she nodded, and blew out a heavy breath.

"Yes. Yes, you may see him."

He followed her to the Burneson spread, a modest but thriving operation, with outbuildings and a two-story main house protected by fences on two sides, and a high cliff on the back side.

As if he'd expected them, Martin Burneson came out to meet them, a dark-headed boy in his arms. The child was squirming slightly, impatiently demanding to be allowed to go and play with Pedro and Fidelito.

"In a moment, Matt. We have a visitor. Remember your manners."

Steve dismounted, aware of Elizabeth anxiously watching him as he moved toward the child. Martin had set him down, and now held out his hand to Steve.

"You're welcome for a short visit, Mr. Morgan."

He nodded understanding and shook Burneson's hand. When he turned, the boy, a sturdy youngster with dark-blue eyes and surprisingly long lashes, held out his hand in a perfect imitation of Burneson.

"How do you do, sir?"

It was said with a slight air of impatience, the blue eyes cutting toward the side of the house where a small Mexican boy was playing with a large, shaggy dog.

Steve shook his hand solemnly. He recognized some of Franco in the boy, in the set of his eyes and the dark hair and skin.

"I have a son a lot like you," he said, and smiled at the look of polite disinterest the boy gave him. "Maybe you can meet him one day."

"That would be very nice, sir." Obviously having gone the full extent of his social duties, Matthew glanced up at Martin. "May I go now to play with Pedro, Papa? He's been waiting on me for a very long time."

"Yes, son. You did well."

With a glance of happy pride, the boy scampered down the steps and fled across the yard, hurdling a low fence to reach his playmate more quickly. Steve watched him, reminded again of Franco's impulsive, reckless nature. He glanced back at Elizabeth, standing now beside her husband, and shook his head.

"I've always blamed Franco's daring on his mother. I see I may have been mistaken."

Elizabeth smiled, though there was a hint of strain still left in her face. "He's very well-behaved, just full of energy."

"So Ginny says about Franco." He glanced around, then back at the couple standing awkwardly on the porch. "So Fidelito is still with you?"

"Oh yes, and Domingo, too, though he's not as spry as he used to be. He won't admit to it, of course."

"No, he wouldn't."

It was suddenly far too uncomfortable now that he had achieved the purpose of his visit, and he could tell that they wished him gone.

"Will you let me know if he ever needs anything?" He looked directly at Elizabeth, holding her gaze, and knew that she understood.

"Yes, of course. But he's very happy and healthy. We love him very much."

"It shows. Well, I'm thankful you let me see him. And if it means anything to you, I won't intrude."

Martin Burneson nodded, relief in his eyes. "I rather thought you'd do the honorable thing, Morgan."

"He has your name," Elizabeth blurted suddenly, then colored. "His middle name. Morgan. Martin insisted, said that one day he should know about you and his real lineage."

Steve nodded. "When the time is right, I'll be glad to answer any questions he may have."

As he turned, gathering up the reins to his horse, he heard a shout, and paused to see Fidelito running toward him.

"*Señor! Señor!* You have come back!"

It was the first true welcome he'd had since coming back to Prayers End and Steve grinned, bracing as Fidelito—now a sturdy adolescent—threw himself at him like a cannon ball.

"I saw you, and I thought to myself that you looked so familiar, but it wasn't until I saw your face closer that I knew it was you," the youth chattered in idiomatic Spanish, and grinned when Steve answered in the same dialect.

"I hope you haven't been hiding under any sidewalks lately."

"Ah, but if I had not, they would have hung you, so you should be grateful. Now, I am too big to hide in so small a space."

"You're nearly a man."

"*Sí,* so I tell my grandfather, but he says I am still young enough to beat for insolence."

"Fidelito! Fidelito! Come and get our ball down from the roof of the smokehouse. Pedro has put it up there again when I told him not to throw it so high!"

Young Matthew's impatient demands snared Fidelito's attention, and he turned to tell him to wait just a moment while he spoke with an old friend. As he turned back to Steve, he wore a puzzled frown, and then dawning recognition lit his eyes as he looked again at the child.

"It's time I go," Steve said quietly, and in Spanish, "I know you can keep a secret well, and that you'll keep this one, too."

Fidelito nodded, eyes huge in a face that mirrored his sudden understanding. "*Sí,* I would never betray you."

"Tell your grandfather hello for me."

He didn't look back this time either, but rode north toward the Prendergast spread. It occurred to him that one day Ginny would learn about the child he'd had with Elizabeth. After all, if Jim Bishop knew—and damn him, he'd found out about it somehow, or he wouldn't have made that cryptic comment about seeing an old friend *or two*—it was bound to come out sooner or later. It wasn't something he could tell Ginny right now, when they were still uncertain of each other, still had doubts. No, he'd wait. The right time to tell her would come around.

16

Sunlight seeped through windows left open to allow in a warm breeze, slanting across ocher walls, spilling bright gold over the mahogany furniture and pretty carpets. At last they were in a decent hotel, new and freshly painted, with the smell still lingering in the air. Ginny and Paco had crossed the border from Presidio, Texas, to the tiny town of Ojinaga in the state of Chihuahua late the night before, and she had gone straight to bed.

But it had been a restless sleep, peopled with dreams of places and faces from her past, and she had tossed and turned the entire night. Maybe she was too tired to sleep, or too frustrated.

I hate waiting! Every day she expected Steve to return, looked for him on the horizon as they rode, expected to see him around each bend in the road and behind every stand of trees. At first, she had lingered in Laredo after Steve left, uncertain what she wanted to do despite Paco's obvious impatience. Finally she had decided she would travel on to the new *rancho* after all, too restless to remain in Laredo, and unwilling to go to Zacatecas without Steve.

Damn Steve. Damn Bishop, and damn the rebellion that made it unsafe to travel right now! If it wasn't so risky, she would go on by herself. And why not? She'd done more dangerous things before, had survived it all.

But now she had other things to consider. Her children

would be motherless if she miscalculated, and she had just begun to know them, just begun to win over Franco. Laura was easier, accepting her with a sweet, guileless trust that was at once comforting and terrifying. How could she ever betray that faith?

So she waited, restless and miserable, while Paco tended to some business he had here in Ojinaga, deviling him when the days passed and the tension grew too strong to bear.

"Please, Ginny, wait for Steve's return," he begged when she joined him downstairs one morning, frustration prompting her to announce her intention to leave immediately for Mexico City. "I don't deserve this. Save it for him!"

"He's not here, so you'll have to listen." Irritation edged her voice, gave a sharp bite to her words. "It's been two weeks since we left Laredo. I'm ready to leave tomorrow. Steve still isn't back. Why did he have to go to New Mexico *now?*"

"A thousand times you have asked me this, and a thousand times I have said I do not know." Paco looked almost desperate. "If he does not join us soon, I will hunt for him myself."

"In two weeks there has been no word from him. He could have at least sent a telegram to let us know when he'll meet us. This wouldn't be the first time he's disappeared."

"Are you more worried that he won't join us, or that he's joined someone else?" Paco asked bluntly, startling her into silence.

"I don't know," she admitted frankly after a moment. "I just...just feel that something has happened. Or that it will happen. Maybe I'm worried that, now that the fighting has escalated, he'll be caught up in the rebellion."

"Steve's too smart to be dragged into something he can avoid. I doubt he'll be conscripted into either army."

Paco's dry assurance was surprisingly comforting. She smiled.

"Oh, I know I'm being foolish, Paco. But so many times before, we've been separated. I just don't want to take the chance that it will happen again."

"I have finished what I came here to do. We can leave in the morning for the *rancho.* By the time we get there, Steve will probably be waiting on us, madder than hell that we took so long to get there."

She laughed. "Yes, that would be his reaction!"

"Then tomorrow we leave. Once we reach the *hacienda,* all will be well. You'll see."

"Tell me about Señor Valdez," Ginny said then, more to change the subject than from curiosity. "He has come here to see you three times, and each time he looks at me as if he knows what I look like without my clothes."

"Valdez?" Paco looked startled, a reaction swiftly hidden as he lifted his shoulders in a careless shrug. "He is a minor official, unimportant. And he no doubt would love to see you without your clothes, but if he comes again, I will be sure that you do not have to deal with him."

"Yes, he waits in the lobby, and approaches me even when I am eating dinner. A rather forward man. He reminds me of...of someone very unpleasant."

Devereaux sprang to mind, a man puffed up with a sense of his own importance, and far too eager to ingratiate himself with higher-ups in the command. The French colonel had lied to her, had tricked her into his bed to save Steve. But Steve had still been condemned, still whipped and sent to prison. She'd learned to recognize men like Devereaux, to see the motivation behind their smiling faces and too polite reassurances.

As the sun slowly sank behind the ragged horizon, light lingered in a reddish haze that made the stark hills glow. Ginny dressed for dinner in her yellow silk, coiled her hair atop her head and secured it with fine Spanish combs and pins. Paco had other plans, he'd said, and suggested she eat dinner in her room, but she didn't feel like it. What did it matter if she was alone tonight? She certainly could take care of her own needs.

Dusk was balmy, the promise of winter's chill a distant bite in the air. Above the folded creases of the Chinati Mountains, clouds hung low to cloak serrated peaks. It was the end of the rainy season in Chihuahua, when the desert received most of its rainfall. Flat-topped ridges and gap-toothed passes lined narrow, twisting trails westward; it would be the most difficult, dangerous part of their journey.

But tonight, Ginny thought restlessly, I am not going to think of that, or of anything but what I want to do!

She paused in the arched doorway of the *cantina,* absorbing the loud, gay music of Mexico that drifted in from the patio. Cottonwood *vigas* and *rajas* formed the framework of the *cantina,* sheathed with creamy adobe. Torches shed cheerful orange light on walls, chasing away shadows and chill as effectively as did the bottles of tequila and wine upon scattered tables. It was a fiesta night, and laughter and noise filled the air. With Presidio just across the border, Tejanos mixed among the Mexicans, dancing with pretty *señoritas* garbed in bright skirts and blouses, watched over by indulgent parents or sharp-eyed *dueñas.*

The spicy scent of chili burned the air, and *tortillas* sizzled on plates filled with beef, chicken and beans. A fire glowed at one end of the bricked courtyard, more for the patrons than the *cantina*'s use, and delicious smells emanated from just beyond in the kitchens built at the end of the L-shaped building. A profusion of flowering plants swarmed over low walls, and a huge oak spread ancient branches over the patio, dripping lanterns that bobbed erratic light over dancers and tables.

Ginny navigated the two shallow steps down into the courtyard, her skirts lifted in one hand as she swept the area with a glance. She recognized no one, but hadn't really expected to, after all.

"Señora Alvarado," a voice behind her said, and she turned in surprise to see the round-faced, smiling man she'd discussed earlier with Paco. "It is very pleasant to see you again, though I had not expected to see you so soon."

"Nor I you, Señor Valdez."

"Ah, it is an unexpected pleasure to find you here on such a lovely night. The rain has stopped at last, and it is time to celebrate. Tell me, *señora,* where is your escort? I had thought to see him here with you. Such a beautiful lady should not wander about alone in a strange town, heh?''

Her brow lifted in a gesture of haughty reproof that he would be so forward. ''He is to meet me here later. I thought perhaps he had already arrived. Now if you will excuse me—?''

It sufficed to keep him at arm's length, a small lie that she didn't regret in the least, and Ginny was relieved when Valdez murmured his regrets after escorting her to a table in the corner of the courtyard. From this vantage point, she could see the entire *cantina,* including the gate.

She could also see Señor Valdez, across from her at a table with two other men, their glances in her direction a constant irritation. One of the men, tall and swarthy, with a penetrating gaze, never took his eyes from her. Pah! Let them stare and wonder. She did not care what they thought.

Besides, Señor Valdez was involved in the business with Paco and Steve somehow, and she suspected it had something to do with the mysterious shipment of cargo that had been unloaded when they disembarked at Point Isabel. She had not seen the long wooden boxes again. A lingering suspicion that perhaps Steve was bringing in guns and ammunition to fuel the rebellion was a niggling worry.

Despite several discussions on the topic, she had no idea if he favored Lerdo or Díaz as Mexico's next leader. But when had her opinion ever mattered? Not often. Not when it came to war or political intrigue, both of which she detested as much as Steve seemed to enjoy them.

She sipped wine, the rich, fruity *sangria* that she found so refreshing, and ate sparingly while she watched the dancers grow more lively as the night progressed. Then the melody changed a bit, from *El Chinaco,* a song of the *Juarista guerrilleros,* to *La Malaguena,* then to the music of the peasants, wild and abandoned, a plaintive melody that soared higher than the leafy branches of the towering oak, a paean to the night sky and lost love. It had been so long since she'd heard the true music of Mexico that she'd almost forgotten how the guitars could sound like a woman's sobs. Now it was a reminder of her own sobs in those days of marching, apathy and sullen resignation, with only the dancing to make her forget for the moment. The fiery peasant dances of Mexico—the *jarabe, corrido* and sometimes even the *fandango*...

It had been the only thing then that allowed her to forget that she had become dirt, lower than the whores who walked the streets of the cities. And she had despised herself then, for continuing to live, for even wanting to survive, to endure.

But that was a long time ago.

There were so many memories in this country; some of them she tried to forget, but never would. Even during the worst times, when she had survived brutality and horror, the music had kept her feeling alive. It was one of the few things from that time that she *wanted* to remember.

She sipped more *sangria,* watching and listening, her slippered feet beating a rhythmic tattoo against the tiled floor. Bright skirts were a whirl of color, the men clad in short jackets and snug-fitting pants, heels clicking against stone in the dance steps, the music a hard, driving throb.

"It is too lovely a night for a beautiful woman to sit alone," a deep male voice murmured. Ginny glanced up to see a handsome young *caballero* smiling down at her. "I will be happy to show you the steps if you will dance with me, *señorita.*"

"Yes," she surprised herself by saying, suddenly reckless, desperate to escape darker memories. "Yes, I would like to dance."

A combination of *sangria* and frustration fueled her heedless response. She gave him her hand without hesitating, as the young man swept her into the center of the patio. In the far corner, the musicians played the traditional *Jarabe Tapatio,* and Ginny turned, her feet swiftly finding the rhythm.

"You know our dances, *señorita?*" He sounded surprised that a *gringa* would know the steps, but his black eyes gleamed with satisfaction.

She answered in a Mexican dialect. "Oh, yes, I have not forgotten how. I used to live here, you see, in Mexico, a long time ago."

As they joined the circle of dancers, Ginny forgot her surroundings, Steve's absence and her frustration. She forgot everything but her love of the music and the moment.

Her partner kept up with her, his young, lithe body supple and eager as he smiled at her appreciatively. As the rhythms changed from fast to slow, then back, they danced face-to-face, eyes meeting, movements alternately inviting and then rejecting. She felt free, released, as her feet kept the rhythm, her body a lissome flame in her yellow silk gown, copper hair atop her head slowly coming loose from the careful coils to drift around her face, cling damply to her neck.

Despite the slight chill of the night, it grew hot as she danced, aware, womanlike, of the glances of admiration she received from the men watching, aware of Señor Valdez sitting still in the corner and watching her so intently. Oh, let him watch her. She did not care. It had been so long since she had been in Mexico, much too long since she had allowed herself to dance like this, with the driving tempo of the music filling her body and blotting out everything but the rhythm.

Her partner grew bolder, closer, the edge of his short jacket almost brushing against her breasts as they danced, until she stepped back, whirling away from him. His black eyes reflected hot flames, speculative and admiring.

"*¡Caramba!* But you are magnificent!"

Ginny smiled distractedly, lost in music and memories of other times, lost in dreams. Night chill was banished by the feverish steps of the dance. Her skirts whirled around her legs, up above her knees, as her feet moved in steps so familiar to her, from one partner to another.

As the circle of dancers widened, the black-eyed youth was replaced by another man, older but with the same hot gaze. Lanterns flickered and bobbed, casting patches of light over the patio and dancers while, beyond the low stone wall that encompassed the courtyard, shadows cloaked the street. A pale sliver of moon snagged on a distant mountain peak, a crescent of light between shreds of cloud.

Despite the cool night air she was flushed with heat from her exertions; perspiration damped her gown so that it clung damply to her curves, the thin material like a second skin.

Like a firefly among lanterns, she flitted from partner to partner, losing herself in the dance, in the heady rush of memories that accompanied her return to Mexico where so much of her life had been changed. It was both exhilarating and melancholy at the same time, these memories of her past, the past she had shared with Steve, and the future that was theirs.

I have to have faith in us she thought distractedly, I have to have faith in Steve....

"Beautiful lady," a low voice as smooth as fine brandy murmured in her ear. She looked up to see the tall man from Señor Valdez's table taking the place of her last partner. She whirled away, ignoring him, but too aware of his eyes on her, black and reflecting light from torches.

He followed her, persistent, his lean body graceful in the steps of the dance, but too close, too intimate. She could feel the heat from him, powerful, almost threatening.

"Are you afraid?" he taunted, and flashed a white smile at her when she stamped her feet and lifted her arms over her head, snapping her fingers with contempt.

"Of you? You flatter yourself, *señor,*" she replied in the same flawless Castillian Spanish he had used. He did not seem to be a part of these men here, though he had the same swarthy look about him. His features were more refined, with no trace of the Indian forebears that graced so many Mexicans.

He laughed softly, and there was a hint of approval in his eyes. "Little butterfly, you intrigue me. What is such a gracious creature doing in Ojinaga?"

She only smiled. Her body, shoulders a gleaming white above the yellow silk, moved with sinuous grace and utter abandon to the dance. The smile lingered, lashes lowered slightly to hide the green of her eyes, a provocative, seductive expression on her face as she danced.

There was not a man watching who did not think what it might be like to possess her, to have her naked, satiny body beneath him.

From the shadows just inside the courtyard gate, Steve watched with a wry smile. How many times had he come upon her like this, dancing with teasing abandon, her gypsy eyes half-closed and a dreamy smile on her mouth? More times than he could count. There were things about both of them that never seemed to change with time or tragedies.

And yet there were so many things that *had* changed. He knew now that he loved Ginny too much to give her up.

What would she say, and do, when he told her he had to leave her again, even if it was only for a little while? Would she trust him enough to accept it?

When she swirled in a blur of yellow silk and flashing legs, he stepped in, a hard glance challenging her partner to resist. For an instant, Steve thought he recognized the man, but that impression was swiftly banished as black eyes lowered, and with a murmured, *''Señor,''* the man relinquished his place and backed away.

As Ginny turned, her brows flew up in surprise and she faltered when she saw Steve. Then a smile curved her mouth. Silently, she gave him an alluring glance from beneath her lashes, provocative and teasing, the trick of a practiced courtesan. Moving to the driving tempo of the music, she tossed her head, then began to remove the pins from her hair one by one, scattering them carelessly on the stone tiles as glorious copper strands fell free. It was an invitation, seductive and arousing, and every man there was riveted to the sight.

Of all men, Steve understood it most. Ginny, dancing with abandon, her heavy mane of bright red-gold hair framing her face, was the lure that kept him coming back.

''Little baggage, are you trying to start a fight out here?'' His murmured comment only earned a wicked smile and careless shrug, and he grinned. ''I should know better than to leave you on your own for longer than an hour. When will I learn?''

She danced close to him, her breasts brushing against his chest in a silken promise before she whirled away again. When the steps of the dance brought them back together, he grabbed her hands, held them above her head as his feet stamped against stones in a rapid staccato, his body so close to hers he could feel the dampness of her gown. Green eyes widened up at him.

As the music ended in a crashing flourish of guitars, he

pulled her hard against him, one arm bent behind her back to hold her. He grazed her ear with his lips as he murmured, "Come upstairs with me, *bruja.*"

Ginny leaned into him, breath coming in little pants of exertion. A teasing fragrance emanated from her hair, all too familiar and tempting, her favorite perfume, a blend he had bought for her in France. Her hand splayed against his chest and she looked up with a faint smile.

"I thought you'd never ask."

The night air became sweeter, softer. Now that Steve was here, her worries and fears proved groundless. He had brought her jewels—fire opals, gleaming with lustrous brilliance in a velvet box, set into ornate silver filigree. A lovely bracelet for her wrists, and a magnificent ring for her hand, looking much too large but so very beautiful.

"Tears of the Moon, the Aztecs called it," Steve said when she admired the artistry of the silver setting. "Now that Mexico has even more silver veins being discovered, I thought you'd appreciate some native ore."

Delighted, and deliriously happy that he was back, she slipped on the jewelry, admiring the radiant gleam in the soft swaying glow of lanterns overhead.

"You spoil me, Steve Morgan."

He smiled as he took her hand to guide her from the patio of the *cantina,* and they passed beneath fragrant vines and night-blooming flowers, huge white blossoms like full moons crowding heart-shaped leaves that tumbled haphazardly over walls and archways.

"Oh, Steve, I really did miss you," she said softly.

Steve's eyes, so dark blue and intent, regarded her with careful scrutiny. "You didn't seem to miss me that much, green-eyes, or you wouldn't have been dancing when I arrived."

Her laughter was soft and teasing. "A lady must take her pleasures where she finds them, you know."

Steve paused, pulling her to him in the shadowed alcove beneath the bower of moonflowers. "So must a man, my sweet."

"Steve!" she gasped out, shocked by the swift pressure of his hands on her as he pushed her back against the vine-covered wall. "What are you doing?"

"It's been two weeks. Don't turn shy on me now, Ginny. I seem to recall a more adventurous spirit."

Grasping her skirts, he pulled them up, leaning forward with a gleam in his eyes that she recognized. His mouth crooked in a smile and his face was half-shadowed by the filtered light that barely penetrated this shaded bower.

It was risky, dangerous—exciting. What if someone came and caught them? But it only added a certain titillation to the moment, the threat of discovery nearly as exhilarating as the sensation of his hands on her, sliding up legs that were bare under her skirts, finding her, caressing her with a teasing, shocking friction that sent shivers down her spine. She clung to him, drowning in familiar desires.

With her back pressed against the wall, cushioned by the thick mat of vines, the sweet, heady scent of crushed flowers beneath her, Ginny hungrily responded to his kisses and caresses. Such sweet, dangerous desire…the need so compelling and urgent, the response so instant to his touch that she felt herself swept away.

All thinking halted. His hands moved over her, his lips following, until finally, with her arms clasping him closely as he lifted her by the waist, he slid inside her, a searing thrust that made her breath catch in her throat, sent her senses spinning out of control. As he drove into her, the leafy bower whirled in a kaleidoscope of green and white, faster and faster, until she arched against him in exquisite release, whispering her love, the words rising to the very top of the pergola.

Finally Steve went still, his body taut as he pushed her harder against the wall, straining into her. His breath was hot and fast against her cheek, his head bent to nuzzle her ear.

"Christ, Ginny," he muttered, "you make me crazy. I'll never get enough of you."

"Good." She squirmed slightly, arms around his neck. "I want you to always want more of me, to never be completely satisfied unless you're with me."

"Witch woman...you've bewitched me."

A throaty laugh purred as she murmured, "No, voodoo. I picked up a few tricks in New Orleans."

"I don't doubt it." He stared down at her with a wry smile. Deep grooves bracketed his mouth, and his eyes were dark with lucent shadows, reflections of diffused light a pale gleam. He touched her hair gently, his hand a tender caress as he dragged his fingers through the softly curling mass that waved around her face. "It wouldn't surprise me at all to learn that you'd put a spell on me, enchantress mine."

Ginny's breath caught, and she thought then that they had never been so close before, never felt the same emotion at the same time as they were now, this meeting of more than just the flesh, but of the hearts....

Oh God, let it last forever!

17

"Where did you go, Steve? Why did it take you so long to get back to Mexico?" Ginny slanted a glance at him, her body satiated and lethargic, replete.

They lay wrapped in a damp cocoon of tangled sheets and lamplight, still flushed from lovemaking. Her hand lay upon his chest, fingers spread and pale against skin dark as any Comanche warrior.

Arms crossed behind his head, Steve shifted lazily, bringing one leg up and over to lie across her thighs. "Do you ever run out of questions, green-eyes?"

His thick murmur was teasing, but there was a serious tinge to his comment.

"Yes. When I'm asleep." Her hand curled into a small fist, knuckles grazing the shadowed angle of his jaw in a light, mock blow. "Answer me. Did you talk to Sam Murdock?"

"A lot longer than necessary. He sends his regards."

"I'm sure he does." She frowned slightly. "I know he's your partner and very astute. He also happens to be a friend of my father's. Does this have anything to do with the new silver mine the senator bought in New Mexico?"

"You talk too much."

Moving swiftly, he caught her by surprise, pushing her into the mattress and sliding his body over hers to look down at her with a familiar hot gleam in his dark-blue eyes.

"Steve...stop it."

He bent his head, black hair tickling her bare breasts as he began to kiss her, washing his tongue over quivering flesh in a leisurely torment until she closed her eyes, forgetting Sam Murdock and William Brandon, forgetting everything but the sweet, heady sensations he was provoking with his mouth and hands....

It wasn't until later the next day, when they rode out well into the morning on the next leg of their journey south to Don Francisco's, that Ginny remembered their conversation of the night before. She turned to look at him, where he rode his big black gelding next to Paco, both of them deep in a low-toned conversation that she was certain had to do with Steve's recent trip.

"Well?" she said when he nudged his mount alongside her a little bit later. "Are you going to answer my question?"

"Which one, love? You fire so many at me I feel as if I've been ambushed by an Apache war party."

Though he said it in a teasing tone, his eyes narrowed slightly at her, glinting a dark blue beneath long lashes.

"Damn you, Steve Morgan, don't pretend you don't know what I mean! You were with Sam Murdock for a week. Was his gypsy protégée there, or has she remained in England with her viscount?"

"If you mean Concepción, as far as I know, she's still basking in the English countryside. Or as she puts it, 'molding in the rustic wasteland.'"

"I'm devastated to hear she doesn't appreciate the beauty of the Cotswolds, but hardly surprised. There aren't many men there who would appreciate her brand of coarse entertainment."

"Ah-ah, your forked tongue is showing, Ginny. You and I have never been able to discuss Concepción without it degenerating into name calling, so let's talk about something else for a change."

"That's fine with me." Her hair had come loose, blowing across her face, the wind brisk and smelling of dust and the lemony-sharp scent of sage. She tightened the strings of her hat, a serviceable wide-brimmed *sombrero* that kept out sun and rain. "Did Murdock mention my father?"

"His name came up." Steve's mouth flattened to a grim line. "Stop trying to get information out of me, Ginny."

"Stop avoiding my questions."

It's no use, she thought when he ignored her. He has no intention of answering me.

Philosophically, she accepted momentary defeat. And after all, he was here now, so what did it really matter if she knew why he'd been gone or why she couldn't go with him?

I must be mellowing with time, she thought with a wry smile that earned her an assessing glance from Steve. Before now I would never have surrendered so easily. But perhaps it shouldn't matter if I know everything. We're together finally after having been apart for so long.

The Chihuahua Trail ran through Presidio and Ojinaga, then cut a wide loop through rugged mountain passes to the city of Chihuahua. It was the main route from San Antonio, arid and dry most of the time, except in the rainy season when dried up riverbeds could become raging, dangerous torrents without warning.

In daylight, the sun beat down fiercely, heat shimmering in waves from rocks and hard-packed trail, though at night it could be cold enough for several blankets. For miles, the only sounds were the clopping of hooves, the creak of saddle leather and the jangling of metal bits. Finally they stopped beneath an overhang to let the horses drink.

Ginny dismounted, stretching muscles finally becoming more accustomed to hours in the saddle. She plopped down on a flat rock in the shade of the overhang. The musty smell of damp earth and baking rock was potent.

Paco approached where she sat fanning herself with the wide brim of her hat, and propped his foot against the side of the rock.

"Guess I'll be heading off in another direction now. I have a *compadre* who lives on the Conchos River a bit north of here."

"Why is it that I've been expecting this?" The air stirred

by her hat was only slightly less hot. She stared up at Paco, who had the grace to look sheepish.

"If I do not join you before, I will meet you at Don Francisco's *hacienda,*" he said, but his furtive glance in Steve's direction convinced Ginny he had other reasons for splitting up.

She shrugged, her only comment the customary, "*Vaya con Dios.*"

With Paco gone, Steve kept to the more traveled trail, riding at a swifter pace than they had before. They stopped in the occasional village, sleeping in missions when there was no *cantina* or inn available, sometimes sleeping out under the stars.

"Ever think about the first time you rode in these mountains with me, *chica?*" he asked her once, when they were bedded down in a copse of gnarled trees twisted into shapes resembling grotesque animals.

"Yes, but usually only in nightmares." She watched his face in the erratic glow of the small fire between them, saw him smile.

"You were the meanest little hellcat I'd ever tangled with until then."

"You weren't exactly charming yourself. If I recall, you had a nasty habit of dragging me everywhere, like some primitive beast with a trophy."

"Yeah, you kinda grew on me after a while. I got used to you."

"Is that why you refused to free me?"

Firelight made his eyes gleam like hard jewels. "No. If I'd let you go, there would have been no reason for your father to bargain with me. As it was, he was out for my hide anyway."

"I don't think he's ever forgiven you for besting him. He's used to winning."

"Yeah, sometimes losing can build a man's character. Or so I'm told."

She stared at him curiously, suddenly grateful for more time alone with him, the opportunity to understand him as a man provided at last. With nothing to distract them, it was the perfect time. But what could she say that wouldn't seem like prying, or an attempt to ferret out more information?

Silence fell, comfortable, filled with night sounds—a shivering wail of a coyote, plaintive and lost against the vast sky; small scuttling sounds of nocturnal creatures that came out after the heat of the day melded into cooler gloom. The moon was higher now, and nearly full, a silver disc that spread ethereal light over the mountain ridges but left deep purple-black shadows in the crevices.

On nights like these, the Comanche were said to take advantage of the light for their raids. She held her hands out to the warmth of the fire, shivering at the thought.

"Do you ever miss riding with the Comanche, Steve? I know you lived with them as a boy, but did you—"

When she stopped, he finished, "Go on raids with them? It would be a good night for it tonight. Plenty of light to see by." His teeth flashed in a grin. "You'd make some brave a good prize, but once he tried to tame you he'd probably prefer to have your scalp at his belt, instead."

"You just say things like that to annoy me. If I was such a bad hostage, you would have drowned me in a sack."

"Don't think it didn't occur to me more than once. Ah hell, Ginny, sometimes it seems like only last week when I first saw you—"

"And mistook me for a whore."

"Understandable if you take into consideration that I'd been told a red-haired Frenchwoman would be coming to my room for the night, and there you were."

"Yes. There I was." She caught and held his gaze. "And here I still am. Do you ever get tired of moving around so much, Steve? Don't you ever want to just *stay* in one place, know that when you go to bed, it's your own bed? That when you wake up the next day, you'll see the same faces of the people who love you?"

He was quiet for such a long time, she thought he did not intend to answer her, and moved to rise from the rock where she sat, intent upon finding her bedroll.

But then he said softly, as if to himself, "It's not that I don't want that. Part of me does. But there's a part of me that's never satisfied to stay in one place for long, always restless, looking for something else. I don't know why. I don't know if it's forever. And sometimes I think that maybe I've found what I've been looking for with you. I know that I don't want any other woman, but I'm just not too sure what I do want."

A shiver traced down her spine, and she clenched her hands tightly together in her lap. "Well..." She forced a laugh that sounded hollow. "That's honest, at least."

"Yes. I think you deserve honesty. Ginny." He stood up and stepped around the fire, pulling her close to hold her against him. His hand clenched the hair at the back of her neck to pull her head backward until she looked up into his eyes, an inexorable tug that would not allow her to look away. "You know I love you. I've told you so over and over again. I mean it when I say it. It's not something I would ever say if I didn't."

"Yes, I know." A lump in her throat prevented her from saying more, and she took comfort as he held her hard against him, the thud of his heartbeat a steady rhythm beneath her cheek.

The next day, a line of squalls moved across the mountains, rendering the pass slippery and dangerous. Steve took them up into the rocks off the trail, picking a spot carefully in case of a rockslide.

"Sometimes the ground gets too soft, and boulders the size of a two-story building come crashing down the slope, taking everything in the path along with them. A rockslide can bury an entire village in minutes. I saw it once, from a ledge overlooking a valley. There wasn't a damn thing I could do but watch as people tried to run. Few escaped. It was over too quick. Later, we could hear the cries of those trapped in the rubble, and pulled out the ones we could find."

He said it dispassionately, but she had a sudden image of him pulling aside jagged rocks and digging through the mud to rescue those trapped. It was an image that contrasted sharply with some in her memory, of him facing a man in the street, drawing his revolver so fast it was a blur, killing without evincing regret. Two completely different images of the same man. Could he be both?

She thought then of Matt Cooper, who had taught her how to use a knife when she was a *soldadera* forced to follow the army with Tom Beal, and his careless kindnesses when it was convenient for him. And she remembered, too, that Steve had killed him for it, for using her as he had, even though Matt had been the only man who was kind to her during those long, wretched days of torment.

There was a kind of justice in it that she appreciated, though she'd felt a faint sense of regret when he told her.

They rode on again when the rain stopped. It was drier up higher into the mountains, where the air was thinner and it was harder to breathe. The view was breathtaking, a network of yawning canyons patchworked with furiously twisting rivers across a landscape ribbed with green-and-brown hills. Fresh-scrubbed by the rains, emerald-green basins cradled picturesque villages, the missions tiny white beacons of hope when seen from such a high altitude.

The ride down was more harrowing than the arduous ascent, as the trail seemed to drop through narrow gorges rimmed by steep spirals of rock that made her think of stalagmites. In places, no sunlight could get through. The walls were so high that only a thin ribbon of light could be seen high overhead.

Halfway down, Steve took a detour down a rocky ledge edged with thick brush and stunted mesquite. The air grew cooler, and she could hear a loud, muffled roar, like the approach of a train. Vegetation became thicker and almost tropical, reminding her of the trees near Oaxaca.

When they rode around a bend, the low roar suddenly turned into a deafening crash, and Ginny sucked in a sharp breath as she saw the source.

From high above, cascading over gray rock formations like graceful wings, water poured in a thundering rush to a wooded pool. Spume rose into the damp air, and sunlight glinted from the curve of a rainbow that disappeared into the mist.

Steve grinned at her, and beckoned for her to follow him, words useless in the noise of the falling water.

They were to spend the night here, a short distance down from where the water bombarded rocks and the shallow basin. Ginny immediately took off all her clothes and splashed in the water that was crystal clear and breathtakingly cold. She scrubbed her body, then her hair, standing waist-deep in the natural pool, toes curled into the pebbles on the bottom for balance against the swirling current. She felt like a mermaid, bare breasted, hair heavy wet ropes draped down her back and over her shoulders.

Steve was downstream a bit farther, investigating the most likely spot for them to spend the night, and she took advantage of his absence to lay down on a warm, mossy rock in the sun. There was something so sensual and free about being totally naked, and she closed her eyes against the glaring light beating down.

It had been far too long since she had enjoyed such freedom; Nassau, perhaps, when she had discovered the bathing pool surrounded by palm, pomegranate and orange trees, a veritable paradise. She stretched languorously. Perhaps her skin would tan to a peachy gold color again if she lay here long enough. What would Steve say when he came back and found her like this?

She almost laughed at the thought of his face, then thought that he would probably strip off his own clothes and join her. He'd looked hot, dusty and tired, but determined to find a place he deemed safe to spend the night. Why could they not stay here, by the pool?

Oh, she really was entirely too much of a sensualist, for she was certain she could go about without clothes all the time if it wouldn't shock everyone who knew her. Wasn't it true that Benjamin Franklin had been what they called a freethinker, preferring to sit in his own parlor as naked as the day he'd been born? Of course, men could get away with doing such things and not be regarded by society as loose. Eccentric, perhaps, but not immoral.

But then again, Franklin was known to enjoy many ladies

in his time, though public record did not chronicle opinions of his habits. Ginny thought she would probably have liked him for his autonomy of spirit, if for no other reason.

It was so pleasant, being lulled into tranquility by the rushing sound of water and the heat of the sun on her body. Her breasts were warm, the nipples tightly beaded. It was strangely arousing to lie beneath the sky in such abandon.

Droplets of water spattered on her belly and thighs, and over the noise of the waterfall she heard Steve say, "You look like a virgin sacrifice."

She smiled blindly, relishing the damp heat that rose from the rocks, arching upward when she felt Steve's hand on her belly, then her breast. It was exquisitely erotic, lying atop the rock while he stroked and caressed her, her eyes closed as she gave herself up to pure sensation.

His hands moved over her leisurely at first, touching her with familiar assurance, palms spread over her ribs, then testing the cushion of her breasts, his skin abrasive enough to send delicious little shivers through her at his caress. With the heat of the sun on her bare body and the stroke of his hands along her thighs, then between, Ginny felt wanton, a purely sexual excitement throbbing inside her, turning her blood to liquid heat and her flesh to malleable clay in his hands.

He molded her, hands clever at finding the spot that elicited the most intense response, fingers sliding over her mist-dampened skin with unerring accuracy. The moss beneath her was a soft, fragrant cushion. Sunlight was displaced by the heat of his hands as he skimmed her thigh, up to the crevice between her legs. His thumb found her in a heady, potent kiss across her quivering center, and her hips arced up into his hand.

"Keep your eyes closed, Ginny," he murmured when she started to open them. "Don't think. Don't talk. Just *feel.*"

The steady, loud collapse of water plummeting from two hundred feet above was a constant roar in her ears, the air alive with a damp mist that permeated muscle and bone. His hand moved, his thumb an erotic friction across the aching, melting heart of her until the heat of the sun coalesced into a blinding white flame to ignite a shuddering release that swept through her like wildfire and left her boneless, drained as she reached out for him.

"Oh God, Steve..."

Her hand encountered bare flesh, fingers finding old scars on his back, sliding up over taut muscles and smooth skin to curve around his neck, tangling in the crisp dark hair that was slightly damp.

"You drive me to distraction, Ginny. I should have known I'd come back to find you as naked as a woodland nymph." His laugh was rueful, swallowed as she pulled his face down to hers to kiss him deeply.

"I could live like this," she murmured dreamily, eyes still closed against the light. "I'd love nothing better than to go naked all the time."

"You should live in the Pacific where there are islands filled with people who wear little or nothing, then. I'm afraid we're too civilized, even out here."

She opened her eyes the tiniest bit as he straightened, raked a hand through his hair and glanced around them. Then her eyes widened slightly.

When had he taken off his clothes? She watched through slitted eyes as he loomed above, silhouetted against sunlight, a dark golden god with an aura of light behind him, familiar and beloved. He was the only man she had ever loved so passionately, ever risked her life for, or would again if necessary....

Her throat ached suddenly, with love and yearning, and all the things she wanted to say. Reaching up, she lay her palm against his lean jaw as he gazed down at her, his eyes slightly narrowed, the lashes making long shadows against his dark skin.

"I don't want this moment to end, Steve. I wish we could stay here forever—oh, I don't mean abandon our children, of course, but wouldn't it be nice if we could stay a little longer, at least?"

Instead of replying, he scooped her into his arms, startling a gasp from her as he carried her from the rock to the edge of the pool that seethed with lacy froth.

She thought for a moment he intended to drop her, but as a protest formed on her lips, he stepped down into the pool with her in his arms, laughing as she clutched at him. He said something, but she couldn't hear him over the pounding crash of water pummeling dark rock, splashing back up in delicate geysers that sprayed over them. It was surprisingly shallow where they stood, the water so clear she could see pink, brown and black rocks lying on the bottom.

The world closed in around them, enveloping them in spume and sound. With her arm still around his neck, Steve released her legs and she slid down him in a sensuous glide of damp skin against damp skin until her feet gained purchase in water that came just above her waist. Sculpted muscle drifted under her palm as her hand coasted over his body in a light skimming exploration, over the taut band of muscles on his chest, then the corded ropes of muscle on his belly, lower until she found him in a brazen caress.

He sucked in his breath as she held him. She didn't need to hear the words to decipher his mood, for his body was willing evidence that he wanted her.

As water lapped around them and spilled over high black knees of rock studding the cliff, Steve put his hands on her waist and lifted her to straddle him, his legs apart and braced for balance. She understood immediately, and put her arms around his neck. Her breasts were against his chest, her legs clamped around his hips.

Then he was inside her, filling her with a swift, hard thrust of his body, his hands guiding her movements as she shuddered. Warm sunlight, cool water, heated friction and the rhythmic noise of crashing water combined in a collage of exquisite sensations that Ginny knew she would never forget.

"*Bruja...mi corazón....*" His husky endearments were whispers in her ear, the thundering roar of the falls muting words and world, drowning her in pleasure and aching love.

Later, she would remember their hours on the mossy rock and in the pool with wistful longing, for it was the last time for quite a while they were to be so carefree....

18

Zacatecas at last. The ancient grove of trees still stood sentry, heedless of time and the elements, casting deep shadows in the blue light of late evening. Dogs began to bark, a scattered sound in the soft dusk. Splinters of light like huge fireflies flickered behind thick-boled trees and dusty leaves. Their horses picked up the pace, sensing the end of the journey.

Home. There was the sense of returning home, to a familiar beloved place, Ginny thought. Yet she had felt this way the first time she had come, strangely enough, as if she were coming home after a long journey.

Now it was true, in a way.

Vaquera rode out to greet them, armed and grinning, acting as both an escort and a guard. "Don Esteban, you are expected!"

"So I see. Luis, where is my lazy cousin, that he will not come out to greet us?" Steve rode a little ahead, lapsing into the dialect of the *vaquera,* laughing with them when it was drolly observed that Don Renaldo was no doubt unaware of the time again.

"He reads all the time, that one! The *señora* must always coax him out of the house, or he would never be seen about."

But when they neared the house, the door opened and Renaldo came out to greet them with his wife at his side.

"*¡Hola!* Cousin," he called cheerfully, his tall, rather stooped frame silhouetted against the welcoming lights inside.

The two-story house sprawled at the end of a long, curving drive flanked by tall shrubs. Nightblooming flowers clambered over a trellis and lent a fading fragrance to the air. Twin lanterns illuminated a shallow flight of steps to the narrow porch that wrapped around the house.

Aching, unaccustomed to the long ride, Ginny dismounted stiffly, then yielded her reins to the small boy who came running up to greet them.

"Don Esteban, Doña Genia!" the boy said, grinning from ear to ear, his teeth white in a dark, shining face.

Steve had already dismounted, and passed a hand over the top of the boy's head to ruffle his hair. "*¡Hola,* Juan! You have grown since last we saw you."

"*Sí,* Don Esteban!"

"Esteban," Renaldo said, stepping down from the porch to greet his cousin, "we received your telegram just yesterday, but the little house is ready for you. Missie and Rosa saw to that."

"Rosa is here, too?" Ginny smiled with pleasure as she went forward to greet Melissa Carter Ortega, Renaldo's wife.

Missie was smiling, her pretty freckled face as young as it had been when last she saw her, untouched by years or tragedy.

"Ginny, it's so good to see you again," Missie said, and it was obvious she meant it. She came to her, arms enclosing her in a hug that was both affectionate and warm. Then she stepped back, laughing. "But come inside! You must be exhausted after your trip, and I want to hear all about Laura and Franco. I can't believe that they're nearly four now. I miss them so. Oh, and you must meet our Alejandro. Why, he's not yet a year old but so big...well, you'll see."

Half turning when she reached the top step, she said to her husband, "Don't you let Steve go off anywhere with Luis. I know how they are, so you just bring them on inside with you. Later, you men can catch up on everything."

Missie took control so efficiently and good-naturedly that no one complained, but instead complied with her wishes as easily as if it had been intended all along.

Ginny soon found herself divested of outer garments and trail dust, ensconced in a huge stuffed chair that bespoke comfort and welcome, sipping fruit juice from an iced glass. Missie certainly had blossomed after marriage to Renaldo. She was confident now, mistress of the house and her own nature, and quite obviously still terribly in love with her husband.

There was an inner glow to her that Ginny envied. A sense of peace emanated from her, imbuing the house with it. Even the heartbreaking loss of their first child had not shattered her new serenity, it seemed. Bruised it certainly, but not destroyed it.

"Tell me about Laura and Franco," Missie begged, perched on the arm of a fat chair near Ginny. "Are they big now? Oh, I wish I could see them again. I cried for a week after they left here. I felt as if I were losing them forever."

Smiling, Ginny told her about Laura's new puppy and how Franco had climbed to nearly the top of a huge tree, scaring her and Tante Celine.

"He is so reckless, it frightens me."

"Like his father, it seems." Missie glanced at the far end of the room where the men stood, and there was something in her eyes that reminded Ginny that once she had been in love with Steve, just a little. It had not been mentioned, but on occasion, a casual comment had reminded her that the girl had loved him once. Another ghost from Steve's past; they were as numerous as her own, she thought.

"Yes, I have thought the same thing myself. Tell me about your Alejandro. Does he have your red hair?"

Laughing, Missie nodded, and for a time they discussed their children as easily as if they had been old friends. Perhaps they were in a way. Missie Carter had accepted Ginny without reservation, if not without a bit of shock. After all, to the innocent Melissa, Ginny had been a cosmopolitan creature far removed from her experience and world. She had been half fascinated, half afraid of the elegant young woman who seemed supremely confident.

It had been a revelation to Missie to discover that beneath the facade she showed the world, Ginny Brandon was as uncertain at times as she was, and as unhappy. It was Manolo—Steve—who had made her that unhappy, of course, as once he had even made her.

But that had been so long ago. She'd met Renaldo, and realized that the kind of man like Steve Morgan would destroy her woman's soul if she fell in love with him. Oh, but he had been so exciting, so *dangerous,* and while she did not regret for a moment that he loved Ginny and not her, there was a bit of her that wondered with a delicious shudder what it would be like to be with him.

It had almost happened once, but she had been so naive, expecting tenderness and starlight, not the kind of harsh, ruthless *invasion* he intended. Perhaps he had known that, had done it only to show her that he was not at all what she wanted. He was right, of course. He'd terrified her.

But she never intended to allow Ginny to know any of that, for it was so long ago, and she'd been just a child playing at love, playing at passion. Renaldo, with his steady, honorable love and fierce desire to protect her, was what she had really wanted all along.

"Do you travel to Mexico City often?" Ginny was asking her, and Missie smiled and shook her head.

"Not as often as I would like. Oh, I love it here, you know I do, but there are times I want to see other places, go where I've never been before and see new things. I envy you your travels. You've been everywhere, and I've hardly left Texas or Mexico. Though Renaldo has promised me a trip to El Paso soon, as he has some business for his *abuelo* up there. Something to do with cattle." She laughed. "I don't pay much attention when they talk market prices, I'm afraid. I prefer to think of the hotels and shops and the theater. El Paso has a new theater and Renaldo has promised to take me. Why, they even have opera now, though not often."

"Why El Paso and not San Antonio?" Ginny asked. "It seems much too far to go for cattle business, when you're much closer to San Antonio from here, or even Brownsville, where you can ship beef from the port."

Missie shrugged. ''As I said, I don't interfere in the business aspect. I just enjoy the few trips I get to make.''

When Ginny nodded with a faint smile, Missie said, ''Did you bring the new styles with you from France? Or the Lady's Book? I'd love to wear something no one has seen yet, and be in fashion.''

''Fashions don't reach here for two years after they come out in France,'' Ginny murmured, and her lovely green eyes were a little dark as she glanced across the room toward Steve. There was a pensive quality to her, though she attempted to hide it.

Missie wondered what could be bothering her, or if they had quarreled again. It certainly wouldn't be the first time!

Ginny turned to her suddenly. ''But I *did* bring some new gowns. Has our baggage not arrived yet? It should have been here long before now.''

Missie shook her head. ''No, I don't think so. Unless, of course, it has come and no one thought to tell me. We can ask Señora Armijo tomorrow. She will certainly know. She knows everything.''

Ginny laughed. ''I suppose she's beside herself with the preparations for the *fiesta.*''

''Oh my…'' Missie spread her arms out, shaking her head. ''It has been impossible while we waited for word from you that you were on your way. Now that you are here, she had no doubt gone into a complete frenzy. But it will all be perfect, no doubt. Have you seen Don Francisco yet?''

''No, I imagine we will see him tomorrow. Is he well?''

''He's quite well, and I credit his wife for that. Doña Teresa is very efficient, and the only one I know who can deal properly with Señora Armijo.''

''I suppose I'll meet her tomorrow as well,'' Ginny said, then rose from the chair with a faint smile. ''It's late and I really must go to bed. I'm afraid I'm not at all accustomed to traveling so much by horse. I miss a well-sprung carriage!''

Early the next morning, Ginny and Steve rode up to the main house to visit with Don Francisco. They were greeted by Don Francisco's longtime bodyguard, Jaime Perez, still imposing despite his age, with gray at his temples and sprinkled through his hair.

"Don Esteban, your grandfather awaits you in his study. And Doña Genia, there are refreshments in the *sala.*"

Ginny's brow rose, but she did not comment as she took the hint and went to the tiled *sala* that was filled with light and lush plants. It looked different than when last she had seen it, with clearly a woman's touch at decorating with greenery and pretty vases, and a few paintings by European masters on the walls. She paused before a huge oil painting.

"Degas," a voice said behind her, and she turned to see a dark, trim woman with vibrant eyes and skin approaching. "I find his work intriguing. *L'Orchestre.*"

"Yes, he loves to paint everyday scenes of life." Ginny surveyed the older woman, and returned her radiant smile.

"I am Doña Teresa, though you may not recognize me, as you suffered from blindness when we first met."

"I would recognize your voice, Doña Teresa, for it is soft and lovely," Ginny replied graciously.

Doña Teresa smiled. "I am relieved to see you are so well. Francisco admires your courage and strength greatly, you know."

"Does he?" Ginny accompanied Teresa to the small patio off the *sala* where freshly squeezed orange juice waited in tall, frosted glasses of ice. Fruit overflowed a bowl; cakes dusted with thick sugar were arranged on a large flat plate.

To her surprise, Ginny found Teresa to be very charming and not at all stiff, as Steve had once said she was. Their first meeting had been so brief, her mood then so dark, that they had spoken little. Now they spoke of the children, and of everything but where Ginny had been the past few years. It was difficult to reconcile the fact that this woman was Richard Avery's mother, for she was so petite and fragile in appearance, with lustrous dark hair gleaming among the strands of silver, a reminder of her Persian ancestry. It was easy to understand why Lord Tynedale had rescued her so long before, and then married her, though she had been but a girl at the time.

Easier still to understand why Don Francisco had fallen in love with her, as well.

As if sensing the direction of her thoughts, Teresa said quietly, "My son writes often. Before we met, he told me of you and what a lovely young woman you are. It is a pleasure to know that he did not exaggerate."

"Thank you." Ginny took a sip of juice, suddenly uncomfortable. "I am delighted he speaks highly of me, as I do of him."

"It has been a difficult year for him, with his wife's death and the loss of his child. I am so relieved that he is out of danger now, and moving back to Cuba after he returns from his visit to Russia. I had so hoped he would return to Mexico, but alas, he has not agreed to do so. Perhaps I shall have to travel to him if I want to see him again."

"I hope he is enjoying his time in Russia," Ginny said politely. "I know he loves to travel to exciting places."

"Yes, though he did express some concern about the political upheaval there." Teresa laughed softly. "After the revolution in Cuba, and the one here in Mexico, I would think he would be immune to such conflicts, but he seems quite concerned. He even suggested I warn you to be cautious in the future, as there is a fanatical fringe that seem quite intent upon damaging the Tsar. Richard seems to think they might even attempt to harm you."

"Me? I hardly think they would go that far. After all, I'm half a world away!"

"Yes, so I think, but Richard has always been one to worry unduly about those he—admires."

Before the conversation grew too uncomfortable, Teresa adroitly changed the subject, much to Ginny's relief.

"But how long do you and Esteban intend to stay here? I know Francisco has been looking forward to your visit for some time. Despite the fact that they may not always get along so well, he adores his grandson, as I am certain you realize."

"Yes, I've also recognized that their relationship is rather—volatile. I fear that Franco is growing to be much like his father in that way...."

This was safer ground, and they talked for a while of the children, until finally Ginny heard Steve and Don Francisco approaching down the hallway, their boots clicking against the polished tile floors.

"Next week," Don Francisco said after greeting Ginny, "is the *fiesta!* Already guests have begun to arrive."

"What of my baggage?" Ginny asked. "Has it arrived?"

"Your baggage? I'm afraid that I know nothing of your baggage, but—"

"Apparently it's been delayed," Steve said then, "but Ginny is determined that she not shame you in front of your friends. I told her we must travel light."

"I have an excellent seamstress," Teresa said, "and if you have nothing suitable, she can alter one of my gowns. We are very close to the same size, I believe, though of course, I do think some of your gowns may still be in storage here. Did you not leave some here some time ago?"

Ginny smiled mechanically, but even as she replied to Teresa and Don Francisco, she was convinced that Steve's excuse of sending her baggage ahead had all been a ruse.

"God, Steve, what are you up to?" she demanded when they were alone in their spacious room on the second floor of the main *hacienda.* He gave her an impatient glance.

"Christ, don't start that again, Ginny. You know I can't tell you."

"Yes, I suppose I do, but you must admit that all the uncertainty is maddening. How can I relax if I think you're entangled in one of Bishop's dangerous intrigues?"

Frustrated, she yanked at the laces of her gown, snapping one in two. "And now look! My limited wardrobe is in danger of being entirely depleted."

"It just gives you a good reason to buy more, my love. When we get to Mexico City, I'm sure you'll make up for lost time. They may not have the very latest fashions, but there are seamstresses there who can create anything you like from a drawing."

"That's not the point, Steve. You can laugh at me if you like, but I feel these terrible premonitions, as if truly awful things will happen to you. To *us*. Please, tell Bishop that you're through, that you no longer want to be the ambassador, and we can live on one of the estates and raise cattle for the rest of our lives...."

Turmoil seethed inside her, a simmering anxiety that he couldn't assuage with anything but the assurance he wouldn't work for Bishop anymore. But Steve had no intention of agreeing to that.

His gaze was flat and opaque, telling her nothing as he shrugged off her demands. Ginny gave up, for the moment. Why allow it to mar her time here, where she was made to feel so welcome? Still, there were times in the days that followed when she could not shake off the feeling of impending doom.

The *fiesta* was gay, and friends and acquaintances came from miles around to stay at the *hacienda* and show their respect to Don Francisco. Ginny drank too much champagne, and was able to forget everything but the music and the beauty of the night.

How wonderful it was to be in Mexico again, where she felt so free and alive! Even Steve seemed different, more relaxed without his gun belts. Don Francisco would not allow guns to be worn, of course, and Steve acquiesced to his wishes, knowing the futility of defiance. The old martinet had lost none of his authority, and made certain all knew it.

Though he seemed more stooped and used a cane since his stroke, and his gray hair had turned white, Don Francisco looked happier than ever before. It was his wife who made the difference, her serenity and elegance a welcome addition to the *hacienda*.

"I like her," Ginny told Steve, and shrugged when he scowled. "You have nothing against her except that she's married to your grandfather."

"And bore his child to be raised by another man."

Amused, Ginny said, "A fine time to remember morals, Steve Morgan! You know why she did that. Oh wait—I see.

You resent the fact that your grandfather has a son. Is it your inheritance that worries you?"

"Don't be stupid, Ginny." His voice was harsh, and though she knew she should stop, she couldn't help tweaking him a little.

"No, it can't be that, since you inherited your mother's portion.... I know, it's that Richard is heir to a title and you aren't—"

He grabbed her arm, fingers tight on her wrist, and said softly, "Enough, Ginny."

She recognized the steel beneath his soft tone and shrugged, rubbing at her wrist when he released her. A curl of music drifted from the patio to where they stood beneath an archway covered in vines. She was suddenly sorry that she had provoked him.

"Dance with me, Steve."

"Little hellcat. You insult me one moment, want me to dance with you the next. I ought to go dance with fat Rosa."

"She can dance rings around you," she teased, and tucked her hand into the crook of his arm. She could feel his muscles tense. "I want to dance with the most handsome man here, and that's you. Don't tell me no, or I might have to choose another partner."

"You would do it, too." He slanted her a faint smile. "I may end up having to fight before the night is over if you continue to drink champagne. It makes you a flirt."

She laughed, flashing him a glance from beneath her eyes as they reached the cleared spot where a dance floor had been laid beneath trees strung with bright lanterns. The music was familiar and lively, and she began to snap her fingers, her feet moving almost of their own volition. One of the things she loved best about Mexico were the dances that were so much a part of the culture, of the *peónes* and the *gauchopines* alike, peasants losing themselves in the music as much as the aristocrats.

To her surprise, Steve did join her in the dance, his lean body supple and controlled, matching her steps with an expertise she had forgotten. Oh, it was just like Steve to try to match her, and she danced until she was breathless, until even the musicians were ready to stop.

Señora Armijo was shaking her head, eyes reproachful, her words reproving when they finally paused. "Both of you should be more careful of your reputations," she scolded, but there was a note of admiration in her tone. "You dance like gypsies!"

With a wicked smile, Steve said, "And how is Señor Sanchez these days? Does he still come and visit you?"

Señora Armijo flushed, her mouth pursing in disapproval at his teasing, but there was a light in her eyes that belied her denial. "No, no, Esteban, you are too wicked to even suggest such a thing!"

"Ah, no, you must admit that there are few who can dance as beautifully as the gypsies, especially the women." He shot Ginny a swift, teasing glance. "If I did not see an old friend over there, I would stay and dance with you, Señora, but as Don Francisco's host for the evening, my duty calls."

Ginny ignored him. He was only trying to tease *her,* of course, to remind her of Concepción. But she refused to let him see how it stung, and said only, "I feel the need for more champagne. If you will excuse me?"

It was crowded, and older guests sat around tables that were set up beneath vine-shrouded galerias, drinking wine or *aguardiente* while keeping a sharp eye on the younger couples and their *dueñas.*

Ginny paused beside one of the columns that held up the second floor galeria. Inside, the long tables of food were piled high, and there was a steady stream of guests coming and going, laughing and talking, the women garbed in lovely gowns, their hair pinned up in elaborately decorated Spanish combs. It all seemed so festive, yet there was a strange undercurrent that she didn't quite understand, evident only when she saw a man that she was convinced was Butch Casey meet with Steve at the fringe of the crowd.

That must be the *old friend* he had seen, his duty! Ginny frowned.

But if he was here, that meant her baggage had arrived. Or

had it? Had he just arrived? If he was here, after all, then some of her worries were proven groundless. It should be a relief. So why did it leave her vaguely unsettled?

It was with a faint sense of shock that Ginny heard Steve tell his grandfather of their impending departure the next day after breakfast had ended.

Don Francisco frowned, brushing his mustache with one finger, a gesture that betrayed agitation. "But why must you leave so soon after arriving?"

"I apologize, sir, but I must get to Mexico City. The situation has escalated, and it's only a matter of time before Díaz drives Lerdo out of Mexico."

"What has this to do with you? Are you still involved with that Mr. Bishop? I sense his fine hand in this affair."

"You know I have duties as an ambassador." Some of the old impatience crept into Steve's voice, and he cleared his throat. "It's unexpected, but not a shock. Ginny can stay here with you—"

"No." She looked up at him, eyes steady. "I told you that I will not be separated from you again. I'll go to Mexico City with you. Besides, in case you've forgotten, I am acquainted with both Lerdo and Díaz."

A faint smile curved his mouth. "I've not forgotten."

They left early the next morning, before the sun had risen above the mountain peaks.

19

A strange, oppressive air hung over the small village as they rode down the main track, dust-grimed and weary. Most of the inhabitants were Tarahumara Indians, some of whom lived in caves on the valley floor at the foot of the high cliffs.

Ginny barely noticed her surroundings, she was so weary and sore. Horses might be the swiftest method of traveling the Sierra Madres, but they were certainly not the most comfortable. Next time—if there was a next time—she would go by carriage or stage, a circuitous route that would take much longer but not leave her so exhausted.

She was so tired she did not at first notice Steve's frowning tension, the hard set of his mouth and narrowed eyes as he accompanied her inside the small, rough *posada*. The dialect spoken by the *posadero* was unfamiliar, an Indian dialect that she didn't understand but apparently Steve did.

After a few minutes of conversation, he took her by the elbow and escorted her to the rear of the adobe building. "It's not much, but it's all there is, unless you want to sleep outside again."

"Oh, Steve, I don't think I can take another night of sleeping on the hard ground. I've gotten soft, I suppose. I don't care if it's a bed of straw, as long as it's a bed!"

The room was tiny, with one window and a bed, a table against the far wall that held a water pitcher and a basin, and an oil lamp. There wasn't even a chair, and Steve slung their saddlebags to the hard-packed dirt floor.

"It's not the Astoria, but it will keep the rain off our heads. Is that a bed or a donkey's breakfast?" He gave the offending item a kick, and chaff dusted the floor.

"I don't care." She peeled off her hat and loosened the buttons of her shirt.

It wasn't much better than a hayrack, but at least it was fairly clean. Ginny spread her own blankets atop the crude bed formed of pine planks and a thin mattress, and lay down. She was asleep almost instantly.

Down the street from the shabby *posada,* Steve entered a small *cantina* and slouched against the bar, his hat shadowing his face as he waited. It was late; Paco should have been here long before now. All the arrangements were made. Señor Valdez in Ojinaga had met with Paco for the final shipment of rifles to be transferred from Casey's possession to an agent for Díaz. Paco was to have shown up at the rendezvous with Casey, but hadn't made it. With most of the rifles already passed on to Díaz's army, there had been only the last of them to distribute.

Ginny had been right, of course. The rifles were hidden beneath garments in her trunks, the empty crates filled with straw and dishes once they'd left the ship. It was an uneasy alliance, a dance with the devil.

He remembered General Díaz well, had ridden with him for a while. He had been an efficient general, and would be a ruthless president. The human qualities of Benito Juarez had been evident in his presidency, a certain compassion mixed with the necessary regimen imposed on a man who ruled a country.

Díaz had none of those qualities, but he was capable of winning a revolution and controlling Mexico. If he could be tempered by his cabinet, the country would prosper, but that remained to be seen.

If Steve was wrong about Díaz, he would be instrumental in creating disaster, but it couldn't be helped. Lerdo had been too weak to hold Mexico, and even with the help of the United

States, had failed. Steve's job was to play the odds and pick the victor and he'd done what he had to do.

Conversations around him abruptly ceased, as if a door had been shut. Steve glanced up, swearing softly under his breath as he recognized the uniforms. He kept his head down; he'd had trouble with Lerdo's men before. They were growing too desperate, sensing the end, and were more brutal for it.

They crowded into the small *cantina,* loud and unruly as they ranged through the room, eyes scanning frightened faces that turned toward them, then away, quickly, afraid to be noticed. He could feel the tension; it crouched in the low-ceilinged room like a feral beast, ravenous and dangerous.

There was no escape without drawing unwanted attention. Steve remained still, his cup of whiskey untouched.

Prowling through the crowded *cantina,* the soldiers took their time, obviously enjoying the fear they incited. Then, at some furtive signal, they suddenly pounced, jerking up men from stools to shove them toward the door, denouncing them as rebels.

"You are under arrest as a traitor to the government! Pig!" Cuffing a man who was slow to respond, one soldier laughed when the man sprawled to the floor, then viciously struck him with the butt of his rifle, again and again until the peasant lay still and bloodied. It effectively quelled any possible resistance by others.

Christ, just my luck to be in the middle of one of their roundups! Steve thought. He slid one hand down his side, skimming the heavy outline of the .45 in its holster and rearranging the heavy woolen folds of the serape he'd draped over his shoulders.

One of the soldiers paused beside Steve, waited for a moment, his very presence menacing. Steve didn't react, even when the man nudged him.

"You are from San Luis Potosí?"

Steve shook his head and answered in the same rough dialect, "No, I am from La Junta."

The soldier moved on, but returned in a few moments, this time with two other men. "You will come with us."

Appearing to accede, Steve accompanied them without comment, but when he reached the doorway, he hung back to let them clear the opening first. He expected to be ambushed as he stepped outside, but was ready, the butt of his gun already filling his palm.

As he moved to the open doorway, muscles tensed and ready, a shadow detached from the wall and lights exploded behind his eyes before he could evade the blow. His pistol fired, the bullet slamming into the dirt at his feet, and he was only vaguely aware of boots and rifle butts slamming into his head and body as he curled into a knot to protect his belly.

When Ginny awoke, it was dark and Steve was gone. Light filtered in through an open shutter, along with the drone of flies and a barking dog. Somewhere, music played, a guitar lending soft melody to the night. She lay there a while, listening.

Where was Steve? Gone for food, probably, or a drink. She should get up, wash her face and hands. The pitcher and basin were cracked, but serviceable. When she finally rose and lit the lamp, a pool of wavering light showed her that there was no water in the pitcher.

Wearily, she searched for her shoes by the bed, and grabbed up the pitcher. Surely there was a well close by, so she would not have to go to the village well they had passed on their way in. Damn Steve, he should have seen to this, and not left it up to her to go out on her own in a strange place.

But it was a small village, after all, and it was unlikely that she would get lost. There was only the main street, and a ramshackle collection of mud huts with thatched roofs. The *posada* was the most elaborate building she had seen, boasting a patio as well as rooms built at an angle to the main structure.

Squares of light dotted the street, streaming through windows left open. Shadows darkened the street at this end, and the well was a bulky dark silhouette against the glow of distant lanterns. She crossed the dusty courtyard and street to reach the stone well. Water trickled from an iron spout in the shape of a lion's gaping mouth, collecting below in a shallow basin of stone.

The *cantina* music grew louder now; a burst of laughter was shrill. Clutching the empty pitcher, Ginny's head came up, and she frowned. It sounded odd.

Then her hand tightened on the handle of the pitcher as she saw the horses bunched in front of what must be the only *cantina.* So many horses! A uniformed soldier stood guard, obviously unhappy as he slouched against a wall with his arms crossed over his chest.

Soldiers. From Lerdo's army, no doubt. Ginny stirred uneasily. None of her experiences with Mexican soldiers had been pleasant, though she had lived with Colonel Miguel Lopez a long time ago.

As she stood there, uncertain and listening, there was a volley of gunfire followed by screams and shouts. Her heart began to thud erratically and she dropped the pitcher with a crash. Oh God, not again, not again... Where was Steve?

Panic set in, and she ducked into the shadows behind the well, her spine pressed against damp stone as men spilled out of the *cantina* and into the street. Feeble bars of light slanted across unmistakable uniforms and shouts of anger filled the night.

Hiding in the dark, crouched down so she wouldn't be seen, she watched for Steve. As more time passed and there was no sign of him, only the chaotic milling of soldiers rounding up citizens and shoving them into a line, linked by chains that she could hear clinking heavily, she had the rending thought that he might be among them. Oh God, no!

No, she told herself, Steve's too smart to get caught like that. He's hiding somewhere until the soldiers are gone and it's safe to come out....

A hand descended upon her shoulder, startling a scream from her that she quickly muffled with one hand. Relief flooded her, and she rose to turn, knees weak with reaction. Of course he was too wary to be taken....

But the dark face that loomed out of the shadows was not Steve at all. Instead glittering black eyes pinned her like a helpless insect. Recognition dawned slowly, then she blurted, "You were in Ojinaga! We danced...."

"*Señora,* an unexpected pleasure to see you again. But I am afraid that you are in danger."

"I...who are you? And what is happening? Are you with the soldiers?"

Gently but inexorably, he pulled her with him, ignoring her resistance. "Come, come, do not be afraid, for I will see that no harm comes to you."

He spoke in the same flawless Castilian Spanish as before. It was incongruous. What was he doing out here, in this isolated village far from everything?

"No, I will *not* come with you!" She jerked free, taking him by surprise, so that he wheeled around and reached for her, his fingers a hard vice on her arm.

"You are being foolish, *señora.*"

"Hardly! I don't know you at all, and I have no intention of going anywhere with you. My husband will be back soon, and he will see to it that I am kept safe. Now be so good as to release my arm."

"Ah, I am afraid I cannot do that. And your husband has been unavoidably detained, I think, or he would already be here with you, is that not so? Don't be foolish, Señora Alvarado. It will only make things worse."

Trembling, Ginny managed to keep her voice steady as she asked again, "Who are you? You know my name, but I have not been told yours."

He escorted her back to the *posada,* and she glimpsed the *posadero*'s face peering at them from the door as she was halted. Lanterns had been lit, and crimson and gold light illuminated a strong face, with defined mouth and high jutting cheekbones—the features of a *criollo*—one of the Spanish aristocrats.

"Many pardons," he said with an exaggerated courtesy that grated on her temper. "Allow me to present myself to you. I am Rafael Luna de Gonzalez, Adjutant General to el presidente Lerdo de Tejada."

"What do you want with me?"

"El presidente requests your presence in Mexico City, and I have come to escort you to him."

20

It was happening to her again. Ginny sat stoically in the closed carriage that rocked over rutted roads leading to Mexico City. Luna had forced her to accompany him, and if he knew where Steve was—or if he was even still alive—he would not tell her. How infuriating that this should happen to her again!

"I will tell *el presidente* exactly how rude you have been," she told Luna, who did not seem a bit bothered by the threat, "and he will see to it that you lose your commission in the army!"

He merely lifted a dark brow and smiled. "Such a fiery woman you are, *señora.* It is most remarkable that your passion has not faded with time."

He knew things about her, even lovers from her past. He was subtle, casually mentioning Miguel Lopez, even Michel Remy, as if he knew them, when it was obvious he was only trying to intimidate her. She'd quickly learned that silence was the only way to deal with him, and she retreated behind a wall of indifference.

Today he had told her, they would reach Mexico City.

"It has been some time since you were last there, I understand." He sat directly across from her in the black lacquered carriage, his long legs deliberately brushing against her knees. Occasionally, he allowed his knee to push her legs apart, suggestively subtle.

Ginny eyed him coldly and refused to rise to the bait.

"You are very lovely, Señora Alvarado," Luna said, and smiled when she merely looked at him. "Can it be that you do not like me? But why? I have done nothing to you. I have been only courteous and respectful. Did you not have a room to yourself? I have not attempted to force my attentions upon you."

Turning her head, she stared out the window. Her pointed silence should be enough to dissuade him, but it wasn't.

"Tell me," Luna said when the silence dragged on for a time, "when you were known as Madame du Plessis, did you also sleep with Maximilian? I had heard he was one of your conquests. But then, you seemed to prefer the lower caste to the more aristocratic lovers. It was said you were even once married to one of those dirty *Juaristas,* a half-breed mongrel like a mad dog."

She faced him then, green eyes narrowed and sparkling with anger. "He has more nobility in his little finger than your entire family has ever possessed, I am certain. Please excuse me if I don't care to continue talking to you. I feel quite nauseous suddenly. There seems to be a noisome stench in the carriage."

Luna laughed, but behind the smile his black eyes glittered with fury and menace. Ginny stifled a sudden shudder. He would not *dare* harm her! She had already reminded him that her father-in-law was the very influential Don Francisco Alvarado, and that she was well-acquainted with both Sebastian Lerdo and Porfirio Díaz. They would definitely take it amiss should she be insulted.

By the time they reached Mexico City she had developed a loathing for the handsome officer.

It was obvious to her that Lerdo was losing control of the country; Mexico City showed all the signs of an imminent invasion. Troops were scattered and looting was rampant. Those loyal to Lerdo were taking what they could while they could, for once Díaz came into power, they would be lucky to escape with their lives.

This beautiful city was a sad reminder of the doomed emperor and his wife. Poor Maximiliano…he had not deserved to die for only doing his duty, but perhaps that could be said of every soldier, even those who were elected president of the country.

And what on earth could Lerdo want with *her?*

Luna offered no clues to the reason for her summons, save the implication that her father was involved. That would be one reason, of course; wasn't he backing Lerdo in order to keep his Mexican properties? No doubt he had sent him money as well.

But Lerdo de Tejada wanted more from her than her intercession with the senator; he wanted an escape route.

"It seems that my term as *el presidente* is coming to a rather precipitate end," he told her dryly, "and I must make my plans. I wish to go to New York, and Senator Brandon has very graciously agreed to lend his assistance."

"But el presidente, how can *I* help?"

"You are also acquainted with Díaz, and your husband was once a captain in his command. I wish to get a message directly to the general, and there are few I can trust to deliver it for me. Every man thinks only of himself at a time like this, and I admit that I am doing the same. When I heard that you were in Mexico again, I implored General Luna to find you for me and ask you to come here."

"I wasn't asked, I was abducted," Ginny said sharply, "and I don't even know where—where my husband is or if he's still alive. Luna will tell me nothing. He is detestable."

Shrugging, Lerdo said, "He is a Spaniard, and they are all very arrogant. I would not have allowed him to be here were it not for the fact that he has high connections in Madrid. Ah, I had thought to make a difference in Mexico, to see my country become wealthy again, as she was long ago."

Ginny remained silent. She had heard different tales of Lerdo's rule, of his squandering tax money on personal vices instead of the reforms he touted so highly.

But eventually she found herself agreeing to speak to Porfirio Díaz for him, to secure a safe escort for his retreat from Mexico.

21

A steady pounding thud penetrated slowly into his numb brain. It sounded like the slam of metal against metal, loud and heavy. Steve tried to move, but was pinioned as if by a large object, his arms and legs splayed.

Gradually, he surfaced from the prolonged sleep that had rendered him unconscious, his brain struggling to assimilate the noise with the cause. Panting, he lay still.

Thick, noxious fumes clouded the air, stinging his nose and eyes. He blinked against it. Something struck him on the arm, and he realized that he could move after all, though it was slow and painful.

"It is time you woke up."

The voice came at him from the darker shadows, a casual observation. He blinked again, and his vision began to focus better, distinguishing between the shadows around him.

"What…where the hell am I?"

"Don't try to talk yet. Just listen."

A familiar darkness broken by wavering patches of light from creosote torches…the stench of urine and sweat…the rattle and clink of chains…a steady moaning like that of a wounded animal…

Suddenly he knew where he was, and an irrational panic rose up in a choking wave. He'd worked in a mine once before and knew that smell, knew those sounds….

"Christ! No, I've got to get out of here!"

"*Por Dios,* stay down," the voice muttered, urgent now, "or you will leave here bent over the end of a sword!"

It took all his will not to leap up, and a cold sweat broke out. Bile rose in his throat, memories suddenly stark and real. *The doctor...*

But the face that hovered over him with an anxious expression was not the smiling, unctuous face of his old tormentor. The doctor was dead now...*dead.* No, whatever nasty trick of fate that had brought him here, it was not the same.

This time, there had been a trial, a farcical exercise in frustration and futility as soon as he had recovered enough to make an appearance. He was taken from his cell to a room, where he was swiftly condemned for the crime of smuggling.

It was almost laughable.

The rifles he'd smuggled across the border were not the ones presented to the *magistrado* as evidence, but it didn't really matter anyway. Someone knew about it and had betrayed them. Who would have known? Had Butch Casey and Paco been caught as well?

It was all still so fuzzy, most of the details still foggy...the soldiers entering the *cantina,* ranging around the room like scavengers, hunting.

Thinking back, he would almost swear that the soldiers were interested in him alone that night, had been *looking* for him. Only a few peasants were arrested; they had ignored most there, save the few men they scooped up and charged as bandits.

"Guilty," the *magistrado* had pronounced with barely a glance at the prisoner standing before him in shackles and bruises. He had rifled some papers, then scrawled his signature across the bottom and motioned for Steve to be taken away.

The sentence was predictable—thirty years hard labor. A guard had nudged him, laughing when he stumbled, then slammed a fist against the side of his head as he struggled for balance.

"*Gringo* pig! You will be with us a long time, so you had best learn your duty now, filth! The price of resistance can be painful...crawl back to your cell like the dog you are!"

The lash of the whip had cracked against his back and he had sucked in a deep breath, forced to go on hands and knees the long way back through the tunnels, while the guards beat him and prodded him with whips and clubs. By the time he was returned to the tiny cell, his hands and knees were shredded and bleeding, and his back and ribs ached where the whip had flayed him.

Panting for breath, sucking in huge gulps of fetid air to fill his laboring lungs, Steve had crouched on the cold rock floor of his cell like the dog they had named him.

Like before, only his pride sustained him, that and a stubborn will to live. This time he was better prepared for what lay ahead. He had learned through the years that compromise was not the same thing as surrender, that if a man lived to fight another day, it was a victory of sorts.

The other two men in his cell moved slightly, silently, as if conserving their energy just to breathe. He had been like that once, had almost willed himself to die. Had even tried to kill himself rather than submit to a fate worse than death. That he had failed at it had been a triumph he had not then recognized. He did now.

For he was still alive, and the doctor who had brought him to the point of suicide was long dead—killed by one of the young men he had forced to submit to his advances, gutted like a fish and left to die in his own blood.

A fitting end for a man who had caused so much misery and death.

"Men who live by the gun, die by the gun," his grandfather had told him too many times to count. Maybe he'd end one day as the doctor had ended, dying the way he had lived. But for him it would be with a gun in his hand.

But not now. No, not now, by God!

"*Amigo,*" came a whisper in the dark, "there is water to wash your cuts here...."

It was an offer out of despair, an act of humanity in an inhumane place. Steve looked up, saw in the fitful light that filtered through the bars of their cell the face of his cell mate, and nodded.

"*Gracias, amigo....*"

As his cell mate gingerly washed his back, sluicing a small amount of their precious drinking water over the raw cuts, Steve reflected on his situation.

It was all too familiar to him, the dark days of tedious back-breaking labor deep in the mine shafts. All he had to do was wait. He would have plenty of time to do nothing but think and plan. Like before, he would escape. And like before, he would kill the man who had put him here.

LA CORTESANA

22

How unnerving it all was. It was the end of autumn, the end of a presidency, and the air of death permeated the entire city. Ginny was given an apartment in a little house off the main plaza, and since she had brought only the barest of necessities with her, Lerdo generously saw to her wardrobe.

"It is the least I can do for you, Señora Alvarado, since I am the cause of so much inconvenience to you. Luna should not have overstepped his bounds."

Rafael Luna would do much more than overstep his bounds if she gave him even half a chance, Ginny realized, for he was at her heels at every opportunity. He was her escort—a guard for her own safety, of course—but she knew that it was much more than that. While it was obvious that he wanted her in his bed, there was an underlying reason for his constant attendance on her as well. Why else would be go to so much trouble? And why else would he stop her from finding Steve?

Steve. She was sick with worry for him, and had not been able to get a message to Don Francisco, though she had certainly attempted it. Luna, of course, for reasons of his own, intercepted her messenger. She shuddered to think of the man's fate, for she had not seen him since.

"Señora, as you are on a mission of some delicacy, you must not continue to attempt sending messages. Surely, you realize the danger to *el presidente* should you be so foolish as to say the wrong thing." A faint smile curled Luna's mouth, and his eyes were watchful, regarding her with the same hot gaze that made her feel as if he knew what she looked like beneath her gown.

"I am not a fool, General Luna, but I am worried about my husband. Since you profess to be ignorant of his fate, I must find him myself."

"Should you continue, you may find to your sorrow that he has been lost forever. Do not provoke trouble, *señora.*"

"Are you *threatening* me?" Ginny was furious, her hands knotting into fists at her sides. She clenched them into the silk of her skirts and snarled, "I refuse to be intimidated!"

"There is a vast difference between intimidation and warning, but you will do as you see fit, of course." Luna observed her coolly, and she bit her tongue to keep from lashing out unwisely. Why warn him of her intention?

She wanted to ask, *why?* but was too stubborn to give him the satisfaction. An indifferent shrug was her only reaction to his intimidation, and that sufficiently annoyed him.

It was a duel between them, and she had the despairing thought at times that she was being forced into retreat.

Fretfully, she insisted that Lerdo discover what had happened to Steve, and told him that she suspected Luna had something to do with his disappearance.

"I have no sound basis other than intuition, but I am certain he not only knows what happened to Steve, but he is somehow behind it."

Lerdo looked surprised. "But what reason would he have for harming him? They have never met, you said."

"Not to my knowledge...no, they must not have known each other or Steve would have recognized him in Ojinaga. Oh, I don't know why Luna would want to get rid of him, but he did. I know he did. There is no other logical reason why Steve is not here at this moment. As the Mexican ambassador, he may have incurred Luna's enmity without meeting him."

"And is it not possible that your husband had his own plans, Doña Genia?" Lerdo smiled gently. Deep circles under his eyes bespoke his sleepless nights, and he held himself with the air of a man resigned to his fate. "It is far more likely that the nature of his business would call him away, is it not? This is not the first time he has suddenly disappeared, you must admit. I remember him in California. He had a reputation for being a man of danger and mystery then, too."

"There is a vast difference between mystery and sudden disappearance, Your Excellency." Ginny kept her tone calm with an effort. "I realize that Steve is prone to vanishing from sight for a time, but this time, he was abducted. I am sure of it, as I am sure that General Luna knows more than he will divulge to me. Can you not investigate?"

With a sigh, Lerdo nodded. "I will do what I can."

It would have to suffice for the moment, but Ginny held little hope that Lerdo, with his world collapsing around him, would expend much energy in finding one man.

A week passed before she was once more summoned to the palace and a meeting with *el presidente.* He looked even more tired, deep lines engraved into his face by sleepless nights and strain.

"It is time, Señora Alvarado. My tenure is done, and the battle lost. You must travel swiftly now, and inquire from General Díaz if I am to be granted safe passage from Mexico. General Luna will accompany you."

"General Luna? Your Excellency, I must protest. I do not trust the man. He is *not* to be trusted!"

"Try to put aside your personal feelings about Luna," Lerdo said quietly. "As an emissary of Spain, he has access to Díaz where many do not."

"Then perhaps he should make the arrangements for your escort to New York," she said tartly, and saw the reproach spring into Lerdo's eyes.

"Luna has access, not trust, *Señora.*"

Trapped and frustrated, Ginny could do little else but acquiesce, but she once more took to wearing a dagger strapped to her thigh beneath her skirts. It gave her more confidence, a reminder that if she had to, she would use it against Luna. Or any man who tried to hurt her.

General Luna looked at her with barely concealed triumph

when she climbed into the carriage early the next morning, his black eyes glittering.

"I trust you slept well, Señora Alvarado?"

When she did not answer, he persisted, "And Carmen, she is an adequate servant, I trust."

Sitting back, smoothing her hand over the deep green velvet folds of the cloak she held around her, Ginny said tartly, "It must be dreadfully tedious to be so bored with life that one must immerse themselves in all the petty details of another person's life. I pity you, General, for your lack of diversions."

He laughed softly. "Oh, do not waste such a sentiment on me, *señora.* I have my diversions. Yes, I have some most interesting diversions. Perhaps, one day, I shall share them with you. I think, somehow, that you might appreciate them more than most women."

"Do not waste your time or mine, General. Now, if you please, I would prefer to ride in privacy. Be so kind as to ride with the driver."

"I have my orders, fiery little cat," he said in a low, intimate tone, "and one day you shall learn what it is to take orders from *me.* I think you will learn more swiftly than you like what it means to court discipline."

A feeling of nausea churned in her belly as she stared at him, and Ginny knew that should she ever fall into this man's hands, she would regret it.

"If you ever come near me," she said slowly, each word distinct and deliberate, "I will do my best to gut you from neck to navel."

To her angry surprise, he only smiled. "You will be a challenge for me, *señora.* I await the day with great anticipation."

Before she could respond again, Luna shut the door, and to her relief, did not ride inside the carriage with her.

I do not think I can take another moment of his nasty innuendoes! she fumed. *When I return to Mexico City, I will* insist *that Lerdo find me a safe escort home! Even if I have to wait until Díaz himself is president, I do not dare remain near Luna. He is dangerous.*

But now she had to convince Porfirio Díaz, the man who would be the next president of Mexico, to show clemency to his predecessor. It was not an interview she anticipated with eagerness.

23

The silver mines were rough passages cut deep into the heart of a mountain, with tiny cells hacked into dank corridors off the main artery. Rickety wooden frames were built into the sides, clinging like vines to the rock walls that rose a hundred feet high.

It was Steve's worst nightmare come true, an endless litany of labor and wretched conditions. Before, when he had been sent to the mines by Devereaux, he had resisted the guards' attempts to force him to work. This time, he was a model laborer, blending seamlessly into the anonymous file of men.

But he waited.

The right time would present itself, and he would grab it. Then he'd be free again.

The man who had befriended him upon his arrival was manacled to him, their leg shackles tearing flesh but not their fierce desire to escape.

"When you go," he said softly one day, waiting until the armed guard had passed them, "take me with you."

Steve slid him a wary glance. "What makes you think I intend to escape?"

"You have that look about you. But you, I think, are much smarter than the others who have tried and failed."

Juan Rodriguez was a political prisoner, a man who had spoken out too boldly and found himself arrested and sentenced to twenty years hard labor.

"I miss my family most," he said bitterly. "My wife was pregnant when I was arrested. I do not even know if I have a son or a daughter. Or a wife any longer."

Steve thought of Ginny, and he thought of their children. What would happen if he didn't manage to escape? But Ginny must be looking for him; she was resourceful. She would find him, or at least go to his grandfather.

Ah, Christ, I hope she doesn't think I have just gone off on business for Bishop again! Where the devil is Paco?

He was supposed to have met him there in that tiny *cantina,* but all hell had broken loose when the soldiers had come in "looking for escaped rebel prisoners," though the men they had taken were only honest civilians.

It was war. Being in the wrong place at the wrong time could get a man killed if he wasn't careful.

Or earn him freedom if he was bold enough to take a chance....

Steve had been in this exact same situation before. He'd seized his chance then, and he would do it again. This time, at least, there was no doctor with unnatural desires to drive him to the brink of surrender. No, this time he knew how to survive what must be tolerated, and just wait for his chance. It would come. Sooner or later, it would come.

Days blended seamlessly, night no different than day save for the thin edge of light beyond the dank, dark walls that smothered them. Leg and wrist irons were not welded this time, but fastened with locks and keys, dragging in heavy metallic thuds as they worked. There were three men to a cell, all shackled together, sharing space and scant food that was little better than fare fed to livestock. Water was provided in a small bucket with a battered dipper, and more often than not, fetid.

Work was a blur of darkness barely broken by flickering torches and the orange-yellow glow of lanterns that illuminated sweating, straining bodies streaked with soot. Tunnels stank of rank sweat, creosote and urine, almost overpowering at times.

And always, as before, there were the sadistic guards who

enjoyed meting out punishment or reminders of who was in charge.

Steve plodded on, forcing his mind to think of more pleasant days, anything but the reality of his situation. It was the only way he could survive at times, the only way he kept from doing something careless or stupid.

One of the guards paused behind him, and the hiss of the lash was a brief warning before it struck.

"You! Get back to work. *El jefe* tolerates no idle *gringos!*"

Head bent, he ignored the fiery bite of the lash into his back and kept working, refusing to be provoked. Chains rattled as he toiled, dragging at his wrists and ankles in a cruel reminder that he had been careless enough to repeat a lesson he should have learned well the first time.

But this time, there was the certainty that Ginny would do whatever it took to find him.

"Where are we?" he asked one day when they had been taken back to the tunnel from their tiny cell. Juan gave him a strange look.

"You do not know?"

A wry smile twisted his mouth. "I wasn't exactly awake when they brought me here. It's hard to keep up with where you are when a dozen soldiers have managed to bash your skull in for you."

Juan nodded understanding, a sympathetic gleam in his eyes. The steady smack of steam machines filled the black passageway with a racketing sound that muffled their conversation.

"We are in Chihuahua. This is the Galena, a silver mine owned by *el jefe,* the rich norteamericano who promises to pay *el presidente* but gives most to himself and the men in his employ. Greedy bastards!" He spat to show his contempt.

"*El presidente* will soon find himself needing silver if Díaz succeeds, and I think he will," Steve replied, and when he saw a guard approaching, bent again to his work. Head down, he endured the brief stinging bite of the lash as the guard passed by.

The Galena. It struck him like a heavy fist that he was no doubt working in the mine owned by William Brandon—U.S. senator and Lerdo's supporter. God! If it wasn't so damned infuriating, it would be ironic. Did Brandon know that his son-in-law was a prisoner in his mine? Hell, it may very well be at his instigation. After all, Brandon wasn't exactly a stickler when it came to eliminating obstacles, and lately Steve had proven to be a most irritating block to getting what he wanted—Mexican silver.

Just how rich did a man have to get to be satisfied? And how low did a man have to sink to justify using these methods of getting cheap labor?

By God, he would pin the senator to the wall for it this time! Ginny would just have to understand.

24

Don Porfirio remembered her well, of course, and Ginny was glad that Lerdo had so graciously presented her with new clothes for the meeting. It would have been too embarrassing to meet the man who was to be the next president wearing the rags that Luna had abducted her in, and she had told the Spanish emissary so in no uncertain terms.

"You are a boor, Señor Luna, and I do not care to be associated with you on any level but in the capacity of envoy for *el presidente.*"

Luna had merely smiled, eyes appraising her with a steady confidence that made her want to slap him for his insolence. The man was disgusting!

But now that she was here to speak to Díaz, who was preparing for his triumphant return to Mexico City since the defeat of Lerdo's army, she realized that she was nervous. If he did not grant Lerdo safe conduct, would he consider her part of the rebellion? An enemy?

After eleven months of fighting, the revolt had succeeded despite initial reverses, just as Steve predicted. It was time for the victor to claim his prize.

Once in the presence at last of Porfirio Díaz, Ginny lost some of her nervousness, remembering the man she had met years before. They spoke congenially about their work together after the last revolution, and she was careful to avoid mention of Juarez and his renunciation of Díaz.

"But you have changed hardly at all, Señora Alvarado, except, of course, to grow more beautiful."

He swept her a gallant bow, his eyes frankly admiring as he stared at her elegant, stylish gown, a shot silk of emerald green to match her eyes, with full skirts pulled up and draped at the rear over a wire cage. The gown's bustline was accentuated by white lace edging that fringed her bare skin and emphasized the faint shadow between her breasts.

"As always, you are far too gallant, Don Porfirio. Or I should call you *el presidente* now?"

"Not quite yet, but soon, very soon." An expansive smile curved his mouth as he poured an excellent French wine into crystal glasses. Stocky, with intense dark eyes and the broad features of his Indian heritage, Díaz smiled at her over the gold-trimmed rim of the glass. "It has, at last, come to fruition. My years of work and planning, my time in exile—now is to be rewarded. I shall lead Mexico, champion liberal principles, more municipal democracy. Lerdo was too soft, and granted far too many concessions to the United States railway interests. It profited my country nothing, but I shall change that."

"You intend to stop all foreign investments?"

"On the contrary, *señora.* I intend to make foreign investments more profitable for Mexico. First, we must have internal stability. Banditry is rampant, so much so that it frightens away foreign investors. Already I have started to scour the country of many of these bandits. Others, however, will be more useful to me."

As he talked, Ginny took careful note of an unobtrusive cleric seated at an ornate desk in the far corner of the room. He scribbled constantly in a ledger, head down, seemingly absorbed in his work. In taking up the reins of power, Díaz would be assailed by many requests for favors; and now she must make her own pleas as well.

At a pause in his outline of proposals for Mexico's future, Ginny asked, "And what of Lerdo de Tejada? Do you intend to imprison him?"

"Ah, now we get to the heart of the reason for your visit,

I see. You are escorted by Rafael Luna, who is known to Lerdo as well. Do you come to ask a favor for yourself or for Lerdo?''

''Both.'' Boldly meeting his shrewd gaze, she stood up and set her nearly untouched glass of wine on a table. ''As a man of honor, I assured Lerdo that you would treat him with the respect due a man who has fought well for his country. A difference in politics may make men enemies, but should not make them dishonorable.''

Díaz regarded her thoughtfully. ''What is it that Lerdo requires of me?''

''Safe passage from Mexico.''

''Ah, and that is all? Should I give him his freedom so that he may go and conspire against me, plot to retrieve the power he wielded so badly? I think not, *señora.*''

''He will be an exile, and no threat to you. He wishes to leave Mexico, to go and live with friends.''

''Such as an American senator, perhaps? You seem surprised, *señora.* Did you think I would not investigate, would not find out that your father has received many beneficial concessions from Lerdo? While I see the definite advantage to American investments, I do not approve of granting so much power to men who only a few years ago were our enemies.''

''That war is behind us. So is the revolution that has earned you the presidency, if I may be so bold as to remind you of that, *el presidente.* It is time to look to the future and let the past be forgotten.''

''A woman with brains as well as beauty—an anomaly that I admire, Señora Alvarado.'' Díaz smiled slightly. ''I do not agree that the past should be forgotten, for men who do not remember their own history often find they must suffer the same fates again. But I will grant Lerdo safe passage, upon my own terms, of course.''

He drained the last of his wine. ''And as for you, what is it you wish to ask of me? I know there must be something, for you have the look of a desperate woman about you.''

''You are very perceptive, Your Excellency. Yes, I do have a request of my own.''

She told him about Steve, and how he had disappeared from the village the night Luna abducted her, and the men she had seen weighted down in chains and escorted by Lerdo's soldiers.

"I fear he is in a prison somewhere," she said, keeping the tremor out of her voice with an effort. "And I have not been allowed to get a message to his grandfather, for Luna treats me as if I am a prisoner as well!"

"I think General Luna will have his uses, but in this he has erred. We will make inquiry and find your husband if he has, indeed, been made a prisoner. But tell me, why would he be arrested? He is not one of the notorious bandits, is he? No?"

"I don't know why...I only know that he has disappeared and I believe that Luna knows what happened to him."

Rafael Luna, however, disavowed any knowledge with a shrug and deprecating denial. "No, Your Excellency, I do not recall an Esteban Alvarado, or a Steve Morgan the night we routed the *cantina.* It was only a routine raid, you understand, for we learned that there were men who smuggled many rifles across the border. Bandits, of course, seeking to sell them to whoever would pay. There was a trial, and the men were convicted of smuggling."

Ginny's heart dropped. Was that why Steve had been there? It must be true...all those heavy crates, the baggage that he'd sent ahead, with Butch Casey and the other men to guard it.

Oh, Steve! Oh, damn you, Steve Morgan, for being so reckless!

He had been caught smuggling rifles, and there would be nothing she could do to save him—unless Díaz granted him clemency.

25

When Ginny returned to Mexico City and the small apartment on the Calle Manzanares, a summons from Lerdo awaited her. Though exhausted, she went immediately to the palace, where she was given a telegram. It was from her father, a terse message that she must contact him at once.

Surprised that he knew where she was, Ginny wrote him, telling him about Steve, begging for his help in finding him. Now that Lerdo had his promise of safe conduct from Mexico, he had no more use for her, and granted her the permission to leave Mexico City at her convenience.

Ginny returned from the palace near midnight, hopeful that her father would receive this message, and wished she had dared contact Don Francisco as well. The interview with Lerdo had been draining. The former president was gone from Mexico City now, fleeing before the triumphant entry of Díaz, his passage from the country to New York arranged.

With Brandon's assistance, he would safely reach refuge in New York. But what of *her?* Perhaps she should have left with him, but could she abandon Steve? If she left Mexico now, she might well never find him, never be able to discover what had happened to him. Men were all too frequently lost in the corrupt judicial system, and with the change of presidents making things even more chaotic, delay could be fatal.

No, she would stay in Mexico, though not here. Not with

Rafael Luna so close and dangerous, though Lerdo was skeptical of the man's intentions.

"He is merely Spanish," he'd repeated as if that reason excused and explained Luna's blatant threats to her.

Frustrated, Ginny knew that flight was her only protection from him. She would go to Don Francisco at once.

But when morning came, Rafael Luna was at her door with a message from Díaz. "He requests that you remain in Mexico City, *señora,* for he recalls your assistance to him before."

"I'm afraid that won't be possible." Already dressed to leave, Ginny stared back at Luna with defiance and growing dismay. Three uniformed *policia* were behind him, and moved to stand on each side of the door, as if guarding it.

Luna intercepted her glance and smiled. "And I am afraid that you have no choice at the moment."

Seething, Ginny refused to give him the satisfaction of seeing her rising panic, and merely nodded coldly. "I will be glad to meet with Díaz at his leisure."

There was no point in arguing with Luna; only Díaz would be able to help her now.

But an audience with Díaz grew impossible to achieve in the following days, while Ginny grew more desperate. Luna became more persistent, more bold, too confident in his invulnerability.

He has his feet in both camps, she fumed, and whichever way the wind blew was the way he leaned. He was only in Mexico to further his own interests.

It mystified her why Díaz did not dismiss Rafael Luna and send him back to Spain, but he was allowed to remain in the country and in the employ of the president. The switch of his allegiance from Lerdo to Díaz was immediate.

"You are a traitor," she accused Luna, and he laughed.

"I prefer to think of myself as a chameleon, *mi bella,*" he had murmured, "able to change colors as needed. But then, is that not true of most men involved in politics? What of your father? Your *husband?*"

"Don't you dare mention them to me! I know you know where Steve is. Why won't you tell me?"

"Is it that important to you? But I had understood that it was a marriage of convenience, a union merely for appearances' sake. You have both had many lovers, and the marriage is a farce. It is true, is it not?"

Biting her lip, Ginny stared at him in frustration. She could not deny the truth of the past, but it was the *past,* not the present. Not the future.

"Steve and I have not always been close, no," she said at last. "But our children have brought us together."

"Ah, the children. Of course. There are three, are there not?"

"Twins," she replied stiffly, "but I refuse to discuss my children with *you!*"

"Only two?" Luna frowned, shaking his head at her. "Ah no, I could not be wrong. I was told there are three."

"Not unless there's another one I don't know about," Ginny said irritably, turning away to walk to the long window that looked out on the street.

Behind her, Luna's laugh sounded rueful. "But, of course, that is it. I had forgotten. My apologies, *señora,* for forgetting that you are not the mother of the other child."

Ginny turned slowly away from the window to stare at him. "That is a lie. There is no other child."

"Ah, but you are mistaken. There is a child, a son, I believe, who lives in New Mexico Territory with his mother."

Suddenly cold, Ginny began to shiver uncontrollably, and moved to stand in front of the fireplace where a low blaze cast a small pool of heat beyond brass firedogs. It wasn't true, *couldn't* be true! They had no more secrets between them, had told each other everything. But she recalled with a sudden sense of nausea that it had been she who had confessed, she who told Steve about all the others in her past. He had told her nothing.

Oh, she hadn't wanted to hear about the women, for she knew there were many, but this was different. This was something important, something she should have been told. A child was not just a casual affair, a night or two in another woman's bed. A child changed everything.

Had that been the reason for his trip to New Mexico? Not Sam Murdock, but the mother of his child? Oh God!

Luna stood there watching her with that faint, supercilious smile on his mouth, as if he *knew* she had not known.

And, of course, he did. That was the reason he had told her, the reason he watched her so carefully to gauge her reaction. She refused to let him see the depth of her devastation.

"Really, Señor Luna, you are not so foolish as to think I would consider another woman's child as my own, I hope. My husband and I have led *separate* lives much of our marriage and I simply cannot keep up with everything."

"You are very European, Señora Alvarado. Not many women from America would be so casual about their husband's child with another woman."

"Perhaps because I was not reared in America but in France, or perhaps because I have not always been uninvolved myself. But you know that, as you seem to have made quite a study of my life. Really, General Luna, I cannot understand why you have this strange *obsession* with me. It is unhealthy to be so deeply engrossed with the life of someone you do not know, nor will ever know."

"Ah, but I intend to change that." He moved toward her, eyes gleaming in the light of lamps and the fire. "When I first saw you, dancing there in Ojinaga, I decided I must have you. You have the soul of a courtesan, the fire of a Spanish gypsy. And I," he said softly, "make it a point to get what I want."

Coldly, she said, "You are too insolent! It is time for you to leave, before I summon Artur to evict you."

"That old man?" He laughed contemptuously. "He could not throw out bathwater, *señora,* and you know it. No, I will stay as long as I like, long enough to convince you that you need my favor to find your husband."

"And I presume that your favor comes with a price."

"Ah, you are very clever. Yes, all things worth having come with a price. It is up to you to decide what is worth more to you—your pride or your husband."

Bitterly, Ginny thought that it always came down to this, and always she was presented with intolerable choices.

"I refuse to bargain with you, General Luna," she said icily. "A man who would make such a bargain would not keep it. I have had experience with men like you before. I will not sell myself."

"Not even for your husband?"

"Steve would not wish to be free at such a price."

"A pity." Luna reached out to touch her cheek, smiling when she stepped back to avoid his caress. "I would have kept my bargain. But your refusal does not lessen my desire for you. It would have been better if you came willingly to me."

"That will *never* happen, General."

"Ah, do not be so certain, Señora Alvarado. One never knows what may happen in a moment of passion."

"I seriously doubt you have ever known real passion. You seem more the type to demand it, when it is meant to be freely given. But perhaps no woman has ever felt it for you without it being demanded, so you would not know that."

A hot light sprang into his eyes, a glitter that made her take a step back. A muscle twitched in his cheek as he stared at her. "It is true that few women have felt the kind of passion that I require, but you are a woman who is accustomed to passion. You were born for it. You will not disappoint me."

To Ginny, it sounded like a threat.

26

Steve Morgan had lost track of time. Endless days and nights were separated only by routine. In the deep recesses of the mine, he survived by sheer will alone.

The sting of the whips came less frequently now, though often enough. Food was scarce, just enough to keep grown men alive and able to work. His belly growled constantly. Was anyone searching for him yet? They would eventually realize that he had disappeared involuntarily. By now Paco would have managed to find out what had happened to him. He and Bishop would probably be forming a strategy plan.

But Ginny could very well be angry, thinking that he'd left her again, as he had so many times before.

Christ, it's no more than I deserve if she does....

Regret dogged him, an unfamiliar emotion. He tried not to think, not of Ginny, or escape, but only of survival. And when it was at its worst, he again used the method Gopal had taught him so long ago, and focused on pleasant memories.

It was liberating, the illusion of being free, in a sun-dappled forest, or by a clear, running stream with the sharp sweet scent of pine in the air....

Reality came with a murky blackness broken by the fitful yellow glow of lanterns or the sputtering flame of creosote torches that served to illuminate silhouetted figures of straining men heaving pickaxes, bodies saturated with sweat, mouths open holes gasping for air. The air reeked with despair. The whips of the guards were a constant hissing pop, curling around backs, bellies and thighs. If a man failed to cry out under the lash, it was applied until he did.

Days dragged into nights, an endless monotony, until he lost track of time, until he dared not think of anything other than the mechanical response of his body. But like a small, niggling worm, at the back of his mind was the reminder that he would not have to endure this long, that soon it would be over.

And then I will kill the man who put me here....

That memory was still vague, a tall, dark shadow half-hidden in a corner who Steve somehow knew was behind it all. An air of smug confidence had emanated from the man, catching his attention just before lights exploded behind his eyes and everything was plunged into darkness.

When he had awakened to the familiar nightmare of hell, he had known who was responsible for putting him there. In the days—weeks—that followed, the certainty grew.

I am here for a definite reason, and it has to do with the man in the cantina.

"You! *Gringo!*" The guard's shout was accompanied by the stinging lash of his whip. Steve straightened, careful not to move too fast or the whip would only bite more deeply. "*Gringo* pig. Lucky for you that more men are needed outside, or you may soon begin to look like these others here, eh? Move faster!"

A flurry of activity was the only warning he had before he was taken, along with Juan, to the mouth of the mine. He winced against the sharp stab of light into eyes far too accustomed to the turbid shadows.

The guards were impatient, brutal, freely applying the lash to those who stumbled or didn't move fast enough.

But then they were outside, where the air smelled of something besides musty air and creosote, and he dragged in a deep breath to fill his lungs. God! He was almost drunk with the feel of the sun on his face, warming his skin, burning his eyes. They stumbled along, still manacled at the legs, the chains a weighted constant clanking as they bent to the tasks of moving the ore cars along the gleaming lines of track.

It didn't matter that they were forced to work from sunup to sundown as long as there was fresh, clean air to breathe, nor did it matter so much about the brutality of the guards. That could be borne.

He began, surreptitiously, to gauge the odds of escape.

Guards were posted on the rock walls that ringed the mine, others roved the work area. All were heavily armed, as if expecting trouble. Escape would be difficult, at best. Christ, it would be damn near impossible. While he worked, he scanned the area, marked the routine of the guards. It would take a miracle.

But the idea had taken root, and it sprouted and began to grow. All he needed was a diversion, something to distract the guards long enough for him to grab a weapon.

By now, if his grandfather or Ginny knew where he was, he would have been freed. No one knew. If he didn't take the steps to freedom, he could end up spending years here, lost in the nameless, faceless mass of men forced to work.

There were so many of them, political prisoners some, others innocent of anything but the ill fortune to be taken by soldiers or *Rurales.* It hadn't changed since he had been a political prisoner, a revolutionary spared from death and given a living hell instead.

Hate had kept him alive then, and a need for vengeance.

This time, it was thoughts of Ginny, his copper-haired wife who drove him to distraction so much of the time, but who was in his blood. It was a luxury to think of her, to recall the soft feel of her skin beneath his hand, the gypsy slant of her green eyes and the provocative pout of her sensual little mouth.

When he lay on the cold floor of his cell at night, he thought of their time at the waterfall, remembered Ginny's delight at going naked, the way her body gleamed beneath the sun and glistened with rivulets of water streaming over her breasts, belly and thighs. She embodied passion, life and love. She represented his past and his future. Without her, he had only gone through the motions of living.

The other women—Francesca, Concepción, Beth—had never sparked a tenth of what he felt for Ginny.

When he escaped from here, he would tell her that. Now that he had time to think, he knew that until he took the risk of telling her everything he felt, there would always be barriers between them.

I'll tell her…I'll tell her everything….

27

Senator Brandon stared out the windows of the carriage that narrowly missed scraping against high stone walls rising on each side of the trail. When had he become an old man? It seemed to have happened suddenly, yet here he was, having to ride in a carriage instead of astride a horse like a man. The bullet in his back still crippled him at times, but the doctors had shaken their heads and informed him it would be there forever.

"To remove it would be to kill you. Or leave you unable to sit up or walk again."

So he endured it as best he could, riding when once he could have walked, taking trains instead of carriages wherever possible.

His fingers drummed impatiently against the velvet-padded side of the carriage. There was enormous need for a railroad out here in this godforsaken country that was good for nothing but mesquite and the purest ore he had ever been privileged to see.

It was the last that would make his fortune, would give him a legacy to pass on to his grandchildren.

He frowned. In his later years he had come to the realization that such a legacy would be all he would leave. How had it happened? He'd struggled so hard during the disastrous Civil War to keep the Virginia estates that his father and his grandfather had left him. There were times it looked as if all would be swept away by the fortunes of war. So he had compromised. He had compromised his principles and compromised his promises, and had managed to hold on to them when others lost everything.

Such a dear price to pay.

At first, he'd wrestled with his conscience about the decisions he'd made, before consoling himself with the thought that it wasn't just for his own use, his own pride that he had lied, cheated, even stolen. It was for his only child, his beautiful daughter Virginia. One day he would be able to tell himself that he had founded a dynasty, not ended it.

Yet it had all begun to unravel. The tapestry of deception and power he had woven during the years after the war was fraying rapidly. Virginia wasn't his flesh and blood but the child of another man. The wife he had loved so much loved another man, and his second wife had slept with Steve Morgan. Even the grandchildren he claimed were not really his, but another man's blood.

There were times it all seemed so futile, a pissing contest in the wind.

The analogy made him smile.

As the carriage slowed, he heard the unmistakable sound of money being made, the raw ore dug from the bowels of the earth rattling up on ore cars that would be conveyed to the smelter. Some of the purest damn ore he'd ever seen lay in the Galena mine—named after the high quality lead-silver ore.

The carriage's well-oiled springs dipped gently as he emerged to stand in a canyon ringed by high rock and guards. If nothing else ever went right in his life, he was going to make certain that this mine made him wealthier than any man in America.

The mine foreman came to greet him, his manner polite but brusque, as if he were too busy to give the *norteamericano* owner his time.

"The labor force is larger than I thought," Brandon observed with a frown when he saw the straining men hauling ore. "I prefer to keep costs down."

"Ah, many of these men are on loan from the government,

most of them rebel prisoners, Senator. They cost us next to nothing. Some food, perhaps, and blankets. When they have served their sentences, there are always more to take their place.''

''Does Lerdo's successor have the same attitude toward these rebels?'' Brandon asked dryly. ''I would think he would feel some sort of obligation to men who risked lives and liberty for him.''

''President Díaz is, above all else, a practical man. And many of these rebels were nothing more than outlaws before they were apprehended.'' A shrug lifted his shoulders. ''That will not change. Cheap labor supports the country—and you, Senator.''

It was said slyly, with a sidelong glance at him, and Brandon understood. If he expected to continue making profit from the Galena, then he could not question the method.

But it was more unsettling than he expected, to see the ragged condition of the men forced to work in the mine. Their heads were bent and they were covered with soot. A few of them wore little more than the most essential of garments, loose, tattered pants that did nothing to protect them against the cold or heat. He was sure it was even worse below the earth's surface. At least these men had fresh air.

Victor Delgado escorted him on an inspection of the rough cars of ore ready to go to the smelter. The tour took them down into the mines and into the tunnels lit by lamplight that was thin and wavering. The eerie light against corbeled black walls and the moaning sounds of men punctuated by snarling commands from armed guards was like a scene from Dante's *Inferno.* A cold chill shivered down Brandon's spine, and he moved stiffly, carefully picking his way across the rough rock passage hewn into the mountain. A misstep may well put him flat on his back—or cripple him for life.

The blunted end of his black, lacquered cane provided a steadier footing, but the dense air and lack of light made him clumsy. The sharp crack of a whip split the air, and was followed by a string of curses and a pained cry. Brandon put a hand against the wall to steady himself, suddenly sick.

"Take me back outside," he ordered abruptly, and turned back toward the front of the mine shaft. His gaze swept over a line of men with eyes gleaming in the fitful light of glass lanterns. Like animals in the night, he thought, the same waiting, feral gaze....

Delgado escorted him to the offices where the ledgers were kept. Here, it was private. Here they could speak more frankly, he was assured.

Away from prying eyes that might report the exchange of money and collusion, he thought wryly, and took a seat behind the desk in the only comfortable chair. It left Delgado standing as if he were only a *peón*—which, in all truth, he was, whether he would admit it to himself or not. There was never a dearth of men ready to sell souls and country for personal gain.

"So," the senator said, "show me the ledgers."

Delgado's mouth tightened slightly, but he produced the ledgers. These were the second set of books that were kept in a hidden compartment behind a heavy set of shelves, and he spread them out on the desktop.

After an hour of perusal, William Brandon sat back in the chair with a grunt of satisfaction. It always paid to do your own investigations.

Locking his fingers together over his chest, he smiled. "This is much better than I expected. You have done well."

"*Sí,* we have been careful. What of Díaz?" he asked. "Do you intend to maintain the same...standards?"

"I intend to do what I must, as always. Your reward is well-earned. Do you wish to share with Díaz? Ah, I thought not. Neither do I. We will, as I said, do only what we must to ensure that the silver gets safely to the United States."

It was, he thought, a perfect, profitable arrangement. Cheap labor provided by the Mexican government, and a high grade quality of ore. Just perfect.

A sudden loud noise outside jerked him upright. As he lurched from the chair, he heard Delgado begin to swear furiously in Spanish as he leaped for the door.

He understood only a few words, but enough to know that

an insurrection of the prisoners was creating havoc—and it had begun with a blue-eyed *gringo.*

Uneasily, Brandon limped to the door Delgado had left flung wide open, and stepped out into utter pandemonium.

28

It had all happened so quickly. One moment Juan was working beside him while Steve stood staring with frozen disbelief at the tall, dignified form of his father-in-law, the next a guard had brought down his whip to prod the prisoners back to work. Brutally, he slashed down again and again, the whip a fiery tongue against the bare chests and backs of the prisoners.

Straightening, Steve met the guard's angry gaze with a brief glance of utter contempt. His hands tightened on the handle of the shovel he'd been using to scoop ore into the heavy buckets for the smelter.

Beside him, Juan stumbled slightly, the chains making a metallic rattle as he tried to regain his balance. Another guard stepped in swiftly, coming from behind to curse at them.

"Filth! Move! Back to work...what do you dare to stare at, *pendejo!*" This last obscenity was accompanied by a clip of his rifle butt that caught Juan on the cheek, laying it open.

When Juan staggered and went to one knee, his weight pulled Steve off balance as well so that he also fell to one knee. The guards reacted as if they had been attacked, viciously using the whips on not only Juan and Steve, but randomly striking other men manacled in the line.

"Christ, leave him alone!" Steve said to the guard as Juan moaned under the savage beating. "Can't you see he's nearly unconscious?"

"*¡Cierra el hocico!*" The guard's swarthy features grew

dark red with fury at the insolence of the blue-eyed *gringo* prisoner who dared to address him. The rifle butt came down in a swift, sharp chopping motion as if to hit Steve, but at the last moment, descended with a crushing blow on Juan's skull.

Steve heard it crack, heard Juan's soft, almost gentle sigh as he collapsed in a lifeless heap. For an instant, a rational reminder that there were too many guards kept him from reacting, but when the guard laughed, any logic was replaced by gut instinct, and a fury born of deep hate.

The shovel in his hands sliced out and upward, the edge of the heavy metal scoop catching the guard by surprise as it slammed into his throat. Blood spurted out in a geyser; it spattered on his grime-streaked clothes, warm and sticky.

Steve Morgan, goaded by fury and frustration, now moved with reckless efficiency to snatch up the guard's rifle even as it fell from abruptly limp hands. Whirling in the same fluid circle, he swung it around and fired from the hip just as the other guard began to comprehend what had happened.

The sharp report ignited instant chaos. Prisoners rioted, leaping for their guards with murderous cries of pent-up pain, rage and hate, overpowering many despite the overwhelming odds. Shovels, pickaxes and wooden staves were used as weapons. The canyon resounded with the echoes of gunfire and screams of wounded and dying men.

Somehow, Steve managed to grab a ring of keys from a fallen guard, and unlocked his manacles before tossing them to the next man. He paused only for an instant to ascertain that Juan was truly dead before moving on with grim purpose.

It will soon be a bloodbath if I don't get to the senator and make him rein in the guards.

Bullets smacked into rock, spraying him with hot, sharp shards that stung as badly as the lash of the whips as he crossed the narrow, rock-rimmed ravine at a run, bent over to provide a less stable target, bare feet tearing on sharp rock.

Brandon was only halfway down the steps, his face ashen in the chaos, when Steve took the steps two at a time to meet him. The wooden staircase vibrated from the force of his ascent and he paused a few feet from the senator.

He's got nerve, Steve thought cynically when Brandon leveled a pistol at him with cool aplomb. The hand holding the weapon shook only slightly.

"Damn murdering swine—Stop!" He repeated it in Spanish that no Mexican would have recognized, and Steve laughed.

"You'll have to do better than that, Senator."

"Don't come any closer or I'll shoot you where you stand. Tell the others to halt this riot before the guards kill them all!"

Gunfire was sporadic but loud, filling the canyon with thunder. Brandon looked grimly determined, white lines carved beside his mouth, the pistol steadier now. Steve saw the resolve in his eyes.

"You'll have to stop it, Senator. You're responsible for this, but for the love of God, do it quickly before even more men are killed. Isn't it enough that you're getting rich off the slave labor of these poor wretches?"

Balanced on the balls of his feet, he calculated that he could reach the senator with the butt of his empty rifle if necessary, but it would probably knock him off the steps and over the railing. It was a good twenty feet to the ground below.

Brandon sucked in a sharp breath, and his eyes narrowed into thin slits as he stared at Steve, then blurted, "My God! It's—*Steve Morgan?*"

The last was said with disbelief. Steve ignored that, snapping, "Call off the guards! *Now!*"

"If you think I have any influence, you're mistaken." The barrel of the pistol wavered slightly. Brandon looked uncertain. "Delgado is in charge here."

"Then for chrissake, tell him to put a stop to it! He'll listen to you. It's not likely he'll be in any mood to listen to me."

The senator gave him a swift, frowning glance before he moved down one step. "I'll tell him, and when this is under control, you had better come up with a damn good explanation for why you're here, Morgan. My daughter has been worried sick about you."

"If she was that damn worried, I wouldn't still be here."

Steve had the impression that Brandon was genuinely surprised to see him. But then, the man was a consummate politician and capable of disguising his real intent extremely well.

When the brief rebellion was subdued and the few prisoners that were left once more secure, Steve sat across from the senator in the mining office. His voice was hard.

"I'll accept that you had nothing to do with me being here. For now. If I find out differently, you know I'll come back to you for an explanation."

Brandon paled. His hands clasped atop the silver head of his cane trembled slightly, but he nodded, his mouth set into a harsh line. "As I just told you, I had nothing to do with it. I may be a lot of things, Morgan, but I'm not a fool."

"And I had the little idea that you wanted to be rid of me lately, that you've been unhappy with some of my actions. Guess I was wrong."

"No, you're right about that." Brandon grimaced. "I will admit I haven't been pleased by your efforts to ruin my plans. And I have tried to stop you. But not this. Not what amounts to kidnapping and slavery. I leave the abductions to you."

"Ah, yes, you're referring to Ginny, of course. That was a long time ago, Senator." He flexed his hands; they ached, the skin callused from wielding pickaxes and shovels. He felt suddenly weary, and disgusted. Blue eyes hardened, and he said softly, "You have no scruples when it comes to making a profit, why would it bother you to get rid of a man who gets in your way?"

"It wouldn't." Brandon's flinty gaze held his. "But you have influential friends and contacts, men who could ruin me. I have worked too hard to take the chance of losing it all now. This mine promises to be the most profitable venture yet. With a railroad to get the ore out more efficiently, we stand to be the richest men in America. You could profit as well."

"I don't think I could stand the stench of the blood on my hands." Steve stood abruptly, saw Brandon brace himself, and said softly, "These men are treated as little more than animals. If you insist upon using prisoners, at least treat them as men instead of beasts."

"Until I arrived today, I had no idea they were being ill used. For the love of God, Morgan, I'm not uncivilized!"

"I'd like to believe that. Recent events, however, make it a bit difficult. What are you doing here?"

Brandon gave him a sour look. "I came to investigate my interests. A man cannot always trust subordinates to take care of his business as well as he would."

"I suppose you learned that from Hearst."

"A consummate businessman, you must admit."

"Better than Jay Gould," Steve replied cynically, "but not by much. One of your investors, I presume, another shark in the waters. I would think a man such as yourself, worried about his reputation with the voters, would be more careful about who he went into business with. It would be a shame if it became known that you condone the use of virtual slavery in your mines. What would your constituents have to say about that? Seems to me the stigma of using slaves has a nasty connotation to it lately. Maybe some of the men who put you here condone slavery, but that war is over. How would it look if they found out about these conditions?"

Clearly irritated, Brandon's knuckles whitened on the head of his cane and he scowled. "I pay the Mexican government for workers, and they provide them. I cannot dictate their policies toward prisoners."

"No, but you can alleviate their suffering or refuse to use them." Steve moved closer and saw in the senator's face an uneasy awareness of his appearance. A tight smile slanted his mouth, and his blue eyes were hard and ruthless. "Maybe if you had to work below ground for a day, you'd know what it's like to be treated inhumanely. If you think my choice of garments is my own, you're wrong."

"I know that, Morgan." Testily, he added, "We can talk later after you're cleaned up. You smell foul."

"Senator, so do you."

Anger tightened Brandon's mouth, but he was wise enough not to comment.

Delgado was summoned, clearly unhappy that one of the prisoners—the very one who had started the riot—was now being treated as a guest. He complied with the senator's request for decent food and clothing, but lodged a protest.

''But he is a bandit, *señor!* A prisoner!''

''By mistake. I'll deal with the authorities. You just do as you're told and provide him with food, clothing and a bath—the latter being the most important at the moment.''

Muttering under his breath, Delgado showed Steve to a small room to one side, but kept a wary eye on him, leaning against the door frame. ''Crazy *norteamericano,*'' he spat. ''It would have been better had you been killed.''

''Perhaps for you,'' Steve said softly in a Mestizo dialect that he knew the man would understand and Brandon would not. ''You know I would like to kill you, eh?''

Delgado glared at him silently.

When Steve was washed and dressed, and had rejoined Brandon, the senator dismissed Delgado.

''See to the others. There are matters I must discuss with my—guest.''

Delgado nodded stiffly. ''*Sí, señor,* but if you should need me to shoot any vermin...'' His hand on the pistol he wore strapped to his hip was ample evidence of his meaning.

''Most of the vermin here are already wearing guns,'' Steve said before Brandon could reply. ''If I were you, Delgado, I would be more concerned with my own neck. I have a feeling the authorities will not be too happy with you.''

''I have done my job well, *gringo* pig! No man can say that I have not done what I was told to do. And if you think to make trouble for me, you may find that you have a tiger by the tail. I have friends in high places, much higher than a *norteamericano* who thinks he is so important.'' He made a contemptuous gesture, slicing his palm into empty air. ''You will soon discover who really owns Mexican silver. It is not all for *gringos* who care nothing for this country, only for their own pockets!''

''I see we have a patriot in our midst, Morgan.'' Senator Brandon's eyes were half-lidded, his tone dry. ''A well-paid patriot, I should add. I wonder if his scruples suffer when he takes my money?''

Delgado made a strangled sound, started forward, then came to a swift halt when Morgan pinned him with a hard, gimlet stare. There was something intimidating about the blue-eyed *gringo* who moved with such competence, even as weak from hunger and mistreatment as he was now. It was in the way he carried himself, a competence that had been weighted down with chains since arriving at the Galena, but was far too obvious now.

Backing away, Delgado reached for the door handle behind him, keeping his eyes on Steve Morgan. "Keep in mind, Señor Brandon, that the new president may not be as agreeable as the old one."

When they were alone once more, Brandon said harshly, "Why in hell *are* you here?"

"If you mean in Mexico, the answer should be fairly obvious. There's been a revolution."

Steve prowled the small room, glanced at maps and plats scattered on tables, noted the leather bindings of ledgers locked behind glass doors. A sense of wary tension pervaded the room, was obvious in the senator's eyes. Damn him. He bought and sold men like cattle and then had the nerve to ask questions! Steve swung around to stare at him, saw him recoil at the sudden movement. "It's not just coincidence that I was brought here after being ambushed."

Brandon made an impatient sound. "You don't still think I had something to do with that? You're wrong. I had no idea where you were or what happened to you. Virginia is in Mexico City, but has not returned my wire or letters. No one seemed to know what happened to you. Even your partner, that Paco Davis, has just dropped out of sight. Hell, you have a habit of doing that yourself."

"I have a bad habit of running into folks who want me to drop out of sight. Sometimes permanently." He paused, then frowned. "What is Ginny doing in Mexico City? She should have gone back to my grandfather's."

"Surely you've realized by now that my daughter does as she pleases, and that we are usually not advised of her reasons for it. No doubt she changed her mind on a whim, or whatever motive she may have. Probably something to do with that damn Luna.''

''Luna?'' Steve's head snapped up and his eyes narrowed, nearly missing the senator's quick frown and tightened lips.

''Yes. A General Rafael Luna, emissary from Spain or some such nonsense. He sent me a damned impertinent telegram telling me that I should focus on my business interests and leave my daughter's welfare to those who could assist her. A damned insolent man.''

''Yes.'' Steve rose from the chair and let the front two legs slam back to the plank floor with a loud smack. ''I've had the dubious pleasure of meeting Señor Luna.''

''I'm not surprised. Is there anyone in Mexico you do not know?''

''Actually, I met him in Italy a few years ago. He was quite taken by…an opera singer.''

''Ah.'' Brandon's gaze was assessing. ''Signorina di Paoli is a lovely, fiery young woman, if a bit…headstrong at times. Tell me, does she still provoke gunfights?''

''If she can. I'll need some weapons, food, a horse.''

''Of course. I'm sure Delgado will provide them, whether he approves or not.'' Brandon drummed his fingers on the wood surface of the desk, a soft sound. ''You're going to Mexico City, I presume.''

''Where is she staying?''

''Calle Manzanares. Give her my regards.''

Steve didn't answer. He was remembering Rafael Luna and their last meeting, and thought of Ginny with the man.

Christ! It had been Luna in Ojinaga dancing with Ginny that night. He should have remembered him. But he had been too intent on his passionate, tempting little wife to pay more than perfunctory attention to her dancing partner. Now Luna had Ginny. And if he did to her what he had tried to do to Francesca, this time he would kill him. He should have done it last time. Now it might be too late.

29

Winter had come to Mexico City, with warm days and cool nights. President Díaz entered the city in triumph on November 21, and the citizens celebrated. Ginny was invited to palace balls, to the elegant, grand affairs honoring the new president, but found to her dismay that General Luna was her assigned escort.

Ginny struggled in a familiar nightmare, caught between pain and anger, old memories dredging up doubts. *Oh God, not again!* Should she even *look* for Steve? He'd disappeared so many times before, and yet she had the persistent feeling that this time, it wasn't by choice. If only she could talk to Paco, or even Bishop, but of course, she had no idea where they were, either.

And now to find out that Steve had another child... *Why* had he not told her?

She had vacillated between despair and rage since Luna had told her of it. If only she could believe it wasn't true. But somehow, she knew it was.

Rafael Luna was too exultant, his satisfaction far too obvious for her to cling to the fiction that he was lying.

''Even your husband's friend, Jim Bishop, knows of the child, Doña Genia. There are...reports on these things, and I have excellent resources to discover what I wish to know about a man I consider dangerous.'' His lips pursed. ''It is too bad he did not tell you about it, but I could help to soften the blow, should you need comfort.''

''You made a serious error if you thought my discovery of this child would entice me to your bed,'' she told Luna, her tone icy. ''Now I have little reason to *want* to find my husband.''

It wasn't true, of course, and Luna must have sensed it for he only laughed. ''Ah, but you will change your mind soon enough, Doña Genia, for being a woman, you will want to see his face when you tell him that you know, eh? Do not bother to deny it. I know the female mind well enough to suspect your purpose for being so angry and full of denials. Shall I tell you her name, perhaps, or do you wish to wait and ask your husband?''

Would putting a name to the betrayal really make it better? Or would it only engender more questions, more images of *her* with Steve? When Ginny hesitated, Luna smiled.

''Elizabeth Burneson. Her name was Cady when he knew her in New Mexico Territory. Now she is married, to a dull man who is most besotted with her, I am told, but then, he must be besotted to accept another man's child as his own.''

''Perhaps he is only noble, Señor Luna, something you would not understand.''

''Would I not? Ah, perhaps you are right. I am so often puzzled by such men. Or the women who live with them until the man they really want comes back—which is what happens quite frequently, I have observed. But that will not happen this time, I am sure, for your husband is loyal to you now, and the children you have. He confides in you, yes? You are very certain of his love and fidelity, or you would be most dubious as to his reasons for running off to New Mexico Territory under the pretense of seeing an old friend again. I believe that was the reason he used last time, when he met this Elizabeth Cady....''

''Oh, stop it. Don't you think me clever enough to see what you are trying to do? It won't work. Steve and I have been through too much to allow silly doubts to come between us now, and I refuse to allow *you,* Señor Luna, to create suspicions between us. I will ask Steve about it when I see him again. That brings me to another question. *When* will you tell me where he is?''

''Why do you think I would know where your husband is?''

''Because it would appeal to your sick, twisted sense of justice to find out, to withhold the information from me. If you did not know, you wouldn't be so certain I cannot find him.'' Anger and frustration sharpened her voice, made it rise as she said, ''For God's sake, *tell* me! Stop playing your sadistic little game! What do you hope to gain from it?''

''All. I intend to gain all,'' he said softly, and there was such a note of menace in his tone that she recoiled, a warning knell sounding in the back of her head. There was so much more to this than she had realized, but she could not allow him to guess her sudden fear.

''President Díaz himself has suggested that you do all in your power to find Steve, General. Would you deny him? After all, they are acquainted, as both used to fight for Juarez.''

''Yes, and you know how the friendship between Juarez and President Díaz ended, I presume. Have you thought, Doña Genia, that perhaps it is *el presidente* who wishes to remove men who may recall too much about his time with Juarez?''

''Don't be ridiculous!''

But was it so ridiculous? Since Díaz had come to power, he had systematically and ruthlessly removed all obstacles to his complete governance. Already, men who had once been outlaws were being installed at his direction in the new police force, given the power to decimate those bandits who had plagued Mexico for far too long. Even Juan Cortina—the scourge of Lerdo's office who had escaped prison and made a fool of *el presidente*—was being pursued again. Díaz did not wish trouble with the United States of course, and since Cortina had the rather embarrassing habit of conducting his cattle raids into Texas as well, Díaz must at least give the appearance of pursuit of the popular rebel leader.

Aware that Díaz was ruthless in his quest for absolute power, Ginny wondered uneasily if Luna might be right. If Steve knew too much about the new president, he could be viewed as an inconvenience best dealt with as unobtrusively as possible. His disappearance may well be beneficial, if a bit awkward to explain at first, as he was an ambassador.

Yes, she saw how it might be unpleasant for a new president to have an ambassador near at hand who reminded him of his former servitude to a man who had become his nemesis.

As if sensing her misgivings, Luna moved forward, his tone unctuous as he murmured, ''Now you are distressed, Señora Alvarado. How unfortunate.''

''Spare me your false sympathy.'' Ginny moved away from him, uncomfortable with his close proximity. He was always putting a hand on her somewhere, her arm or her shoulder, a hand at her waist to guide her forward—any excuse to touch her, and she disliked it.

''Stop hovering! You put me in mind of a buzzard, with the same hot gleam in your eyes as if you cannot wait to feast upon my flesh.''

''In a way,'' Luna said with a smile, ''that is very accurate. I would love to feast upon your beautiful flesh, taste your soft skin beneath my lips, run my tongue—''

''Enough!'' Ginny whirled to glare at him. ''You are entirely too bold. I insist you leave at once. What are you doing—''

''Taking what you offer with your eyes...your lips. Do you think I do not hear what you want me to hear? It is not what you say, but what you do not say that intrigues me most, *perdida.* Ah, did you think I do not know everything about you by now? I do. I have made it my business to find out.''

Ginny's muscles tensed as he held her arm tightly, his fingers squeezing cruelly. There was a frightening intensity to his grip and his words, and his dark eyes were almost black as he stared down at her. She forced her muscles to relax, and saw an almost imperceptible shift of his body as he reacted.

''My, my, General Luna, you are very *intense* tonight. Whatever has happened to unsettle you?'' Her head tilted slightly to one side and her mouth curved into a deliberately teasing smile as she lowered her lashes in a flirtatious glance sideways. ''Surely you are not going to let our difference of opinion matter? I have my opinion, and you have yours. It should not be allowed to come between us.''

As she talked, she leaned back so that her hip rested against the wall by the window. Light slanted through the open shutters, glinting in Luna's eyes and illuminating a faint scar that curved across one high cheekbone. A handsome man, admittedly, but cruel beneath his suave exterior. It was a perception she had learned far too well at the hands of men like Tom Beal, who had not had Luna's sophistication. There had been others, with all the surface veneer of wit, education, intelligence and sophistication, men who had been just as ruthless and brutish as Beal beneath the facade they showed the world.

Luna was one of them. She knew it, felt it in every fiber of her being.

Rafael Luna put his hand on her throat, forcing her chin up so that she had to look into his eyes, his fingers a light clasp that was vaguely threatening.

"I hope you are not planning anything foolish, *chica,* for it would make me very angry." His grasp tightened the smallest bit, restricting her breathing. "I am afraid that I would have to punish you were you to misbehave...."

A spurt of fear rendered her momentarily unable to do more than stare up at him, eyes wide and absorbing light from the windows so that she felt dazed, blinded by it. Her right arm dropped to one side, fingers curling into green silk like claws. The outline of the dagger hilt was buffered by her skirts. It fit snugly against her thigh. She touched it lightly for reassurance.

Luna's eyes narrowed fractionally. She forced herself to go still, returning his stare with what she hoped was a cool gaze.

"If you think you can intimidate me—"

"Ah, I know I can intimidate you, *chica.* But I wonder, has any man ever conquered you? This husband of yours, this Steve Morgan who is so competent, so fierce and noble that you love him so much, has *he* ever conquered you? Has he made you beg for him, made you yield all to him when you did not want to?"

"As a matter of fact, yes. You could not begin to understand what I feel for him. Do not even try."

"You think I do not know about love? I do. I have felt it myself. It burns like a fire inside, makes a man do things he should not. Is it that way for a woman, too? I think it is. And you, passionate little gypsy with the hair like flame and eyes so green, you would do whatever you must to have your man, would you not?"

"If you are asking me to go to bed with you to find out where my husband is, I have told you before that I refuse."

Ginny held his gaze. Her jaw tightened against the subtle pressure of his fingers cradling her throat, but she did not attempt to struggle or pull away. Defiance lit her eyes, and the cleft in her chin deepened as her mouth thinned to a taut line.

"Let go of me, General Luna. I would hate to have to explain to President Díaz how I got bruises on my face. And I must begin to get ready, for the ball at the palace is this evening and I haven't made proper arrangements."

Despite her bravado, a frisson of fear shivered down Ginny's spine. Luna only looked at her with a small smile on his mouth.

"I think that I am done with waiting, fiery one. If you please me well, perhaps I shall tell you what I have learned about this paragon of a husband of yours, eh?"

"And if I do not please you?" Her hand slid downward, crumpling silk beneath her fingers as she tugged her skirt upward. A seductive smile played upon her lips, and she gave the general a glance from beneath her lashes. "I am married, and have tried to be a faithful wife to my husband. You ask of me what I do not wish to give, General Luna. What if Steve should learn of our...liaison?"

He sucked in a sharp breath, and his clasp on her throat loosened as his palm slid down over the bare skin gleaming above her scooped bodice.

"It is not necessary that he know." Sharp sunlight reflected in his black eyes so that they gleamed like pieces of jet, a cold glitter warmed by desire. Boldly, he cupped her breast, and when Ginny did not move or offer a protest, he molded it into his palm, fingers stroking her. "Since seeing you in Ojinaga, dancing with all the abandon of a Spanish gypsy, I have dreamed of having you. You are like them, you know, the fiery ones who have such passion in their souls. Only one other woman has ever intrigued me as you have— *¡Te quiero mi alma!*"

She allowed him to press hot kisses over her face and throat, his hands working at the low scooped bodice of her gown, hard and demanding against her breasts. Stifling a shudder,

Ginny forced herself to relax, to lure him into heated complacence.

If only I can keep him busy until I have a chance to free the knife....

There was no question of yielding to him. Not even for Steve could she barter her body again. She had learned her lesson well. It was a sacrifice that Steve would not want from her, and when had it ever worked anyway? Men like Luna were without honor. He would tell her nothing once he had used her. Or worse, he would do as that fat Colonel Devereaux had done so long ago, trick her into giving him what he wanted in exchange for Steve's freedom, then refuse to honor their bargain. No, if she gave herself to a man, she had vowed that it would be because she wanted to, and for no other reason.

But now she had to play the part Luna expected of her, lure him into a sense of false security before she could use her knife.

"Wait," she murmured as he freed her breasts from their prison of silk and lace. "I must have your promise that you will tell me what I want to know."

"You want to know where your husband is? Ah, such a devoted little wife. How unexpected." His hands were large and dark against the milky skin of her breasts; her nipples were tight beads between his fingers. "Perhaps, my dove, if you please me well enough, I shall tell you everything."

Where was Artur? Carmen? Oh, if only someone would come to the door of the sitting room, interrupt them so that she could think. She *had* to think, to delay Luna until she could get away from him....

Luna continued to caress her, a teasing massage that made her shiver with revulsion. He laughed softly.

"I think you like that. You cannot deny your own nature after all, *mariposa*...exotic little butterfly. See? I can make you squirm, make you beg for me...no, do not back away. You will like how I make you feel, though you may pretend that you do not. Yes, close your eyes if you must, but do not run away, little one."

A feeling of panic engulfed her as he held her much too

tightly, his arm around her preventing her from reaching the knife strapped to her thigh. She remained calm with an effort.

"You are hurting me. Has no woman ever told you that you must pursue her with gentleness instead of pain?"

"But pain is part of pleasure, is it not? You know that, for you have experienced it. Did you not find it exciting? There is more pleasure to be found in passion if one is aware of the body's limits, and the delight in going beyond them."

"I do not equate pleasure and pain on the same level," she said sharply, and this time shoved hard at him with the heels of her hands. "If you persist, I will summon my servants to show you to the door."

"Ah, but your servants have gone for the day. I took the liberty of telling them that you wished to allow them to join the festival in the main plaza, and that they need not return until tomorrow. But you look so unhappy, my sweet. Are you not pleased?"

"You know I am not! How dare you take it upon yourself to direct my employees. Perhaps it is best if you leave, General Luna, for I find that I do not care at all to be in your company any longer."

He only smiled. Sunlight behind him created a hazy glow that left his face shadowed. Outside, she could hear the tolling of church bells, and the muted sounds of celebration that filled Mexico City. No one would hear her screams if she tried. She had only her wits and her weapon to keep him at bay.

Casually, as if it were his house, Luna strode across the sitting room to open the door to her bedroom beyond, then turned to look at her.

"We have the afternoon before us, *chica.* Come, let us begin to discuss our bargain."

Ginny remained by the window, turning now with her back to the light, angled so that Luna could not see her right hand. With her left, she tugged her bodice up over her bare breasts and said coolly, "I have changed my mind. A woman's prerogative. It is time for you to leave. I must begin to get ready for the ball tonight at the palace. President Díaz is expecting me. He'll be worried if I do not arrive on time, so don't think my absence will be unnoticed."

"The day belongs to us. *El presidente* does not expect you

until much later this evening. We are alone. I will wait no longer for you, for I have waited too long already.''

As he moved toward her, long swift strides that brought him to her in only a few steps, Ginny reached beneath her skirts and whipped out the wicked dagger. It briefly caught the light, a sharp glitter of warning, then sliced across Luna's arm as he reached out for her.

It brought him to a sudden halt, and he drew in a hiss of pain, staring in disbelief at the bloody gash opened in his sleeve and arm.

''Little bitch, do you think that will stop me!''

''It was not meant to stop you, only to warn you. I am not a novice with this knife, General, and you would do well to remember that should you try to come any closer.''

Anger glittered in black eyes, and his mouth twisted into a sneer. But he inclined his head in a surrender, and said harshly, ''I yield for the moment.''

Ginny did not relax her guard when he moved a step away from her and pulled off his coat to examine his arm. It oozed blood, dripping to the carpets on the tile floor, bright-red splashes that slowly diminished.

''You will forgive me, General, if I request that you tend your wound in your own home. Circumstances being what they are, I would be more comfortable if you left at once.''

''I am certain that you would.'' Luna slanted her a disdainful glance as he moved to the sideboard that held crystal decanters. ''But surely you will be civilized enough to allow me a drink before I leave?''

He poured a liberal amount of brandy into a small snifter and turned to face her, his white shirt stained with blood as he lifted his arm in a mocking salute.

''To a beautiful gypsy whore!''

Before she could anticipate it, he tossed the brandy into her eyes, temporarily blinding her as he leaped forward agilely. A crushing blow of his hand disarmed her, and she heard the knife clatter to the tile floor as Luna captured her arm.

''And now,'' he promised softly, ''I shall have to punish you for your insolence. But I think you may learn to like it before I am done.''

Half-blinded, struggling, Ginny screamed only once as he

dragged her across the sitting room toward the door of her bedroom. Outside there was too much noise, too many shouts and even fireworks to celebrate Don Porfirio's triumphant arrival. No one would hear her.

As if reading her mind, Rafael Luna said against her ear, "Scream if you like, *chica,* for no one will come. The celebrations will last for days, and so, perhaps, will you. Would it not be entertaining, to lie in your wide bed for the next few days and explore all the ways that pain can add to pleasure? Yes, I can see that you want it…fight me if you like, for then I will have the pleasure of subduing you…."

Ginny did fight, desperately, and with a savagery dredged from panic, but it did her no good. Luna countered her ineffectual blows with an openhanded viciousness that left her dazed, her mind reeling. She was only vaguely aware that he had stripped away her garments, leaving her only in a thin chemise that hid little of her body from his prying eyes.

And, humiliatingly, he tied her to the four posts of the bed, using silken drapery cords to bind her wrists and ankles, leaving her spread-eagled on the mattress.

Vulnerable, exposed to his lewd gaze, she lay helpless and waited for the inevitable. In a way, it was much worse than anything she had endured before, this waiting and knowing what was to come. She had seen men at their worst, and knew that Luna had waited too long for this moment.

Rafael Luna came to stand beside the bed, smiling down at her. "You are even more lovely than I had hoped. Such soft white skin…. I will make you ready, make you want me as I want you."

"You will *never* make me want you!"

"Little liar, I will soon prove to you the foolishness of your thinking. You will be surprised, I think, to find that your body responds to me whether you wish it to or not."

Straining futilely against her bonds, Ginny shuddered as his eyes narrowed at her, his expression intent as she raged at him.

"You'll never keep me! When Steve learns of this, you will wish you had not been so foolish."

"Pah! I have taken care of your estimable husband, and he will not be learning of this unless I tell him! Perhaps I will take you with me when I visit him, and he can watch while I take you. It would only be fair, as he once took a lady from me. Do you not think so, *chica?* He thought nothing of that, but I was in love with her. I swore vengeance upon Steve Morgan then, but I did not know it would be so sweet!''

''Is that all this is? Vengeance?'' She tried to turn her head to look at him, but he moved to stand slightly behind the bed, tightening her bonds. Silken cords dug painfully into the flesh of her wrists and ankles. ''Then you have risked much for vengeance, because Steve will kill you for this one day.''

''He will have to save himself first, and I do not think he will be able to do that.'' The palm of his hand came down in a caress, making her wince. ''But while he languishes in a dark prison, I will keep you with me. When we go to the palace to meet with *el presidente* tonight, you will be with me. All in Mexico City will know you are mine now....''

''I belong to myself, not to you, not even to my husband. You may use my body, but you cannot own my soul.''

Viciously, swearing at her, he loomed over her, but if he thought to break her, he was disappointed. Not even the humiliation of being at his mercy could do that.

She had endured worse than this before, and she would survive Rafael Luna as well.

30

Night fell at last, the time of the president's ball near. "Get up," Rafael told her harshly, and pulled her from the bed. "And get ready to present yourself to President Díaz. I will choose your gown. And if you should think to tell him that I am holding you against your will, you might recall that I am the only man who knows what happened to your husband. It would be such a pity for you if he were to languish forever in a dark prison cell, would it not? Or perhaps it would not be so terrible after all, for you could then be free to have many lovers."

Prison! Ginny stood silently as he untied the silken cords around her wrists, freeing her at last. She gasped as blood rushed back into abused flesh. Luna smiled cruelly.

"It will be said throughout Mexico City that you are my mistress. Do not disappoint those who want to see the famous Madame du Plessis, once a famous *cortesana* who has become an ambassador's wife—and who now belongs to me."

He made her wear a daring gown; the bodice was cut far too low, the boned corset pushing up her breasts to reveal the edges of her nipples.

"If it is your intention to have a prostitute on your arm today, you have succeeded admirably," Ginny said with angry dismay when she saw her reflection, "for I resemble nothing so much as a street whore!"

The gown, a copper silk shot with gold that turned different colors in the light, could have been beautiful, but it showed far too much of her, cut low in the back as well as the front, and worn off the shoulders. The skirts were slit, with gauzy petticoats beneath that were nearly transparent so that when she walked, the outline of her legs was clearly visible.

And instead of being coiled neatly atop her head, her hair was loose, a coppery cloud around her face, held back on the crown by exquisite Spanish combs. Only her jewelry was modest, a topaz necklace and matching earrings.

"I do not think President Díaz will appreciate my appearance at his palace," she murmured, and ignored him when Luna only laughed.

"Do not be so modest, *chica.* Every man there will notice you, and every man there will want you. Perhaps I will allow you to choose a lover to bring home with us tonight when the ball is over. Have you ever been with two men at the same time? Would you like that?"

"I would like to put a knife into your heart," she replied coolly, and reached for a silk shawl to pull around her shoulders. It was the only concession to modesty she was being allowed to take with her, and that only because the nights were chilly and they would not be back until well after dark.

It was near Christmas, and the air was crisp, the earth slowly baking under a warming sun during the day. People milled in the streets, and the mood of the city was festive now that the rebellion was ended and Díaz was in power.

"Like mindless cattle," Luna murmured as their carriage rolled through the street. "They do not care who leads them to the trough, only that there is a trough."

"Yet these *mindless cattle* are people with dreams, love and hope, Rafael. If they are forced to concessions to live, then they concede. That does not mean they are mindless."

"You are a strange kind of woman, *chica,* an aristocrat with the philosophy of a peasant."

"Perhaps because I am as they are," she replied, "at the mercy of ruthless men who care only for their own desires and not for what is just and fair."

"How noble. Did you learn that sentiment from your *Juarista* husband?"

"Don't sneer. Juarez was a good president."

"Juarez is dead. Díaz is now president. Will you say the same of him?"

"I suppose that depends on what he does as president." Ginny turned to face him, and said boldly, "You promised to tell me about Steve. I have done as you wished. When will you tell me where he is?"

"You will know soon enough. While you may prefer not to believe it, I am a man of my word." A strange smile played on his lips, and she narrowed her eyes at him.

"Damn you, if you intend to play some sort of trick on me. Do you even know where he is?"

"At the moment, I'm not at all certain. I do know where I left him, however. Ah, do not look so angry, *chica,* or I shall have to show you what happens to naughty girls. But if you behave, you will know very soon where your husband has been. Perhaps then you can ask him how the mother of his other son is doing, eh?" He laughed when she drew in a sharp breath of outrage, and reached out to stroke her. "How lovely you are when you are angry, my butterfly. I shall miss you when I have left Mexico."

"That will be very soon, I trust."

"My business here is almost done. It may be more swiftly than even you hope. Now come. Put on a pretty face, so that no one will know that you are not happy to be with me. Remember what happens when you are defiant."

She turned to gaze out the window. The streets were overflowing with people. With the lanterns lit it was beautiful, the plaza alight with laughter and music and celebration.

Would she have the opportunity to be alone with Díaz, to tell him Luna was holding her prisoner? If necessary, she would say it publicly, but she hoped that it would not come to that. It could be embarrassing for the president, as Luna was Adjutant General from Spain. There was always the chance her complaint would be treated lightly if she chose to make a public issue of it.

The palace rooms were crowded with guests, but few of them were familiar to Ginny. Her days here with Maximilian's court were so far in the past. All traces of the French occupation were nearly gone, but a faint poignant sadness still seemed to her to shroud the rooms.

There were whispers, some of recognition, others of shock when Ginny appeared on Luna's arm. She ignored them as she had once done. Her chin was held high, her gaze directed straight ahead. But inside, a curl of shame burned so hot and bright, that she was nearly nauseous with it. All that sustained her was the thought that perhaps she would escape from Luna before the night ended.

I will not go back to that house with him! He will have to drag me screaming down the street, and I don't think he is truly prepared to risk that. Surely, there is someone here who can help me?

But hope dwindled, for in the crush that thronged the rooms, she recognized no friendly faces, no one familiar enough that she would trust to ask for aid in escape. With her fingers lying lightly on Rafael's arm, she floated at his side like a bronze shadow with haunted eyes.

A huge topaz strung on a thin gold chain circled her neck. It nestled into the valley between her breasts, drawing the eyes of many men to the alluring shadow and high globes of flesh. But then, she would draw attention even without the necklace, and not just because of her daring attire.

Indeed, in such a huge crowd she might have gone almost unnoticed if she were not so striking. Lamplight glinted on her fiery hair with a rich golden sheen, and her pale skin gleamed with flawless, translucent beauty. Only when one drew close enough to see into her slanted green eyes, was it apparent that she was unhappy and desperate.

From across the room, she had an air of regal, aloof beauty. A tarnished rose, perhaps, with her shocking gown and low décolletage, but a rose of incomparable beauty, even in this sea of beautiful women.

Luna kept her close, his hands occasionally brushing casually against her breasts, a proprietary touch that did not escape notice. It branded her as loose, and the women present drew aside when she passed, as if afraid of contamination should she get too close.

Men noticed, eyes staring as he toyed with the edging of her low bodice, hopeful gazes waiting for it to fall away and expose her to their lecherous gazes. Ginny began to feel quite nauseous, and focused instead on the others in the huge room, so many there that it was difficult to see the walls opposite where they stood.

It was not as surprising as it might once have been to find a liberal sprinkling of Americans celebrating Díaz's ascent to the presidency, for Mexico's future was closely intertwined with that of the United States. New policies were crucial.

Still, as her gaze drifted around the room, it was a shock to Ginny to see Jim Bishop in attendance, and she had the inescapable feeling that Rafael Luna had known he would be there.

''Is this my answer?'' she murmured just before Bishop reached her side, and heard Luna laugh softly.

''General Luna,'' Bishop acknowledged with his usual imperturbable smile, ''and, of course, it is always pleasant to see you again, Mrs. Morgan. Or should I call you Señora Alvarado?''

Relief flooded her, and she was almost giddy with it as she greeted Bishop, edging away from Luna, who let her go without a murmur. There was a slightly hysterical edge to her laughter as she said, ''Mr. Bishop! Perhaps I should not be so surprised to see you here, but I am. You have met General Luna, I see, and you must know President Díaz. Why, it sounds as if I'm babbling, when I am only glad to see you again....''

''May I speak with you privately? I am certain that the general will not mind, will you?''

Jim Bishop gave her his colorless smile, nodded to Rafael Luna and steered Ginny to an alcove half-hidden by a huge potted palm.

''I am glad to see you safe,'' he said before she could speak, "for everyone has been worried about you. You are well, are you not?"

"No, but now is not the time or the place to confide to you all the details, except that you must rescue me from Rafael Luna!"

"Yes, I rather thought you looked unhappy." He gave a discreet cough. "It was reported that you were in his company willingly. I had to be certain, you understand. You'll not have to go with him, I'll see to it."

Ginny grasped his arm, her tone urgent. "Steve is in a prison somewhere! You must find him. General Luna may know where he is. Oh, you have to find him, Mr. Bishop, before Luna gets to him. He hates Steve, and wants to kill him!"

"I don't think we'll have to worry about that. No, don't look at me that way, and please, if you will, keep your voice down. It has come to my attention that Steve has already freed himself, and should soon be in Mexico City."

Her knees began to quiver, and the hand she had put on his arm trembled as she said, "He is safe?"

"As safe as a man like him can ever be."

"Why, Mr. Bishop, is that humor I hear?" She smiled, nearly giddy with relief. A trace of a smile touched Bishop's thin lips, slightly warming his gray eyes as he regarded her.

"That is a most *interesting* gown, Mrs. Morgan."

"Yes." The swift glance she shot Luna was filled with loathing. "It was *suggested* I wear it this evening."

Bishop merely nodded, not asking any embarrassing questions, and Ginny wondered if he had known about Luna all along. It would be just like him, to wait until the time was convenient for his own plans before he interfered!

"I think it would be wise if you were to leave very soon," Bishop said. "I will have one of my most trusted men escort you home."

"Oh, yes, I would like to leave as soon as possible," she said in a low voice, "but there is the matter of General Luna.... If he decides that I cannot, he is not above creating an embarrassing scene and making trouble."

"I will see to all the details, and deal with General Luna myself—unless it becomes unnecessary." Bishop's attention was suddenly directed over her shoulder, and she knew him well enough now to recognize his abruptly altered tone as a clear sign of perturbation.

Ginny, half-afraid that Rafael had come up behind her, set her chin in a defiant slant and turned, steeling herself for a public confrontation that would only be humiliating. It was the final degradation, but it would be behind her and she would be free of him!

Luna stood behind her, elegant and saturnine, his handsome face a mask to hide his cruelty. But he was not facing her and Bishop, his back turned to them as he looked toward the front of the room. His frame vibrated with an intensity that was so thick it was almost palpable. She recoiled slightly, fear coursing through her veins though she knew he could not hurt her here, not in front of Bishop and the crowded palace.

Yet her heart pounded painfully against her rib cage, and she felt Bishop stiffen beside her as Luna took a step to one side, his hand sliding beneath the edge of his black coat as if to draw a weapon. Ginny had the wild thought that Luna meant to force her to go with him after all, that she would not escape him...

"No!" she hissed between her teeth, and felt rather than saw Bishop's swift glance at her. "I will *not* allow him to take me again!"

The walls seemed to shrink around her and the world closed in. The cacophony of noise escalated and receded in a blur of indecipherable noise and words so that she was only vaguely aware of Bishop reaching out for her, of his restraining hand on her arm. She shook it off, the urge to flee so strong and intense that she felt like a wild animal backed into a cage. Ginny moved swiftly to one side.

"Señora Alvarado," Bishop said in a warning tone, and she gave him a blindly panicked glance. His eyes were colorless, his tone unruffled, but the warning punctured her brief panic and she paused.

And then, somehow, she knew. Steve Morgan was there in the president's palace.

31

It was, Steve thought with a trace of irony, a reminder of all the other times he'd found his wife on the arm of another man. But that she was here tonight with Rafael Luna was infuriating—and dangerous. *Damn Ginny!*

When he arrived, he had seen them across the room, a group of men leering at Ginny while Luna caressed her. She had not seemed to mind, but stood docilely under his touch as if slightly bored, like a jaded Jezebel. It should have reassured him, but somehow it hadn't. Like a cat, she always seemed to land on her feet. Didn't he know that?

He had gone through three horses to get from the mine to Mexico City, riding as fast as he could, certain Ginny was in danger. Now he found her at a dress ball for the new president, wearing a smile and drinking champagne. He had thought… Ah, hell, it didn't matter what he'd thought.

He was here, and Luna was here, and there was other business to settle now that he knew Ginny was safe. The Spaniard was staring at him with satisfaction gleaming in his black eyes, a faint, smug smile touching the corners of his mouth. Steve didn't even glance at Ginny.

"You're just where I thought you'd be, General Luna. Still stirring up trouble, or did you come to Mexico to line your own pockets?"

Bishop didn't move from Ginny's side, but murmured that

it was not the time or place to settle old scores. Steve ignored him.

Rafael Luna merely smiled coldly, regarding him with a triumphant smirk. "You remember me now, I see."

"I remember you well enough. It's been a long time since Milan, when I had to remove you forcibly from Francesca's dressing room."

A small space had cleared out between them, men and women scattering as the two faced each other. Tension vibrated in the air. Rafael Luna's eyes had narrowed, and his mouth twisted into a smile that was more of a snarl.

"It was not your place to *remove* me from her dressing room or anywhere else. You took advantage of my inattention at the moment."

Steve allowed a slow smile to touch the corners of his mouth. "You were cowardly enough to run, as I remember it."

Luna went rigid; his arms fell to his sides, hands curling and uncurling, fingers flexing as if he held a weapon, but he only bowed slightly from the waist.

"As crude as usual, I see. I demand satisfaction for your insult."

"Name the time and place."

"Tonight!" Luna fixed him with a fierce stare, and a strange light glittered in his eyes. "So that your lovely wife will be a widow. Not that it matters so much to her, I believe, as she has spent some time in my *company* of late. A most lovely and compliant companion."

Slow rage gathered at the back of his throat and behind his eyes, but Steve allowed nothing to show in his face or in his tone. His brown face was as impassive as an Indian's, but his cold implacable stare conveyed a ferocity and danger that penetrated even to Rafael Luna, who betrayed himself with a swift, faint flicker of uncertainty shadowing his eyes. It was the first sign of weakness, a chink in the armor Luna had erected.

"You know why I've come, Luna. And it has nothing to do with my wife."

How many times had he faced a man intent upon killing him? Across a dusty street or a marble floor, it was always the same. The man who allowed emotion to weaken his reflexes ended up making new dust. Not even the sight of Ginny—with her green eyes all wide and glazed, her breasts almost bare in that damned gown and her lips wet and parted—not even that would distract him.

''What is this in my palace?'' The commanding voice cut through the crowd as if a hot knife through butter, parting them to make a path as Presidente Porfirio Díaz strode to the two men. ''A quarrel? Between my Spanish envoy and my so excellent ambassador? This will not do, gentlemen, for we must not start my term off with violence. It has been too long since we have had peace in Mexico, and there should be peace now.''

A murmur ran through the crowd, approving but with an undercurrent of excitement and disappointment that the show had been momentarily quelled. Still wary, his muscles tense with the need for violence, for vengeance against the man who had sent him once more to the hell of the mines while he toyed with his wife, Steve managed a courteous nod.

''It will be as you wish it, of course, Your Excellency.''

Díaz smiled. ''We have been comrades in arms for far too long for me to believe that you will submit so meekly, Esteban, but I will accept your promise that you will not fight with General Luna here or today, eh? Now come, where is your beautiful wife? She has not come to see me as she promised me she would. I hope that she is feeling much better now that her illness has passed. Is she here with you?''

Steve's jaw set. Ginny, trembling visibly, gave him a beseeching glance as she stepped forward when he didn't reply to the president's query.

''I—I am here, Your Excellency. Many pardons for my absence of late. As you mentioned I have been—indisposed.''

''Of course, of course. Now that you are once more well and we are all in a better mood, we shall celebrate! General Luna, do not be so distant. Come. Tell me news of Spain.''

Though he seemed congenial enough, there was a steely

undercurrent to his tone that left no room for dissent. Luna bent an ironic bow in Steve's direction, swept Ginny with a glance and accompanied Díaz as he moved away.

Ginny. She didn't move but stood there watching him, slanted green eyes slightly wary. The seductive gown clung to her body, skirts parting with her movements to give a glimpse of her legs. It was a *cortesana*'s gown.

The tension that had gripped Steve for the past hundred miles was slow to ease. His muscles were taut, his nerves and temper on edge. Ginny was alive, unharmed, staring at him with brimming eyes, but all he could think at the moment was that he was too tired to give her the explanations that she deserved. Not now. There would be time enough later.

With only a slight bow from the waist, he gave his wife a parting smile, pivoted on his heel and left the palace. Bishop could explain it all to her. It was his game. Let him field her questions for a change.

I need a bath and a drink, not necessarily in that order, Steve thought grimly, and was quickly lost in the crowd filling the plaza.

32

Lanterns bobbed erratic light over the streets of Mexico City. Ginny stared blindly out the carriage windows, not seeing them as she was escorted home.

Steve…oh, God! Had that been contempt in his eyes? His deliberate dismissal of her was as scorching as the flush that heated her face when he'd raked his gaze over her with studied precision. He could at least have stayed long enough to hear her explanation! Damn him…and damn Rafael Luna!

By the time the carriage rolled to a halt before the shallow steps of the rented house, she had made up her mind what she would do next. Her escort, Butch Casey, was as taciturn as he had been the first time she'd met him, and coolly polite as he handed her from the carriage.

"You will remain as a guard, as Mr. Bishop asked?" She was loath to go inside, the memories of the past brutal hours still sharp and painful. She caught and held Casey's gaze. "If— I want to be certain that I am not bothered by anyone."

"I have my orders, ma'am, and you won't be bothered by anyone you don't want to bother you."

Was that a trace of contempt in his voice? But of course, it was ridiculous to expect respect when she was wearing a gown that left her almost naked. Casey's cool blue eyes reminded her somehow of Steve, perhaps because there had been the same icy regard in his gaze.

Oh God, he hates me. It's all for nothing now, the closeness we shared…but at least I'm free of Rafael Luna! Steve will listen. I'll explain it all to him tomorrow.

Carmen met her on the landing, fussing over her with soothing hands, her chatter a steady stream that required no thought and no reply.

"Ah, *señora!* I have been so worried.… That horrid man, he sent Artur away and I was so worried about you. I do not like that arrogant Spaniard. But you are well, and I am so relieved. Here, I will untie your laces for you, though they are already loose enough. And this gown—it is lovely, but so thin, so daring…"

Ginny sank down into the high-backed copper tub, the water fragrant with oil of roses and a hint of musk, the scent filling her nose, the steamy waves of heat curling around her in a comforting shroud. A fat sponge floated in the water, and she scrubbed herself with it, raking it over her arms, legs, breasts and belly as if trying to scrape away the residue of the past hours, rubbing until her skin was bright pink and almost raw.

"More hot water, Carmen," she demanded when it grew cool, suddenly seized with the urgent need to wash away all traces of Rafael Luna, of her humiliation and anguish. She washed until Carmen protested that she could not bring any more hot water up the narrow stairs for her bath.

"There is no more water in the cistern, *señora,* and no doubt in the entire city after tonight!"

Worry creased the maid's face, and she stood wringing her hands, anxious that her *señora* was so perturbed.

"It's hot enough, Carmen, *gracias.* Lay out my dressing gown, and I will get out of the tub in a moment."

Ginny closed her eyes and lay her head back against the edge of the tub, her skin tingling all over from the harsh abrasion of the sponge. Why did things always go awry? Was she ever to know peace? Ever to feel safe?

And Steve— *Oh, I wish he had killed Rafael Luna!* A feeling of nausea washed over her, tinged with regret, with a suddenly fierce yearning to find Steve and tell him that she loved him, that it had not been what he might think.

Why did I just stand there and let him walk away? Why didn't I follow him, make *him listen to me? Just* once *I would like for him to believe in me without having to defend myself!*

Damn him. It wasn't as if he were so very innocent, after all, was it? No, there was Francesca, the woman whom Luna loved so much he was willing to destroy the wife of the man who had taken her from him—and there was Elizabeth Cady.

Elizabeth Cady...

What did she look like? Did she still love Steve? Had he left her behind as he had so many others, without a promise, only a careless farewell, or perhaps the gift of a dress or some trinket...?

Anger began to replace the heartache, a slow fire igniting, the embers fanned to a steady flame.

I might as well know everything about him.

Why should she not? He knew everything about her—and what he didn't know, he could certainly guess. *God, the look in his eyes when he saw me standing there, that horrible Luna with his hands on me like that. What does he think of me now!*

Ginny allowed Carmen to towel dry her hair, then brush it until it glowed with burnished light in the soft gloom of the wall lamps. Seated at the small marble-and-ivory inlaid dressing table, Ginny sipped from the cup of cocoa the maid had brewed for her, finally relaxing under Carmen's anxious ministrations.

"You must sleep well tonight, *señora,* for if you do not, you may become ill again. I will keep watch over you, and that so fierce *hombre* at the door, he will guard your rest. I have changed the sheets on your bed. No one will disturb you."

"I will not sleep in that bed," she said abruptly. The thought of it made her ill, reminded her too vividly of Rafael Luna. She met Carmen's startled gaze in the mirror. "I would like to sleep on the settee in here. It's quite comfortable."

"Sí," Carmen murmured, but it was plain that she was bewildered. Still, she dutifully tucked sheets that smelled of lavender atop the cushions of the settee, along with a plump pillow and a light coverlet.

With the drapes drawn and windows closed against the muted sound of revelry in the streets, Ginny stretched out on the comfortable cushions.

It was, she thought as a luxurious languor began to seep through her body, a relief to feel safe again, if only for a single night.

33

It was nearly dawn. Pale light streaked the eastern sky, tingeing mountain peaks a hazy gold. Steve sat in a *cantina* near the plaza. He'd been there most of the night, nursing a drink.

Paco found him still sober, his mood foul.

"You are about to be even more unhappy, *amigo,* when I tell you what has happened to your wife." Paco didn't bother to sit down, but stood watching Steve closely. It was no surprise, the way things stood between Steve and Ginny, but he had learned to be wary and not to get involved. It was much safer that way, for him, at least. *¡Dios!* but matters got complicated quickly, and it always seemed that he was the one to have to tell Steve...

"What has she done now?" Steve drawled, sitting back in his chair to look up at Paco with a cold gaze. "Danced with veils for Díaz? It wouldn't surprise me."

"It seems that General Luna has taken her. Tige found Butch Casey nearly dead, his throat slit, though he is still alive. Missed the jugular, but just barely. Ginny is gone."

"Christ!" The chair was pushed back so quickly it fell to the hard-packed dirt floor with a crash as Steve stood up and reached for his rifle. "Which way did he take her?"

"No one is certain, but it looks like they headed north toward Chihuahua. If what you told me is true about Luna and Senator Brandon, you can guess where they're going and why."

"Hell, yes. The Galena."

The sun was well over the mountain ridges by the time they rode north out of Mexico City. Paco was quiet for a while, reading his partner's mood from long experience. Ever since he'd met Ginny Brandon, Steve Morgan had changed. He'd always been a man who attracted women, but he could take them or leave them, when and how he pleased. Only with Ginny things had been different.

In a way, Paco understood. There was a fiery quality to her that matched Steve's stubborn nature, even conquered him at times. He'd seen him do things for Ginny that once he would have sworn Steve Morgan would never do for anyone, man or woman.

But for Ginny, he had. He'd turned himself in to the French for her—and nearly died for it. Flogged to within an inch of his life, then relegated to the mines to die a slow, anonymous death, he had still survived it.

It hadn't been easy for Ginny, either. Not in those tempestuous times when *Juaristas* were still fighting the French, and Mexico seethed with revolution. Betrayed and taken hostage, she had suffered terribly. It was a miracle they had both survived.

Steve reined his mount to a halt in the shadow beneath a rocky overhang that jutted beside the trail, and pulled the cork on his water pouch, squirting a stream into his mouth before he offered it to Paco. It was quiet, the only sound the wind and muted clink of curb chains and creaking saddle leather. The smell of baking rock thickened the air.

"Bishop doesn't like this." Paco handed him back the water pouch, his eyes thinned against the glare of the sun beating down and warming the damp earth. "He seems to think this could endanger the shaky relationship between the United States and Spain, for some reason."

"I don't think Luna has that kind of influence, though he'd like to pretend he does."

"How does he figure in all this? Luna, I mean. What does he have to gain by taking Ginny?"

"Revenge. Guess you'd call it that." Steve shrugged. "I

met him a long time ago in Italy, when I was there with 'Cesca. Luna fell for her in a big way. She was mad at me, decided that I needed to be taught a lesson, but Luna took her flirtation seriously. He viewed me as a rival for her affections. When he became too insistent and a problem for her, I had to convince him she didn't want to see him again."

"So now he is taking your woman as revenge?"

"Ginny wouldn't go with him willingly."

Paco hesitated. "Bishop said she had met him before, in Ojinaga."

"How would he know that?" Astounded, Steve swore under his breath. "Damn Bishop, if he knew all the time that Luna meant to use her to get at Brandon— Where is he?"

Paco cleared his throat. "I believe he is on his way to San Antonio. He said you would know what to do."

Steve swore again, long and feelingly, angry that he had not been warned about Luna a month ago. "If Rafael Luna harms one hair on her head, I won't give a damn about diplomatic relations with Spain."

Time had not improved the road between Mexico City and Zacatecas. The beaten-down ribbon of dirt snaked through San Luis Potosí and Salinas and up to the province of Zacatecas. If Luna had gone that way, it was possible Steve could head them off. He knew the land like the back of his hand, had been exploring the *arroyos* and flat-topped ridges since he was a boy.

Steve let his horse set the pace. It would be a grueling ride, and he was pretty sure he knew where Luna was headed. It was unlikely he would do anything to Ginny until he reached his destination. He'd be too pressed for time, knowing that he was pursued.

Green-eyed gypsy—his love, his life. It had all been a mirage, an illusion...his assumption that he could keep her safe from harm a dangerous fiction. He'd failed her, and he had failed himself. It made him nauseous, reminded him that he couldn't control everything, that there were times he'd lose. It was humiliating and humbling. It was frightening.

How could he face her again, with the knowledge of his

failure between them? Christ, he'd chased her across half of Mexico and even the world at times, angry with her, too damn stubborn to admit even to himself that he loved her. But he had never once considered that he might lose her with his arrogance.

He remembered Concepción's wailing lament so long ago when he had ridden after Ginny, a futile noble gesture to save Ginny. *''He goes for her, that green-eyed woman.''*

It seemed that he was always going after Ginny, always trying to catch her.

Would he never learn to hold her tightly?

34

It was cold that high up in the mountains, and Ginny shivered beneath the thin blanket draped over her shoulders. Rafael Luna seemed quite comfortable, even lighthearted as he sat by a fire built under an overhang of rock.

"As a soldier, I learned survival in any situation, *chica,* so do not worry that I cannot properly care for you out here. Of course I can. It is not so bad, eh? We will be at the end of our journey soon enough, once I am certain we are being followed."

"You *want* us to be followed?"

Luna chuckled. "But of course! Why do you think I brought you with me? It would do me no good to leave on my own, for then, it may well be thought of as good riddance. But with you, my lovely *puta,* I am assured that I will have what I want soon enough."

"I don't understand." Ginny stared at him in the faint flickering light of the fire; Luna was stretched out, his long legs crossed negligently at the ankles, and the tip of a cigar glowed bright red in the night air. "Why go to all this trouble?"

"I have my reasons. But you look so sad, *pequeña.* What is the matter? Are you afraid I will hurt your husband?"

"Hardly," she said in a cutting tone that made his eyes narrow. "Steve Morgan will slice you to ribbons and filet your heart before you have the chance to move. Don't make the mistake of underestimating him. It could be fatal for you."

"And so you warn me. Is it possible you have developed a little softness for me? Ah, I see you glaring at me as if I insulted you. But it is true, is it not? I know women like you. You have the nature of a true whore, passionate and fiery."

Refusing to allow herself to be goaded, Ginny looked away from him; stunted trees were misshapen silhouettes against the night sky, assuming fantastical shapes that made her think of monsters, the stuff of nightmares. But it was the real nightmares that were so dangerous, the men like Rafael Luna.

Within three days, they were high in the mountains of Durango. They had ridden through Zacatecas, as familiar to Ginny as her own face in the mirror. Was Steve following them? Oh God, did he even *know* that she'd been taken hostage by this madman?

By now, surely he should have overtaken them. But what if he wasn't coming? Doubts tormented her, and even when they stopped in a small village *posada* for the night, with a bed and decent food, she was tense and on edge. It didn't help that she was sick, wracked in turn by fever and chills. She tried to ignore it. Her very survival depended upon concentration.

"Where are we?" she asked, and he surprised her by answering.

"Not far from Parral. Ah, you know it?"

She nodded. "Yes. I went there once, several years ago, when it was occupied by the French. Where are we going?"

"That depends on how swift your husband is. If all goes as I plan, this humble abode may be our final destination."

When she stared at him, he laughed. "You may soon have a chance to see your husband alive. Are you getting anxious? Perhaps he will be so obliging as to reach us tonight. If not...there is tomorrow night. But he will come. I have made certain of that."

A chill went down her spine at the malevolence in his tone, and she prayed for rescue. Oh, what was taking Steve so long? He *would* come, wouldn't he? Did he suspect that Luna planned an ambush for him? Surely he must realize that the Spaniard was consumed with jealousy, deranged enough to go to elaborate lengths just for vengeance. Oh God, if only she could get a message to Steve!

Luna brought a bottle of wine to the dingy room in the cheap *posada,* and with a faint, sneering smile, set it on the scarred table beneath the window.

"Tonight, *chica,* we shall celebrate."

"I'm in no mood for a celebration," Ginny said tartly.

Luna crossed the room to where she was tied to the bed—his first action upon bringing her inside—and squeezed her chin painfully between his fingers.

"But I am in a mood to celebrate, so you will humor me. Ah, if your eyes were daggers, I would be pierced to the heart! Such lovely eyes, so green...and your mouth—it has been too long since I have enjoyed you. Are you feeling lonely or abandoned? I will rectify that soon, I promise, my sweet. Before this is over, we will enjoy each other. I know how you wait for it, and how you long for me."

Ginny shuddered and he laughed, then flicked his fingers against her cheek before he sat back. He used her small dagger to slice the leather straps tying her to the bed, then stabbed it into the wall, as if to offer her a challenge. The hilt quivered slightly as Ginny glanced at it, temptation casting a shadow against the cracked surface.

"Do you wish to use it on me, *puta?*" His laugh was soft. "Do you recall what happened the last time you tried to do such a thing?"

A shudder went through her, and she nodded silently.

"I thought you might. If you wish, I shall leave it there, and if you try it again, I will know that you truly appreciate the punishment you receive when you disobey me."

His hand moved over her face, long brown fingers a dark sacrilege against her pale, gleaming skin. Finally, with a laugh that told her he knew she was too frightened to attempt escape or resistance again, he rose and went back to the table.

A lamp burned with a steady, subdued glow, casting pools of rosy light and wavering shadows. The room was surprisingly large. Through the open window she could hear a dog bark, and far away, the plaintive sounds of a guitar.

Ginny lay supine upon the bed, marshalling the ebbing reserves of her strength as the fever rose higher, blurring her vision and nibbling at the edges of consciousness. It was no time to be sick! Oh God, if only she could hold on long enough for Steve to come. She'd be of no help to him if she was incoherent with a raging fever.

''I wanted you,'' Luna said suddenly, walking back to the bed, ''from that night in Ojinaga. You intrigued me, with your sultry beauty and the way you danced—like a Spanish gypsy. Such abandon, such fluid grace. I realized then what I had to do, how to set a trap for Steve Morgan. I did not think I would find his wife so lovely, so tempting. But you are accustomed to the admiration of a man. Of many men. Oh, yes, I saw your true nature in your eyes that night. You expect men to want you, to fall under your spell.''

Reaching out, he slid his hand over her face, then the arch of her throat, his fingers a light caress that made her shudder. Luna laughed at her reaction.

''How many times have you traded your body for favors? I am just one more man to use what you offer.''

''I never offered you anything!'' Ginny glared at him. ''I detest you. I find you repulsive!''

''Perhaps. But that is of no consequence. You are just an instrument to me, a method of gaining what I want.'' He stood up, stared down at her a long moment, his dark eyes glittering in the gloomy shadows. ''I have a special fate in mind for your husband, *chica.* This time, he shall see how it feels to watch another man take what is his—to spoil it, to desecrate that which he holds sacred. It shall give me great satisfaction to watch him suffer the same torment he gave to me.''

''Francesca di Paoli is hardly worthy of such devotion,'' Ginny said calmly. ''She is much more of a whore than you think me. She pursues married men—''

''Enough!'' Luna slapped her, a vicious blow that stung her cheek and caused lights to explode in front of her eyes. As if from a distance, Ginny heard him say, ''Never speak ill of such perfection, such talent! She is blameless, a victim of

Steve Morgan's careless attention. He abandoned her, and now will die for it."

His words came in overlapping waves, descending through a dark haze of sound and the roaring in her ears, but Ginny could perceive that Luna's determination to avenge the Italian diva was as warped as he was.

Crouching down beside her again, Luna grasped her chin between his thumb and fingers, a brutal hold as he turned her to face him. Dazedly, Ginny focused on his mouth, watched his lips form words that struck terror into her heart.

"When Steve Morgan arrives to rescue you—he will be surrounded by Rurales. Then he will watch while I strip you of your garments and give you to them. There are only a dozen, but they are very eager to taste your charms, *chica.* These Rurales once rode with Juan Cortina, who was called an outlaw and persecuted by gringo Texans like your husband. They will be quite happy to avenge Cortina."

The fever made her shudder. Luna watched her with a faint smile, his eyes narrowing at her reaction.

"It is warm in here, is it not, *chica?* I can see you are too hot. Would you like to take off your *camisa?* It is just us, and I have already seen your beautiful body. No, do not protest, I will help you, eh?"

Ginny resisted, but it was a futile effort; Luna easily combated her attempts to kick him. She was at his mercy as he undressed her, leaving her in only the thin silk shift she had been wearing the night of the ball. Asleep on the settee, clad only in her dressing gown, she had been awakened by Luna sometime in the middle of the night. He had given her no time to dress, to do no more than snatch up a garment from the back of a chair before he had dragged her from the house. In the murky light, the shift had been all she saw.

Luna was laughing, his dark eyes filled with a kind of grim satisfaction as he perused her.

"You are so lovely, little Ginette, so very lovely. I am almost sorry I must do this to you, but it is necessary. I wonder what it might have been like if I had met you first, before even the lovely Francesca? But I shall never know, shall I. No! And it would never be enough to have you now, for you will never truly be mine. A curious thing, but I find I am not content with just your body. I must have the woman's heart as well, must have her love and loyalty or it means nothing to me."

"What—" She licked dry lips, her chest heaving as she panted for air to fill her lungs. "What are you going to do to Steve?"

"Kill him. But only after he had watched you share your lovely body with the Rurales, of course. And perhaps even me, though that is not necessary. I made certain he knows that I have already tasted your charms. What a charade that was, parading you before all of Mexico City, rubbing Steve Morgan's nose in the fact that you were mine, just as he flaunted his affair with Francesca before me."

"No, no...." Her moan was soft and low, and she shuddered again as the horror of her situation was made so clear. At the back of her mind, she had suspected what he planned, but now she knew he would kill Steve.

The music had drawn closer, the guitars louder now, a sobbing, plaintive melody that was familiar. Ginny was pulled from the bed, her mind screaming rebellion but her body refusing to obey her commands to flee, to resist. Luna caressed her a few moments, laughing softly when she strained away from him, too weak with the encroaching fever to fully resist.

"Do you hear the men outside? They wait for you. They are so impatient to see the beautiful *gringa* that I promised them as a reward for their vigilance. Perhaps it is not fair to make them wait.... Shall I let them preview what it is they will fight for tonight?"

She felt so hot, her vision blurred and her tongue thick with fever; her throat ached as she forced words past parched, dry lips.

"Rafael, no...please...I'll stay with you if you forget about Steve. Let him go."

"Why should I? I have already had you, and could keep you even if you don't agree to stay with me. No, I have waited too long to avenge Francesca. Nothing must go wrong tonight."

Holding her by one arm, he moved to the door and swung it open. Ginny saw a dozen uniformed men waiting in the lantern-washed courtyard outside the door. They snapped to attention when Luna said, "As I promised you, here she is, the most famous *cortesana* in all of Mexico!"

Hoarse murmurs of lust and admiration filled the air, and one of the men, bolder than the rest, stepped forward. His black eyes were hot, probing, as he said, "We will have her now."

"Not yet, my eager *compadre.* Not yet. There will be plenty of time later. First, I am paying you to do a job. You know what you must do, and you will remain in the shadows until it is time. But if you would like to see your reward, I shall allow you just a small sample...."

Pulling Ginny in front of him, her back pressed against his chest, Luna curled one arm across her throat to hold her, and slowly began to pull up the silk shift. It rose higher and higher, a thin wisp of material that bunched in his fist as he slid it above her knees, up to her thighs.

"Higher!" came the hoarse demand. Luna laughed.

"Do you wish to see all her treasures at once? She is as beautiful as I told you, is she not?"

She felt their eyes on her, greedy and hot. Relief washed over her as she heard Luna deny permission for them to touch her, and she strained against his grip.

"Be still, or I shall give you to them now, *chica.* Are you tired of waiting? Shall I let them have you? Look at them, so eager to stroke your soft flesh.... Yes, you may have her later. She is most impatient for you."

Nothing could erase the shame she felt at being so exposed. She closed her eyes, forcing herself to remain still when all her instincts urged rebellion and flight.

One of the men laughed. "*Ay di mi!* she is a hot one, this! She will be mine first, for I won the toss. And I shall use her well, the famous Madame du Plessis! She is not so noble now, eh? Yes, I used to see her ride by with Colonel Lopez, her skin so white and pure, but her eyes! *Ay!* I knew she was only a *puta.*"

"And tonight," Luna promised, "she will be yours. He will be coming after her, so prepare for him. You have your orders. Remember the prize that waits for you."

Reluctantly, the men retreated as he took her back inside and shut the door. When he released her, she stood trembling until he put his hand beneath her chin and lifted her face to his.

"Are you afraid? But it will not be the first time you have been shared with so many. Yes, I know it all, as I told you. I have my methods of gaining information, and you would be most surprised by the things I know. Your father is an interesting subject as well, and your stepmother— She was once your husband's mistress, but you know that."

Ginny closed her eyes, shutting out the sight of his leering face. He continued to taunt her, telling her things about her past that she had tried to forget, about Ivan, and even Andre Delery.

"I would think you would be relieved to have your husband meet his fate at last, *chica.* He has been most cruel to you."

"Please..." she heard herself whimper in a desperate plea. "Please...no...I'll stay with you if you let Steve go...."

She stood panting, wracked with fear for herself and for Steve, her hair a wild tumble about her face and shoulders. A damp sheen misted her bare arms and legs, gleaming in the light of the lanterns as Luna moved to the table to pour more wine in a cup. Then he came back to stand before her. His breath was ripe with the smell of the red wine he'd been drinking.

"Little *puta,*" he said softly, "do you want me?"

"No...no!" It was a breathless moan, ripped from her throat despite her efforts. She wanted to scream at him, to strike out, but knew it would be futile. She had to remain calm; how else could she warn Steve?

Revulsion rippled through her when he dragged his hand across her face, moving lower, fingers grazing her throat in silent intimidation.

"But you will tell me that you want me, *puta*...loudly! If

you want to save your husband, you will do what I tell you to do."

She knew with a dim part of her barely conscious mind that she was saying what he wanted her to say, parroting the words he had whispered to her, hating him but compelled to obey in the hopes that she could stall for enough time to warn Steve of his danger.

Then Luna's hand clamped down on her shoulder, pushing her down until her knees struck the hard floor. Her heart pounded furiously and there was a ringing in her ears like fire bells.

Kneeling on the rough floor, her knees pressed against hard planks, she curled her fingers into her palms until the nails dug half-moons into her skin.

"Perhaps," he said, his voice penetrating the thick mist of her fear, "you need some wine to cool you off."

Ginny tried to twist away, but he forced her to drink some of the wine. It splashed over her white silk shift, over her ribs and belly, and onto her thighs. She swallowed some, choking on it before he took away the bottle. A coughing spasm wracked her. In a moment he came back to her and knelt in front of her, his hand bringing her chin up so that she had to face him.

"Now, perhaps you will be more agreeable, *chica.*"

Ginny swung a hand at him. He grasped her wrist, bending her arm backward, and laughed at her gasp of pain. She was pulled swiftly to her feet, falling forward into his arms.

He held her hard against his chest, ignoring her struggle to free herself as he laughed softly. "Ah, it is time, I think, for it to begin...."

It was then that Ginny heard the door slam open and heard Steve Morgan say, "Let go of my wife."

35

It was all a horrible blur after that. Later, she would vaguely recall watching in numb, silent horror as Steve and Rafael fought, viciously, with a savagery that held her unwilling gaze.

Rafael Luna had planned well. With the *Rurales* he had hired posted just outside the door, Steve Morgan had walked into a trap, and Luna smiled triumphantly.

"It is customary for you to choose the weapons, I admit, but time has not permitted me to be so generous. You will pardon me for the breach of etiquette, Morgan, but I have taken the liberty of providing swords for our duel. I find pistols so…crude."

"It doesn't matter to me. Just get on with it."

Steve sounded impatient, hard, his lean body and dark, piratical face reflecting nothing but hostile competence.

A faint, mirthless smile touched Luna's mouth, the dark shadows behind him illuminated by a leaping red-and-orange glow of lantern light that seemed hellish and terrifying to Ginny's dazed mind as she huddled on the dirt floor and fought waves of burning nausea. In her befuddled state of mind, she thought for a moment that it was Ivan Sahrkanov who stood staring at Steve with such a cruel smile of grim satisfaction.

But then the images swam away again and she shuddered as a new wave of nausea washed over her. She closed her eyes against it. When she opened them again, the two men each held a glittering saber, the lethal blades sparking faint glimmers of lamplight in tiny starbursts.

It was obvious that Rafael Luna was a master swordsman and confident of his ability. He moved with the fluid grace of a dancer, the gleaming tongue of his saber darting in and out, the clash of steel against steel a ringing, brittle sound in the turbid air of feeble lamplight and shadows.

But if Luna had thought he had the advantage over Steve Morgan by using the sword—after all, it was the acknowledged weapon preferred by gentlemen and aristocrats instead of hard-eyed American mercenaries—he discovered that he was very much mistaken. As proficient as Luna was, he quickly saw that he had grossly underestimated his opponent.

Air gusted from flared nostrils as Luna parried the smooth, seemingly effortless kiss of Morgan's blade against his own. What had begun as a swift, methodical and efficient execution became a fight for survival. Beads of sweat dotted Luna's brow and upper lip, dampened his skin so that his thin shirt clung to his chest.

They fought silently, moving across the floor of the room with savage intensity. At the door of the *posada* men crowded to watch, necks craning as they made bets on how long it would take the so excellent Spanish *criollo* to disarm and kill the blue-eyed *norteamericano*.

"*Dios!* He fights well for a *gringo,*" one of the *Rurales* muttered, disappointment in his tone at the thought of losing his bet—and perhaps the lovely *puta* crouched on the floor. "But no matter, for there is only one of him and there are many of us, eh? We have our orders, after all, and there is the woman..."

Sergeant Rameriz laughed softly. "We take no orders, even from Spain. The woman is ours, whether he wins or loses. We will have her and the silver he promised. Then we will take her to *el capitán,* and be rewarded for our generosity. Perhaps we will even visit with Cortina, eh?"

Rubbing his crotch with one hand, the sergeant shifted the rifle he held beneath his arm forward, a casual gesture but significant. The others laughed.

Ginny heard them and shuddered, terrified even in her fog of confusion.

These were men who had ridden with Juan Cortina, the ginger-haired Mexican who had been the scourge of the Rio Grande and Texas until recently, the bandit who had killed white settlers and collected hefty ransoms until the Texas Rangers pursued him across the border. To be at the mercy of these men—! Pressing her fist against her mouth, she fought back a scream, teeth digging into her knuckles until she tasted blood.

The two men moved in the glow of lamplight and shadow. The sound of pants for air, feet scraping across the rough floor and her own strangled breathing were so loud, everything such a blur of images imposed one atop another, that it took her a moment to comprehend what she was seeing. Steve suddenly lunged, his blade catching Rafael's saber just beneath the hilt and flipping it from his hand in a smooth, almost indolent sweep to send it flying through the air. It clattered against the wall, then to the floor. Before Luna could move, the point of Steve's saber was at his throat, a deadly pressure.

"Call off your hired thugs, Luna."

Blanching, Rafael Luna's lips were drawn back from his teeth in a grimace. He swallowed, and the saber tip cut a small gash into the skin of his throat.

"Sergeant Rameriz..." he sucked in a breath between his teeth as the blade shifted slightly, and got out in a choked gasp, "you are dismissed!"

There was a heavy silence before the sergeant said, "I do not think so, General Luna. It is unfortunate that you have lost your battle and your honor, but we were made certain promises. We do not like being disappointed." He levered the rifle up slightly, the barrel pointing at Steve as Ginny watched with glazed comprehension. "We will take our money and the woman, and leave you alive if you allow it, but if not..."

The unfinished sentence was eloquent in intention.

Crouched by the bed, Ginny slowly slid upward, her spine pressed against the wall. The loose mass of her hair tumbled over her shoulders and back, then caught on an object stuck into the wall. Terrified, with a madly beating heart and fear coursing through her in a flood, she did not comprehend what had snagged her hair. Then she realized—it was her own little dagger, the one Rafael had taken from her in Mexico City.

The *Rurales* attention was focused on Steve and Rafael; no one noticed as she pulled the dagger from the wall. It was a comforting weight in her hand, a promise that she would not have to endure what the Rurales had in mind for her. There were things worse than death. Didn't she know that well enough?

She felt so sick. Mixed with the fear that beat through her was the strange, thundering *heat* that was unabated, the fever that left her in torment. It was all such a blur of sensation and sound, washing over her and then receding. The only thing real was the dagger in her hand and the perception of danger.

Then it all grew loud at once, with men shouting and gunfire racketing in the room, deafening explosions, spurts of orange flame and the smell of sulphur a terrifying blur. A man lurched forward, his uniform identifying him as the enemy, and grabbed her, hand digging painfully into her flesh as he spun her around and in front of him.

''Halt!'' he shouted. ''Or you will hit the woman!''

He held her against him, one hand clamped down on her breast, his fingers squeezing cruelly so that a wave of nausea shot through her, cutting through the haze with swift clarity. Ginny had brought up one hand instinctively to grab at his arm, fingers plucking at his sleeve in a futile effort to remove it. He only squeezed tighter, until she cried out. He laughed.

She remembered him then, the hot-eyed man named Rameriz who had watched her earlier, one of the *Rurales.*...

Rameriz was saying in a reasonable tone, ''See? You will only kill her if you do not put down your weapons.''

Vaguely, through her red mist of pain and outrage, she saw a man who looked familiar standing in the doorway, but her mind would not identify him. She lifted her other arm to push at her tormentor, but there was something in her hand.

As Rameriz started to move forward, Ginny shoved hard at him with one hand, and heard his grunt of shocked pain. She pushed him again and again, the heat inside her building with each blow as he released her and fell away, collapsing into the shadows that spread around her, shadows tinged red and black and yellow-orange, encroaching on her field of vision.

Half sobbing, wet and sticky with something on her hands and arms, Ginny waited until she could see again, then looked up, pushing her hair from her eyes.

Panting, with blood streaming into his eyes from a cut on his forehead, Steve came to kneel down beside her, his voice soft.

"Ginny, it's over."

He sounded so faraway, the words drifting to her through the heavy layers of fever that raged through her body.

When she said nothing, Steve reached down for her and pulled her to her feet, reaching at the same time for a blanket to pull around her, his hands swiftly efficient.

"Christ, Ginny, are you all right?"

He sounded so angry… Why was he angry? The moment of lucidity began to fade. She clung to it desperately, her muscles shuddering beneath Steve's touch as he slung her over his shoulder and strode from the small room. With her head bobbing, she caught a glimpse of Rafael Luna's body sprawled bonelessly on the hard floor in a spreading pool of blood. Then the dark shadows came to claim her, washing over her in clouds of black streaked with crimson.

There was a vague impression of men in uniform, and she thought she recognized one man who wasn't in uniform. Steve went to the man and talked to him in a hard, low tone before she was thrown atop a horse. Steve mounted behind her, and there was a jarring, jolting motion as they rode out of the village and into the night beyond the cluster of buildings.

When she glanced back, the wool blanket tilted into her eyes, she thought she saw flames licking at the sky, but it was probably just the fever working, turning the world to crimson and heat, to a fire that was consuming her.

It seemed forever until they stopped. A night sky so purple it was almost black held thousands—millions—of tiny pinpricks of light that glittered overhead. She was pulled from the horse and went sprawling on the ground. Unable to do more than stare upward, she felt the world wheel around her in a slow revolution that left her reeling. Her fingers clutched at something solid, but only found the blanket beneath her, and bunched it in folds.

"Ginny!" she heard, and knew it was Steve. He was always so angry with her. She wanted to say something, but no words would come and nothing made sense. It was the heat that made her so confused, the pulsing need that made her ache so badly.

Unmoving, she lay atop the blanket, shivering in the cold night air, her hands clutching fistfuls of wool. She was afraid to move, afraid she'd fall off the edge of the world where she was balanced so precariously.

From above, his voice lashed her again, sounding so strained, so sharp.

"Be still, Ginny! You've got blood all over you. Where are you hurt? Damn Luna, death was too easy for him."

Another wave of heat engulfed her, and the wool was a harsh scrape against her back, making her cringe. He was saying something important, something she should comprehend...if only she could think straight! But the fever and chills overwhelmed everything else.

Her head tilted back, and more stars swam in front of her eyes. The night air was cool and silky, washing over her endlessly but not easing the heat that engulfed her. There was something important she should say, should do, but what was it...?

There was such a pounding in her head, a steady roaring sound that seemed to come and go, drowning out his words so that she heard only a few at a time.

"...lie still, Ginny...I don't see a wound and you don't seem to be hurt...did he hurt you? Jesus, so much blood on you...what's the matter...?"

"Oh God, Steve...please...help me! I feel so sick!"

"*¡Chingate!* Ginny! That bastard! Did he give you something to make you sick?"

He didn't wait for an answer, but stood up and pulled her

with him, swearing softly. His hands were gentle, and she strained toward him, grasping at coherence.

"It's so hot... Why are you putting that on me? Stop it!" Crossly, she shrugged aside the blanket he draped over her shoulders. He held her still, his grip firm as he wedged her between his thighs.

"Be still, Ginny. I've got to get you to a doctor. It won't help if you fight me. God, you're burning up with fever! How long have you been like this?"

But she was beyond answering him, beyond even fighting as the struggle to make sense of everything dissolved into a suffocating cloak, as if someone had pulled down a black curtain that made everything abruptly disappear.

The next thing she knew, she was in a bed in someone's house, a real bed, with springs and an iron frame. Steve was slumped in a chair beside her. Beard stubble darkened his jaw, and he dozed, his chin digging into his chest.

Somehow, it was comforting. Ginny closed her eyes again and slipped back into a sleep that was much easier. If Steve was there, it would be all right.

It took days for the fever to subside, and she was incoherent and nauseous by turns, drifting between reality and vague, frightening dreams. Steve tended her with a gentleness she had never expected from him. He said nothing of how he had found her, nothing about Rafael Luna, and in her moments of lucidity, Ginny could not bring herself to mention him, either. When they talked, it was of mundane things, of the children or the weather, or of the little village in a green valley surrounded by hills where he had taken her to recuperate.

Ginny grew stronger every day, physically if not in spirit. As her body healed, she became more withdrawn. She wanted to hide from the world, from Steve, even from her own memories, and retreated behind a carefully erected barrier where she felt nothing. She wanted only to sleep, to dream of nothing. How could she bear it? She felt adrift, wounded, emotionless. Nothing penetrated the shell she built around herself like a high wall.

Early one morning Steve woke her from a deep, dreamless sleep to tell her they were leaving the village. Perhaps it was the way he said it, or the sudden dread of leaving the quiet village nestled in the palm of a ring of mountains where she felt so safe. But she rebelled.

"I want to stay here." She lunged from the bed to face him with arms akimbo, chin lifted in uncertain defiance. "I have no intention of being dragged around the entire country without even knowing why, or where I'm going."

A black brow arched in amusement. "Get dressed, Ginny. Or are you waiting for me to help you? It's a surprise, and I don't want to spoil it for you."

Ginny gazed at him uncertainly, her brief defiance vanishing. There was something so different about him now, the way he watched her, helped her so tenderly, ignored her when she was ill-tempered. While she'd been mending, he had not left her side, but watched her with something like—like shame in his eyes.

I can't bear it! After all that has happened, he must think me so loathsome, so defiled....

Turning away, she said without looking at him, "Oh, yes, you never miss a chance to show me that you're stronger than I am. I suppose you'll drag me kicking and screaming all the way to...to wherever it is you're taking me."

"Ginny, don't make this hard on both of us. We can't stay here forever."

Agitated, she began to pace the floor, moving from the window to the door which was always closed at her request, a barrier to protect her from the world, from danger.

"Why can't we stay here? I don't want to leave, Steve. I don't think...I don't think I can!"

After a moment of quiet, he came to her. He put a hand on her arm and kept it there even when she flinched away from him. "Ginny, I wasn't there for you last time, but I am now. Luna is dead. He can't hurt you anymore."

Drawing in a ragged breath, she turned blindly toward him and felt his arms go around her, holding her against his chest.

She heard the steady beat of his heart beneath her ear, his words muffled.

"Christ, Ginny... Oh God, I don't think you know how I regret that I wasn't there for you. Come with me. I won't force you if you don't want to go now, but you have to leave here one day."

"Yes," she said against his shirt, "I know. You're right. I'll go. I'll go with you."

It was late in the afternoon the day they reached a trail that was little more than a thin ribbon of rock overgrown in places with bright-green moss. It looked vaguely familiar, and she frowned. It was quiet here, and dark despite the narrow thread of sunlight high overhead that insistently pierced the barrier of rock and thickly intertwined branches.

Leaves brushed her face. The silence was dense and heavy, as if a curtain had been drawn over the world. There was only a faint trickling sound, distant, musical, as if all other sound had been absorbed by the lush growth of trees and vines.

As they rounded a bend in the trail, she knew suddenly where they were—back at the falls that plunged from high rock into the clear, cool basin below. The noise burst upon them like fiesta fireworks, sudden and deafening.

"Steve—?" Her voice was smothered by the noise of the falls, but he turned in his saddle to look at her. His blue eyes were remote beneath his long lashes.

"We need a place to stay for a while. It's safe here. I don't want you to worry, and I need to stay out of sight for a few weeks."

His tone was soothing, as if he were talking to a child.

She was quiet for a moment, ducking a branch as they rode down the wooded trail. The drowning remnants of apathy began to lift, buoyed by hope. It was secluded here, a paradise refuge from not only the world, but her own dark memories.

They rode down the steep decline into the rocky basin formed by a volcano thousands of years before, their silence demanded by the very thunder of falling water crashing over the high black rocks to the pool below. Cascades formed by dozens of smaller rocks made a lacy veil of froth and spume that dampened the air so that Ginny's hair curled gently against her cheeks.

Oddly, it was warm here, when the water should have made it cool. Perhaps it was because towering, jagged rocks held warmth from the sunlight that glittered on the water. Tiny rainbows arced, forming bridges across the swirling pool.

To Ginny, the falls represented a time of great contentment. She drew in a deep breath. She was glad they had come back here, where they had enjoyed each other before, like two carefree children. Whatever happened, she would always have those memories.

36

Cascading water had become a constant, soothing sound that blotted out everything else close to the pool. Ginny moved downstream a bit, slipping a little on the slick surface of rocks worn smooth by centuries of water currents washing over them. Her feet were bare; she wore the loose garments of a peon, a billowing *camisa* and baggy pants that reached her ankles.

Peace dwelled within this timeless valley where no one else came except birds and small mammals that peeked curiously from behind fallen logs or tangled vines. It was remote and hidden, a sanctuary from the world.

I feel like Eve, Ginny thought with a faint sad smile, after she was tricked into eating the apple.

Earlier, Steve had climbed one of the rock walls, scaling it with practiced agility while she watched. Bright sunlight had gleamed on the bare skin of his back and shoulders until he had disappeared into the brush that clung in a ragged fringe to the ledge. Ginny had watched with idle curiosity.

It was much easier to think of him with detachment now. To think of him any other way was too painful. Oh God, was it all ruined? Would she ever be able to forget all that had happened?

There was an agreement between them at the moment, a silently acknowledged pact that they would wait until the moment was right to discuss what their future held once they left this valley.

It was a tentative peace, fragile and uncertain. At night when they sat across the fire from one another, Ginny wondered what he was thinking, if he hated her for what Luna had done, if she disgusted him now. Despite his careful kindness, she knew there was something he was keeping from her. He would look away at times, a muscle leaping in his clenched jaw, his mouth a taut, hard slash.

Until her bruises, huge purple and yellow marks, had faded, he'd gone quiet every time he saw them. Silence was awkward between them, the courtesies strained and fractured, as if they'd become strangers again.

Even at night, when the air was cold and invasive, they shared blankets and body heat but nothing else.

It was difficult, lying beside him all night, listening to his deep, even breathing and feeling as if they were farther apart than ever before. Anguished, she lay in the dark and thought of what might have been, of how far they had come and how close they were to finding themselves, to finding the happiness she wanted so desperately.

Some nights she lay awake until the sun rose steeply to banish shadows and shed light into the rocky bowl nestled beneath the waterfall.

Was it all over? Was there no chance now?

It seemed as if everything she touched dissolved, even while she was trying so hard to keep it. But Steve had been right about coming here, for the past week had made her feel safe at last, tucked away from the world.

But tonight, there was a difference. It was subtle, a lessening of Steve's detachment as he regarded her across the fire. "You look tired, Ginny. Your skin has that peachy gold color that I've always liked, though. It makes your eyes look even more green."

Cradling a bowl of stew—it was best not to ask what kind of meat it was, and she much preferred not to know what he had caught in this dense wilderness—she regarded him with a solemn, unblinking gaze.

"I like to lie on the rock and feel the sun warm me. At times, it feels as if I cannot get warm enough, as if…as if I'm cold and empty inside."

"Are you?" A black brow slanted upward. Firelight was reflected in the deep blue of his eyes, leaping. "Are you cold and empty inside, Ginny?"

"I—I don't know anymore. It seems that every time I—we—try to salvage something of ourselves, we're driven apart. Oh, Steve, I don't know if I can take much more! I want to…to run away, and yet at the same time I want to hold on to you with all my strength."

Pausing for breath, she waited when he lapsed into silence, regarding her with unreadable eyes, his gaze betraying nothing of what he was thinking. The fire popped and crackled, and the stew slowly cooled as she sat quietly, nerves on edge and heart pounding furiously, waiting for his response.

Finally he said, in the familiar monotone she heard most often since he had rescued her from Luna, "It's late. We should get some sleep."

Ginny's hope dissolved as quickly as it had ignited, turning into a leaden acceptance. Irrelevantly, she thought suddenly of the time Steve had lost his memory, when he had looked through her as if he didn't know her at all. Was that the way he felt about her now? As if she were a stranger?

A brisk wind sprang up, and they both crawled into the lean-to shelter Steve had built; huge leaves formed the top layer of the roof, and the windblown water made a rhythmic pattering melody. It was mesmerizing, a soothing lullaby.

In the distance, the high-pitched scream of a mountain lion pierced the night shadows. When she jerked, Steve put a hand on her shoulder.

"A mountain cat," he muttered sleepily.

"Yes. I realize that now. It just…startled me."

He moved beside her, and the warmth of his body and drowsy assurance brought a sudden surge of yearning that was so powerful it left her breathless, dispelling the sense of lassitude that had gripped her for so long. Her heart clutched painfully as she dredged up her barriers. No, it could hurt to be vulnerable again, to allow herself to *feel.*

But he rolled over, one hand reaching out to slide along the length of her arm, slowly, as if stroking a tame cat. Ginny stiffened, but before she could move, Steve bent swiftly, his mouth finding hers in the dark, dense shadows.

It was so familiar, so achingly familiar for him to kiss her. But these kisses were gentle, not the almost harsh kisses of her experience with him, and oddly unsettling.

Ginny clung to him tightly, her fingers spreading over his bare back, feeling the familiar play of muscles under his scarred skin, the heat of his body so close to her…

But when he touched her intimately, a shock of searing fear blotted out the passion she felt, and she was suddenly screaming, pushing him away, her entire body trembling from head to toe.

''Don't! I can't bear for you to touch me! Oh God, just don't *touch me!*''

''Ginny—''

''No! Oh God, *no!*'' It was a sob, a plea. Revulsion and misery clogged her throat and tears spilled from her eyes.

''It's all right, Ginny,'' he said in the same soft tone that she was growing to hate. ''It's all right.''

''No! It's *not* all right! Don't you see? I'm ruined! I can't feel what I should feel. I don't feel anything but fear, shame for what's happened to me....'' Her breath caught in a half sob of anguish. ''And I feel that it was partly my fault, that I should have somehow been able to stop him, to get away from him.'' Sitting up, she hugged her knees to her chest, rocking back and forth in the dense black night that hid her. ''You'll never know what it feels like to be degraded like that, to be forced to submit to things that no one should endure—''

''Ginny, I understand.''

''No, you don't! How could you? How could you know what it's like to feel so helpless, to know that you've done your best to escape and it's still not good enough?''

''I know.'' There was a peculiar note in his voice. ''I know more than you think.''

Shivering, she shook her head, copper strands of hair sticking to the wet tear tracks on her face. "No, I don't think you could..."

"Did you choose to be with Luna?"

"No! Oh, how can you even suggest it—"

"I'm not suggesting it, Ginny. I'm pointing out that you had no choice in the matter. Don't you think I know that? Don't you think I know how it is to feel powerless? I was chained in the dark like an animal, treated worse than an animal at times. I know what it feels like to be forced to the brink of madness."

"That's not the way it was— Oh God, it was worse than being chained..." She choked on a half sob, shuddering.

"No? Then tell me how it was, Ginny. If that's not the way it was for you, explain it to me so I'll understand."

She pressed her face against arms that were folded over her drawn-up knees and rocked in silent misery. She tried to form the words, tried to put into coherent phrases how the nightmare had returned to haunt her, all the memories of those long-ago days as a *soldadera* returning so sharply, the degradation like a knife in her soul.

Panting, heartsick, Ginny lifted her head at last, her frustration thick in her throat. "You have no idea what it is to be a woman, to be a *thing* paraded on a man's arm, to be forced to do things you never dreamed existed and be unable to escape...no, you're a man used to taking what you want, doing what you want, and you have *no idea* what it is to be so helpless, to be so frightened of what will be done to you next that all you can do is obey like a trained dog whenever fingers are snapped. You will never, *never* understand because no one has ever done that to you! You've no idea what it is to be touched when and how you don't want to be touched, or the shame of having your body exposed to the eyes of a man you hate. God, it makes me sick to think of it!"

Breathless, sobbing now, she was barely aware that he had sat back on his heels and was staring at her, his eyes a pale gleam in the shadows. The night was filled with the sound of falling water and the thunder of her own heartbeat.

"Maybe I understand more than you think, Ginny."

It was said so quietly she almost didn't hear it, but the words lingered somehow, an offering and a confession.

He laughed, a hollow sound. "I never told you—never told anyone—but in the prison where Devereaux sent me, there was a doctor... He's dead now. I wish I had been the one to kill him, but someone else he tormented had that particular pleasure. He made me feel the way you just described...as if I were a *thing* to be used for his own gratification. He used to taunt me, bring me into his office where he sat behind a white linen tablecloth spread with hot food and wine, knowing that if I'd had anything at all to eat, it was not enough, just scraps of moldy bread or dirty water. He tried to break me down in *other* ways, as well. I know what it is to feel powerless, to be touched when and how I don't want to be touched. To be afraid."

She could feel his muscles tense, feel a vibration shudder through him, hear the fury and disgust in his tone as he said, "I wasn't as strong as you are. God! I tried to hang myself in my own chains one night... I couldn't stand the thought of him touching me, and preferred death."

"Steve—"

"No. No, Ginny, you see, I do understand more than you think. You, with your woman's soft body and tender heart, have survived far better than I could have. You have come through it all with your soul intact. I lost mine. I gave up but survived in spite of myself. Sometimes, I find it damn hard to forgive you for being stronger than I am."

Trembling, she put a hand up to touch his face, her fingers skimming over the abrasive stubble of his half-grown beard, tears clogging her throat and slipping down her face as she murmured, "We can't surrender, Steve. We have to fight, for ourselves and our children. We have to *win.*"

"Ginny..." He gave a short laugh as he caught her hand in his and held her palm against his jaw. "You have the heart of a Comanche warrior in that soft woman's body of yours. I guess I've been ashamed. Every time I saw your bruises and heard you whimper in your sleep, I felt the extent of my failure in keeping you safe. I let Luna ambush me in that village, was careless enough to risk you, and you suffered for my inadequacy. It was more than humbling—it was torture of a kind I've never felt before."

"Oh, Steve..." She faltered, realizing what had been behind his silences, the furtive, shamed glances he gave her. It wasn't her humiliation that so chagrined him—it was his own.

She drew in a deep breath, the shadows that had clouded her for so long dissipating.

"It's behind us now. It's been said that if we do not acknowledge our past, we will never get beyond it. Let's not dwell on what we can't change, Steve, only what we can. Please...I don't want to spend the rest of my life wishing for what I'll never have."

"Ginny—I don't know. I don't know if either of us can forget, can live with the knowledge of what we've done and had done to us. It's a lot to put behind us."

"If we don't try, we'll never know if we could have done it, Steve." Her fingers moved to touch his jaw. "Give me some time. Give *us* some time."

After a moment of long silence, he said softly, "We can try."

A dying ember popped in the fire, slowly turning to gray ash, but neither Steve nor Ginny noticed.

He held her all night, an arm draped over her body, her spine pressed into the angle of his chest and thighs. He didn't try to touch her again, but the weight of him at her back was reassuring. She slept that night without dreaming, without waking in fear, slept in Steve's arms where she was safe.

37

How many days had they spent here, dwelling in this enchanted valley that was so far away from the rest of the world? Ginny lost track of time, drifting in a confusing haze of peace and passivity.

It was warmer now, the sun a burning orb above. She went frequently to her favorite spot to sunbathe, lulled to serenity by the steady melody of water against the rocks, a fine mist diffusing the heat of the sun on her face.

Once, she would have lain atop the mossy rock without her clothes, but not anymore. She felt too exposed, too vulnerable. Now she remained covered from neck to ankle in the loose peasant garments. The restrictions of proper society that she had once chafed against were now harshly self-imposed.

"You look like a Mexican peon," Steve said one evening as high peaks cupping the valley slowly swallowed the sun. A soft hazy light lingered, tinting the world in rose and saffron. His eyes narrowed slightly, his mouth curled into a rakish smile as he regarded her attire. "I remember when you once preferred going about like a bare-breasted Amazon."

"I'm sure you do. But that was a long time ago."

"Not so long. You wore more in that scandalous painting that the Prince of Wales purchased. No wonder he urged you to remain in London instead of accompany your husband to Mexico."

"I should have listened to him," she blurted, then lapsed

into silence when Steve cocked his head and frowned. Why were her emotions so tangled lately, so contradictory?

"Ginny—talk to me. You can say what you want. I won't get angry. Hell, I can't stand seeing you like this, like a damned ghost drifting through this valley. I thought by bringing you here, you could feel safe."

"I feel safe." She sounded defensive even to her own ears, but couldn't summon up the courage to confide in him. It was too devastating to talk about the elusive emotions that lurked beneath her outward calm. It was much easier to ignore what had happened, to drift along, thinking of nothing but the moment.

"If you do feel safe, you have a hell of a way of showing it." Steve got up, his long legs eating up the space between them in two steps. He knelt in front of her so that she was forced to look into his eyes, compelled by his soft tone and the unexpected gentleness. "I won't let anyone or anything hurt you again, green-eyes. Let me protect you. Let me bring you back from that ledge you've been on for the past month."

"Oh, Steve, don't be so melodramatic." She brushed hair from her eyes, and leaned away from him to gaze at the silvery spill of water that cascaded like a delicate bridal veil from the high rocks. "I'm perfectly fine."

"Are you? Is that why your hand shakes and you won't let me get close to you without backing away? Are you frightened of me?"

Her chin came up defiantly, though she could feel her lips quivering with suppressed emotion.

"Perhaps I am, a little bit."

"I'm not Luna, Ginny. Or Beal, or Devereaux, or any of the others who have hurt you in the past. Hell, I know I've hurt you, too, but don't you know how I feel about you? You said our mistakes were all in the past... If that's true, then you'll have to trust me now."

"Yes, I know. And I do.... I'm just not ready to leave here yet."

"I understand your need to be away from everything for a while. But not forever, Ginny. We have to go back soon. It's been over eight months since we left England and the children."

"Yes." She swallowed the sudden choking lump in her throat, and whispered, "Yes, I know. I've thought about them every day. Oh, Steve, I know you're right but I'm so afraid." She forced a shaky laugh. "I've never been so afraid, not even when I was with Devereaux, not even when Tom Beal dragged me with him— Perhaps it's because now I know what can happen. Back then, I had no idea how brutal men can be."

Steve was quiet for a long moment. Frogs harrumphed a bass symphony and insects hummed accompaniment. Peace settled in a flimsy veil over the valley again as they sat silently.

Finally Steve said softly, "We have to put the demons behind us. If we don't, we won't ever have the peace that you want and deserve. You know that."

She dragged in a deep breath spiced with the rich scent of humus. Thick foliage dripped from towering trees, a green mantle of peace and protection spread around them. "It's so lovely here. How did you ever find this place?"

"It belongs to me." Steve smiled slightly when she looked at him in surprise. "Thank God Hearst never saw this valley, or he wouldn't have sold it to me. It's on the ranch I purchased from him. See? You can come back and bring the children with you."

She said nothing, only stared at him in the deepening gloom as the silence stretched far too long. How could she tell him that she *couldn't* leave? That the very though of going back terrified her? He'd think her weak and foolish. She *felt* weak and foolish.

"It's all right, Ginny." He said it softly, his voice only slightly lifted to be heard over the muted thunder of the falls. "We won't leave until you're ready. You know you're safe here for now, just as you know we must leave. I know you're strong enough to make that decision soon."

"Nooo…" It was a kind of moan, torn from her as she fumbled for elusive control of her tricky emotions, craving his reassurance but not quite believing it.

Steve rose slowly, his words careful and calm, as repetitive as if he were speaking to a small child. "You're safe, Ginny. No one is going to hurt you here."

Feeling foolish, she managed to nod. "Yes. I know. It makes no sense, but there are moments when…when it all comes back to me and I'm so afraid. I feel as if I'll never forget it all…not just Luna, but all he represents." A shudder ran through her. "There are times I don't want you near me, that even when I know it's not true, I feel as if you're a danger to me."

He was watching her closely. Light from the fire cast a glow on his face, leaving one side in shadow, while the faint haze behind him slowly deepened as dusk melded into night.

With the shadow of beard stubble on his lean jaw and the reckless slant of his mouth, his bare chest gleaming in the soft dusk, hard muscle and tawny skin marred by tiny scars, he seemed ruthless and predatory.

Oh God, he looks so dangerous! she thought wildly, her heart thumping madly in her chest as the fear surged through her in pounding waves. But Steve was unmoving as he studied her in the half light, staring at her with his wicked blue eyes narrowed and intent. *Steve*…her husband, the man she had loved for so long.

Yet she was terrified of him, even though she knew he would not hurt her.

Finally, moving in a slow, deliberate motion, he spread his arms out to his sides, watching her closely.

"Ginny, you're safe with me. Nothing will happen to you here that you don't want. Would it make you feel any better if I told you that I won't touch you unless you give me permission?"

"That would be a novelty," she said with a shaky laugh. "I don't think you've ever asked anyone for permission to do anything."

"Then this will be memorable."

Ginny's eyes widened. He sounded so serious. If it was anyone but Steve…

As if sensing her skepticism, his mouth quirked upward in a faint smile. "A new beginning, Ginny. Don't you think it's time we tried something different? Nothing else had worked in the past.''

Firelight was reflected in the deep blue of his eyes, diffusing the shadows. Drawn by powerful emotion, trembling with the need to be close to him and the fear that still lay just beneath the surface, Ginny put out her hand.

Steve's fingers were warm and solid as he curved his hand around hers. He held her firmly but not tightly, and when she withdrew her hand he didn't try to hold on.

''Ginny, fear won't end until you face it, until you conquer it. I know.''

''You can't know! You can't know how terrifying it is to feel so vulnerable, to feel as if it could happen again at any time! That I'm helpless to prevent it.''

He studied her, his eyes dark and unfathomable. ''Tomorrow I will teach you how to use a gun.''

''I know how to shoot.''

''Yes, but you should know how to hit what you're aiming at. There's a difference.''

Despite her nervous confusion, she smiled. ''Trust you to put things in perspective.'' She paused, then added, ''Do you think knowing how to shoot will make me feel safer?''

''It will make *me* feel safer,'' he said dryly, and when his eyes crinkled slightly at the corners, she found herself laughing at him.

''If improving my aim makes you feel better, then I'll make the sacrifice, I suppose.''

''Ever the martyr, green-eyes.''

This was safer ground, a familiar banter that put her back on solid footing. Ginny's tension eased.

By the light of the fire, with blankets spread upon a cushion of moss, they ate their evening meal, the customary beans replaced by a delicious stew Steve had thrown together in the huge iron pot over the open fire. Fresh vegetables were scarce, but there was usually an abundance of fresh meat. Ginny had learned long ago how to cook decent meals over an open fire, usually *frijoles* and corn tortillas.

Relaxed, she sat with her legs curled beneath her, leaning

on a thick wad of blankets propped against a rock. The night sounds grew louder, only slightly muffled by the constant din of falling water. The air was crisp and damp enough for her to pull an edge of the blanket around her shoulders.

Steve came to sit close, facing her with his legs bent under him. He was near enough that she could feel the heat radiating from him, smell the faint scent of the soap he'd used earlier and hear the soft rasp of his breathing.

"Ginny," he said when she tensed, "I only want to be close to you."

Awkwardly, she sat in stiff silence as he lifted her bare foot in both his hands and pulled it onto his lap. A faint smile crooked his mouth, and she stifled a moan of pure pleasure as he began to massage the aching tendons of her foot.

"A technique I learned from an old Chinaman I knew in San Francisco," he replied when she dredged up the energy to ask where he had learned such magic.

Blissfully relaxed, Ginny closed her eyes with a sigh as Steve continued to massage her foot in strong, circular strokes. His fingers worked up to her ankle, kneading the calf of her leg with sure efficiency. Then he turned his attention to her other foot.

The fire hissed and popped, and in the distance she heard the low howl of a coyote. The cry trembled on the night air as if suspended, then faded, muffled by the constant drum of falling water.

It had been so long since she'd felt this at peace, with the music of the night around her and Steve's hands working magic on her tense muscles. All of he fears began to subside, replaced by a growing confidence that he would not hurt her, that he would do as he said and protect her as best he could.

"Um," she murmured when he asked if she was relaxed, and heard him laugh.

"I'll assume that means yes." Deftly, his hands moved up her leg, gently kneading the skin of her calf, then skimmed higher to massage her thigh.

Ginny offered no protest. It was too easy, lying there with Steve, his hands familiar and yet foreign to her now, gentle despite the rough calluses that still marred palms and fingers. Had he gotten those calluses in the mines? It was painful to envision him forced to such brutal labor, agonizing to think that he might have died there.

Oh, she was such a coward, when Steve had survived the ultimate horrors of enslavement and degradation without disintegrating into a weak, sniveling wreck. Never before had she yielded to the kind of fear that had gripped her these last weeks.

The pressure of his thumb against her inner thigh was firm, sliding beneath the loose *calzones* she wore, rotating with slow stroked that were sweetly tender. She opened her eyes, gazed at his downbent head as he concentrated on what he was doing.

This was a different Steve than she had ever known before. There was only tenderness in his touch, not the arrogant dominance he had always exerted. They had both changed so much....

"Steve?" He glanced up, firelight reflected in his eyes as he met her gaze with a quizzically lifted brow. "Steve, I want honesty from you. I want you to tell me only the truth."

"Haven't I always?"

Irritation knifed through her, displacing the serenity. "No, you haven't, as you very well know. Always before we've degenerated into recriminations or excuses. If I ask you something that's very important to me, will you give me an honest answer, even if you don't want to?"

His hand stilled, heat and hardness against her thigh. "If it's important to you, it's important enough to me to be honest with you, Ginny."

"A politician's answer."

"Christ, Ginny. Yes, I'll answer honestly. What do you want to know?"

She thought of Elizabeth Cady Burneson, but could not bring herself to ask him about her. Instead, she thought of all the times he had made her feel so powerless, so helpless and at the mercy of his whims.

"What would you have done if I hadn't come to London for the children? Would you have looked for me?"

"Yes." His thumb rotated against the sensitive curve of her knee for a moment before he glanced up at her. "I did come after you, but you'd already fled Stamboul, remember?"

"Yes, I remember you telling me that." It was an answer yet not an answer. Disconcerted, she closed her eyes again and gave herself up to the soothing sensations he created with his massage.

"Ginny, if you're worried that I'll drag you somewhere you don't want to go, or make you do something you don't want to do, I won't."

Not daring to open her eyes, she murmured, "What's happened to change you?"

"All the times I forced you to go with me, made love to you when you fought me—yes, even raped you—I was wrong. My grandfather nearly disowned me because of how I treated you, and he was right. I can't undo everything I've done, but I won't force you to do anything against your will ever again."

Her eyes slowly opened. Steve was staring at her, his eyes level with hers, his hands still now, resting on her knees. Then he leaned forward.

He drew his hand down her face, his fingers lightly skimming the sculpted bones of her cheeks, then the slope of jaw. He dragged his thumb over her mouth, smearing moisture over the curve of her lower lip. The fire crackled and popped, curls of smoke drifting skyward, and the sound of the waterfall was a constant drumming rhythm.

"I want to kiss you, Ginny."

His whisper fanned against her cheek, and she tilted her face upward.

Leaning forward, he kissed her, his mouth traveling from her lips to her ear, then down over the arch of her throat to linger, his tongue washing over her in leisurely, heated circles. When her breath grew a little ragged he said against her throat, "I want you to kiss me, Ginny. Will you?"

His soft question was unexpected. She hesitated, then found his mouth with her own. She kissed him, let him kiss her, his free hand moving behind her neck to hold her in a light clasp. Breathless, some of her restraint melted away.

For the first time in their relationship, she felt in control of herself and the situation. It was a heady emotion after all the years of uncertainty, of frustration and defeat.

As her breath came faster, the hot sweeping rush of desire rose high, so that when Steve lay her gently back on the blankets, she made no protest. The fire was lower now, its light faint and wavering, rosy pools ringed with shadows. His hand explored her body, slow velvety caresses followed by fierce, needy kisses, a stimulating contradiction that sent shivers of desire through her.

When he began to pull the *camisa* over her head, she put a hand on his arm. Immediately, he paused.

"Only if you want it, Ginny."

"If I tell you to stop, you will?"

"Yes. If that's what you want." He released the light cotton, watching her in the soft gloom of fire and shadows.

"I'm not sure what I want." It was true. Part of her wanted to yield, to give herself up to the exhilarating oblivion he could so easily induce, but another part of her was still testing the boundaries of their relationship.

Steve sat up, raked a hand through his hair, his smile taut as he blew out a breath. "I know what I want, but what is more important is how you feel, Ginny."

Amazed, she laughed softly. "I never thought I'd hear you say anything like that, Steve Morgan!"

"That makes two of us, green-eyes."

Relaxed again, sharing laughter, she leaned into him, this time with no reservations as he held her and stroked her gently. When his hands moved to cup her breasts, teasing her taut nipples until they swelled, she reveled in it, in the power she had to make Steve's breath come swift and harsh, to see the naked passion in his face. Her breasts throbbed, and a slow, steady pulse ignited between her thighs, spread through her body when he kissed her burning flesh gently, drawing the taut button of her nipples into his mouth, until she forgot everything but the delicious sweep of sensations.

At last he stretched out beside her, and she arched her body up for his touch. Her earlier fear had vanished forever, the nightmares fading at last. There was only room for Steve now, and he filled the night with his caresses, her world with reassurances.

"Oh, yes, Steve...please...?"

He answered her plea with his body, as he had so many times before, their joining one of mutual need and passion.

He kissed her. Then the delicious friction of him sliding insider her was a vivid reminder that this was *Steve,* the man she had loved for so long, the man she had never been able to forget for even a day.

For the first time since she had met him, she was confident they could work through anything—their doubts and fears, even anger with one another—and manage it in a way that wouldn't destroy them.

Later would come the true test; now, there was only Steve, his hard, lean body over hers, his hands teasing her breasts, exploring her everywhere.

This was familiar, the aching tension inside her that escalated to an almost unbearable pitch before he eased it, before he took her from twisting, panting need to a sweet, exultant release that made her forget everything for the moment but how much she had always loved him....

Drowsily replete at last, she took a chance, risking it all to murmur her love for him over and over, in French, and Spanish and English, her lips moving against the damp skin of his neck and shoulder until he said it back, the words a harsh groan against her ear.

"Green-eyed witch, don't you know I've always loved you?"

It was true, and Steve recognized it with resignation. She was in his blood, as he was in hers. No other woman had ever excited him like Ginny, or intrigued him, or infuriated him as she did.

He loved her for her courage, for her dignity even when her back was to the wall. He wanted to kill Luna all over again, watch the lights fade in his eyes as he died, for what he had done to her.

He could see the emerald sheen of her eyes in the soft shadows that enclosed them, the lustrous color faint but still recognizable…remarkable eyes, cat's eyes, that haunted his waking hours and even his dreams. he scraped his palm up her body, over her flat little belly to cup her breast, felt a shiver ripple through her at his caress.

"Such soft skin…like satin… Ginny, you should know by now that I'll never let you go. Don't you?"

A fierce surge of need to protect her nearly swamped him, made his hands clench tightly in her hair, that glorious mass of copper fire that had tantalized and tormented him since the first day he had seen her.

"She is an obsession with you," Paco had once told him, and he'd been right, known it then even though Steve denied it.

One day, he'd tell her everything. He'd tell her about Beth and what had happened to him at Prayers End years ago. He'd tell her how, when he'd thought she was dead, he hadn't felt life was worth living anymore. That he'd only survived because he had not been able to accept her death.

And he'd tell her that he had another child, one he felt an obligation to assure his life was all it could be. Would she understand? With her fierce mother's heart, would Ginny accept the knowledge that he'd created a son with Beth Cady?

Damn him for being a coward, he just couldn't tell her about it now, not when she still seemed so fragile.

38

"Before we leave here, you'll learn to shoot well, Ginny. I'll give you a pistol, and you can learn to use it as expertly as you do your knife."

"With practice, I'm sure I can."

Steve spent three days working with her until he was satisfied that she could at least hit a target. Gunfire sent birds screeching into the air of the small, rocky valley at the bottom of the falls as Ginny aimed at pieces of wood.

One after the other, the chips Steve hung from a tree branch were shattered, bullets smashing them to splinters. The Colt he'd given her was heavy, so that she had to use both hands to hold it steady. Steve, his swift draw so graceful and easy—and deadly—could put two bullets into a wood chip in the time it took her to put one. But she was accurate enough.

"If you don't kill 'em you'll sure as hell scare 'em to death," he said, spinning the chamber of his revolver and loading it with quick efficiency. A black brow cocked, and there was a glint in his dark-blue eyes as he surveyed her. "Just hope you get the drop on a man, because by the time you get the pistol out of the holster, he'd have you so full of lead you could be used as an anchor."

"Your faith in me is touching." Disgruntled, she arched a brow and smiled. "But you might keep that in mind the next time you get the notion to intimidate me again."

"Ginny, your arrogance never disappoints me!"

Too soon, Steve said they were to leave the valley. She met his gaze with a steady stare that refused to yield.

"I still have some unfinished business to attend in San Antonio. Paco should have been able to report Luna's death as an accident by now—an unexpected fire in his room."

She remembered the fierce glow on the horizon, a hazy memory of that night, and understood now what it was. She nodded. "Yes. I'm sure any inquiries have been settled by now. Steve, don't leave me behind. Take me with you."

"Ginny, you'd be safer at my grandfather's house."

"No, Steve. What difference does it make if I go to San Antonio or to Zacatecas? We were together last time, and it didn't help. I'll stay with you. Whatever happens to us, at least we'll be together. Besides, I'm ready for a change. San Antonio sounds very inviting right now."

When dubious shadows darkened his eyes, she lifted her shoulders in a light shrug. "I won't interfere with your plans, Steve. I just want to feel safe again."

"San Antonio is not necessarily a safe town," he said dryly, but didn't offer any more arguments.

Relieved, Ginny wondered what he would say if he knew what she planned. He wouldn't be happy, but she was determined to exorcise all the old ghosts, rid their relationship of any lingering specters from their past.

It's the only way we'll ever be able to go on....

THE JOURNEY

39

When they rode out of the valley early the next morning, Ginny looked back only once, a faint sense of regret filling her that they were leaving behind what had come to represent to her a romantic interlude in their lives.

Paco rejoined them in Chihuahua, finding them in the *sala* of a small *posada* in Santa Rosalia near the mineral springs where people went to bathe in the medicinal waters.

"Those *Rurales* gave me a hard time," he grumbled when Steve asked what had taken him so long. "Díaz may be getting rid of the bandit problem, but he'll end up having a bigger problem on his hands unless he keeps a tight grip on his police force. They have too much power, and since most of them are former bandits themselves, they have no scruples."

"Creating a climate of confidence is *el presidente's* way of coaxing in more foreign investment. He hopes to lure European as well as American investors."

"Hearst is buying up a lot of cattle country. And we know who has invested heavily in mining interests."

"Yes." Steve nodded thoughtfully, blue eyes narrowed and hard as he met Paco's troubled gaze. "I heard rumors that American Smelting and Refining Company will set up ore smelters as soon as the plans are approved. The Galena Mine has laid more track and feeder lines from the mine to the smelters, with plans to join a major railroad."

"And we know who is behind that, *amigo.*" Paco sat back

in his chair. ''Brandon switched loyalties before Lerdo could even reach the Rio Grande. He's become quite friendly with Díaz now, as well as Hearst. Díaz's policy of paying foreign employees more than Mexicans for the same work will start trouble before long. And Bishop informed me that *el presidente* is playing one side against the other by encouraging British and European capital to counterbalance the U.S. investments.''

''I wonder how Brandon is dealing with the possible loss of his profits to British investments?'' Steve said dryly. ''He intends to dominate the silver market, and he's close enough to the border to get his ore to the smelters quickly, then get it on the market. He's managed to do it without a lot of interference by the Mexican government, but I have a feeling that's about to change.''

Paco laughed softly. ''*Sí, amigo,* I think perhaps his luck is about to run out.''

William Brandon was beginning to think the same thing, and frustration battled with anger as he realized that his son-in-law was behind this most recent turn of fortune. He crumpled the telegram in one fist, eyes smoldering as he regarded the messenger.

''No, there is no reply.''

Damn Steve Morgan! Swiveling around in the leather chair, he leaned back to stare out the window of the office that looked over the San Antonio River. Cottonwood trees thrust bare branches over the slow winding curve of the river. A willow swayed in the wind. It would be spring before long, and he had to get the ore out of Mexico before the rains started in May.

Now, it seemed the new president had been informed of the Galena's profits and had politely and firmly reminded him he was a guest in the country. A Mexican envoy would be made available immediately to survey the mine and offer any government assistance.

How much did Díaz know? Was he aware that only three months ago Steve Morgan had been a prisoner in the Galena Mine? And that he had killed four guards before their brief rebellion was over? It was not something he wanted known, especially in the United States. If the newspapers got wind of it, they would have a field day with that bit of knowledge. He could see the headlines now if they learned that a United States senator was involved in the operation of a Mexican mine that had imprisoned his own son-in-law. Thanks to influential friends, nothing had yet been leaked, but should a journalist get wind of it…

And now *this!* It was easy enough to recognize the fine hand of Steve Morgan behind Hill's withdrawal from the plan to expand a railroad through Mexico. Suddenly, the rights to prime land through one of Hearst's ranches had been yanked away, access denied. It meant excruciating delay and much higher costs. The country was too rugged in places, the land brutal and almost impossible to lay tracks through. Now he learned that the railroad rights he had thought finalized ran through the ranch that Morgan had purchased from Hearst. To go around could take months, time he didn't have.

How long before Díaz increased his discreet taxation on the silver production? Already, the governor of Chihuahua had been ousted, Terrazas having supported the erstwhile president instead of the victor.

Disgruntled, Brandon heaved himself up from his chair. Perhaps it was time to compose a telegram. Jay Gould and Dr. Thomas Durant were both influential men who knew how to get things done. And they weren't squeamish about crushing their opponents when necessary.

Steve Morgan would soon realize he had gotten in over his head. He may be ruthless, but he was a mercenary more than a businessman. He would never be able to withstand the combined forces of three of the most powerful men in all of America.

It had taken over a month for production to improve at the mine after Steve's interference. But Luna was responsible for *that* fiasco! It had nearly caused an international incident with Spain, but Luna's untimely—or timely, if one chose to see it that way—death in a mysterious fire had put a swift end to the problem.

Odd affair, that, Brandon mused; a fire in some remote village in the mountains killing the man so conveniently. It was almost *too* convenient. Why was it that Morgan seemed to attract coincidences far too often?

It couldn't be just coincidence that he and Virginia had disappeared right after Luna's death, nor that railroad rights had abruptly been blocked immediately after Steve escaped from incarceration in the Galena.

Damn Luna…he'd warned him to be careful even while approving of his plan to get Steve out of the way, but he had never thought the Spaniard fool enough to imprison him in the Galena! No doubt Luna had planned all along for the blame to fall elsewhere should the authorities or influential friends come to Morgan's rescue. God, he'd been a dupe, a convenient scapegoat for Luna's own schemes of vengeance.

After sending a telegram, William Brandon went to the Vance House Hotel and took his usual seat at the table by the window. The river wound in a distant, placid curve through the town. When the rains came, it could turn from tranquil to turbulent in a matter of moments, boiling over riverbanks to sweep along everything in its path.

But now it was calm enough, winding through stands of cottonwood trees and scrub willows, with new construction springing up precariously close to the banks as the town limits spread. San Antonio had been settled since the early 1700s and gone through as many changes as the landscape.

A rough town still, it boasted burgeoning commerce and a reputation as a place where one could buy almost anything, legal or illegal. Since the arrival of the new railroad in February, San Antonio had become a boom town. New industry was pouring in every day. Cattle lots sprang up, and even more saloons, hotels and mercantile stores were being built to handle the influx of cowmen.

He made an appointment to meet with Thomas Pierce of the Galveston, Harrisburg and San Antonio Railway. Pierce and his associates had organized a new company, but Pierce had since bought them out and the Pierce Line was operating under the nickname of the Sunset Route. Pierce, Brandon had observed, was eager for expansion, a man with vision—a man willing to take chances in business.

A man who might be willing to take the Sunset Route across the Rio Grande…

It would be perfect. He had already managed to lay tracks almost to the border, feeder lines that would get his ore to market more quickly and safely. Bandits had taken a toll at times, stopping silver convoys to steal the ore. Another expense had been incurred to hire guards to get it out safely.

Satisfaction replaced Brandon's earlier pique, so by the time he finished his steak and had a brandy in front of him, he was in a much better frame of mind. Leaning back, he only smiled when he recognized the man coming through the door.

Shanghai Pierce, an obstreperous Texan and owner of some of the richest land in the state, strode into the dining room as if he owned it.

With a sigh, Brandon braced himself with distaste for Pierce's imminent companionship.

"I heard you were in San Antone," Pierce said as he plopped down in the chair opposite Brandon. "You oughta come down my way. I know how to treat a guest, by God! So what's this I hear about your new venture, heh? Still plannin' on runnin' a railroad into Mexico?"

The temptation to excuse himself was great, but the senator merely smiled politely, his tone low in the hope that Pierce would lower his own voice.

"I'm always interested in new commerce, of course. I like to diversify."

Pierce cackled, slamming his open palm on the table with a loud smack. "Hell, don't we all! Damn, but it ain't no coincidence that I done bought me some more land in Wharton County. Gonna see about puttin' up some sites on it to load and unload cattle. Got the Texas and Mexican Railway in mind to run a line across it, name me a town, maybe. Pierce's Station sounds damn good to me."

Nodding, the senator debated involving Pierce, but it seemed a better bet at the moment to court Thomas Pierce. He'd never really liked the brash Texan across the table. Nor did it endear the man to him when Pierce grinned slyly and brought up Steve.

"Where's that son-in-law of yours these days? He still running from the law? Damn, but he's the fastest gunslinger I've ever seen work! Took ole Jed Langley without a blink, by God, and Jed's the fastest around. Or was. Got hisself killed a while back, plugged in the back by some cowpuncher he pushed just a bit too hard. Had a temper, Langley did. I always knew he'd end up dead instead of making old bones.''

Irritated, the senator managed to say coolly, ''I have no idea where Morgan is at this moment. We don't keep in touch.''

''No? Well, he gets around, that's for sure. Thought you might be meeting him here, since your daughter's arrived. Wheeoo! I don't mind sayin', Morgan has good taste when it comes to women! Damn, I thought that Italian gal was a looker until I saw your daughter. She's a beauty!''

Brandon felt his face freeze into a polite smile that he hoped masked his surprise at finding out Virginia was in San Antonio.

''So you've run into Virginia?''

''Senator, I had to stop myself falling off the sidewalk tryin' to get close to her! Lord, those green eyes and that red hair—like a cloud, by God!'' He chortled. ''That's about as fanciful as I get, though I wouldn't mind giving Morgan a run for his money for that one!''

A trickle of sweat dribbled down under his high collar, and he fought the urge to swear. If Virginia was here, then Steve was no doubt close by. It could be very awkward!

While Shanghai Pierce talked about Virginia, Brandon busily constructed a plausible reason for being in San Antonio. It would never do to allow Steve Morgan to know too much about his plans. He knew too much as it was. Damn him! Why was he *here?*

It wouldn't have made Brandon feel much better to know that Steve was wondering the same thing.

Just his luck, Steve thought, to ride into trouble again. He should have sent Ginny on to his grandfather's despite her objections. Now there were bound to be problems he hadn't anticipated.

Most of all, with Ginny.

''Did you know *she* was going to be here?'' Ginny eyed him skeptically. ''Is that why you wanted me to go elsewhere?''

''Don't jump to conclusions, Ginny. I had no idea that Francesca would be here. San Antonio is not exactly the kind of place she likes to visit."

"Ah, I'd forgotten. The great Signorina di Paoli seems to prefer singing in London or Paris...yet here she is. What a wretched coincidence!"

"Believe it or not, it *is* a coincidence. In case you've forgotten, I've been out of touch lately."

"Oh, Steve, I know that. It just...surprised me that she is here, that's all." Ginny smiled but she sounded uncertain as she moved to the window of their hotel room. Across the street, the marquee of the Majestic Theater advertised the world-famous opera singer, Princess Francesca di Paoli, in San Antonio to celebrate the grand arrival of the Galveston, Harrisburg and San Antonio Railway.

It didn't make things any better that Shanghai Pierce was in town as well. The man was unscrupulous. A perfect match for Brandon, but even the senator had enough scruples not to get too involved with him.

Ginny turned away from the window. With the light behind her forming a hazy halo, she looked to Steve like a seductive angel.

"You needn't look so wary, Steve," she said. "I don't intend to make any kind of a scene."

"I'm relieved to hear it."

She smiled slightly, and moved to the wardrobe where her new clothes had been delivered earlier. "These will do," she said now as if there were nothing more important, "until I can have some made. I suppose I should be accustomed to having garments strewn all over Mexico, but somehow, I never quite adapt to misplacing my beautiful gowns. Such a waste, when all of them were sewn especially for me."

She turned suddenly, eyes wide and innocent. "But then, you probably left them in New Orleans anyway when you packed contraband instead."

Amused, he said as he buckled on his gun belt, "You have no faith in me, Ginny love. I sent them to my grandfather's, but maybe not as we had planned."

"So I found out. Honestly, Steve, I constantly surprise myself with how much of your plans I can guess. You forget, I've worked for Bishop, too, and can always discern his fine hand mixed up in your plans.'' Her loose hair brushed against her waist, and she pulled it over one shoulder, combing her fingers through it. ''Should I ask where you're going?''

''You can if you like. Paco is waiting on me. You're getting skinny, my love. You need some meat on your bones. Have a good meal tonight, and don't wait up for me.''

Before she could do more than splutter a protest, he grabbed her by the shoulders and kissed her, his mouth effectively cutting off any more questions.

''Behave yourself,'' he said when he lifted his head, ''or you'll upset Missie.''

Some of the anger leached from her stormy face. ''Missie and Renaldo are here?''

''In the restaurant we passed—and so was your father. It looks like a reunion in town. Just what I need. Since I'll be busy for a while, do you think you can stay out of trouble?''

''Steve! My father is here, too… I wonder what he's doing here still? I mean, he was here before Christmas, but I assumed he'd rejoined Sonya in Louisiana by now. Oh, I must go and visit him, then. I have some things I want to discuss.''

''You'll have to wait your turn. I have business with him first. Besides, you'll want to see Missie. You'll be traveling back to my grandfather's with them when they leave.''

As he expected, her eyes narrowed at him. Before she could reply, he added, ''I'll meet you there as soon as I can.''

''You're not leaving me *now!* We just got to town. You haven't been here an hour yet, Steve Morgan!''

''Ginny, the sooner I take care of what I have to do, the sooner we can send for the children. Keep that in mind while you're badgering me.''

Two bright spots of color flamed in her cheeks, but she said with prim resignation, ''I have no intention of *badgering* you, Steve, so you needn't look so expectant. I know you have to finish whatever it is Jim Bishop has sent you to do, and I know you have no intention of taking me with you. It should make you happy to know that I'm quite content to stay here. I'm just rather surprised to discover that Renaldo and Missie are here, as well as my father. Quite a crowd. Are you sure you didn't send for all of them, just to keep me busy?''

He grinned. ''Maybe I did mention to my cousin in a telegram that we would be visiting San Antonio and suggested it was a good idea for him to get Missie away for a while. You like Missie well enough, don't you?''

"You know I do. And I see through your plan. You're quite obvious, you know. I'll go back with them, don't worry about that. And I will wait for you, Steve Morgan, but I won't wait forever! Don't forget where you left me, because I may not be there if you take too long to come back!''

Even though she had said it with a faint smile, he thought about that, and of all the times he'd left her before as he stepped out of the hotel into the street.

The wheel always seemed to swing back around, bringing everything full circle. It wasn't so long ago that he'd run into Francesca in Dallas, too, but then Toni Lassiter had been there. Vicious, depraved Toni—the beautiful blond bitch who had tried to destroy him.

If not for Francesca's help then, Toni may very well have succeeded. And then Ginny had been there, come to find out what she could about him. After everything, he had gone to her rescue, taking her from Toni and Matt Cooper before they could hurt her.

Ginny, above everyone else, still had the power to seduce him into forgiving her transgressions, however unwillingly. He hoped that, this time, she did what he told her and went home with Renaldo and Missie.

The back of the Majestic smelled like new paint and grease, with stale odors he'd just as soon not identify. Steve slipped inside, finding the dressing rooms by instinct more than memory.

He heard her before he reached the closed door, and grinned to himself. The long-suffering Costanza was the recipient of one of Francesca's famous tirades, her Italian temper flaring into heated invectives, the gutter speech of her youth more familiar despite her outward elegance.

He opened the door slightly, leaned his shoulder against the frame and waited.

"Am I to wear a gown without a sleeve?'' Francesca was demanding shrilly. "It is too much, this! I am not some simple actress who does not care how she looks. Bah! I do not know why I bother! This town has never appreciated my talent, and is full of crude men who leer at me as if they have never seen a woman before!''

''They have never seen a woman like you, *carissima.*'' Costanza's answer was mechanical and dutiful as she bent to pick up the sleeve her precious *bambina* had carelessly discarded on the floor. ''I will sew it back on. Take off the gown now, before you rip the other sleeve.''

''Oh, it is not the sleeve! It is this *town!* I do not think I can bear it here.'' Pacing, her dark hair loose and held from her face by a glittering diamond comb, she swept regally across the carpet, angrily snatching up a glass of champagne and downing it in a single gulp.

''It is not the town you hate,'' Costanza observed with a sniff. ''It is a man.''

''No! I never think of *him* anymore. I am happy with Lord Lindhaven, you know I am.''

''So? You do not seem to miss him when we are away.'' Costanza's sturdy body quivered with indignation, and when she looked up, her dark eyes widened with incredulity and then dismay. ''Ah, it is the *banditti!*''

''I told you *no,*'' Francesca said irritably, flouncing around to glare at her companion, but as she caught sight of him in the doorway, the words died in her throat and the empty champagne glass dropped to the floor with a tinkling crash.

''Stefano! Oh, it *is* you!''

''Still making poor Costanza's life miserable, I see. Don't you ever get tired of being angry?''

His lazy stance in the doorway, and the slow drift of his gaze over her, made her laugh throatily, her dark head tilting back so that her long dark hair swung seductively.

''I never tire of being angry at you, my *banditti.* What are you doing here, in this hellish town?''

''I could ask you that.''

''Yes.'' Her glossy lips curved into a smile, and she moved to him to press them against his mouth in a lingering kiss that made Costanza mutter under her breath. ''Leave us,'' Francesca commanded, ignoring her protests. The older woman stalked from the dressing room, banging the door loudly behind her.

''She still hates me, I see,'' Steve said, his arm having gone automatically around Francesca's waist. "I feel quite at home again."

"Do you? I think not." She drew back a bit, eyeing him with a critical frown. "You look—dangerous. Is that a new scar I see on your so beautiful face?"

He caught the hand she put against his jaw, turned it over to kiss the palm, then held it. "I just came by for old times' sake, 'Cesca. I can't stay."

A note of sadness crept into her tone. "It is your wife, *caro?* She is with you?"

"Yes, but that's not the reason. Ginny will be staying in town. I'd like it if you avoided her. She doesn't need any reminders of recent problems right now."

A dark brow arched. "And how would seeing me remind her of recent problems? Oh, have you two been quarreling about me? How provincial, *caro!*"

"Nothing so mundane, 'Cesca. Do you recall a persistent admirer of yours by the name of Rafael Luna?"

Francesca waved a dismissive hand. "So many men follow me persistently. I cannot remember them all, Stefano!"

"But perhaps you recall the man who accosted you in Florence. I had to throw him bodily out of your dressing room after he saw us together."

"Perhaps I recall him. Has he followed me here? How intriguing. Should I see him, do you think?"

"That would be rather difficult. I had to kill him."

Francesca laughed. "Such a vicious *banditti!* Did you kill him for me?"

"No. He abducted Ginny to get to me. She went through hell because of him—and because of you and me."

"I had nothing to do with this Luna!"

"No, but he blamed me for keeping him from you. And Ginny suffered for it."

"So you want me to avoid her." Francesca stared at him for a long moment, then shrugged. "I shall not seek her out, if that concerns you. But should she confront me, I will not play the role of a coward. I warn you now."

"I don't think Ginny will be confronting you, 'Cesca. I hate leaving her behind, especially now, but I must."

"So you try to wrap her in cotton wool so she does not see

anything unpleasant? I see. Do you recall that I once told you to go back to your wife, that you must love her? I was more right than even I knew.''

Sighing, Francesca stepped back; her luscious figure was flattered by the gown that hugged her curves, and she looked every inch the princess she claimed to be.

''I knew the day would come, Stefano. I felt it. You were never really mine. But then, I was never really yours. It was always a fleeting thing between us. I do not have time for a man in my life.''

''Not even Lindhaven?'' Steve's mocking reminder of her most faithful protector made her shrug.

''He accepts me as I am, and makes no demands upon me. I am free with him.''

''He's the kind of man you need in your life.''

''Yes.'' She gazed at him with a faint smile. ''You and I, we learned not to give too much of ourselves. Lindhaven is willing to settle for little. But I think perhaps you have given all this time. There is a difference in you, Stefano. Is it because you are a father now?''

''Partially.'' He released her hand, and she put it behind her, leaning back against the dressing table scattered with bottles of perfume and face powder, waiting. ''Mostly because of Ginny. She's gone through a lot. Some of it is my fault, some of it's hers, but we've both realized that we need each other. Hell, we love each other.''

''So, it is true. She is a lucky woman to have you.''

He walked to the back door with her on his arm, and stood just inside. ''Your performance begins soon. Go back inside, 'Cesca.''

Genuine tears sparkled in her eyes, and she kissed him, a long, passionate farewell kiss.

''Ciao, mi amore.''

He had gone only a few steps when he heard her behind him again. She flung her arms around him, heedless of her costume. ''I will never forget you, my *banditti!*''

Steve kissed her again. ''Try not to make Lindhaven's life miserable, *cara.*''

Half laughing, half sobbing, she took a step back. ''And for you, Stefano, I wish much happiness.''

* * *

Ginny tied the sash of her dressing gown around her waist. Still damp from a long, soothing bath, she looked into the long mirror tilted on a stand by the tub. No sign of the bruises remained on her body. All traces of her recent ordeal were gone, except that Steve was right—she *was* too thin. Now her eyes looked too large for her face, and there were hollows beneath her high cheekbones.

The silk dressing gown she had purchased in a dress shop upon their arrival in San Antonio clung to her damp curves, drifted around her legs as she walked to the window to pull down the shade. Sunlight poured into the room in broad swathes that made her eyes narrow against it as she fumbled with the shade. To her irritation, it snapped loose from her hands, spinning up around the wooden roller with a brisk hum. She reached for the cord to pull it down again, but paused suddenly as a glitter caught her eye.

Across the street, just visible from her third-floor window, was the alley that ran beside the Majestic Theater. Sunlight reflected from a huge diamond comb tucked into the dark hair of Francesca di Paoli. Ginny would recognize her anywhere. And the man with her was Steve, of course, his lean frame far too familiar to her. His back was to the street, and the opera singer was glued to his front, her arms flung about his neck in a passionate embrace.

Suddenly cold inside, Ginny stepped away from the window.

I should have known…should have remembered that he can never resist a beautiful woman!

But it didn't mean that he'd been unfaithful, she told herself. *I have to trust him! Oh God, I cannot let the doubts destroy us again….*

40

Steve was still thinking more of Francesca than he was Ginny when he found Senator Brandon in the office he had taken in a two-story building overlooking the river.

"I've been expecting you, Morgan."

Brandon looked at ease, his manner cordial and even friendly as he gestured him to a chair. "I was told you were in town with my daughter. How is Virginia? I trust she came to no harm while in Mexico City. She never listens. I did my best to get her to leave, even offered to send an escort for her. She refused, of course. Apparently, President Díaz treated her quite well."

"That made it convenient for you."

Brandon frowned slightly, and there was a wariness in his eyes that told Steve he was on the defensive.

"If by that you mean that I was relieved, yes."

"I had the thought that you might have been more relieved to learn that Díaz is willing to allow you to operate your mine as long as you pay for the privilege."

"Ah, the mine. It has become an expensive luxury I am not sure I can afford any longer." Brandon's shoulders lifted in a slight shrug, and he held out a carved lacquer box of cigars. Steve took one, clipped off the end and ran his fingers over the smooth tube of tobacco; it was fragrant and distinctive, a good Cuban cigar.

"So you intend to close the mine?"

"I've had an offer." Brandon eyed him for a long moment before saying, "I think there is more money to be made in railroads. Tell me, you own a large chunk of Union Pacific stock, what are your thoughts?"

Steve narrowed his eyes at him. "Railroads are risky. You know that. What do you have in mind?"

"I've recently met with Shanghai Pierce. He told me about the Texas Western Railway Company. It's a narrow gauge railroad, recently amended to change the name to Texas Western Narrow Gauge Railway Company. The amended charter also gave the company the right to build west, to cross the Rio Grande at, or near, Presidio del Norte and into Mexico. The plan is to eventually cross Mexico to Guaymas on the Gulf of California. It sounds feasible, since the charter grants authority to construct a branch line from the northwestern border of Texas up to connect with the Denver and Rio Grande Railway Company."

"Right now, they've only got tracks laid between Houston and Pattison," Steve said bluntly. "Not close enough to your mines to do you any good."

Brandon's brow rose. "Perhaps I'm not as worried about that as I once was. I applied for government funding to run tracks all the way across Copper Canyon eventually."

"That will take more money and time than you can get, Senator." Steve met his gaze calmly. "There are *barrancas* and *arroyos* there, hundreds of feet deep. Peaks are so high that even birds get dizzy. It's not practical any time in the near future. Maybe not in our lifetime."

"You need a grander vision, perhaps."

"Senator, you'll need financing. And you'll need the Mexican government's permission to lay your tracks. Even if I believed that's what you intend to do, I wouldn't advise it."

"It's comforting to know that you're so worried about my investments, Steve."

He stood up, a slight smile slanting his mouth. "If you're planning on calling in Durant or Gould, you might want to be certain that President Díaz will allow you to continue mining ore, Senator."

"I don't think that's going to be a big problem. I have

become acquainted with Díaz, and I find him to be quite agreeable.''

''If he learns that you intend to remove silver and not pay him his share, he won't be quite so agreeable, I can assure you of that. But take your own chances, Senator. You have been warned.''

''I trust you would do nothing to interfere, Morgan. I have told you that I knew nothing about your being at the Galena until I saw you that day.''

Steve recognized the angry frustration in Brandon's eyes. He held up the unlit cigar he'd been given. ''Thanks for the cigar, Senator. I'm leaving town tonight, but Ginny will be here for a while. I'm sure you'll want to visit.''

He left, smiling when he heard Brandon cursing as the door slammed shut behind him. That should give him something to think about for a few days, Steve thought.

Within an hour, he and Paco left San Antonio.

Heat shimmered from flat expanses of brush-studded hills, closing in like a heavy fist on the riders. The Rio Grande was behind them as they left Texas and crossed into Chihuahua. Their eventual destination was the capital city, El Paso del Norte, that lay to the northwest.

''Brandon will never be able to finish what he started,'' Paco said flatly when they paused beneath the welcome shade of a scrub oak. Rugged hills and canyons stretched red-and-dun folds on each side, high crags gnawing at the horizon like jagged teeth. ''Getting rails laid through Copper Canyon will be impossible.''

''I don't think that's his main goal.'' Steve squinted against the glare of the sun, drew a shirtsleeve across his brow to wipe away the sweat stinging his eyes. ''He wants to get his ore to a seaport, and rails are the quickest method of transport. It's all a cover. He doesn't give a damn about laying tracks anywhere else.''

''Then the government funding—''

''Will be used for his own private enterprise, is my guess. Thomas Durant is an old crony of his, associated with innumerable accusations of bribery, fraud and scandal, from the president on down through the halls of Congress. He and Senator Brandon make a good team, acquiring venture capital at the expense of everyone else.''

''So how is Brandon going to get his ore to the U.S. without the railroad?'' Paco hefted a skin of water to squirt a stream into his mouth before offering it to Steve, then held it out. ''By pack mule?''

''Maybe. You know what Copper Canyon's like, and the country is just as rough going around it. He can take his ore across the border into Arizona, even Texas, but either way, he risks running into *Federales* always on the watch. It's my guess when he's run rails as far as he can, he'll pack it out of the Sierras to a seaport. With Durant's help, he'll end up getting the ore out of Mexico more efficiently, and both men will make enormous profits at the expense of the Mexican government and politicians.''

''What about Terranzos?''

''Right now the governor has his own problems worrying about his future since Díaz came to power. We have to worry more about Gould and Durant providing capital to the senator for his Mexican railroad.''

''Durant—we met him with Murdock out in California, right?''

''He's an acquaintance of Murdock, but not an affiliate. Sam Murdock prefers not to maintain close association with men identified with virtually every accusation of scandal connected to railroad construction. Durant is as dirty as Senator Brandon, and as adroit at escaping consequences for his actions. With politicians like Brandon behind him, he'll continue to get wealthier while the people he exploits go out of business.''

''Politics is a bare knuckle kind of fight,'' Paco said as he rolled a cigarette with one hand, his leg hooked over the horn of his saddle. ''Too rough for me. I'd rather face a band of screamin' Apache than a roomful of diamond studs and bowlers.''

''At least the Apache make no bones about wanting your scalp. Men like the senator and Durant are sneaky about it.''

''So what are the chances of Brandon getting his silver overland to the coast?''

''I'd say they were damned good. No one's around to stop him.''

"Except you."

"Yeah." Steve nudged his mount into a walk. "Except me."

"What will you tell Ginny?"

Steve was quiet for a moment, the only sound that of hooves scrabbling on hard rock, the smell of dust and baking earth pungent and suffocating as they left the shade and rode into hot, searing sunlight.

"Hell," he said finally, "she can figure out what kind of man Brandon is. It's pretty obvious. And she knows that he's not above cheating or lying to get what he wants. Only now, she doesn't honey-coat it with some fantasy of noble intentions, but sees it as it is—pure greed. If she gets angry at my interference, she'll get over it."

"She sure didn't like being left in San Antonio."

"With Ginny, protest is as natural as breathing. She liked it well enough. She's safe there, staying with Renaldo and Missie, and can shop and go to the theater anytime she wants. I think she was relieved to be in a civilized town again, but just wouldn't admit it."

Paco laughed. "You might be bankrupt by the time we get back to San Antone...."

Ginny was, in fact, having a fine time. It was a relief to be in a real bed again, with clean sheets that smelled of sunlight and soap instead of bedbugs and lice, and a feather mattress that actually cushioned her aching muscles instead of the hard rope cots of her most recent experience.

The hotel boasted as fine accommodations as would any hotel in New York, with private bathing rooms and huge tubs, and a sitting room with bolstered boudoir chairs and mirrors hung in ornate gold frames. It was comfortable, even luxurious, and Ginny realized that she wasn't afraid any longer. Even if she did keep the pistol Steve had given her under her pillow or in her purse, she thought that she had finally overcome the gripping fear that had hounded her after Luna.

Thanks to Steve...his patience and understanding were what had helped her most. How had he known that she would feel much better knowing Renaldo and Missie were in town? When she thought of how he had felt responsible, filled with regret for his own failures, she vowed to give him the benefit of the doubt about the Italian diva. An embrace was not the same as an affair, she reminded herself when the image cropped up to haunt her. He loved *her,* not Francesca.

And didn't she know well that appearances were so often deceiving?

On her very first trip to San Antonio she had watched out her hotel window while Steve Morgan faced another gunman across the street, and in just a split second, his opponent lay dead. Then, she had been appalled at the raw, ruthless way of life in this sprawling new country.

It was so long ago. A lifetime. Little shocked her now, though she had learned enough to be wary of situations that once she had considered exciting. There was nothing exciting about a desperation to survive.

In the days following Steve's departure, she filled her hours with shopping, or lunching with Missie, who stared at her with big reproachful eyes when Ginny laughed gaily, determined not to delve below the surface of anything. She spoke only of shallow topics, such as the cut of a gown, the new fashions from the *Lady's Book,* or the latest play at the Majestic.

The great di Paoli had left town not long after Steve, and Ginny would not allow her imagination to take her to uncertain possibilities.

"Ginny, you have changed," Missie said softly, her small face reflecting concern. "Are you all right?"

"Of course, I'm all right. Why wouldn't I be? If you mean because Steve has gone off again, this time it's quite all right. I don't mind at all. In fact, I'm grateful." She took a sip of chilled white wine, a French label that was light and refreshing, and smiled gaily. "It gives me time to myself, to do the things that he doesn't like to do. We were able to talk quite a bit while we were in that lovely valley I told you about. I've finally realized that I cannot change him, and that to try only makes us both miserable. Oh, don't look at me like that, for you know yourself that Steve Morgan is not a man adaptable to any law but his own. I've just finally come to accept it."

"I see."

"No, I can tell that you *don't* see. But it's all right. We've come to a truce, so to speak. I've learned to give him room, and he's learned to be a little more honest about how he feels.''

''And this...this works well for you?'' Missie sipped at her lemonade, having refused a glass of the wine, and stared at Ginny with a troubled frown. ''I know it's none of my business, and Renaldo is always telling me I must not interfere in people's lives, but I know how you both feel about each other.''

''And you're worried that we'll stop?'' Ginny smiled. ''If we are still together after all this time, I don't think it's going to end overnight.''

''No. Of course not.'' Missie looked slightly embarrassed as she finished her meal. Sunlight through the glass windowpanes of the Menger Hotel highlighted the elegant sculpture of her face, the open honest expression appealing and attractive.

It was too easy to remember that she had once been in love with Steve, too. Ginny reached again for her wine. Was there no end to the women who had loved him? And how many of them had he loved in return?

And what of Elizabeth Cady? What of the woman who had borne him a son? Did he love her?

Like a worm, the thought burrowed deeper into her mind, tormenting her, until finally she decided to seek answers from the only other person who could give them to her—Elizabeth Cady herself.

The Prendergasts lived very close to Prayers End, where Steve had told her he had met Elizabeth. Perhaps if she went for a visit— Her cousin Pierre and Lorna Prendergast were practically engaged. It was the perfect excuse. Then the uncertainty would be behind her at last. It wouldn't matter that Steve had not been the one to tell her. At least she would *know*.

''Ginny, you don't need to travel without an escort,'' Renaldo said when she told him of her intention. A frown lowered his brow, and he looked so worried that she put a hand on his arm and smiled.

''It's not as if I have to worry about my reputation. I doubt seriously that anything more dramatic than a late train will happen. Besides, it's not at all far from the train station to the Prendergast ranch, and Mr. Murdock has put his private coach at my disposal. Don't worry so much, Renaldo. You drive poor Missie to distraction."

Despite his protests, his threats to tell Steve, Renaldo had little choice but to let her go. He couldn't hold her by force, and Murdock *had* put his own private Pullman coach at Ginny's disposal. She'd be safe, but what on earth would he tell Steve?

"You'll tell him that I decided to visit an old friend, Renaldo," she said when he despaired. "It's not as if Sam Murdock is only *Steve's* friend. He was quite kind to me in San Francisco, and I've never forgotten it."

Yet when she arrived at the Prendergast ranch and was greeted by big Jack Prendergast, his bluff heartiness not quite masking his open curiosity about Steve's wife and her unexpected appearance in New Mexico Territory, Ginny had to fight sudden qualms. *Was* she doing the right thing? Steve would be furious when he learned what she had done!

Ginny needn't have worried about Sam Murdock; he greeted her graciously.

"It is very good to see you again, Mrs. Morgan. I trust you are well," Murdock said with his faint Scottish burr.

Despite feeling awkward, Ginny smiled at him, her green eyes betraying none of her discomfort.

"I am quite well, Mr. Murdock. Really, we have known each other for a while now, do you not think we have progressed to a first-name basis? It's very American of me, don't you think?"

He smiled, transforming his features from rather severe to quite attractive. Murdock was tall, with broad shoulders and gray liberally streaking hair that had once been red. A thick shelf of brows nearly met over the bridge of his nose, and his clean-shaven jaw was square. It was a strong face, yet kind.

Ginny remembered that Murdock had once *sponsored* Concepción, taking her under his wing to teach her the rudiments of proper etiquette at the request of his friend, and partner, Steve Morgan. At first, Ginny had wondered about the relationship between Murdock and the Mexican gypsy. Had it been more intimate than it was presented?

But she had become convinced that Sam Murdock behaved with the utmost propriety, and felt comfortable with him herself.

"Ginny, then," Murdock said as he took her hand and tucked it into the crook of his arm, walking her across the wide verandah of the rambling Prendergast house. "And you will call me Sam, of course. It's such a pleasant surprise to see you again. Did you become well-acquainted with Jack's daughter Lorna and, of course, her beautiful mother, Françoise? Their letters from England have been full of news about your cousin Pierre. It seems that he and Lorna have grown quite fond of one another."

"Yes, so I gathered. Pierre is delightful, and would make any woman a fine husband."

However, Lorna Prendergast Ginny thought, was a spoiled willful girl, who had set her sights on Steve for a time, no matter that she now pursued Pierre. But it wasn't Lorna or her designs on Steve that concerned Ginny now.

To broach the subject at once would have been too obvious, so she waited until after breakfast the next day.

Garbed in a riding habit that fit snugly to her curves and accentuated her slender waist, she smiled up at Murdock as Jack Prendergast had a carriage brought around for her.

"There is so much beautiful country around here. I'm glad I came. I really needed a change, and of course, to renew our acquaintance."

Murdock smiled down at her, but behind his shrewd eyes was a glimmer of polite curiosity.

Delicately feeling her way, Ginny brought the conversation around to Steve's time in New Mexico Territory, and his brush with death.

"Steve told me that he had some accident here, and that he was cared for by a very kind woman. Elizabeth Cady, I believe he said. I am quite grateful for her care of him."

"Ah, yes."

Murdock did not elaborate, and Ginny relinquished any pretense when she saw that he had no intention of giving away information.

"I wish to visit her while I'm here, Sam. Do you know where I can find her?"

"Are you certain that's what you want to do, Ginny? There are some things best left in the past."

"Not this time." Her gaze was direct as she recognized that he knew her reasons for visiting. "I came all this way, and I want to see her. I have to *see* for myself. You do understand that, don't you?"

"Not everything is black-and-white, you know. There are times and circumstances that alter perceptions and our actions." Murdock leaned against the smooth wood of the white-painted post that held up the long gallery roof. He smiled slightly. "When I first met you, I recognized your innate honesty and courage. Nothing has changed. You have grown more confident, perhaps, and more wary, but you are still the same woman. Steve is still the same man. Your habits and surroundings have changed, but neither of you have altered your ultimate goals."

"Yes, it would seem that a leopard cannot change its spots, after all," Ginny said tartly.

Murdock shook his head. "You are deliberately missing my point. You're a clever woman. Don't disappoint me."

Sam Murdock had offered her nothing but friendship since the time of their first meeting several years ago. He had never shown her anything but respect, and had been instrumental in extracting her from the difficult tangle of her brief marriage to Prince Sahrkanov. He knew more about her than most people, and did not disapprove of her as had so many around her.

Even her father, and Sonya, had given her little approval.

Now she looked up at Murdock and said quietly, "I will do nothing to embarrass or hurt either Steve or Elizabeth Cady, but if I do not meet her, I will always wonder. It will eat at me, the uncertainty, the suspicion, until it ends up destroying anything I have left with Steve. I can't explain it. I only hope you understand."

After a long silence, Murdock nodded. "There are some things you need to know first, Ginny. I don't know if Steve has told you all of it or only a little, but Elizabeth Cady was married to the man responsible for nearly getting Steve killed. Jared provoked a fight, but as you can imagine, Steve prevailed. Unfortunately, Jared had friends with him who decided to finish the job. They swore Steve had drawn first, and if he hadn't been wounded so badly, they would have strung him up then and there. Mrs. Cady nursed him back to health so he could go to trial. She wanted him to pay for what she believed was her husband's wrongful death."

He watched her face as she talked, and Ginny nodded. "I can see how she would feel that way. And I'm not really surprised that Steve managed to convince her otherwise."

"Understand that there were other things going on then, too, between the cattlemen and Prendergast. Land rights and water rights are vital here, and a balance is needed so that all can coexist in harmony. A full-scale range war was developing until Steve took over. Once he was cleared of Cady's murder, he prevented that war, and no doubt saved quite a few lives in the process. During that time when he thought you were dead, he and Mrs. Cady became...close."

A vise seemed to squeeze her heart, slowing crushing it as she thought of Steve with another woman. This was so different than all the others—he had a child with this woman! How could she bear it if she didn't find out, if she didn't *know* whether Elizabeth Cady wanted him? She had a bond with him, a blood tie of their shared child. Would she use it to draw Steve back? Could he be induced to return to her?

The noise of carriage wheels on the crushed rock of the curving road in front of the house grew louder, then stopped. Springs squeaked slightly as the driver stepped down to the road and waited in courteous silence.

Ginny took a deep breath. "I understand what you are saying, Sam, but I must see for myself."

"I will have the driver take you there. I hope this resolution gives you some peace."

"So do I," she said as she turned to the waiting carriage. "So do I."

Serrated ridges were cushioned by shreds of cloud, faint wisps that wreathed the crisp peaks like a woman's lacy shawl. It was spring, but it was still early enough not to trust a sudden snowstorm to descend upon them and bury the ranch in drifts of smothering ice.

A single carriage approached at a fast pace, stirring a faint haze behind huge wheels as it navigated the deep ruts of the road leading to the Burneson ranch.

Fidelito had summoned her, excitement in his voice. "A visitor comes! Shall I ride out to meet them?"

"No, they'll be here soon enough, Fidelito. Go and help your grandfather. Oh, and ask Matthew to come back to the house, please. It's nearly time for the noon meal, and he's to help Emily."

Elizabeth Cady absently wiped her hands in the folds of her apron, eyeing the approaching vehicle with a slight frown. It was not familiar to her. On occasion, they had visitors to the ranch, but not usually in smart black broughams with drivers to handle the horses. It was too bad Martin had gone into town for the day. She always felt better when he was here, especially lately.

The baby was due any day and she tired easily now. There just wasn't enough time in the day, and there was always something to do, cooking or cleaning or repairs. She didn't resent it, and truly loved her husband and family, but there were moments when she longed for time to herself, time to read a book or just sit alone beneath a tree and dream.

Patting a loose curl back into place behind her ear, Beth smoothed her hands down her plain skirts and stepped off the porch to greet their visitor as the carriage rolled to a stop before the neat, two-story house.

The elegant young woman who stepped down took her by surprise, and she suddenly felt dowdy and clumsy in comparison to this exquisitely groomed creature. A lustrous cloud of copper hair was crowned with a small emerald-green hat tilted stylishly forward. The green velvet riding outfit she wore hugged slim curves in such a fashion as to appear provocative, though there was nothing inappropriate about the high neck. Her matching gloves and trim riding boots were the same rich shade of green reflected in the pair of exotically slanted eyes that regarded her curiously.

In a voice that bore faint traces of an unusual accent, the woman asked, "Are you Mrs. Burneson?"

Stifling the urge to rearrange her hair and try to hide the inevitable stains on her apron, Beth nodded. "Why yes, I am. But I'm afraid you have the advantage."

"Yes, of course. This is rather unprecedented, but I feel that perhaps we should talk privately, if you don't mind."

Uneasy, Beth frowned. Her glance shifted beyond the carriage to the stableyard and she was relieved to see Domingo and Fidelito pretending to work while they watched over her. Her gaze moved back to the woman.

"I'm afraid that—"

"Please, Mrs. Burneson. It would mean a great deal to me if you would agree. My name is Virginia Morgan."

"I'm sure I don't know—" Beth stopped suddenly, the words sticking in her throat. *Virginia Morgan...Steve's wife!*

As if reading her mind, the young woman's head tilted slightly. "I think you have heard of me."

"Yes. Yes, I think I have. Really, Mrs. Morgan, I cannot imagine why you have come—"

"Can't you? I think you can." It was said quietly and without rancor or aggression.

Beth floundered, staring at the composed young woman before her and struggling for words. Finally, she said, "I suppose this is about Steve."

"Yes, in a way. May I impose upon your time?"

Unwillingly, Beth stepped aside to open the door, and thought fleetingly of the dirty dishes in the kitchen and the rug that hadn't been swept in the parlor.

She wondered how this exquisite young woman would view her home, then with a flush of shame at her own thoughts, squared her shoulders and escorted Virginia Morgan into the parlor. It was clean enough, and the furniture was good quality pieces, heavy and gleaming with layers of beeswax polish that had taken her hours to apply. Lacy cloths draped over chairbacks and tables, and the table lamp with frosted globes and tiny dangling crystal prisms had been Martin's before they married. *It's nice enough for anyone!* she told herself fiercely.

A tiny cloth doll with yarn braids lay upon the settee beneath the window, and Beth picked it up, holding it like a talisman as she gestured for her visitor to be seated.

"Is that your daughter's doll?" Virginia Morgan asked, and a faint smile touched the corners of her mouth. "My Laura has a favorite. It is worn nearly to pieces now, but she insists upon taking it everywhere with her, so we must keep it washed and clean and pray that it does not fall apart before she grows out of the need to keep it near.''

This revelation suddenly made her seem more human, and Beth reminded herself that this woman, too, was a mother.

''Emily has moments of sheer panic if she cannot find it. Martin and I try to keep track of where she leaves it, for the tears are instant when she realizes it's gone.''

As Virginia sat down on the settee, light from the window behind her forming a hazy outline, she peeled away her gloves with slightly trembling fingers. Beth realized with a shock that she was nervous.

Why, how silly I'm being! She is every bit as nervous as I am!

More at ease now, she took a seat on a chair nearby. ''How can I help you, Mrs. Morgan?''

A smile curved the beautiful mouth, and green eyes gazed at her with frank curiosity. ''How gratifying that you are willing to be direct. I don't really know how to begin, but it has to do with Steve. I know you saved his life.''

''At the time, my motives were hardly altruistic,'' Beth said dryly. ''I wanted him alive to hang for what I thought was the murder of my husband. Once it was proven that Jared was responsible for his own death, I was grateful that I had done so, of course.''

The small clock on the mantel ticked loudly; outside, a dog barked and there was a childish shout of glee that she recognized as Matthew's. Beth realized that Virginia Morgan must know about him, and come to see her husband's son. She waited.

Slender fingers twisted around the emerald gloves, and her knuckles were white with strain, but Virginia's voice was composed and soft.

''I am grateful as well that you were kind enough to save him, for whatever reason. We—Steve and I—have not always had a tranquil marriage. I've often thought how horrid it would have been if he had died before we were given another chance to make it work.''

''Then I'm doubly glad that my actions were warranted. It is not always easy to know what to do in situations, what is right and what is wrong, and who you may hurt by your actions. I never wanted to hurt anyone. All a person can do is go on, make their daily choices and pray for the best.''

''Yes. I suppose with all these children—there are three, I understand—it must be rather difficult for you to manage. I'm certain there are times you must feel a bit overwhelmed, and perhaps wish for what might have been.''

So that's it.... Elizabeth's eyes narrowed slightly, and she hesitated. Surprise was slowly turning to comprehension as she realized that this woman in the elegant gown and hat had come more to see *her* than Steve's child. She seemed so poised and self-confident, but beneath that elegant exterior obviously beat the soul of a woman who wondered about her husband's former lover.

''Children can be overwhelming,'' she replied, ''but my husband and I are very happy to have them. *All* of them.'' She put a hand on her swollen belly, the age-old gesture of an expectant mother, and smiled. ''Each new child is another expression of our commitment to one another.''

When Virginia Morgan lapsed into silence, Beth leaned forward and put an impulsive hand upon her arm. ''Steve truly thought you were dead, you know. I knew he was still in love with you. And I knew that it would never work between us, for that reason and others.''

''Others?''

Beth sat back, her muscles aching, and tried to get more comfortable in the straight-backed chair. ''Yes. Steve Morgan's kind of life could never have been mine. I wanted peace and stability in my life, not a life of wandering the world and never knowing where I'd be tomorrow. He's the kind of man who needs a woman to share *his* world. He would never be happy in mine.''

''Yes, I suppose you're right.''

''I am right. Would you like to meet my children?''

It was an offer and a claim, and she saw that Virginia Morgan understood it. She smiled faintly.

''Yes. Did you know that we have two children—twins?''

''Yes, I know. A girl and a boy. Steve told me.'' She struggled to her feet. ''Matthew looks very much like him.''

When the children were introduced, she saw Virginia's eyes

widen, and her lower lip quivered the slightest bit as she gravely returned their greetings.

Matthew, as usual, was restless, and young Emily was wide-eyed with awe at the sight of the beautiful woman in green velvet. To her credit, Virginia Morgan did not try to force her attention on Matthew, but allowed him to respond to her as he wished. Once, she put a hand atop his head, her bare fingers drifting through the glossy threads of his dark hair. It was a light touch, swift and faintly poignant, then she straightened as Matthew took his leave.

Before she left, she turned back to smile at Beth. ''Your son and mine could be twins.''

''But they are not. My son belongs to me. I think you know that I would never do anything to hurt him.''

''Yes, I know. It's as it should be. I'm glad I came. I wasn't sure, you see, if I would be. But I had formed this picture of you in my mind, and...and now I see that I was wrong.''

The well-sprung brougham dipped noiselessly as the driver helped her up into the gleaming cab. When she was seated, Virginia Morgan looked out at Beth where she stood on the top step of her sprawling house. Emily leaned against her legs, and Beth's hand rested atop the curve of her belly as she returned Virginia's gaze.

Relief gleamed in the lustrous green eyes and a smile curved her mouth as she nodded understanding.

''Goodbye, Mrs. Burneson. And thank you.''

41

A thin rut of road followed the edge of the narrow *barranca* leading to the Galena Mine. A hot wind blew over the riders, stirring up clouds of dust that coated leaves and horses in a fine red powder.

Paco rode at the head of the snaking line of mounted men, garbed in a uniform taken from one of the *Rurales.* It was rugged landscape, cratered and stark in places, with sheer cliffs plunging down to twisted knots of river that looped through rock.

As the small force of men moved carefully down the steep mountainside, Paco glanced at Steve, his dark eyes a little strained at their deception, but glittering with excitement.

"*Dios mío!* You are crazy to try this, Steve!"

"It won't be the first time I've done it," Steve said flatly, and it was the truth. Only then, he had gone back to the same prison where he had suffered such degradation of his soul. It wasn't something he wanted to think about, or to tell. It still haunted him at times, worse than his days here at the Galena, where conditions were harsh but not degrading.

Hooves clattered on rock and saddle leather creaked in air that was thick with shimmering heat. Overhead, the cry of a hawk drifted down, absorbed by rock and twisted limbs of pine trees formed into grotesque shapes by the hot wind.

"But it is such a risk. What if something goes wrong?"

Steve squinted against the sun's glare; he wore no hat, a

shapeless serape slung over his shoulders. "Then shoot the foreman first. Make sure I have a rifle as soon as possible after the shooting starts."

When they had drawn close Steve's wrists were manacled, and he rode a horse in the midst of the others, as if he were again a prisoner. Butch Casey—a blue scarf around his neck to hide the raw, red line of his healing wound—rode on one side, Paco on the other. Tige and Charley were to hide and wait, along with a few other men; they'd never pass as Mexicans, not even as reformed bandits.

The men left outside the perimeters of the mine hid in stunted brush and stands of pine that stubbled the red shale and granite rock. A dozen rode forward, boldly approaching the metal gates that blocked the entrance to the mine. A guard stepped out of the shade to confront them.

"*¡Alto!*"

Paco made a convincing *Rurale,* arrogantly announcing that they had brought a prisoner to the mine.

A brief argument ensued, with the first man delaying until finally Paco threatened to send the prisoner back. "The governor will not like that, but I will tell him that you, Sergeant Ruiz, refused to open the gates."

The sergeant's eyes flicked to Steve, who sat on his horse with his head down, swaying slightly as if weak. Paco shrugged and started to turn the horses, but the guard stopped him, a scowl creasing his forehead.

"*¡Ay di mi!* Bring him in. I will allow Capitán Delgado to deal with him."

Paco said slyly, "He has been here before, but this time, you should keep him chained, eh?"

Another guard came up behind the first one, and keys jangled in the lock. "We chain all our prisoners! After the last one escaped, we learned to—*Dios!* It is him. It is the blue-eyed devil who killed four guards! What is he doing here? He is friends with *el presidente,* we were told, and there was much trouble after the owner left last time!"

With a careless shrug, Paco said, "He made the mistake of killing the Adjutant General of Spain, and for his crime he has been sent back to prison. It is fitting that he be brought here, eh, where he caused so much trouble before?"

Laughing, the guards said, "*El capitán* will be most glad to see this one. He was very angry that this prisoner caused so much trouble. Of course, he is too far above himself at times, but it would be foolish to tell him that."

As Steve was led inside, the manacles around his wrists clanking heavily, he slid his gaze around the high rock walls, the armed guards and the ragged men that strained under the lash of whips to drag up heavy ore cars. Wooden staircases crisscrossed the rock face of the mines, rising as high as a three-story building. Chutes and tracks gleamed in the searing sunlight, metal reflecting bright rays of heat.

"There are so many men," Paco commented casually as they rode into the open area below the captain's quarters.

"They are like mules, only cheaper. It is not so big a loss when they die," one of the guards replied with a shrug.

Delgado met them at the foot of the wooden stairs leading to the offices, his black eyes glittering with angry satisfaction when he saw Steve pulled from his horse.

"So, he has been brought back. This time, he will not find his accommodations quite so comfortable."

Steve did not look up as Delgado spoke to Paco; he had begun to sweat beneath the heavy wool serape. Below that he wore a loose shirt that covered the .45 stuck into his belt next to his belly. Suddenly it seemed far too small a weapon for what he planned. He wished grimly he'd brought a cannon, something to annihilate the mines as well as the brutal guards.

He was pushed forward a step, his boots scraping on rock.

Delgado stepped close; he stank of sweat and the potent *pulque* that was brewed by so many Mexicans. Dark patches discolored his brown shirt, and spread under his arms and down the sides. Using the handle of his whip, he shoved it under Steve's jaw to snap his head back.

"Filth, did you think to escape? You have no protector here now. It is only I, Victor Delgado, who has the power of light and darkness over you. Ah, I see you do not like that! You will like even less what I have planned for you, I can promise you that."

Hate gleamed in the man's eyes, the irrational hatred of a sadistic enemy. *Delgado.* Steve broke out in a cold sweat. The metallic taste of fear filled his mouth and throat, though he had no intention of being left at the mercy of Delgado or the guards again.

Once before, when he had gone back to the prison where he'd been forced to slave, Steve had not been able to free the men chained together. This time he would not leave until every last man bound to servitude in this living hell was set free. There were too many like Juan Rodriguez who had died for no reason, like Juan Rodriguez, who never saw his wife again, never knew if his child had lived.

Stripped to the basics of survival, denied their humanity, the hell of virtual slavery in these mines would be stopped for a while at least, forever if he could manage it.

"I will put him in our manacles," Delgado was saying. Paco swiftly objected.

"Not until the papers are all signed, *Jefe,* for I have my orders. He is my responsibility, you see, and I will not take the risk of his escaping you again until he is in your custody."

Delgado sounded displeased, but agreed. "All these rules are unnecessary, Lieutenant, but if it will hasten the process, I will do it. Come with me. You, Perez! Come and watch the prisoner!"

"My men will watch him," Paco said coolly, "until the papers are signed. Then he will be yours to do with as you wish."

Delgado swore softly, but spun on his heel to mount the short flight of stairs that led to the offices, Paco close on his heels.

When the door shut behind them, Steve shifted position, his muscles tense and aching with strain. The sun beat down on his bare head and sweat stuck his cotton shirt to his sides as he waited. The wool serape was heavy, weighing him down. The reassuring press of the pistol cut into his rib cage.

At last Paco appeared in the doorway above them. He held up a small ring of keys and nodded.

It was the signal. Steve twisted his hands inside the loose coil of iron manacles, sliding them free, reaching under his wool serape for his gun at the same time as those with him leaped upon the unsuspecting guards.

The struggle was brief and decisive, the guards brutally overwhelmed. It was done so swiftly that none of the guards across the compound even noticed. Steve bent and took the huge ring of keys from one of the dead guards.

By the time the other guards saw their fallen comrades, they were surrounded; only two resisted, and were quickly defeated. Paco ran to open the gates for Tige and Charley, swinging them wide in a loud shriek of rusty metal.

The prisoners, still manacled, ceased to work, and stared in confusion at the men in *Rurales* uniform as they went coolly about their business.

Shrugging free of the confining serape, Steve gestured with his pistol to the yawning mouth of a tunnel blasted into the rock.

"The silver is down there." It was all too familiar, the walk down a narrow tunnel illuminated by the hot, smoky light of creosote torches set into brackets in the rock walls. The walls closed around them like jaws, swallowing them up as they descended into murky air that smelled of raw earth and desperation.

The iron door set into a wall had a double bolt and lock on it, formidable resistance without the key. Hollow clanks sounded loud in the shadows as the door swung open.

Haunted by memories of the days he'd spent in this dank prison, Steve began to sweat despite thin cotton garments and his breath was shallow.

"Are you all right, *amigo?*"

He didn't look at Paco, just nodded tightly. "Get the silver loaded as quickly as you can. Use their wagons. We'll get it out of here before the second shift of guards arrives from the village. We don't have long."

"I have the feeling that Senator Brandon is going to be mighty upset," Butch Casey observed laconically. In the turbid light, his grin flashed white.

"Yeah." Steve's belly knotted at the unmistakable sound of a muffled, despairing cry of a prisoner locked into one of the cells. "Finish here, Paco. I've got some work to do."

Using the ring of keys he'd taken from the guard, Steve began to unlock doors, flinging them wide. He went from iron door to iron door, and the men too weak to move were helped by their comrades.

"Go back and help him," he ordered one man who tried to

push past, leaving his cellmate. "If he doesn't go, *you* don't go."

In the faint, flickering light, the man gave him a wide stare of resentment, but went back, helping the other man to his feet. Freed of manacles and prison, the men poured out of the mine like ants scurrying from a sandy hill, streaming to freedom.

None were left behind. Not one man remained.

"You probably set free some of Cortina's men or worse," Paco observed, but Steve only shrugged.

"Better than leaving innocent men down here to suffer the torments of hell. Lock the guards in the cells. Too bad we can't stay long enough to give them some of the same kind of treatment they like giving to others."

It wasn't until they were on the way back, the silver weighing down a wagon and their saddlebags, that he felt as if he could breathe easily again, the stink of the mine finally behind him.

This wouldn't stop Brandon—there was more silver in the mines—but it would certainly cost him.

The trek to El Paso del Norte was arduous, long enough that he had time to think, to reflect on Ginny and their past. Their future.

He had done all he could do about Brandon and the mines. There was nothing else to do now except wait and see what Díaz did with the country, to give the new president a chance to bring Mexico to prosperity and her people to peace.

Railroads would come, fortunes would be made, and there would always be men like Shanghai Pierce, Jay Gould and Senator Brandon who would profit from the sweat of others. Steve couldn't change that. He could only do his best to see that his own family was safe.

Maybe it was time he refused Bishop's efforts to draw him into more intrigue and focused on ranching and the pursuit of his own business ventures. He had done enough for both governments.

Now it was time to do his best for Ginny. For himself. And for their children.

When they got this silver to El Paso del Norte, he would wire her to meet him. It was time they told each other everything. It was time for complete honesty.

quick profit, despite his estimates. If he doesn't [illegible]

In the end, the fighting [illegible] the [illegible] gave [illegible] were [illegible] but [illegible], helping [illegible] other [illegible] the left [illegible] and [illegible] the [illegible] of the [illegible] each fully [illegible] to [illegible] him.

Now [illegible] would [illegible] one [illegible].

You [illegible] at the [illegible] of Carranza, [illegible] Obregón, and [illegible] only [illegible].

Better than leaving innocent men down here to suffer [illegible] ments [illegible] the [illegible] in the [illegible]. You had [illegible] could [illegible] enough to [illegible] of the [illegible] and [illegible] like [illegible].

It wasn't until they were [illegible] the [illegible] [illegible] the [illegible] and [illegible] [illegible] could [illegible] of the [illegible] [illegible].

This [illegible] that [illegible] were [illegible] alive [illegible] [illegible] around [illegible] and [illegible].

[illegible] at [illegible] was [illegible] that he had time to think [illegible] and [illegible].

He had done all he could do about Carranza and the [illegible]. There was nothing else to do now except wait and see what Obregón did with the country, to give the new president a chance [illegible] to bring prosperity and [illegible] people in peace.

Landowners would come [illegible] made, and there would always be men like [illegible] Pancho Villa. [illegible] who would [illegible] [illegible] change that. He could only do his best to [illegible].

[illegible] he was done he [illegible] to [illegible] and [illegible] on [illegible] and the [illegible] his own business [illegible]. He had [illegible] enough for [illegible].

Now it was time to do the best for Emily. For himself. And for [illegible].

When they got his [illegible] he would [illegible] to meet him. It was time that they [illegible] each other [illegible]. It was time for complete [illegible].

THE DESTINATION

42

Vera Cruz was humid, the heat pressing down like a damp blanket. In spite of the overpowering heat and occasional tropical thunderstorm that cooled the air only briefly, Ginny preferred to sit outside the *posada,* on the small patio that overlooked red roofs and narrow, dirty streets.

It seemed that she had done this far too often before—waited for a ship that would take her away—but she couldn't escape her aching heart, the memories and a pervasive sense of despondency. She should have gone back to Brownsville, or even Galveston, anywhere but here, where there were so many memories.

She had gone back to Zacatecas with Renaldo and Missie, traveling safely with their escort. A week spent at Don Francisco's *hacienda* had not made it easier to leave, but she had at last informed Don Francisco of her intentions.

"I've been away from my children too long. When Steve wants me, he knows where I will be."

Would he want her? She'd hoped all was resolved between them, their growing intimacy in the valley an achingly tender confirmation of their love.

But the doubt, the uncertainty had returned, swooping down like a vulture to tear at her confidence, threatening to destroy all hope. Faith in their future was no longer certain.

Steve was always going off, always restless and in search of excitement. He did jobs for Jim Bishop because he wanted to, not always for some noble ideal of democracy and freedom for the common man. Would he ever change? Would he ever want to make a stable home?

Ginny closed her eyes, thinking again of Elizabeth Cady. Beth had been nothing like what she'd expected. There was none of the flamboyant beauty of Francesca or Concepción, or any of the other women Steve had been with over the years. Instead, Beth Burneson had possessed a quiet serenity and a beauty of spirit and soul that shone out of her intelligent eyes like a lamp in the darkness. It had taken away Ginny's breath, seeing her pregnant and still so graceful despite her bulk, seeing the way she clung to her children.

And Matthew...so much like Franco, except for the eyes. The boy had his father's eyes; deep blue, with ridiculously long lashes, still innocent, but with light of mischief shining in their depths. There had been such pride in the way Elizabeth regarded her children, mixed with fear that their happy life might be shattered.

It was a life Ginny envied, one of great stability. A contentment radiated from Elizabeth that was deep-rooted, unshaken even by her fears.

Ginny realized she was glad she'd met Elizabeth. It was a revelation that Steve had loved the woman enough to ask her to go with him, and a fluttering twinge in her own heart that he had forgotten her so quickly. It was one thing to share his body, but if he had shared his heart, it would destroy her.

But do I have his heart? Have I ever had his heart? If only she knew that, maybe she wouldn't have found herself here....

Yet here she was, lingering in a town she detested, waiting for a ship to take her away from Mexico again. Here, where the oceanfront held little more than desolate sand dunes shaped by the wind into layered hills scattered with palm trees, the only beauty provided by the beautiful peak of Orizaba in the distance. Snow crowned its summit, white and gleaming in the sunlight.

She went daily to the ticket agent's office to secure passage on a ship leaving Mexico, and each day was told that she must come back.

"*Mañana, señora.* Come back tomorrow."

Finally, restless, impatient to be gone, she heard with relief the ticket agent inform her that the ship would be leaving early the next day.

"Don't be late, *señora,* for there are others who will gladly buy your passage. Space for passengers leaving Mexico is limited, for the captains fill the ships with cargo for other countries. Soon, Mexico will be as prosperous as other nations. *El presidente* has promised it!"

He seemed glad to talk, though rather curious about the *gringa* who spoke the dialect as well as any native, and who looked so sad. Too lovely to be so sad, he told her. Ginny only smiled as she promised to be back early the next day.

"Don't sell my ticket to anyone else," she warned, and he swore on his mother's life that he would never do such a thing.

"To see your children again will be too wonderful a thing, and I would not be so cruel, *señora!*"

As good as his word, the ticket agent saw to it that she had the best stateroom available. She had to admit that it was nicer than she had expected, given the limited space for passengers on the vessel. What did it matter, after all, if the cabin was small? It was only for a few weeks anyway, and then she would be in England, where it was cool and her children would be to welcome her.

Had Pierre married Lorna Prendergast yet? Lorna's father had sent a few trinkets for his daughter with Ginny, a velvet box with a necklace of huge topaz stones to match Lorna's eyes. He doted on her, spoiled her rotten and bragged that she would marry a duke and be a duchess.

Sam Murdock had only smiled, and accompanied Ginny from New Mexico back to San Antonio, his lavish Pullman gliding over the rails with such swift efficiency she had almost regretted the end of the journey.

"I have a meeting with the senator," he said when she expressed her gratitude for his generosity and companionship on the trip, "and thought perhaps you might prefer having my company."

For Ginny, seeing William Brandon again had been a bittersweet parting, for she had never seen him look so distressed or so old, not even after he had been shot. It struck her, seeing him in this new light, that she had never really known him, not the real man, not the man capable of such greed and deception, such careless cruelty.

Perhaps his crimes were catching up with him, reflected now in his face and eyes, in his slower step and the air of defeat that wreathed him.

"Give Sonya my love," she had said when she left him in San Antonio. She wondered if she would ever see either of them again. Time and circumstances took her so far at times, were so often uncertain....

Where would she go once she had her children with her again? Would Steve come after them, or just after the children?

When the steamer chugged slowly out of the harbor, Ginny stood at the porthole watching the shoreline fade into the distance, feeling melancholy and pensive.

Silly of me, she thought, but I had hoped Steve might come after me, as he did before. It's all so futile, when I had such hope....

The heat was crushing, oppressive in the stuffy confine of the stateroom. In desperation Ginny abandoned privacy and made her way above deck. She moved to the rail, ignoring the interested gazes in her direction, grateful for the feel of the cooler wind on her face and in her hair.

Hardly a day out of Vera Cruz, Ginny was resigned to spending most of the voyage in her cabin. Two of the male passengers had attached themselves to her with an annoying tenacity, though the younger man, James Tyler, was more doting than offensive.

Mr. Andrews, a bluff, hearty man with whiskered jowls and a touch of gray in his dark hair, was particularly persistent, insisting that he had met her somewhere before.

"Perhaps in San Francisco? You are not a woman a man would ever forget, Mrs. Morgan."

"You are too kind, Mr. Andrews, but I fear that I have no recollection of our ever meeting before." Ginny rose from her chair, intent upon returning to her cabin. Andrews put out a hand to stop her.

"No, please, I did not mean to run you off, Mrs. Morgan,

I only thought we had met before. Don't leave us. We need another player for a hand of piquet. Say you'll stay."

"You may be sorry if I do, Mr. Andrews, for I'm a fair hand at cards. I don't often lose."

He smiled, his eyes roving over her face in a most disagreeable manner. "Neither do I, Mrs. Morgan. Neither do I."

It was a challenge, and it gave her inordinate pleasure to best Andrews at cards, even at poker, which he boasted had made him his fortune. "I won my land and railroad stock that way!"

"Perhaps you should invest in a more dependable venture next time," she said sweetly as she tucked her winnings into her small velvet purse and pulled the drawstrings closed. "I seem to have beaten you."

Andrews rose politely as she stood, but there was a taut set to his mouth. "You must allow me to recoup my losses, Mrs. Morgan."

"Why, Mr. Andrews, then I will have lost!" She laughed lightly, enjoying his discomfiture, and allowed the smitten Mr. Tyler to escort her belowdecks.

"Thank you," she said pointedly at the door, and he had the good grace to blush deeply and retire.

For the next two nights, out of boredom more than anything else, Ginny found herself in the dining hall with the gentlemen, playing cards and winning a great deal of the time. Though he tried, Mr. Andrews was unable to recover his losses from her, and she could tell that it grated on him.

When the ship docked in Galveston, she left the dining area early, preferring the refuge of her stateroom to the chaos of passengers disembarking. Thank heavens the odious Andrews was one of the passengers leaving at Galveston! The thought of crossing the Atlantic with him was dismaying.

The younger man was more courteous, but she saw with a sigh that he was infatuated.

"Please, Mr. Tyler, I cannot possibly allow you to be alone in my cabin with me," she told him in exasperation when he asked if he could join her for a glass of wine in her stateroom. They stood at the door. The heat was stifling in the passageway; perspiration dotted his upper lip and forehead.

He looked almost desperate.

"Y-you are the m-most beautiful woman I have ever s-seen," he managed to get out in a stutter, "and I consider it an honor just t-to be in your presence."

It seemed like forever since she had been told that she was beautiful in such a sincere, sweet way, and Ginny was touched. Impulsively, she leaned forward and pressed a light kiss on his cheek.

"Thank you, Mr. Tyler."

"Well," a familiar, drawling voice said behind her, "it seems that I always happen to show up at the wrong time, doesn't it, green-eyes."

Her heart leaped, and she turned to see Steve standing in the shadows of the passageway. His dark-blue eyes gleamed with amused lights. Half laughing, half crying with relief, Ginny flung herself at him.

"Steve!"

As his arms went around her, holding her tightly against him, he said softly, "You never do what I tell you, you maddening creature! It's damn lucky for you that this steamer stopped in Galveston, or I would have had to chase you all the way across the Atlantic."

"And would you, Steve? Would you have followed me across the ocean?" She leaned back in his embrace to study his face, her eyes searching for signs of mockery.

"I'm here, aren't I? Ginny love, try not to be so impatient. We've got the rest of our lives to be together."

Bending, he scooped her into his arms and carried her inside the cabin. Ginny belatedly remembered Mr. Tyler as she got a glimpse of his pale, shocked face just before Steve slammed shut the door with his foot.

TURNING POINTS

43

Familiar heat seeped into Ginny's bones as she stood on a small balcony enclosed with delicate wrought iron. The sheer curtains had been pulled back, and a light breeze lifted a heavy strand of her copper hair that was worn loose around her face and over her shoulders. She inhaled deeply. The early morning air of New Orleans was redolent with the scents of fresh pastry and the effusive sweetness of flowering plants. Later in the day, the humid stench of the streets would overpower such pleasant aromas, but now it was evocative of all she loved about the city.

Steve had gone to send a cable to London summoning the children home to America. Tante Celine would bring them, and soon they would all be reunited. At last she would see Laura and Franco again. This time, they would not be parted. They were going home, to Mexico, where they could live in peace and contentment.

A wistful smile curved her mouth. It was almost ten months since she had seen them. How much would they have grown? Impatience filled her, barely contained. But they would be reunited as soon as *Tante* could secure passage to New Orleans.

New Orleans was pleasant this time of year, before the summer heat grew brutal. They were staying at the elegant St. Louis Hotel in the heart of the *carré de la ville.* The small hotel situated at the intersection of Royal and St. Louis Street was very comfortable, a welcome change from the hardships she had so recently endured.

Yet she was not as relaxed as she might have been. An undercurrent of apprehension threaded her mood. Steve was more attentive than he had ever been, their love stronger than she had ever thought possible, yet she was strangely uneasy.

"You'll be fine once the children are safely with us," Steve had said when she mentioned her foreboding to him. "All that's happened in the last months is making you so nervous, Ginny."

"Yes, I'm sure you're right," she'd murmured, but the anxiety did not dissipate.

Sonya echoed her concerns over lunch at Antoine's the next day, her normally placid face creased in a slight frown as she regarded her stepdaughter.

"It's so far for the children to be traveling, Ginny. I do hope your aunt exercises extreme caution with them."

"I'm certain she will, Sonya." Ginny's white china coffee cup trimmed in gold clattered slightly as she replaced it in the matching saucer. The coffee was strong and hot, much too hot to be drinking when it was so warm outside. A lovely breeze wafted in through open shutters, doors flung wide to admit cooler air, but not even the huge fans that whirred overhead could keep the heat at bay. Insects droned fitfully despite the precautions of fly traps and netting. "Tante Celine is quite accustomed to handling the children."

Sonya nodded. "It's probably fortunate that I never had any children of my own. I'm afraid I would be far too protective of them."

It was an indirect reprimand, a reminder that Ginny had been away from her children too often and for too long. Her mouth tightened slightly, and she wished she had not agreed to meet her stepmother for lunch. It was obvious that Sonya was in one of her contentious moods.

"Since you feel that way, it probably is best that you were never able to have children. More coffee?"

Blue eyes narrowed slightly as Sonya shook her head. "No, it is much too warm for coffee. When will you be returning to Mexico, my dear? I don't understand why you insist upon living in such an uncivilized, brutal country when you could stay in Louisiana, or even Texas."

"At the moment, bands of renegade Apache are making Texas a rather dangerous place. With the current situation of raids on farms and even large ranches, Mexico is just as safe as Texas." Ginny glanced up at the sommelier who had brought a bottle of chilled white wine to their table.

Silence fell between them as the wine replaced coffee, and when the waiter had retreated, Ginny leaned forward. "If you have valid reasons for your concerns, please share them with me, Sonya. I know we have never been true friends, but I always thought you generous enough to confide in me."

For a moment, Sonya did not reply, but sipped at her wine, no hint of her thoughts showing on her face. When at last she lifted her gaze, her eyes were troubled.

"I don't know why I feel so…so apprehensive, but I do. Have you spoken with your father lately?"

"No, not since I last saw him in San Antonio. He looked unwell." She lay her fork against the edge of the plate, her salmon mousse barely touched. "Is he still in Texas?"

Instead of answering, Sonya looked down at her hands. A linen napkin in her lap was twisted into a coil as she wrung it with surprising ferocity. Then she looked up, her mouth thinned into a determined line.

"I don't know where he is, Ginny. He's disappeared. I'm afraid he has done something—inexcusable."

"What are you talking about? If you're referring to his business dealings in Mexico, I know all about that now. Steve told me what I hadn't already guessed. But I've always known how unscrupulous he can be, how ruthless, when it comes to power and money. He's not very different from most men, I've observed."

"No, no, that's not what I mean." Genuine distress made her voice quiver. "William may be ruthless when it comes to money and prestige, but he has never been…cruel before."

"Cruel? Sonya, tell me what you're talking about. You are frightening me."

"Oh God, Ginny, I don't know for certain. And even if it's true, I don't know what he intends. It's only a guess on my part. I never thought he would stoop to such duplicity and I'm certain I'm wrong..."

"About *what!* You've got to stop babbling and tell me exactly what you mean."

"William sent for your children several weeks ago."

Ginny stared at her. The implications did not hit her at once, only a sense of perplexity that he would take it upon himself to send for Laura and Franco. Then, as she saw the distress in Sonya's eyes, she knew what he intended. Her hand convulsed on the stem of her wineglass.

In a voice as brittle as breaking ice, she said, "If any harm comes to my children, I will ruin him."

"Ginny...I don't think he means them harm, but I know how angry he was when your husband managed to wreck his business dealings in Mexico. He was so livid. I tried to reason with him—after all, business is just business—but he took it very personally. Perhaps he feels that he can use the children as leverage with you."

"You don't believe that any more than I do." Ginny rose to her feet. "He intends to use them as hostages."

"Not even William would do that." Sonya's lips trembled and her eyes were dark with distress. "He'll be furious with me when he learns that I've told you, but I think he's gone too far this time. Children should not be used as weapons in a personal feud."

"How long ago did he send for them? Oh God, they could be in America right now! I must find Steve...."

"Wait!" Sonya lunged to her feet, her face as pale as the white linen tablecloths. "Please, don't let him go after William. He's in ill health, and it could kill him!"

"I never thought you loved him that much," Ginny said tartly, then was sorry when two crimson smears stained her stepmother's cheeks. "Forgive me, Sonya, but this is too much, even for the senator. My God! To interfere in the lives of two young children surpasses anything he has ever done. It's bad enough that he has lied, cheated and stolen just to enlarge his personal fortune, not caring who he hurt in the process, but now he has gone too far. If Steve doesn't kill him, I very well may!"

Aware that their conversation was attracting attention from

other diners, Ginny snatched up her reticule and left Antoine's, gliding past a rather perturbed maître d' with barely a nod and murmured pleasantry. There was no time to pause for social amenities, not when her children may very well be in danger.

When she reached the St. Louis Hotel, Steve was not there. He'd gone out again, leaving her a short note that he would be back in time for them to attend the opera later that evening.

The opera. Dear God, she'd forgotten all about their plans to attend the Royal Opera House's late performance of *Carmen* with the lieutenant governor. How could she sit through an evening of music and pretend nothing was wrong?

Senator Brandon would not harm the children, she knew that, but they would be frightened, especially if her aunt was upset. Did he really think he could keep them from her? Did he underestimate Steve Morgan that greatly? Or was he just that desperate…?

It was true that the senator had lost a great deal of money after the men working his mines were freed. Díaz had bowed to public opinion—shrewdly surmising that it would cost him little in actual silver and benefit him greatly with the citizens—and proclaimed that foreign employers must pay each man a fair wage for his work. Profits would be drastically cut under such a measure, and some investors had pulled out of Mexico.

It seemed counterproductive when Díaz was attempting to lure foreign business to the country, but Steve had said dryly that, behind the closed doors of the presidential palace, deals were being made that would increase foreign profits but also put harsh burdens on the citizens.

"Senator Brandon just happened to get on the wrong side of *el presidente,* or he'd be getting his share of the take. I wonder how much good I did shutting him down. He's liable to be replaced by someone much worse."

To Ginny, already troubled and saddened to learn that the man she'd always considered her father was so pitiless, it had seemed grossly unjust that more innocent people would suffer because of greed. Despite that, she had been unable to stifle a feeling of pity for the senator. He'd looked so old and weary, a bitter, defeated man.

Now she felt nothing but revulsion for him. How could he be so cruel?

Steve returned to the hotel just before dark. Ginny met him at the door of their suite in her dressing gown.

"Sonya told me that my father sent for the children! They are probably halfway here by now."

Blue eyes caught and held hers, his tone grim as he said, "The ship carrying our children from London docked in Galveston three days ago. We probably passed them in the Gulf."

"You *knew.*"

"Not until about two hours ago when I received a reply from your cousin Pierre. His cable expressed dismay that we had not authorized the children's journey."

Ginny stared at him. "Three days. Where are they? Oh God, where could they be?"

"I have some men working on it. Stay calm, Ginny. I don't need female hysterics right now."

His cold tone was like a dash of icy water in her face, and she recoiled. "I'm not hysterical, just frightened, and I would think you'd understand that."

"I do. Believe me, I do. But this doesn't help."

Steve raked a hand through his dark hair, and Ginny caught a glimpse of silver threads among the black strands. It was hard on him, too, she realized, and took a deep breath to stem the flow of protests.

"Yes, you're right, Steve. When do we leave?"

A faint smile crooked his mouth. "I've arranged passage on a ship leaving for Galveston in the morning."

"This is going to be a long night."

"Then attending the opera should take your mind off the wait."

Ginny stared at him incredulously. "I have no intention of attending the opera now! How could I?"

"It won't change anything to stay here in the room and fret all night. Besides, if we're being watched, we need to act as if everything is normal."

To her horror, huge tears welled in her eyes and slipped down her face. She began to weep in great, gulping sobs, like a broken-hearted child. Steve drew her into his arms, held her against him as she wept, his hand stroking her hair with clumsy attempts at comfort.

"Nothing will be normal until we have our children safely with us, Steve," she whispered between sobs. "Nothing!"

His hand tightened in her hair. "I know. We'll find them soon. If I have to string Brandon up by his heels and beat it out of him, we'll find them. I swear it to you, Ginny."

There was an unfamiliar break in his tone that she had never heard before. Ginny realized that, beneath Steve's carefully intact composure, he was as anguished as she about their children. There was a barely controlled sense of violence in him, in the way his hand fisted in her hair, in the clipped enunciation of his words.

Steve would find them. She knew he would. And God help William Brandon when Steve found him....

44

Galveston Bay was hot, the air thick with humidity and the rank smell of rotting marine life. Out in the gulf, huge stacks of towering clouds rolled toward land, bringing the daily summer thunderstorm ashore.

Steve ignored the rain pelting him. A crash of thunder shook the ground and vibrated the dock, lightning hitting so close he could smell the acrid stench of burned earth.

"What did you find out, Paco?"

Paco Davis wiped a hand over his wet face and stepped under the protective eave of a wooden shack that leaned precariously over the water. His black hair was plastered to his skull, dripping rain into his eyes and down the bridge of his nose.

"Lost my damn hat," he muttered, then shrugged. "You were right. They were on the ship when it docked, and the ticket master said he thought there was a carriage waiting for them. No one else seems to know anything."

"I can't imagine Ginny's aunt going off with anyone she doesn't know. She's too convinced America is full of cutthroats."

"Looks like she's been proven right. I guess whoever met them at the dock could have given her a letter of introduction. That would be easy enough to forge. And if Brandon told her who would be meeting them—"

Steve's jaw clenched. "I still can't figure out what he hopes to gain from this other than vengeance against me. He has to know I'll hunt him down.''

''Maybe he thinks his money and power will save him.''

''From charges of child abduction? Not even Senator Brandon is that delusional. This will ruin him. If he lives through it.''

''Any ideas?'' Paco asked after a moment of silence.

''A few. I sent a telegram to Colonel Prime at Fort McIntosh.''

Paco's brow lifted, and his drenched eyelashes dripped rain when he blinked. ''You think they're headed in that direction?''

''It's just a hunch.''

Heat shimmered up in blurred waves from red rock and stretches of dun-colored ground scattered with clumps of greasewood. It was familiar territory, another long ride, but this time there was a new sense of urgency. Trains, boats and horses had brought them within sight of Fort McIntosh.

The dust coated horses, clothes, skin and even tongues. The three of them wore neckerchiefs over noses and mouths, wide brimmed hats providing scant shade against the searing beat of the sun. Steve and Paco rode abreast, with Ginny riding a few paces behind.

Steve turned in his saddle to glance back at her. She looked like a wilted flower. If not for the taut set of her shoulders, he'd have thought her asleep. Her chin dipped toward her chest, the hat brim hiding her eyes.

Steve nudged his mount closer to hers. ''We're almost there, Ginny.''

''I know.'' The words were muffled behind the yellow scarf covering half her face. ''I've swallowed enough dust to fill the Gulf of Mexico.''

''That's better. When you're complaining, I know you're all right.''

Her head lifted, and he caught a glimpse of narrowed green eyes above the yellow triangle. ''Did you think I would not be? I may collapse after we have Laura and Franco safely with us, but I won't give up until then. I *won't* give up!''

"No, you're not the kind of woman to give up, my green-eyed wife. I know that about you. You're as stubborn as I am when you want to be."

"Steve, we *will* find them. Won't we?"

Couched behind the steady timbre of her voice was a note of uncertainty. Leaning over, he put his hand atop her arm. "We'll find them. I swear it to you."

Her gaze was cool. "I know. I don't know why you think they might be here, but I trust you to find them."

He hoped his hunch would pay off. It was a wild idea, and even Paco thought he was crazy for pursuing it. But he remembered Brandon's certainty in San Antonio, and his smug assurance that he would build his rail line from Texas into Mexico. The meeting with Uriah Lott had occurred to Steve, and he recalled the discussion about railroads that night at Fort McIntosh.

William Brandon had been involved then, too. And he'd blamed Steve for ruining that business deal.

Perched on the high, frayed edge of the Rio Grande River, the fort faced the west and the setting sun. Across the wide band of muddy water, Nuevo Laredo squatted on the flat Mexican riverbank.

A mood of bitter rage curled in Steve's belly, belying his outward calm. He was calm only because he had to be, because the senator wasn't in front of him, but he itched to confront him. The nearer they came to finding Brandon, the more vicious his mood grew.

He'd wanted to leave Ginny behind, but knew better than to try it. She was like a tigress since discovering that her children were missing, as feral and determined as any wild cat. The three of them had ridden like avenging angels since disembarking from the flatboat at Roma, silently and with grim purpose.

Steve's big bay had settled into a mile-eating pace that was matched by the other mounts. As he rode in silence, anger built inside him, the cold, dispassionate mood of a gunfighter. It filled him with icy resolution.

Twilight descended, streaking the sky in colors of rose and purple as they rode into Laredo. The streets were crowded, saloons blaring tinny music and raucous laughter. With a new bridge being built across the river to Mexico, the town had grown swiftly.

Colonel Prime seemed surprised to see them, and was reluctant to help search for the children.

"I don't know why you think they're hidden in this area, but I can't spare a squad right now, Morgan. The apaches have been raiding and I need all my men."

"If the Apaches find a United States senator and his grandchildren before we do, you might find yourself back in the rank and file," Steve said curtly. "It wouldn't look good on your military record to have refused aid."

Prime scowled. "I have a squad returning tomorrow. I'll send them out to scout the hills in two days."

"Two days may be too late."

"It's the best I can do. You don't even know if they're out there, but I damn sure know the Apaches are. It will have to wait, and none of your threats can change that."

Steve leaned forward, fists pressing into the wood of Prime's desk as he said softly, "You're wrong, Colonel...."

"I'm going with you," Ginny said when they left the fort and took a room in a small, secluded hotel. She came to stand beside him, her eyes offering a challenge.

A faint smile slanted his mouth. "Where do you think I'm going?"

"It doesn't matter. I can't stay here alone. I'll go crazy with nothing to do but think and worry."

"Do you still have that pistol I gave you?"

She looked startled, but nodded. "Yes."

"Think you can use it if you have to? This will be a lot different than shooting at tree branches and tin cans, Ginny."

"Do you think it will come to that? I mean, I can't see the senator engaged in a gunfight, Steve."

"It wasn't the senator who picked up your aunt and the children in Galveston. He had someone else do that for him. Hired guns, maybe."

Her eyes widened slightly, dark pupils soaking up light from the wall lamp until they glittered. "I hadn't thought of that. Oh, Steve, the children must be terrified!"

"I'd prefer doing this without gunplay, but I want to be

ready for anything. And Ginny, I can't protect you and be certain the children are shielded as well.''

Silence fell in the small, shabby room. A muggy gust of air drifted in through the open window, rife with the sound of drunken laughter. Tension vibrated between them, and he knew Ginny had just realized how dangerous it was for all of them.

''If a choice must be made, Steve, you know what I want you to do.''

''I know.''

It didn't really need to be said. Laura and Franco came before anyone else.

Neither of them slept that night, but lay awake in each other's arms, the closeness their only comfort.

The early morning sun was veiled by pale, cloudy shreds of mist. The air was cool, night shadows lurking at the base of the hills and in crevices and ravines. Laredo was behind them, an indistinct blur visible in the distance. Hooves kicked up dust, clattering on the sun-baked road that was little more than well-worn ruts snaking across the plains.

Steve kept the pace slow and casual, watching the horizon. They couldn't be that far ahead, and wouldn't be expecting him. If not for the cable he'd sent London, he wouldn't ever have discovered that his children were in America.

All his instincts returned sharply to guide him, the old tricks he'd learned when he was still a youth riding with the Comanche enabling him to cut sign of riders that had veered off the main track. Paco had seen the faint marks of hooves in the hard soil, too.

''You figure they're up in the hills, *amigo?*''

''Makes sense. He'd be close here, able to ride back across the border if pursued.'' Steve shifted in his saddle, frowned slightly as something glittered in the rising sun.

He dismounted, bent to pick it up, turned it over in his hand. His mouth tightened. It was a two penny coin. An English coin. As he stood up, he saw another one a few yards up into the rocks, glinting dully. He turned to Paco.

''Isn't there an old ruin up in these hills?''

Paco scratched his jaw. "Yeah, in a stand of cottonwood trees down in an *arroyo.* I holed up there once in a storm."

"Why would he take them to a ruin way out here?" Ginny asked with a frown. "It would make more sense to take them to the house he has near the mine."

"No one would notice out here." Steve palmed the coin. "It's away from everything."

They rode slowly up through the rocks, horses carefully picking a path through jumbled rocks and brush-studded earth that melded from dun to ocher to red. Steve found three more coins. Shadows grew short, hugging boulders as the sun rose higher. The clink of bridle chains and creak of leather accompanied the dull thud of hooves against hard rock.

He heard Ginny unscrew the lid to her metal canteen and drink from it, the sound loud in the natural acoustics of the rocky canyon through which they rode. Paco slapped at an insect and his horse shied.

Steve heard a faint sound and put up his hand to halt the others, uncertain what had made the noise. Then he heard it again—the treble of a child's voice.

Ginny had heard it, too. Her head came up, and her eyes focused on the ridge just beyond. Lips parted, she waited, motionless, but the silence stretched unbearably.

Steve gestured for them to dismount. They would go the rest of the way afoot. Boots scraped over rock, dislodged pebbles that slid down the slope in a light patter. The wind blew across the ridge in hot waves, wafting the scent of sage.

"Wait here until you hear gunfire," he told Paco, his eyes warning Ginny not to protest. She offered no objection, but only nodded, her posture rigid.

"If you need help, *amigo,* just yell for me." Paco grinned, but his eyes were strained.

Steve climbed the ridge, his boots sliding slightly on loose gravel as he descended the other side and disappeared from sight.

Alone with Paco, Ginny's nerves were stretched taut to the breaking point. A hawk soared overhead, its sharp cry drifting down through a searing sky. The smell of sage and dust was sharp and suffocating.

"This is suicide," she said finally. "They'll kill him."

"Maybe. Though I think they'll be too surprised that he's walking in alone to think of that at first. I don't think the senator wants him dead. That would create too many problems."

Ginny slumped against a rock. The horses tore at clumps of brown grass, teeth grinding loudly.

"I still can't understand why he would do this. It makes no sense. I've never thought the senator was foolish, but this borders on lunacy."

"Greed and desperation make men do strange, stupid things, Ginny." Paco pushed his hat back on his head, his eyes scanning the horizon. "I sure as hell hope Steve knows what he's doing."

She glanced at him sharply. "You just said he'll be all right!"

"Yeah." Paco grimaced. "I know. Sometimes I let my mouth get ahead of me."

"Should we follow him?"

"I had the same thought. We'll wait like he said, but closer."

They made their way to the humped top of the ridge, keeping their heads down. Ginny's heart pounded furiously. Her mouth was dry and her hands were shaking so violently she knew she would never be able to fire the pistol she wore on her hip like a gunslinger. Belly down, they stretched out to peer down into the *arroyo.*

Sun-bleached ruins lifted white walls to the sky. An ancient people had built this structure, most of it having long ago tumbled to the ground, but there were still rock walls tucked beneath the overhang of a huge cliff. Clumps of cottonwood trees shaded a small seep, water trickling over rock.

Evidence of habitation was everywhere. Faded blankets hung over gaping windows, and the smoke of a fire curled up from inside one of the buildings. Two men stood guard, their rifles held at the ready.

Steve crossed the *arroyo* in long, loose strides, casting a short shadow with the sun overhead. Relentless heat shimmered around him, rose in blurred waves from the parched earth. Ginny held her breath as he drew near the guards.

Clearly they had not expected him to walk in so boldly.

They glanced uncertainly at each other. They had the flat, broad faces of *mestizos,* Mexicans with Indian blood.

There was no sign of the children, or of William Brandon. It was eerily quiet.

Beside her, light glinted off Paco's drawn pistol, the blue-gray of his .45 a deadly gleam. She drew her weapon as well, rather clumsily, her hand shaking as she propped it atop gritty rock, holding the butt with both hands.

"Is that how he taught you to hold a gun?" Paco asked softly, amusement evident in his tone.

Ginny shook her head. "No. But it's how I'm holding it today."

Below, Steve was speaking with the guards, and after a moment, they stepped aside. What on earth had he said to convince them to allow him to enter?

Paco was frowning. "They didn't take his guns. I don't like this."

"Maybe they know he won't start shooting recklessly with the children nearby."

"Or maybe—"

A sound behind them made the hair stand up on the back of Ginny's neck, and she heard the unmistakable click of a cartridge being pumped into a rifle chamber.

Paco swore under his breath as a voice said, "Please be so good as to lay down your weapons, *amigos.*"

45

The sun had begun to slide downward, a great orange ball of fire blazing a vivid trail of yellow and rose above the rocky walls of the *arroyo.* It was cooler now, the shadows long and deep, reaching into the ruins.

Ginny hugged her children fiercely to her, shushing their frightened sobs with tender firmness as they huddled in a corner under the watchful eye of an armed guard. Tante Celine looked dreadful, her hair more untidy than Ginny had ever seen it, her garments rent in places and caked with dust. But her spine was rigid, her eyes blazing with contemptuous outrage.

''They are animals,'' she said in French to her niece, and only a slight quiver betrayed her strain. ''But they have not harmed us, though they did drag us across miles of desert. It is *him* I worry about. He looks ill.''

A nod of her head indicated the man lying on a rough cot nearby. Ginny's gaze shifted. William Brandon lay listlessly under a tattered blanket. His cheeks were hollow, his eyes sunken, and he responded weakly when spoken to by anyone.

''Virginia...'' His voice was a grating whisper that she had to strain to hear. ''I'm sorry. My fault.''

Moved to pity despite their circumstances, she nodded. ''Yes, but save your strength. Don't try to talk.''

A short, swarthy man Steve had called Delgado returned to the stuffy chamber, grinning at them as he surveyed the two men bound tightly with rope and held beneath the warning rifles of the guards.

"You do not seem so cocky now, Morgan," he said. "Have you lost your courage?"

Steve shrugged. His eyes were dark blue, ruthless in a face that had been battered by heavy fists.

"It's easy to taunt a man who's tied up, Delgado. Cut me free and ask me that question."

"Ah, no, that would be foolish." Delgado moved to the small wooden table against the far wall and poured dark wine into a cup, then turned to gaze at them, satisfaction glittering in his dark eyes. "This has turned out much more pleasing than I had thought. You have been of great help, Morgan."

"Glad I could oblige," Steve drawled. "What do you hope to gain by this? You can't keep a United States senator captive forever. Every soldier in Texas will be out looking for you."

"But I am not in Texas. I am in Mexico. Even your famous Rangers cannot follow me here." Delgado looked quite pleased with himself, his smile smug. "It was a great stroke of fortune that delivered the bait to lure you. I had not thought of using your children."

Steve's gaze shifted to the senator, a flick of his eyes that made the Mexican grin.

"Yes, he saved me much trouble. I am grateful to him for his thorough attention to details."

"Morgan..." The rasping voice dragged Steve's gaze to the cot as Brandon struggled to sit up. "Not the way I planned. Would not harm them."

"Shut up, old man," Delgado barked. "You are useless to me now that I have what I want. Do not tread too harshly or I will rid myself of your presence."

Steve stretched out his legs, hooked one foot lazily over his other ankle and leaned his head back against the wall.

"I think I'm getting the picture here. It wasn't the senator who planned this. It was you."

"Of course it was me. After you killed Luna, I had to think of some way to keep the senator interested in mining for silver. He thinks only of railroads, of laying tracks into Mexico to take out copper and silver instead of where the true profit lies. Mules are more efficient, prisoners productive in getting the silver out without Díaz knowing how much is produced. Not even the senator knows just how much ore the Galena has yielded. I am a very wealthy man, Morgan. I will not allow the stupidity of one greedy *gringo* to ruin it all for me."

"So you used the senator just like you used Rafael Luna and his desire for vengeance."

"It was much easier. I had no way of funding the mine. Once I had Brandon interested in financing the production, it was easy enough to manage. Luna was quite clever, but he allowed his lust for a woman to cloud his judgment. If you had not rid me of him, I would have had to do it myself."

"And now? You have us all here."

"Yes." Delgado rose from the chair, tilting back his head to toss down the last of the wine. "You are dangerous to me. You know too much, and you have an annoying habit of destroying my plans."

"Let the children go. Killing them won't solve anything."

"It is unfortunate that they must die, but children die every day. By the time your bodies are discovered out here, you will be old bones. Ramirez!" An armed guard nodded when Delgado said, "Take them out and kill them, then cover the bodies with rock."

Ginny's breath caught painfully. Desperate, she hugged Laura and Franco to her, her eyes seeking Steve's in the hope that he could avert disaster. But he was being dragged to his feet with Paco, both of them shoved toward the door covered with a ragged blanket.

Tante Celine moaned softly as the guards motioned for them to rise, and Ginny remembered the knife she still kept strapped to her thigh.

As the children began to cry, she hushed them, her hands trembling as she stroked their small heads. "It will be all right, little ones," she comforted them in French. "Listen to me and do whatever I tell you."

Senator Brandon was hauled from the cot, staggering as he was guided toward the door. The blanket lifted briefly when Steve and Paco emerged, allowing in a shaft of fading light. Then, suddenly, Steve was lunging forward, his arms somehow free of restraint, a gun filling his hand as he tuned, aimed and fired.

Delgado swore harshly, then gave a grunt of surprise as a bullet punched a neat hole in the middle of his forehead. Eyes wide, he pitched forward soundlessly.

Ginny jerked as a volley of gunfire filled the *arroyo.* She heard men shouting and a bugle blare. The colonel had kept his word!

Senator Brandon stumbled, threw his weight into the man nearest him with a piercing howl that Ginny had never heard before. It sounded like a battle cry: it was the perfect distraction.

Moving swiftly, she drew the sharp little knife from beneath her skirt before their guards could react and plunged it into the man nearest her, the blade piercing his heart so swiftly that he dropped like a stone, an expression of shock on his face.

Wrenching it free, Ginny hissed in French to her aunt and the children that they must run and hide. She turned to the other guard and saw in his eyes a flare of rage and fear as her arm lifted. A bark of muzzle fire erupted, smelling of sulphur and heat, an orange spurt close to her face. A sharp pain seared into her shoulder, but her forward momentum drove the knife into the man before he could retreat.

All around her was pandemonium, the sound of gunfire and men shouting washing over her in a blur. Ginny was vaguely aware of a woman screaming when she collapsed atop the guard, her fist still clutching the dagger's handle, the blade imbedded in his throat. The gagging sounds faded and the wash of damp heat over her hand slowed as she surrendered to the encroaching darkness, her last thoughts of Steve and the children.

46

Pain. Intense pain radiated through her body. Ginny slowly opened her eyes, blinking as faces swam into view, then faded. She closed her eyes again, but heard the relief in Steve's voice when he said, "She's coming out of it."

Then all was dark again, devoid of even dreams.

It took several days for Ginny to stay awake long enough to hear what had happened after she'd collapsed. It was Tante Celine who told her, smoothing back the damp hair from Ginny's forehead as she spoke soothingly.

"The children are safe, *ma petite.* Do not fret. All is well."

"Where…where am I?" Ginny licked dry lips with the tip of her tongue, grateful for the small amount of cool water *Tante* offered her.

"Laredo. As soon as you are able to travel, you will be going home."

"Steve? Is he—?"

"Most impatient to visit with you. He has hardly left your side this past week."

A week! Had she been asleep that long?

Tante Celine smiled. "The doctor gave you something to make you sleep as the pain was so great after he removed the bullet."

Ginny's hand reached out, curled around her aunt's arm with surprising strength. "The senator?"

"Better now, though he nearly died from the wound he

suffered when attacking the guard. Foolish man. But a brave one, *n'est pas?*''

''Yes.'' Ginny managed a smile. ''Very brave.''

''And it seems that the bullet already in his back was somehow moved by the new bullet. The surgeon was able to remove them both. Perhaps now he can walk without pain.''

After a moment, Ginny said softly, ''I'm glad. It's a comfort to know that he did not mean to harm the children.''

''No, though he is not blameless. He did misrepresent himself by sending the cable. He claims he meant only to provide a distraction so your husband would focus on them instead of what he was doing with the railroads and mines. Bah! The arrogant greed of men never ceases to amaze me.''

''I'm glad you were with the children,'' Ginny murmured, and *Tante* sighed softly.

''Yes. Though I cannot like this savage country, I will stay as long as you need me, *ma petite.* But I must return to France in time for Pierre's wedding.''

''Wedding? Don't tell me—Lorna Prendergast.''

''Yes. They are very much in love. Perhaps soon I shall have grandchildren to hold close to my heart, though they will never replace Laura and Franco.''

Closing her eyes, Ginny surrendered to her body's demand for sleep again. When she woke, Tante Celine was gone and Steve sat in a straight-backed chair beside her bed.

He looked gaunt, a dark beard stubble shadowing his cheeks, but a smile deepened the grooves on each side of his mouth. ''Awake at last, lazy one?''

''Steve—'' She reached out and he clasped her hand in his, warm and strong, his fingers pressing into her palms. ''Steve, I want to go home.''

''Yes, my love. We're going home as soon as you're able to travel. Just concentrate on getting well.''

With a soft sigh of satisfaction, Ginny drew his hand to her face, lay her cheek in his broad palm. ''I love you, Steve Morgan.''

With his other hand, he pushed the hair tenderly back from her face. ''And I love you, my heart. *Mi alma. Mi corazón.*''

''You won't leave me again?''

"No, Ginny. Not again. We're going home to Hacienda de la Nostalgia. I've decided to raise cattle and children."

Her gaze lifted, and she saw in Steve's eyes the love she had always yearned for, complete and encompassing, a love only for her, for all of time.

At last.

THE PROMISE

Epilogue

Zacatecas, September 1877

A cool breeze blew down from the mountains above Don Francisco's *hacienda*. It shivered leaves on the towering oaks shading the sprawling house, cast dappled shadows over the adobe walls and filtered into open windows to bring the promise of autumn on brisk currents.

Ginny stood at an open window overlooking the courtyard. Her green eyes focused on Laura and Franco, who were happy now, the memories of their recent nightmare slowly fading. They played with a puppy, though Laura still waited impatiently for the arrival of her own spaniel. The dog had been left in Galveston with most of their baggage, but was now en route to them.

While Ginny stood watching the children, unable to get enough of the sight of them, a warm presence behind her drew close and put a hand upon her shoulder, its voice a husky murmur against her ear.

"I feel the same way."

She half-turned, smiling up at Steve. "How did you know what I was thinking?"

"It's obvious. God, when I think of what might have happened—" He broke off, his tone grim.

"But it didn't. We found them. Despite all of the odds against us, we found them. *You* found them. How did you know where they would be?"

"I didn't. It was a calculated guess based on my suspicion of the senator. Seems I was wrong about how involved he was. But he *is* to blame for endangering them. He brought them here. Delgado just took advantage of it."

"I think I believe the senator when he says that he would never have harmed them, that he only wanted them to distract you so you'd stop your determined pursuit of his business plans. He knew you were trying to ruin him, Steve."

"I did ruin him. Those plans, anyway. It's unlikely he would have been able to build a railroad through Copper Canyon any time soon, but I was damned if I was going to let him extract money from backers to try. I'm familiar with how that works, how prices are jacked up too high and the men who started the scheme get rich while those more honest get swindled out of their money."

Leaning against Steve, Ginny put a hand on his chest. He wore a light leather vest over a dark blue shirt, snug-fitting trousers and familiar boots. In deference to his grandfather's wishes, he'd removed his gunbelts.

"I'm glad he's gone back to Louisiana," she murmured, thinking of her father and how old and sick he had seemed. "I feel as if I never really knew him. When I was a child, I used to dream about him. When I finally joined him, I was so proud of him. He seemed to be everything wonderful—a rich, powerful man greatly respected by his peers."

"Maybe he started out that way." Steve's shoulders lifted in a shrug. "He just got too confident, then too greedy."

Turning, she pressed closer to Steve, and gazed up into his face for a long moment. Long lashes briefly obscured his eyes before he slid her a sidelong glance, his lips crooking into the slanted smile that never failed to make her heart beat faster.

"What's on your mind, green-eyes?"

"You. Us. The future. Are you sure you still want to marry me?"

"For the third time? I've heard the third time is the charm."

His teasing made her smile. "It better be. Our children expect it."

His lean fingers tangled in her loose hair, gently drawing her head back so that he could see full into her eyes. "I expect it. So does my grandfather. And Señora Armijo will be quite irritated if we don't show up at our wedding. She's organized a grand *fiesta,* with twenty tables of food, and even had ice brought down from the mountains. I'm not brave enough to ruin her plans.''

''Is that the only reason you'll be there this evening?''

He grinned. ''Oh, I can think of another reason or two.''

''Then share them with me. Just so I can decide if *I* want to stand in front of the priest with you.''

Dragging his hand over the arch of her throat, Steve's smile vanished to be replaced by an intent expression, his eyes a very dark blue as he held her gaze.

''I love you, Ginny. There's never been another woman I've really loved. There never will be. You're all I want. And this time, our wedding vows are forever.''

Her breath caught at the intensity in his tone and his eyes. For a moment, she could not speak. Then she said, softly, ''We've never had a honeymoon, Steve.''

''We will this time, my dearest. I've made arrangements for Laura and Franco to be escorted to the Hacienda de la Nostalgia. They'll be waiting there for us when we return.''

''Return? From where? Where are we going now?''

''Eden.''

Eden. The little valley on the property he'd bought from Hearst. Their own private paradise.

Winding her arms around his neck, she lifted on her toes to press a lingering kiss on his mouth. His hands tightened on her back, sliding down her spine to rest upon her hips. A sultry smile curved her lips as she whispered, ''I love you, Steve. For all eternity. Today is the beginning of our forever.''